Of Wulf and Wynd

White Razor M
Duskgard Keep
Fort Snowfalcon
Fringe Road
Dawnstar Fortress
Leeward
Forgotten T
Treecrown Forest
Oldview
EARNA
Road
Fairview Lake
Razor River
Kin
or Route

Of Wulf and Wynd

Part 1

The Vows of Marriage

The Kingdoms of Gyldren: Book 1

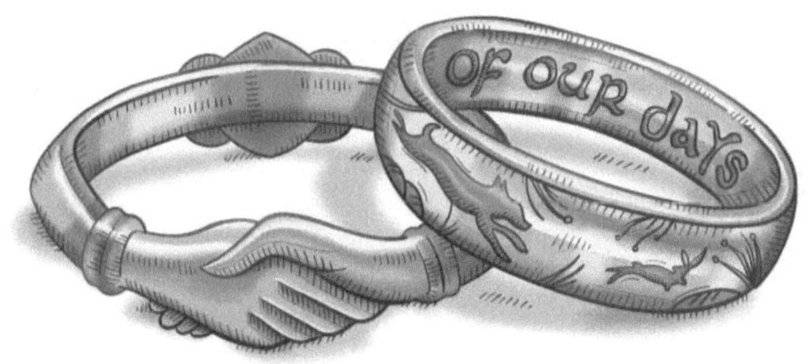

by
Lexa Luthor

Luthor Publishing
2022

This is a work of fiction. Names, characters, places, and incidents are the product of the author's imagination or are used fictitiously. Any resemblance to actual persons, living or dead, business establishments, events, or locales is entirely coincidental.

Books, ebooks, or parts of either, are not transferable. They cannot be sold, shared, or given away without permission.

Contents

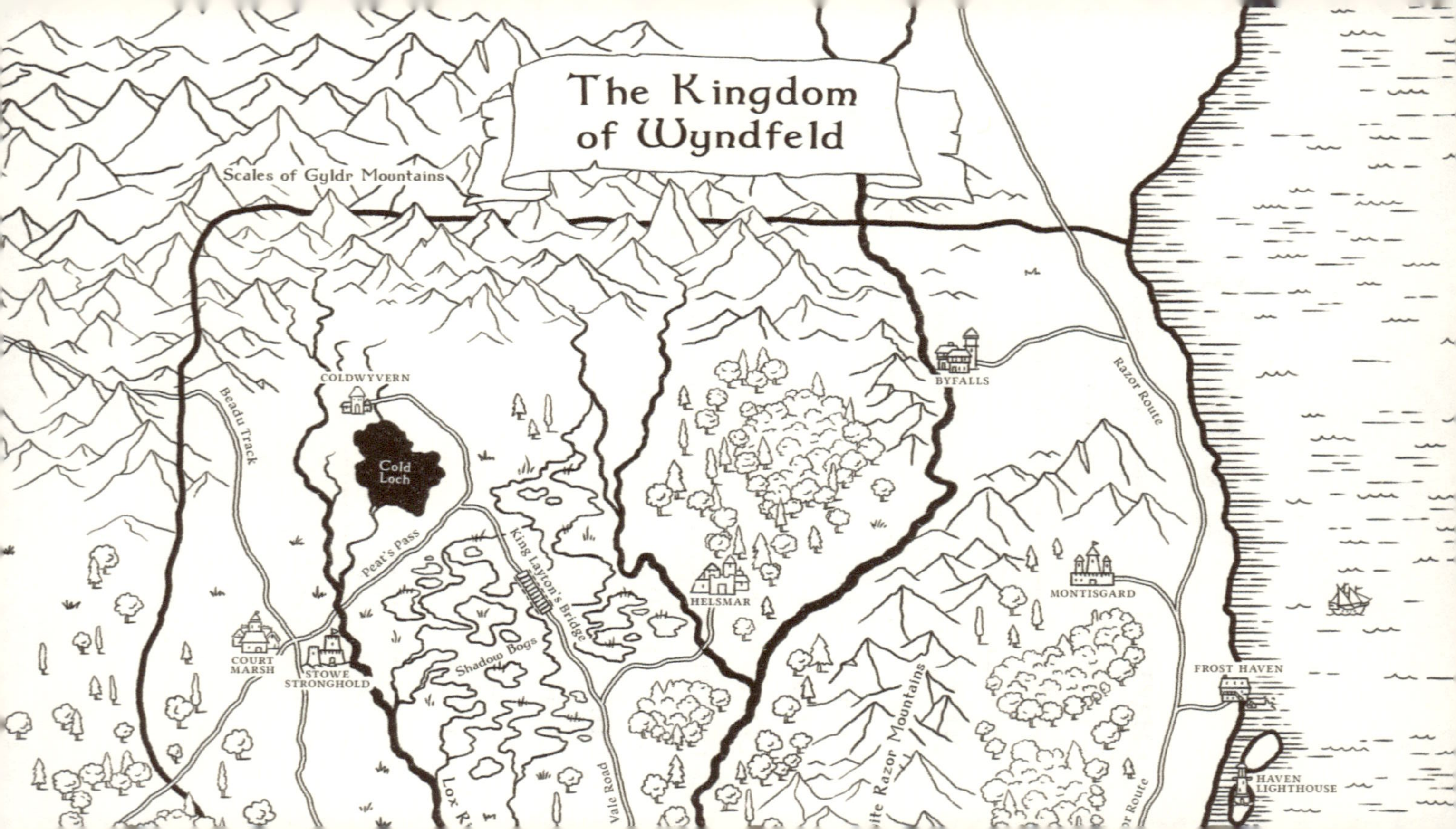

The Kingdom of Wyndfeld
Scales of Gyldr Mountains
Razor Route
BYFALLS
COLDWYVERN
Cold Loch
Beadu Track
Peat's Pass
King Layton's Bridge
Shadow Bogs
HELSMAR
MONTISGARD
The Razor Mountains
COURT MARSH
STOWE STRONGHOLD
Lox R...
Vale Road
...r Route
FROST HAVEN
HAVEN LIGHTHOUSE

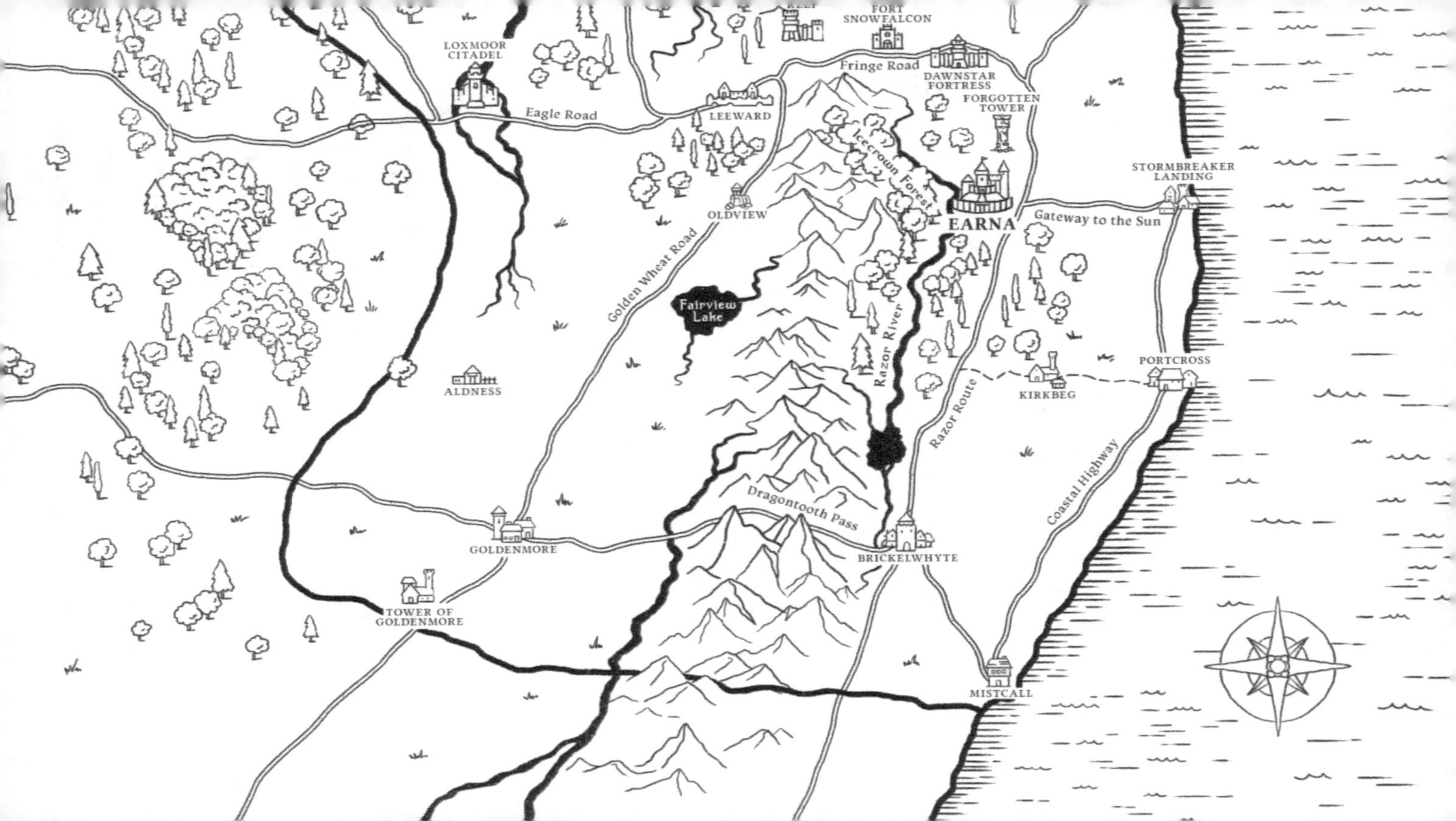

LOXMOOR CITADEL
FORT SNOWFALCON
Fringe Road
DAWNSTAR FORTRESS
FORGOTTEN TOWER
Eagle Road
LEEWARD
Icecrown Forest
STORMBREAKER LANDING
OLDVIEW
EARNA
Gateway to the Sun
Golden Wheat Road
Fairview Lake
Razor River
PORTCROSS
ALDNESS
Razor Route
KIRKBEG
Coastal Highway
Dragontooth Pass
GOLDENMORE
BRICKELWHYTE
TOWER OF GOLDENMORE
MISTCALL

The Calendar of Gyldren

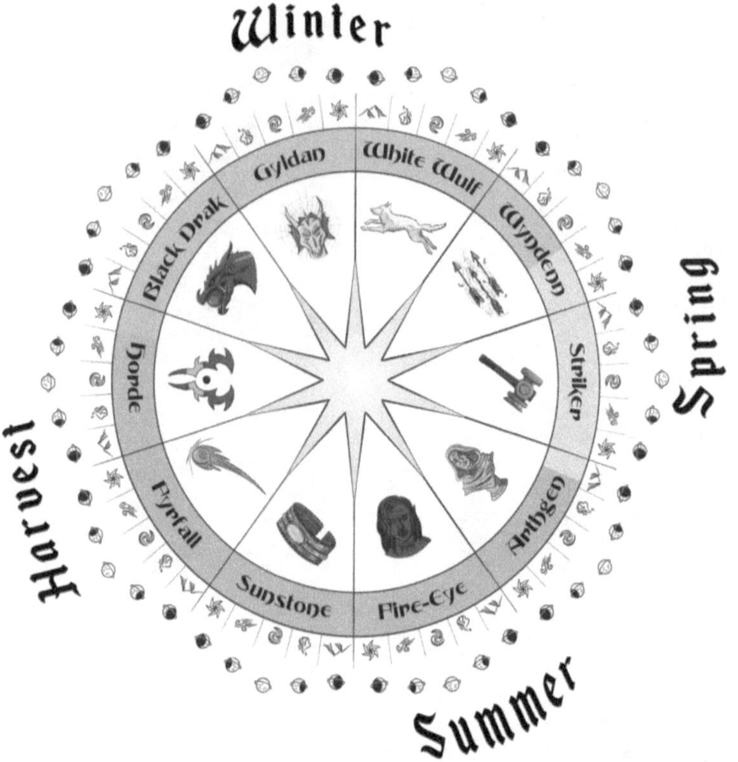

Year
351 Days

Month
35 Days

Week
7 Days

Weeks of the Month

 Week 1: Tharnwice

 Week 2: Furywice

 Week 3: Seawice

 Week 4: Skywice

 Week 5: Driwice

The last month of the year, Gyldan, has
one extra day, totaling 36 days.

Chapter 1

Date: 03 Sunstone 809G
(About 17 Years Ago)

Tharon Blakesley traded several giggles with her best friend, Roswynd Arrington, as they gave the Wyndfeld guards the slip and disappeared into the surrounding woodland. Hitching her dress higher with her right hand, Tharon tightened her left hand's grip on Roswynd's small fingers as they raced between boulders, around trees, and through the brush. The air smelled strong of grass and pine after the recent rainfall. A few rabbits and squirrels scurried away when they burst through the foliage.

Roswynd did her best to keep pace, but one of the boulders was slippery after the morning's summer storm. She squealed and tumbled forward until Tharon's sure arms encircled her.

Blowing out a relieved breath, Tharon kept Roswynd's upper body hooked in her arms and held most of her petite friend's weight.

With a shy smile, Roswynd scraped and dragged her feet off the boulder, then planted them on the soft grass. "Thank you. It was my silly dress."

Tharon admired Roswynd's mismatched eyes that glowed up at her. After years of friendship, she hadn't decided whether she loved Roswynd's blue eye or hazel eye more. The blue eye reminded Tharon of an icy day in the breathtaking White Razor Mountains, and the hazel eye had golden flecks like the summer sun.

"Tharon, I am fine." Roswynd grinned at her blushing friend, who released her steady hold. She laced their hands together and continued their adventure into the woods, familiar with the area. Every summer her family left the capital and spent two or three months at their estate in the Icecrown Forest. For one of those months, Tharon journeyed from the Kingdom of White Sommer, stayed with them, and played with Roswynd day in and day out. It was one of their favorite times together.

"Let us go this way." Tharon turned at a familiar spot by an old, curly willow tree.

"Where are we going? To the waterfall?"

Tharon nodded, then looked at Roswynd and asked, "Is that acceptable?"

"Of course." Roswynd had a bright smile and stayed close.

"We have to be back in time for supper." Tharon searched the canopy of trees, checking for the sun's location in the sky. The sun wouldn't set for another three hours. Of the two girls, Tharon was the more responsible one. It was expected of her, as she was two years older than Roswynd.

"We should hurry, then," Roswynd said with a mischievous glint in her eyes.

Tharon narrowed her gaze at her friend. "You are going to lose, Ros."

Roswynd pouted, then shook their hands free. "On the count of three." She bent her knees and lifted the lower half of her dress.

Tharon mirrored the ready position and said, "One."

Roswynd bolted with a cry of excitement. "Three!"

"Cheater!" Tharon expected it from her friend, who was cackling and running at full speed. With a smirk, Tharon gave chase, and her longer legs ate away at the distance between them. If it weren't for their dresses, they could have run faster. Together, they laughed and carried on all the way to the waterfall's overlook. Once close enough to the open landscape, Tharon pounced on her prey from behind.

Roswynd yelped, but she was scrappy after years of wrestling with both Tharon and her older brother Selwyn. With legs kicking and fists flying, they rolled and tumbled across the grass until Tharon had Roswynd pinned.

"Tsk, tsk." Tharon straddled her friend's waist and held Roswynd's arms above her head. "Cheaters never win."

Roswynd growled, but she was outmatched by Tharon's deeper snarl. As an Omega, Roswynd was supposed to submit to an Alpha like Tharon. But she was a strange Omega, and for the first time managed to toss Tharon to one side.

Tharon yelped and laughed when small hands attacked her sides, tickling her. Thrown off by Roswynd's newfound strength, she failed to stop the assault. "Ros! Please!"

"Cheaters do win!" Roswynd hooted and pumped her fists in the air.

Chuckling, Tharon sat up on her elbows and shook her head at Roswynd's celebration. "When did you become so strong?"

Roswynd placed her hands on her hips and replied, "Wrestling with Selwyn all winter." She climbed off Tharon and held out her hand.

Tharon accepted Roswynd's help, even though she didn't need it. "Well, since you are so strong now, we will try something new." She strolled over to the nearby tree that branched out above the overlook, the waterfall, and the Razor River. Whenever they visited the overlook, they would sit underneath it, talk about their families, each other, and their futures. But often times Roswynd would recant the latest story from a new book that she was reading with her mother. Tharon loved to listen to Roswynd's retellings.

Roswynd followed and brushed off her hands but paled when Tharon grabbed onto a large knot on the back of the tree trunk. "What are you doing?"

Tharon pressed her foot against the trunk and attempted to haul herself up but frowned at how restrictive her dress was. She hopped off, then turned to Roswynd. "We are going to climb." At Roswynd's gaping stare, she chuckled and crossed her arms. "Are you scared now?" Suppressing a grin, Tharon waited for her friend to take the bait.

"I am not scared." Roswynd shot a glare at Tharon but lost it when she scanned the height of the tree. "But… I am not as tall as you."

"I will help you." Tharon grabbed the bottom of her dark blue dress and tore the right side up to her knee. She repeated the same thing on the left side, then tested her new range of motion. It was much better and would make it easier to safely climb. Later she would be scolded for the tears, but rips, dirty smudges, and even blood stains on their dresses were common.

"Wow," Roswynd whispered, eyes big.

Tharon did the same thing to Roswynd's dress before she could protest. "Follow where I go, all right?" She clutched the wooden knot that provided a perfect handhold, then lifted herself and placed a foot on the first low branch. She scooted out on the branch and waited for Roswynd to follow her example.

Roswynd dropped the frayed end of her dress and shifted on her feet, staring at Tharon.

"You can do it." Tharon squatted down and smiled at her friend. Anytime she gave Roswynd a new challenge it was met with enthusiasm. This time Roswynd was hesitant because of the height, but then the look of determination spread across her freckled features.

Roswynd latched onto the tree knot, raised herself up, and put a foot on the right branch. With Tharon's help she balanced herself on the thick branch, then continued to follow Tharon up and up with a huge smile on her face. Occasionally she took Tharon's hand if she was too short to reach the next branch.

"Almost there," Tharon said. "Last one." She knelt again, clung to the branch, and kept her other hand at the ready if Roswynd needed help.

Roswynd was forced to jump, but she caught the overhead branch with both hands. She groaned while lifting herself and pressed her left heel into the trunk. Her flat shoe slipped, causing her to jerk down and lose a hand on the branch. "Tharon!"

With panic buzzing in her ears, Tharon shot out a hand and curled her fingers into the bust of Roswynd's dress. "Grab my arm!" A small hand hooked her wrist, then Tharon hauled her friend up and onto the branch with ease. She pulled Roswynd into her arms and blew out a strangled breath. Roswynd was shaking, but they were safe. "Are you all right, Ros?" A shy nod against her chest eased her racing heart.

Roswynd poked her head out and smiled at Tharon.

"You are a natural climber," Tharon said. She peered past Roswynd and considered a place for them to rest and enjoy the view. "Can you move closer to the trunk, then go over to that branch for a minute?"

Roswynd glanced at the other branch, which was level with the one they were on. "Yes." She took two steps closer to the trunk, placed her hands flat against it, and crossed over to the opposite branch.

Tharon went to the crook between the trunk and current branch, which was thick enough for her to sit on. With her back against the trunk, she held out her hand to Roswynd and assisted with her return. She pulled Roswynd's back into her front, then together they sat, straddling the branch. Roswynd leaned into Tharon, who encircled her friend's petite waist.

"It is pretty from up here," Roswynd said with wonderment. "Thank you for sharing this with me."

Tharon rumbled in agreement and rested her chin on Roswynd's shoulder. "Thank you for climbing with me." The view was beautiful, and the waterfall almost seemed louder. The afternoon sun warmed their faces.

Roswynd shrugged and turned her head sidelong. "I would not let you go alone." They always did everything together when possible. Their friendship was perhaps destined similar their kingdoms, which had forged an unbreakable alliance, joining forces centuries ago. Like Roswynd and Tharon, their fathers had grown up together, and their parents before them. The two Houses went back many generations in a rich history of friendship, family, and love. On occasion an Arrington and Blakesley had even wed each other.

Chuckling, Tharon squeezed her friend and rumbled again.

"The dresses made it difficult, though," Roswynd muttered. "I despise dresses." She plucked at her maroon and brown attire, which was a bit muddy and grassy. "Why are we forbidden to wear trousers?"

After a grunt, Tharon ran her fingers through Roswynd's rich golden hair and listened to the recurring rant. They were considered the softer sex, even though Tharon was an Alpha. But from birth, she was raised as an Omega, although there were differences between female Alphas and female Omegas. Her appearance might be that of an Omega, but there were distinctions between the two, even at their young ages.

"Our brothers can wear trousers, ride, hunt, and use bows," Roswynd said with a huff, then folded her arms against her chest. "It is rather silly, because I could do those activities as well as Selwyn." After a long silence, she turned her head to the side and asked, "Does it bother you?"

Tharon shrugged in response, but she did side with Roswynd. For the past year, she had envied her younger brother, Saxon, for his education and hunting trips. "On occasion," she whispered.

Roswynd huffed, then leaned back into Tharon, resting her head against her friend's shoulder. "I would be better than Selwyn," she muttered.

With a soft laugh, Tharon tightened her arms and thought about her precious time with Roswynd. She had this week and two more weeks, known as Furywice and Seawice, left on the estate before her father returned for her and would take her home. Nuzzling Roswynd, she whispered, "You would be." She pictured Roswynd's big smile and felt her own as she breathed in Roswynd's unique scent. All the Arringtons had a similar scent, but Tharon could distinguish

Roswynd's from the rest of the family. It had become one of her favorite scents over the years.

"I wish you did not have to return home," Roswynd said, voice at a loss. Her shoulders fell and she let out an improper whine. Like Tharon, she was taught not to whine like a peasant or animal, but it was often a natural response and difficult to resist.

"We still have a fortnight together. Then after that, it will be the Howling Eagle Festival," Tharon said but cringed when Roswynd snorted and swatted Tharon's thigh.

"The festival is not until White Wulf, which is *mooonths* away." Roswynd shifted on the branch, groused, and folded her arms. "I refuse to wait that long to see you again. I will pester Father every day after you leave." From the determination in Roswynd's voice, Tharon was certain that Roswynd's family would be taking a trip to the Kingdom of White Sommer to visit Tharon and her family long before the festival.

The Howling Eagle Festival was an old tradition between their kingdoms that began several generations ago. Their parents hosted the special winter festival to celebrate their kingdoms' alliance and their unified families. The festival carried on for two full weeks with a one-week intermission for traveling. The festival's first week was held in Wulfbite, the capital of White Sommer, and the second week was in Earna, the capital of Wyndfeld. The festival was attended by all in both kingdoms and ended with a formal ball, which was Roswynd's favorite part and Tharon's least favorite. Besides strengthening the bonds between the kingdoms, the festival brought merriment, wonderful food, and strong alcohol.

However, the best part about the festival was that Tharon's and Roswynd's birthdays fell during the celebrations. Next year Tharon would turn nine on the last day of White Wulf, then the next day was Roswynd's seventh birthday on the first day of Wyndenn. Celebrating their birthdays over a two-day period was the best.

The Howling Eagle Festival was one of several traditions between their families. Prior to the winter festival, the Arringtons went to Wulfbite and joined the Blakesley family on a hunt to fill the Blakesleys' cellars with meat to sustain them through the cold months. Similarly, the Blakesley family remained in Earna after the winter festival and hunted with the Arringtons to load their cellars. Like her best friend, Tharon wished to join in the hunt, even if it were only to learn how to skin the animals, as all female breeds were taught among their people.

"One day, we will be able to travel Gyldren together like my grandmother," Roswynd said without a thread of doubt in her declaration. "I do not care what our silly prince husbands say." She finished her statement with a firm nod.

Smiling, Tharon canted her head, sneaking a peek at her friend's profile. In the soft sunlight, Roswynd's features were resolute, if not smudged with a little dirt. Tharon thought her friend was beautiful. Similar to Roswynd, Tharon wished to tour Gyldren and see other kingdoms, cultures, and people. The sweet fantasy that they would have such a future was perfect, and flawed. If nothing else, she was certain of one thing. "We will always have each other, Ros."

"Yes. I know."

* * *

Date: 30 Fire-Eye 826G
(Present Day)

"By the end of Sunstone, we *will* take Duskgard Keep."

A heavy silence settled in the tent after the announcement was made by their lord commander. The lower-ranking officers shifted on their boots and looked among each other while Officer Hywel stared at the map on the tall table in the middle of their circle.

"But, Lord Commander, it will be Sunstone in five days' time." Hywel looked up from the map and met his leader's stern gaze. "It is the beginning of harvest now, and the weather has begun to turn already."

"That is why we must capture Duskgard Keep before the first snowfall."

Hywel rubbed the stubble around his chin and asked, "Why not wait until spring? We can rest here in Leeward for the winter, then start our campaign fresh in the spring. Fringe Road will be dangerous enough as it is, much less during the snow and ice." Several officers rumbled or moved their heads in agreement. "I mean no disrespect." He held out a hand toward the other officers and high-ranking knights. "You are our lord commander after all, Prince Tharon. And you *are* the Black Wulf. In the end, we will carry out your orders."

With a puff of her chest, Tharon Blakesley flashed a toothy smile at her loyal officers, who had followed her ever since she became the lord commander of the White Sommer Army. They were in their tenth year of war with the Kingdom of Wyndfeld and were finally carving a path toward Wyndfeld's heart. Two days ago they had captured the prosperous town of Leeward, which resided on the west side of the White Razor Mountains. The mountain range ran north and south, separating the west and east side of Wyndfeld. The kingdom's capital resided on the east side, and so did the House of Arrington. The single major road through the mountain range was Fringe Road, which was heavily guarded by a keep, a fort, and a fortress. But once they secured Fringe Road, they'd be beating down their enemy's front door.

Tharon could nearly taste the Arringtons' blood.

Coming closer to Hywel, Tharon indicated the map and asked, "What is different about Duskgard Keep than Fort Snowfalcon or Dawnstar Fortress?" She rested a hand on one of her sword hilts and waited for his response.

"It is located on the west side of the mountains," a different officer replied.

"Yes, it is on the west side." Tharon scanned her officers' hard features and said, "It is close to us, much too close." She narrowed her eyes and sneered low. "We cannot rest peacefully in Leeward this winter while Duskgard Keep sits over our shoulders." Even with Leeward under her control, Duskgard Keep was a threat to her army. The Wyndfeld soldiers in Duskgard Keep would watch them and perhaps even attack. "The Arringtons are clever," Tharon said in a growly tone. "They will use Duskgard Keep against us if we leave it in their hands. We must capture it and truly secure our control over the west side of the mountains. Only then can we rest for the winter." Rest and then scheme to battle, conquer, and finally capture the House of Arrington.

Hywel gave his agreement first and declared, "Then to Duskgard!"

"To Duskgard!"

Tharon basked in her officers' cheer to capture the keep. Indeed she could have simply commanded her army to march forward. However, she preferred that they understood the purpose behind their battles. A purpose gave them fire and determination to meet a goal rather than marching forward with blindness. For a few more beats, the chanting continued and charged Tharon. Like her knights, she feasted on the war and hated to keep her blade clean for too long.

At the tent's entrance, a newcomer slipped inside and stood to the side near the seating area. He hooked his hands in front of his body and caught Tharon's eye. In his left hand, he signaled the two rolled-up messages but waited in silence.

Tharon recognized both seals on the messages that were in Pòl's hand. The one seal softened her heart for a beat, but she pushed it aside and focused on her officers. "It is late," she said to them, causing the din to die. "Tomorrow we will discuss the plans to capture Duskgard. In the meantime, continue to enjoy the fruits of Leeward." She smirked and said, "I certainly will." Several of the officers laughed and one clapped her on the back on his way out.

One by one, the high-ranking knights filed out of her tent and left her alone with Pòl, who watched the last person exit.

Pòl crossed the distance and held out the two messages. "One is from Wulfbite."

Tharon rubbed her thumb across the wax seal of one message. She would recognize her family's crest anywhere and looked forward to reading the words from her younger sisters, but in private. For now she broke the seal on the other message, which was from her second-in-command. After unrolling the message, she skimmed over the important details from Lord Erland and rumbled at the news. "It seems he will capture Goldenmore by the end of the year. He has already torched many of their granaries."

Nodding, Pòl pursed his lips and said, "That will induce starvation." He was quiet but canted his head when Tharon started rolling the message. "Duskgard Keep will not be easy, Lord Commander."

Tharon sighed and walked away from him. "Are you volunteering to lead the charge, then?" She went to the small table near the entrance to her bedding tent. After she placed the messages on her makeshift desk, she looked to him.

Pòl was an excellent knight. Tharon trusted him without question from the first day she met him. Since becoming the lord commander, she attempted numerous times to promote him, but he refused and remained a knight. Pòl never explained his rejection, but Tharon was certain he wished to stay by Tharon's side rather than leave her and lead soldiers. Somehow Pòl had become her secret guardian despite the clear fact she certainly did not require one.

However, she suspected he vowed to himself a long time ago to protect Tharon, whether she liked it or not.

After a grunt, Pòl took a few steps closer to Tharon but kept his distance. "You are relentless, my prince."

Tharon held back a smile after hearing the endearment that so few were brazen enough to say to her. She allowed Pòl to use it. He was also one of the few Alphas whose scent didn't challenge her own Alpha. "You could do so much more, Pòl. Why do you resist?" She shifted closer to him, taking in his heavy pheromones and not minding them.

"I am happy with my position in life."

With a rumble Tharon accepted his vague answer rather than push him. She folded her arms and held his gaze for another moment.

Pòl chuffed low and changed the topic before Tharon made another attempt. "The same two Betas from last night wish to see you again."

"Oh?" Tharon chuckled and sensed the swell in her trousers. Yesterday evening she had left the encampment and gone into Leeward in search of fun. Many of the locals scurried out of her way, but she heard the whispers among the female Betas. She, Pòl, and a few other knights had settled into a tavern for a meal and drinks. The owner tried to appease them with free food and beer even though Tharon had no malicious intent. By the end of their meal, several female Betas had taken to their group and two of them followed Tharon to her tent. She found it easy to entice female Betas due to her rare nature as a She-Alpha. So many female Betas wanted to see *it* for themselves.

"Shall I fetch them?" Pòl asked even though he knew the answer.

"Yes." Tharon considered her plans this evening and canted her head. After she cleaned up, ate, and read her sisters' letter, she would entertain the Betas. "Bring them here in two hours. I will give them a good fuck then."

Pòl grunted and eyed Tharon, not speaking his thoughts. But his eyes held his unspoken words that told Tharon about his minor disapproval of her sexual exploits. The House of Blakesley wasn't known for being sexually deviant, but Tharon and her brother had proven otherwise in recent years. "I hope one day that cock of yours finds a golden cunt."

Tharon flashed her teeth once at him in silent warning. She didn't need lectures, even if it was Pòl. Without thought, her pheromones grew thicker, yet she reeled it in before she forced Pòl to heel to her. Despite their occasional differences, she respected him and never forced her Alpha's superior dominance on him. "Go," she ordered him and turned away from him before the regret rooted itself in her. Without a word, Pòl departed and left Tharon alone in her tent.

Tharon kept to her plans for the night. She wiped down her body with water and soap, removing the sweat from today's sword practice. Soon she would need a bath, which she could have if she went to Chesford Manor in Leeward. Perhaps tomorrow she would occupy one of the rooms for a night or two, even though she preferred her tent.

After cleaning up she had supper with her soldiers in the dining tent. The conversations were loud, and everyone was discussing the campaign for Duskgard Keep. Tharon smirked at the soldiers' renewed hunger for battle despite the grueling effort it took to conquer Leeward. She bid goodnight to several of her officers, signaling her desire to not be disturbed tonight unless it was an emergency.

Upon returning to her tent, Tharon found the two female Betas waiting for her. They were giggling and eyeing Tharon's crotch without shame compared to last night. Tharon rolled her eyes at their fascination with her dick, but it was normal to her. She allowed them to think she was as keen on them as they were about her.

However, they were all here for one purpose.

After the first hour, one of the female Betas was more spent than the other. Tharon left her alone on the bed and guided the other Beta into her main tent. She shoved the Beta toward the long dining table in the center of the tent. The Beta tumbled forward against the smooth wood, catching herself with her hands.

"Stay down," Tharon snapped and locked the Beta in place with her hand. She pressed the Beta face first into the table.

"Yes, Lord Commander."

Tharon stood tall behind the female Beta, who was as nude as Tharon. Pleased by the Beta's answer, she latched her fingers onto the Beta's bare hips and guided the head of her cock between the spread thighs.

The Beta gave a greedy whine and rocked her hips, until Tharon's pheromones wrapped around her. She stilled, other than digging her nails into the wood under her.

"Be still," Tharon ordered with a snarl. For a second, she tried to recall the Beta's name, but it was lost on her. With one hand, she stroked her hard shaft, which already throbbed again after fucking minutes ago. Battles always left her untamed and hungry for several days.

"Please," the Beta murmured.

The soft plea was exquisite and charged Tharon even more. The Beta's delicate scent continued to linger on Tharon's tongue. But right now, Tharon wanted to hear the little Beta scream under her until her throat was sore. Without warning she buried herself into the Beta, who cried out and jerked against the table.

"Lord C-Commander," the Beta said between gasps, "you are—" She was cut off by a pump of Tharon's hips.

"Be silent or I go back to the other Beta." Tharon finished her threat with a growl. She tangled her fingers in the Beta's unruly hair, twisting and tightening until she earned a hiss. "Good." With one hand still locked around the Beta's tiny waist, she moved her hips and worked the pliant Beta under her. She gave the Beta a chance to prepare for harder thrusts, even though Tharon preferred to get off as fast as possible.

The Beta hissed each time Tharon went deeper, but the increased speed brought her to shame. She begged for more and lifted her ass higher.

Tharon laughed, then slowed and kicked out the Beta's legs for better access. The Beta's arousal was all over the edge of the table, bringing a rumble from deep in Tharon's chest. She spread her own legs, braced herself, and gripped the Beta's hips with both hands. Tharon was finished being gentle. The first thrust was harsh but perfect. The Beta's tight walls hugged the full length of Tharon's cock. They both wanted more friction, more heat, more of everything.

With vigor, Tharon plunged again and again into the Beta, who squeezed Tharon's cock with lust. The Beta's cries urged Tharon on, causing her to pump faster. The table groaned and squeaked under them. Tharon almost lost her hold on the Beta, but her nails tore into flesh, further locking down her prey. They were both so very close, riding the edge of their orgasms.

To the left, the tent flap opened, but it did nothing to deter Tharon. Only one person would even consider entering her tent at this time. For a second, a grunt passed her lips when her younger brother passed her peripheral view. *Fucking bastard*, she told him with her eyes, but then Tharon ignored him and continued her chase for a much-deserved orgasm.

Saxon took a seat in the far corner and waited for her to finish. He cupped his chin and admired the show in silence.

The Beta withheld her cries now that a witness was here, until Tharon smacked her ass. The Beta yelped, then started to scream again. The new presence in the tent didn't seem to deter her anymore, not when Tharon was fucking her so well.

"That is it," Tharon praised and returned to the earlier demanding pace. She could feel the Beta's cunt tightening around her cock. Like the Beta, she ached to come and release the strain in her body. Then she sensed it, the sudden fall. With the next thrust, the Beta gave a deafening cry that tipped Tharon too. With hips forward and cock buried deep, Tharon howled in pleasure and surrendered to the heated waves. A slight stream of slick broke free from her cockhead, but there was no fear of pregnancy. Tharon needed to be rutting for her slick to be viable.

Tharon bent over the Beta's prone form and held up her body with both hands flat against the table. She groaned as the Beta's pussy fluttered around her length. Opening her eyes, Tharon studied the little Beta under her and considered tasting the salty skin. But she'd had enough, and her brother was here. With a huff, she straightened and withdrew from the Beta. As Tharon pulled out, the Beta whimpered but otherwise remained motionless on the table.

"Get up," Tharon said, her voice rough. She pushed off some of her braided black hair that stuck to the damp skin of her shoulders.

The Beta attempted to lift herself off the table, but her arms trembled, and she collapsed with a huff of air.

Tharon grunted, then caught Saxon's chuckle; it dug under her skin. With a growl, she snaked an arm under the Beta's trim waist, lifted her, then tossed her unceremoniously over her right shoulder. The Beta gave a weak squeal, but didn't fight Tharon, who marched into the smaller attached tent to the right. Once inside, Tharon tossed the Beta onto the bed next to the other female Beta, who had a curious look.

"Get dressed and go," Tharon told them. She turned her back on them and went to the washbasin. Wetting a cloth, she wiped down her body and listened to the Betas' movements. The one that Tharon had fucked earlier was moving faster and helped Ffion. *That is the girl's name*, Tharon recalled. She still had no clue about the first Beta's name and didn't know if she'd ever been told. It mattered not at this point.

Wiping her dick clean a second time, Tharon found herself still a bit hard, but she would handle it later on her own. She collected a pair of fresh drawers from the wooden trunk, stepped into them, and tied them off at her waist. In her early years, she hid her body around her brother, but her time being the lord commander had changed that part of her, along with other aspects of her life. No longer bothering with a breastband, she grabbed the one other necessary item, a sheathed dagger.

The two Betas were halfway dressed but paused and stared as Tharon returned to the main tent. They whispered something to each other as Tharon left.

Saxon stretched out his legs, canted his head, and smiled. Tharon wedged the sheathed blade into her waistband before walking to the firepit at the center of the tent, at the far side of the table. She tossed in two more pieces of wood, then approached her brother, who rested comfortably in a fur covered seat. After adjusting the fur, Tharon sank into the U-shaped armchair to see her brother's grinning features. "What do you want, Saxon? I won your battle this month."

Chuckling, Saxon straightened, lifted his hands from the armchair, and cocked his head. "To congratulate you on another successful campaign."

Tharon grunted. "You never visit to simply congratulate me. You did not come out to this slop without good reason." The movement over to the right caught her attention.

The two Betas had slipped out from the bedding tent and paused near the fire. They were both somewhat dressed, but their tops were loose and hanging. Their hair was sloppy, and Ffion hung off the other Beta.

"King Saxon," the unknown Beta said and attempted a curtsy of some type. The Beta's messy curtsy was more of an insult toward royals than a polite effort.

"Go," Tharon said in a snappy tone. She disregarded them, unworthy of any more of her time.

"Yes, Lord Commander." The Beta adjusted her arm around Ffion and hurried out of the tent with a few giggles.

"They are always so enamored with you," Saxon murmured with a trace of wonder. "Why is that?"

Tharon scowled at him and ignored his constant prodding about why Betas fell to their knees for her. It didn't matter where the army marched to within their kingdom or the enemy's territory, there were females ready for her.

"Perhaps it is because you have a cunt too," Saxon whispered, then his dark eyes focused on Tharon. "Tell me if I am right, sister."

Tharon responded with a low growl and a show of teeth. She huffed and asked, "What do you want, little brother?" If Saxon weren't her brother and her king, she would have given him a black eye for his disparaging question. With a deep breath, she controlled her Alpha's desire to dominate, knowing she was the elder Alpha between them. She was certainly the stronger one, too, having earned her fighting prowess early on as a knight. Saxon could hardly keep from cutting himself with a blade.

"Besides the congratulations for capturing our enemy's town of Leeward, I have come with exciting news." Saxon crossed his legs and folded his hands in his lap.

Tharon grunted and asked, "King Garrett is captured and ready to be beaten to death?" Even though she had taken Leeward, which was a huge feat, it still wasn't enough. The crucial town marked the start of an upward battle into the heart of the enemy kingdom. Before they even arrived at Leeward's walls, they had fought their way through enemy lines, clever peasants, bogs, and disease. That in itself had taken them ten years. But the Kingdom of White Sommer was determined on forcing its enemy to heel under its boot.

Saxon grunted, then a shitty grin spread across his face. "That is no way to speak of your future father-in-law."

Tharon blinked and stared at her brother as if he'd grown another head. It had to be a fucking joke, except Saxon had a mischievous glee in his eyes. "What have you done?" she asked, teetering on the edge of rage. Her barrier around her inner Alpha began to crack, especially when her brother chuckled at her. "Saxon!" She was out of the chair, but so was Saxon, who outmatched her height by a hand.

"Easy, Tharon." Saxon grabbed her bare shoulders. "I have done what is necessary for our kingdom to win this war. Now it is your turn to do what is necessary." He was stern, finally sounding like a king. He then rested one hand on the sword hilt at his hip. The firelight glinted off the black gem mounted in the pommel, reminding them both of Saxon's authority as the king. Like all rulers, he wore a crown, but their kingdom's power was held within the Sword of White Sommer that he carried. "We have been at this war for far too long. Our army's might has been whittled away little by little."

Tharon ground her teeth at hearing the harsh truth. No one understood it better than she did, after heading the army for the past three years. But the truth had never smothered her savage desire to defeat the Kingdom of Wyndfeld and destroy the House of Arrington. After a deep breath, she asked, "What horseshit idea have you dreamed up this time?"

Saxon claimed faux hurt, but he chuckled and dropped his arms to his side. "We cannot continue like this, at least not with our army weakened so and our gold mines in enemy hands." He was serious again, and he rubbed the beard that afforded him a few extra years he hadn't yet earned. "I contacted King Garrett under the guise of seeking peace. As you can imagine, he was unreceptive at first, but I told him how earnest we are about a truce. I have offered your hand in marriage to one of his daughters." He continued to speak, but Tharon had lost her mind.

"You what?" Tharon fisted her hands after interrupting her brother's rambling. "I am to wed a daughter from the House of Arrington?" She was breathing deeper, hoping the extra air cooled the fire in her chest.

"Yes." Saxon narrowed his eyes and said, "You are not listening, sister." He grabbed Tharon's jaw, growled and snapped, causing Tharon to focus on him. "Get your little Alpha under control." He searched her eyes and waited for her to accept his authority as king. Once she stopped bristling, he ordered, "Now sit and listen to my great plan."

Bottling her temper for now, Tharon sank into the chair and waited to hear his ridiculous idea.

"As I was saying, you will wed a princess from the House of Arrington. Upon doing so, it will grant you access to the Kingdom of Wyndfeld. We will maintain the fragile alliance through good will, such as returning their lands we have conquered. In addition, you and your new wife will be required to visit both kingdoms on a regular schedule."

"Return their lands?" Tharon laughed, but there was no humor. "My men have given their blood and their lives for these wretched lands." She growled at the mere thought of handing them back to the enemy.

"This alliance will allow us to plant spies," Saxon said in a firm tone. "Those loyal to us who can remain hidden in the Kingdom of Wyndfeld."

"What then?" Tharon slapped her palms against the armrests. "We drink and dance with our enemy, then slit their throats at night? They will not fall for that like our father did." For centuries, their two Houses and kingdoms had been unified; they had been one family. As a pup, Tharon had loved the Arringtons, missed them when she was away from Wyndfeld, and looked forward to every visit with them.

Until the Arringtons *betrayed* Tharon and her family.

Saxon sighed and rubbed the bridge of his nose. He lowered his hand and stared at his fuming sister, then said, "We are losing this war, sister. Do you not see that?" He held out his arms and growled once. "The Kingdom of Wyndfeld has a smaller army than we do, but their terrain is their best weapon. We have pushed through the Shadow Bogs, crossed the open fields, and defeated Loxmoor Citadel, but now we must contend with the White Razor Mountains."

"We have Leeward now," Tharon said and clawed the armrests. "I have formulated a plan to take Duskgard Keep before the first snowfall."

"Yes. But it is merely the beginning of Fringe Road, which is dotted with fortresses and towers." Saxon shook his head and leaned forward, closer to his sister. "It is the month of Fire-Eye, and by the time we are ready to take on Fringe Road, it will be harvest, then winter again. You know this."

Tharon turned her head away and stared at the fire. She had done the math earlier when she looked at the map and considered their current forces. Fringe Road was the main route to Earna, the capital of the Kingdom of Wyndfeld, but it wound up into the mountain range and was littered with defenses that benefited the Kingdom of Wyndfeld. The estimated loss of life on Fringe Road could be anywhere from fifty thousand to seventy thousand, maybe more. If they conquered the west side of Fringe Road, their travels through the White Razor Mountains would continue to be treacherous until they approached the east side of Fringe Road. Then the bloody game would restart on the way down Fringe Road to where the enemy's heart rested in Earna. Tharon was well versed on the Kingdom of Wyndfeld and the journey to Earna, considering she'd spent the better part of her youth traversing the distance.

"Other than spies, what can we gain from this political marriage?" Tharon asked and turned back to her brother.

"Time." Saxon leaned back into the chair again. "Time to rebuild. Time to plot. Time to kill."

Tharon rumbled and pushed her fingers through her wild locks. With a clearer mind, she weighed her brother's plan. The gold mines in northern White Sommer would be returned to them and refill their dwindling treasury. With more gold, they could rebuild their army's numbers, supplies, and weapons. Even health and finances were a concern at this stage. Several years ago, Wyndfeld took control of White Sommer's gold mines. Saxon's plan would indeed give Tharon access to the Kingdom of Wyndfeld, to learn what changes had been made, and what weak points she and her brother could use to their advantage. The House of Arrington would be distrustful at first, but Tharon could charm them.

Saxon chuckled, causing Tharon to glare at him. "I have seen that look before." He gave a triumphant smile because he knew he was winning her over.

After a chuff, Tharon narrowed her eyes at her brother and asked, "Why do you not wed?"

"For those asking, I am the younger Alpha of us." Saxon held out his hand to Tharon and said, "I may be king, but you are first in line to wed."

Tharon snorted. *That did not stop you from easily accepting the sword from Father.* She withheld her scathing thought after her father's voice reminded her why she had to pass the Sword of White Sommer on to Saxon. She had given her blessing after all.

"However, the real reason is that you are wedding because you have the militaristic mind between us," Saxon said. "You will take note of how to bring down Earna. Find its weak spots that we can exploit." He shrugged and said, "Besides, this may be your one chance to marry and sire a pup." His smile was devious and caused Tharon's stomach to churn in response. "At the end of this, if your Arrington wife has an unfortunate accident..." Saxon shrugged and chuckled.

Tharon huffed and shifted in the seat as she considered the next step in Saxon's plan. She worried over the one detail that could derail everything. "Which princess am I to wed?" All the muscles in her body curled, and she gripped the armrest again.

"Myla Arrington," Saxon replied.

"Myla," Tharon whispered, then grunted and chuckled. Myla was the third oldest in the House of Arrington. She was gentle and sweet, if not a bit shy. But Myla was bright, like any Arrington. She was also an unclaimed, pure Omega, who would submit with ease to Tharon. Even though Myla was kind, she was rather different from her sister Roswynd.

However, a marriage to Myla would be a temporary situation allowing her access to Wyndfeld again. Once she and Saxon destroyed the House of Arrington, Tharon could have Roswynd. Just as it should have been ten years ago. But for now, Tharon couldn't show her hand to anyone, especially Saxon, who had disdained Roswynd since their youth. For the first time, both of Tharon's vows could be fulfilled in one fell swoop, if she played her hand correctly. Shaking the forbidden name from her mind, Tharon banished the memories of her once best friend.

"You seem pleased with the arrangement now." Saxon popped out of the wooden armchair. "Then I am pleased."

Lips thinning into a line, Tharon rose and followed her brother to the tent flap. She opened her mouth to respond, but Saxon spun around and beamed at her.

"Tomorrow morning we will meet with King Garrett to finalize the agreement." Saxon adjusted the golden cloak around his body and said, "You will be there."

Tharon rumbled and stared at her brother, who had already set up much of the wedding arrangements with King Garrett without her knowledge. She curled her hands into fists and asked, "What would you have done if I refused your offer?"

Saxon chuckled after tying the upper part of his cloak. His sword hilt still poked out from the opening. "You would not have refused." He started out of the tent but paused and gazed back at Tharon. "I am your brother. And your king." Then he was gone.

For a moment, Tharon stared at the tent flap that settled back into place. "Bastard," she muttered, even though he was her brother. Deep inside, she loved him despite his antics. They both shared a similar goal, to bring down the Kingdom of Wyndfeld. Saxon's ultimate plan included killing each and every Arrington until the House was stricken from the lands. Tharon held little care about the fate of the entire House of Arrington once she conquered the kingdom. However, she was certain of two decisions: King Garrett deserved a slow, excruciating death, and Roswynd Arrington would be hers despite Saxon's desire for her death. If entering a political marriage to topple the enemy kingdom was the best route, then she would follow Saxon's plans, for now. Too many of her soldiers had already died in the war.

At the small firepit, Tharon used a metal poker to separate the few burning logs. She tossed dirt on the remaining flames, then went to the bedding tent. After she cleaned her hands, she took off her bottoms and went to bed with a dagger. She tucked the weapon next to her head while her sheathed swords remained propped up against the bed.

The bed of furs carried the mild scent of Beta, Alpha, and sex. The smell aroused her again, causing her cock to harden some. Tharon clutched the shaft, under the unsheathed head. With her thumb, she rubbed the tip and smeared a few droplets of clear fluid. Even though her cock swelled in her hand, her mind wandered back to her conversation with Saxon.

Tomorrow Saxon would offer her like a prized Beadu oxen, talking up Tharon's abilities as an Alpha, even if she was a degenerate one. She seethed at the slur for her perverted nature as a female Alpha. In the past, she had slit a few throats whenever someone used the slur to describe her. She was an Alpha, and not because of the cock in her hand.

After a growl, Tharon returned to playing with the swollen head that was sensitive to the touch. By tomorrow afternoon, she would be promised an Omega, even if it was an Arrington. Myla was pretty, as Tharon recalled. Her hair was blond similar to all Arringtons. She had hazel eyes, tanned skin, and a lithe figure. As a pup, Myla tried to tell jokes; some were funny. Myla would make an acceptable spouse, albeit a temporary one.

Lowering her hand, Tharon massaged the throbbing length of her cock, enjoying it while she thought more about Myla, who always had a gentle smile. But her smile never compared to how Roswynd's beautiful lips could curl and light up Tharon's heart. Roswynd's eyes were each a different color, always reminding Tharon of the summer sun over the ocean. Roswynd hated her mismatched eyes, but Tharon adored how they glowed whenever Roswynd laughed.

With a groan, Tharon moved her hand faster and dug her fingers into the fur. Somehow Roswynd's voice had snuck into her head. Tharon fought to force it away and think of Myla or even the two Betas from earlier. But instead, Roswynd reappeared and grinned at her. Tharon growled and pumped her cock through her fist, searching for relief. Roswynd's young features were so clear in Tharon's memory, even ten years later. Once, they had shared a delicate kiss. Their lips had been pressed together for a few brief seconds, but Tharon still felt it today.

"Fuuuck." Tharon cast out thoughts of Roswynd, then lifted her head. She sat up, using her other arm to prop up her body. Her glistening cock appeared bigger than normal, but it didn't slow Tharon. She growled and worked the shaft faster, needing to climax. More focused on her own pleasure, Tharon was close and the swollen girth in her hand throbbed. Her inner Alpha keened at the idea that she was indeed larger. It was enough to tip her over, eliciting a howl from deep in her chest.

Tharon continued to fist her cock, milking slick from the head. She needed this, or else she wouldn't sleep tonight. Her body trembled with satisfaction. But Roswynd's beautiful smile invaded her mind again. She reprimanded herself with the idea that Roswynd was perhaps married now, considering her age. *But there has never been any news of a wedding,* she reminded herself. Without control Tharon snarled and ground her teeth. The Alpha inside her ignited her again. Driven by her body, Tharon returned to pumping her firm cock, but this time she didn't deny herself thoughts about Roswynd.

Roswynd should have been hers. For all these years, it should have been Roswynd writhing under her rather than countless unknown Betas. But instead, Tharon had been denied Roswynd and was now being given Roswynd's little sister like a consolation prize. Tharon could almost spit, but she doubled her efforts and stroked her cock with absolute fervor. Tilting her head back, she closed her eyes and imagined Roswynd's adult features: her heart-shaped face, freckly cheeks, and mismatched eyes, all framed by golden hair. It was all Tharon needed to come, releasing the pressure built up in her.

The clear slick pooled out of the tip and ran over Tharon's hand. She stopped moving her hand and smeared the wetness over the shaft, which had gone soft. She was panting and sweaty from the masturbation, but she felt better, even in the empty darkness of her tent. Leaving the bed, Tharon wet another cloth and wiped herself clean for the night. Once done, she returned to bed, turned off the lamp, and settled under the furs.

Tharon needed to have her wits about herself for tomorrow's meeting with King Garrett and about the terms of the arranged marriage. If nothing else, this stupid marriage might give her a chance to see Roswynd one more time.

Chapter 2

Princess Roswynd Arrington stared at her younger sister, Myla, in awe and befuddlement. She stuttered once before she regained control of her mouth. "Pardon me. Did you say you are to marry Tharon Blakesley?" Her heart was in her throat.

Myla shuffled on her feet, then looked away from her sister. Her eyes were puffy and red, and her cheeks were damp. "Yes. Father told me an hour ago."

Roswynd was certain her knees would give out, so she leaned her back against the stable's siding. Her sister's voice was growing smaller, distant until Roswynd shook her head.

"I leave this afternoon with Father. We meet King Saxon and Princess Tharon tomorrow morning." Myla was crying again, edging on a sob. "I am so scared, Roswynd. They say she rapes Betas and th-that she marks them with a dagger."

Pushing off the stable building, Roswynd pulled her sister into a strong hug and held her. Myla tucked her head under Roswynd's chin and returned the hug, sobbing into Roswynd's chest. "Myla, it is going to be fine. I promise." She closed her eyes and continued whispering reassurances, even though she was still overwhelmed by the news.

Myla was to wed Tharon Blakesley.

Tharon Blakesley, who was better known as the Lord Commander of the White Sommer Army and bestowed the title of the Black Wulf. There were other, far less kind names for Tharon, but Roswynd kept them at bay.

Her sweet nineteen-year-old sister was to become the Omega mate of the bloodthirsty lord commander.

With a low growl, Roswynd withdrew from Myla, kissed her on the forehead, and promised her again that everything would be okay. She told Myla to go to her room and rest for a moment. Leaving the stable, Roswynd marched across the castle grounds, entered a hallway, and headed for her father's office. After horseback riding, she typically went to her room and changed from her riding trousers into a dress. Her father was against her wearing trousers, boots, tunics, and anything else masculine. But right now, she cared nothing about appeasing him when he planned to marry off Myla to that enemy asshole.

At the door to her father's study, the guard straightened his back and said, "King Garrett is meeting with the captain of the guard."

"Perfect." Roswynd snarled at the guard, who attempted to stop her. Her burning look made him take a step back before she opened the door herself.

"What is the meaning—" Garrett was standing behind his desk and grew flustered upon seeing Roswynd storming into his office. "—Roswynd! What are you doing? I am busy."

"We must speak." Roswynd turned to the seated knight and said, "If you will excuse us, Sir Donnchad."

Donnchad had risen out of respect, but he turned to his king for actual instructions.

Garrett sighed and said, "You may go, Captain." He waited until the heavy door opened and closed before he turned his wrath on his daughter. "I assume you have spoken to your sister."

"Yes!" Roswynd clenched her teeth, flashing her canines. "How can you do this to Myla?"

"I have little choice!" Garrett's fists clenched at his sides. The furrow across his brow tightened more. His eyes were dark with circles under them. "King Saxon wishes to have peace and has offered his sister's hand in marriage to show good faith."

Roswynd's vision flashed with red dots, but she barked with bitter laughter. "They do not mean such peace, Father! They wish to conquer us, then kill us."

Garrett's pheromones were heavy with a mixture of concern and weariness. He rumbled and said, "I am well aware that may be their true plan."

"Then why fall for the trap?" Roswynd asked, demanding her father use reason. Myla was going to be a pawn who would be hurt or worse by the farce.

"Because we are the better hunters."

Roswynd became wide-eyed. But you taught her how to be a hunter! She reboxed her happy memories of Tharon and their hunting trips. "This is not a game," Roswynd snapped. "This is Myla's life." She waved her hands in the air and continued to reprimand her father. "You cannot trust them! The Blakesleys go back on their oaths!" She knew this better than anyone after Tharon's betrayal.

"Then do you suggest we continue this war? It has carried on for ten years."

"Yes! We have held out for ten years. We can hold out for another ten." Roswynd struggled against the heat in her eyes, but the tears were close. "And another ten after that until they give up."

"They will never give up." Garrett's words were firm and true. He sighed and whispered, "Our resources are dwindling. Now that they have defeated Loxmoor Citadel and taken Leeward, it is only a matter of time before they march across Fringe Road and arrive on our doorstep."

Roswynd released a slight whimper, then took the seat closest to her. It was unlike her father to be honest and open about the effects of the war. The truth left her weak and breathing hard. "I thought Myla was promised to Prince Drust and that they were going to send help to us."

"Yes. But it will take time. Perhaps years." Garrett sank into the chair and tried holding back a groan, but Roswynd heard it. "But if we can end the war now with White Sommer, then this is a better choice."

Roswynd wiped her face, ridding herself of the stupid tears. She wanted to believe that her kingdom was faring better than their enemy, but they had lost the important town of Leeward. Under Tharon's ruthless leadership, the White Sommer Army seemed undefeatable. The previous lord commander of the White Sommer Army had been a pure idiot and easily bested at every turn. After his forced retirement, Tharon was promoted from a knight to the lord commander and proved to be a decisive and excellent tactician, and a strong leader. Tharon was born for it.

The worst part of it was that a ridiculous sliver of Roswynd actually admired Tharon's skills and accomplishments as both a knight and lord commander.

"There is another way, Roswynd."

Swallowing, Roswynd lifted her head and studied her father's grim features. Whatever his second idea was, she would probably like it less.

"You could wed Princess Tharon so that Myla may wed Prince Drust," Garrett said in a calm voice, then fell silent and waited for his daughter's eruption. But it didn't come. The prolonged quietness was interrupted by a pop of burning wood from the fireplace. He pressed on with his thoughts. "If you were to marry Tharon, you could keep a watchful eye on her. You understand her better than anyone else in our family does."

Roswynd closed her eyes and shook her head. "I knew Tharon the princess of White Sommer. Not Tharon the beastly and monstrous lord commander of the White Sommer Army." There were countless wild tales that Tharon transformed into a werewolf on the full moon and slaughtered Wyndfeld soldiers out of pure pleasure.

"Even so, do you believe your sister can handle Tharon?" Garrett asked, his voice gentler now. He was making a difficult decision by giving away one of his daughters to the enemy. From the sour scent rolling off him, he didn't want to do it. There were other ways and reasons to deny the political marriage. But the cost would be the loss of more lives.

Unbecoming of a lady, Roswynd groaned and slouched in the armchair, then rubbed her aching brow. "No." Her father had excellent points about Myla and Tharon. Without doubt, the marriage was a diversion for any plans King Saxon was creating with his clever mind. "What if we were to catch Tharon spying or…" She didn't want to consider what other nefarious plans Tharon might have.

"Or attempting to kidnap or murder someone from the House of Arrington?" Garrett asked and folded his hands on his lap. "We would arrest and behead Tharon, depending on the crime."

Roswynd swallowed and wrenched her fingers together. Images of Tharon's head rolling taunted her, but she chased them off. Was Tharon capable of cold-blooded murder? Were the Blakesleys that determined to defeat their enemy? Considering the lie that started the war, it was possible that Tharon would be willing to murder out of vengeance for the death of Tharon's mother ten years ago.

"Without Tharon, the White Sommer Army would collapse," Garrett whispered, but he sighed and shifted in the seat. "I am sorry you must hear all of this, daughter. These are not conversations meant for your ears." After years of fighting and death, the protective wall between him and Roswynd was cracking. Bits and pieces from the war's strain were bleeding through. Now at the age of twenty-three, Roswynd was no longer a pup who needed shielding.

"I hear the whispers," Roswynd muttered, then straightened. In deep thought, she stared at the mud on her boots from her ride today. The morning had been beautiful even if parts of the trail had been a little messy. She'd packed a light breakfast and ate it at the overlook that she and Tharon had once shared together. Each time she tried to replace her memories of the overlook with better ones, she failed, and instead the thoughts took her back to her heartbreaking childhood. Again, she reprimanded herself for giving in to such bittersweet memories about Tharon.

However, upon returning to the stable, it felt as if an avalanche had struck Roswynd when she learned Myla and Tharon were to wed. She would be idiotic to ignore how deeply her Omega reared up and demanded that no one but her be allowed to wed Tharon. Such an internal betrayal helped her gain control of her silly Omega. Right now she needed to focus on the real problem, which was allowing someone from the House of Blakesley back into their fold to any degree. Especially Tharon, the lord commander.

Her father was right. Myla was too docile and gentle to handle Tharon. Even though ten years had passed, Roswynd still had a fair idea of what made Tharon tick. On the positive side, Myla would be allowed to marry Prince Drust, who was a handsome and kind Alpha, a rare combination. Roswynd's future was marred by her reluctance to conform to the traditions expected of an Omega. Many times her father attempted to pair Roswynd with a prince or noble, but Roswynd did her best to undermine his matchmaking. As a result, she'd earned a reputation as a wild, untamed Omega princess not fit to wed, which pleased Roswynd. But a political marriage to Tharon was a twisted chance to show everyone she was capable, even if it was predestined to fail.

With a sigh, she asked, "Are you not concerned that King Saxon will reject your offer of my hand over Myla's?" Roswynd watched how her father's features made a slight shift, one she couldn't quite figure out.

"No." Garrett hesitated, then lifted a blond eyebrow. He was nearing his fifties, but still had a young face, especially with his beard shaved off in the summer months. "Because even if King Saxon refuses, Tharon will not."

* * *

Roswynd swayed with the motions of her red roan-colored horse, Dragonfly, who was gifted to her on her twentieth birthday. Dragonfly was her second horse after her first had aged beyond any serious riding. The relationship between Dragonfly and Roswynd had been unpredictable and arduous that first year, but they worked through it.

With a pat to his neck, Roswynd minded his footing as they finished the ride down Fringe Road. They were expected at the meeting point about an hour's march from Leeward. The journey through the White Razor Mountains had been enjoyable yesterday afternoon despite their destination today. They'd overnighted at Fort Snowfalcon, which was located part of the way on the plateau between the east and west mountain ranges. They left before dawn and started down Fringe Road's western portion at first light. From their high vantage point, Leeward was easy to spot on such a clear morning.

But as the caravan approached the end of Fringe Road, everyone's mood darkened. The three hundred soldiers were on high alert. King Garrett rode near the front while Roswynd remained in the middle. She was surrounded by soldiers and two knights, who would guard her at any cost. Their duty to protect her dammed the surge of tension inside Roswynd.

At the bottom of Fringe Road, the large unit went to the left and headed south on a smaller road known as Golden Wheat Road. It was well used by farmers from the south. They carted supplies north on Golden Wheat Road, across Fringe Road, and finally down to the capital. As a result, Golden Wheat Road had major divots and potholes from wheels, unlike the cobblestone paving for Fringe Road.

The ride along Golden Wheat Road was about an hour, but it passed in haste, at least for Roswynd. Orders were being shouted, and the unit of three hundred soldiers split into smaller groups. There were no carts or carriages. Garrett didn't want to slow down the unit if a skirmish, battle, or quick escape was necessary.

About half the unit remained near the roadside, spread out and appearing uninviting in case anyone, such as a bandit, was looking for trouble. The remaining portion followed a dirt pathway that was wide enough for two horses.

They were nearing the meeting location, which was at Fairview Lake, about a half-hour march from a nearby village named Oldview. All around them was woodland, but as they progressed, it eventually faded away to grassland, then finally to the quiet lake. The unit started their sweep around the lake, securing the area.

Roswynd swallowed against the forming lump in her throat and stared at Fairview Lake. She was familiar with the lake and wondered if Tharon had chosen this meeting location on purpose. Old promises between her and Tharon echoed inside her, but she packed them away. She dismounted and her two guards did the same. She brought Dragonfly's reins over his head, then they walked over to her father. It was nice to stretch her legs after the journey here.

Garrett was speaking to Donnchad, who was second in charge of the unit for their trip. As the captain of the guard, he was responsible for the safety of the House of Arrington. He always traveled with the king and queen, leaving the lieutenant in charge of overseeing the remaining family's safety.

The conversation paused when Roswynd was close, and Garrett turned to his daughter. "The captain and I feel it is best that you remain on horseback."

Roswynd reached up and pulled back the emerald-colored hood of her cloak. She opened her mouth with an argument, but it fell short. Right now they needed cohesion rather than discord. Her father was worried about her safety. After a second, she asked, "Then I will not be a part of this meeting?" She felt like a showpiece rather than a figurehead with a voice.

Garrett exchanged a glance with Donnchad, who had an uncanny ability to understand his king without words. He stepped away and signaled her two knights to join him.

Now alone, Garrett came closer to Roswynd and softened his voice. "I wish to shield you from this, so if anything goes wrong, you will be able to escape quickly. It is very important that you are here."

"But to be seen, not heard," Roswynd said. She fought to keep the irritation off her face, but she felt it leak into her tone. With a sigh she turned to Dragonfly and petted him in hopes it would sooth her mood. So much was happening at once, and all of it felt out of her hands.

"Roswynd, if you wish to change your mind, it is not too late."

Roswynd listened to Dragonfly's deep breaths, finding comfort in his strong presence. He would indeed burst into a canter to help her flee the area if somehow the meeting became messy or turned out to be a trap. "No." She regarded her father and said, "This is what is best for our people."

"If things turn awry, do you recall where to go?" Garrett asked. Last night, he and Roswynd had gone over a map to work out a safety plan in the event of fighting or separation. Roswynd would continue south to her aunt and uncle's estate. From there her relatives would assist with returning Roswynd back home to the capital. Everyone was on alert, as Garrett had sent out messages to various military figures and relatives.

"Of course." Roswynd touched her hip. "I have the map." She also had enough food and supplies for three days, which was plenty to make it to her relatives. The map remained on her person in case Dragonfly was injured or went lame and she had to continue on foot.

Garrett gave a firm nod, then shifted closer and held Roswynd's arms. "I know we have had our differences over the years, but I am proud of you for shouldering this. It is not something I have ever wanted for any of my pups. This entire war has—"

"I know, Father." Roswynd needed to halt his speech, not ready to hear him crumble right now. She needed him to remain strong. He was tired of the war, similar to all Arringtons. But they hadn't won anything by agreeing to the political marriage. This was simply a new stage of the war that could end very quickly, if they played the game well. The Blakesleys might be persistent and strong, but the Arringtons were far cleverer and smarter. This was the kind of battlefield they could win on.

Straightening his back, Garrett nodded and said, "Thank you."

Roswynd was unsure whether the gratitude was for ending his rambling before he fell apart or her willingness to help find an end to these ten years of madness. She took a deep breath, then did something she hadn't done in years. She hugged her father.

A gust of air left Garrett, even though he was much larger and bulkier as an Alpha. He held her head close to his chest, which rolled with soft thunder. Bowing his head he breathed in her sweet scent, and for a moment they both laid aside their past arguments under one goal, to find peace. Since birth Roswynd knew her father's distinct scent was mixed with sandalwood. As a pup it brought her comfort and security until her adulthood. Then she had craved it less, until now.

"Come along," Garrett murmured, then forced them to separate. The enemy would arrive soon, and they needed to prepare.

After clearing her throat, Roswynd put the reins over Dragonfly's head, mounted, and settled into the saddle. Behind her the two knights mirrored her motions and then flanked her on either side.

Garrett patted his daughter's calf but walked away without a second glance. Donnchad rejoined his side, and they headed toward the lakeside, the designated meeting spot. Within a few minutes, a clamor sounded and drew everyone's attention to the north, beyond the lake.

In the distance outlines of soldiers dotted the field. Wyndfeld soldiers often traveled in formation, but the White Sommer Army was better known for spreading out. Today was no exception as the enemy soldiers fanned out across the field, stomping down the already dead grasses. Farther behind, a small cavalry followed the footmen. There were at least two hundred soldiers, most on horseback, which didn't bode well if there was an attack. Most of the Wyndfeld soldiers were on foot, but they were carrying pikes, which were perfect for spearing horses.

As the enemy unit grew close, Donnchad ordered the Wyndfeld soldiers to reassemble at the southeastern portion of the lake, closer to their king and princess. The path back to Golden Wheat Road was left clear, an easy escape route. Everyone's hands were on their weapons, but no one readied them.

However, Roswynd heard her two knights' swords scrape. She glanced over at one of them and confirmed he was testing it to make sure the blade wasn't stuck in the sheath. Their preparedness gave her some peace of mind. Reaching behind, she drew the hood back over her head and adjusted the long cloak around her legs to hide them. A princess should be transported in a carriage, but Roswynd was more than capable of riding, and she disdained the confines of a carriage. Still, many frowned upon females straddling horses, let alone wearing trousers, as she was now.

With a deep breath, Roswynd allowed the hood's anonymity to play in her favor. She watched with scrutiny as the White Sommer soldiers took various positions around the area. From her older brother's education, she had learned the different types of soldiers that comprised the White Sommer Army. Most of the footmen were common soldiers. A few were crossbowmen, who would have had formal training, but the soldiers on horseback were White Sommer knights. They were considered fierce and extremely loyal to Tharon.

The cavalry flowed to the right and left, parting open for King Saxon and Tharon, who could be seen riding forward, closer to the lake. Saxon tugged on his horse's reins, then dismounted. Tharon halted her black horse next to her king, but she remained astride for a minute. Her gaze was hunting and calculating the enemy. Next to her, several knights dismounted and waited for further instructions.

Roswynd clenched the reins harder when Tharon's piercing gaze settled on her. *She cannot see my face. She thinks I am Myla*, she reminded herself. *Her father didn't have time to send a message about the change in the arrangements.* For now, she wanted to play the dutiful daughter and listen to the conversations. But her own self-reassurances did little to slow the frantic beating of her heart. The black gloves on her hands were sticky against her palms. Earlier the thick cloak had kept her warm, but it was stifling and heavy, feeling as though it would drag her off the horse. She forced herself to not tighten her legs around Dragonfly, but he was already aware of her emotions. He stomped his hoof twice and whined. She hushed him once, then rubbed her hand against his neck.

Finally, Tharon dismounted, then handed off the horse's reins to a foot soldier, who was shorter than her. In fact, she was taller and bigger than most. Roswynd struggled to reconcile her adorable former best friend with the bulky, dangerous knight who equaled her father's size or possibly outmatched him. Tharon carried two swords, one on each hip. She wore no cloak, but her black leathers and midnight armor looked heavy enough. On the chest of her cuirass was a wolf head, indicating her position as White Sommer's powerful Black Wulf, a title bestowed upon one Alpha in each generation of the Blakesleys. After Saxon exchanged a look with his sister, they marched forward. Tharon rested a hand on a sword; her quick and surefooted gait belied the weight of her attire.

Saxon was the first to break the stalemate of silence between the royal families. "Good morning, King Garrett." His deep voice was chipper, as if they were gathering for brunch.

Roswynd's stomach roiled with bile. Even now many years later, Saxon's voice could still climb to a high-pitched volume that reminded her of a mountain fox in heat.

Garrett returned the greeting, then looked at Tharon. "It has been many years, Princess Tharon," he said, his tone formal and polite.

"I am Prince Tharon or Lord Commander," Tharon corrected. Her voice had deepened to a timber that held power and demanded respect. She had done more than grow into an Alpha; she had become the Alpha of White Sommer, even though it was Saxon who carried the Sword of White Sommer.

Roswynd's attention was hyperfocused on Tharon Blakesley, tuning out the conversation for a moment. Her mouth was terribly dry, but she refused to make a scene by reaching for her waterskin. For years she imagined what Tharon looked like as an adult Alpha, never able to match it with the stranger in front of her. But she failed to prepare herself for that commanding voice or the low rumble at the end. It was no wonder the soldiers of the White Sommer Army fell in line.

But just as curious was the fact that Tharon went by "prince" rather than "princess" now. At what age had the change been made? What had finally triggered it? Roswynd recalled a young She-Alpha too scared to wear trousers in the face of backlash. But now, that same female Alpha demanded her proper titles be recognized and used without question. Tharon was a far cry from the timid, cute pup Roswynd once knew. This new game of a farce political marriage was going to be a lot harder now.

"I concur that finding peace is in both kingdoms' best interest," King Garrett said. He matched both Saxon's and Tharon's height, dominance, and assuredness. He was ever the Alpha king.

"Excellent." Saxon was expressive and smiling, perhaps the only person smiling within a league right now. "Then shall we begin conversations about this new beginning between our kingdoms." He shifted and looked at his sister. "And of a beautiful union between my dear sister and your sweet daughter."

"Yes." Garrett pivoted in Roswynd's direction, giving a nod of reassurance. He was telling her that everything was okay, so far, but to be prepared to gallop if his next announcement angered the Blakesleys. "There has been a minor change, I am afraid." His words triggered Tharon to lift her blade, but Saxon's arm shot out to halt her attempt.

Without words, Saxon willed Tharon to relax and sheathe her weapon. With a huff Tharon slammed the hilt against the scabbard and remained silent.

"What change?" Saxon asked, his voice rumbly now, indicating he wasn't keen on any unexpected change being sprung on him.

"My daughter Myla was promised to another about a year ago. The House of Arrington cannot withdraw from that arrangement." Saxon opened his mouth to argue, but Garrett continued without hesitation. "Instead, Roswynd has agreed to take Myla's place and would be honored to wed Tharon."

Roswynd groaned inwardly at her father slathering on the compliment at the end. Such flattery worked well on Alphas, especially a Blakesley. At least, she assumed it would work until Saxon's bark of laughter startled her. Even with her father's back to her, his face hidden, she noticed his shoulders rise and fall. Everyone's attention was centered on the laughing king, except Tharon, who zeroed in on Roswynd as though she were her prey. Roswynd swallowed her panic and gripped the saddle horn with force.

Saxon grew silent and wiped a spot under his right eye. He sniffed once and said, "Roswynd Arrington." His heavy breath formed white in the cool air between them. Like his sister, he now stared in Roswynd's direction, as if noticing her for the first time. "That would explain why your daughter is astride a horse."

Roswynd thought she caught her father's growly response to Saxon's insult. She licked her lips and continued to remain hidden under the hood, still needing it as a barrier.

"The untamed Omega of Wyndfeld," Saxon added but in delight now. He was smug again and said, "She must be twenty-two."

"Twenty-three," Garrett corrected. His chest had risen, showing his protective nature over his daughter, whether she was rumored to be wild or not.

Roswynd rolled her eyes at the continued conversation as if she didn't exist. Her patience with Saxon's game was wearing thin. Plus, she found it impossible to read Tharon, who continued to stare at her, stone-faced.

"Twenty-three, then." Saxon shook his head and pursed his lips in thought. "Quite past the acceptable age for marriage." He was poking and taunting them while building a case against Roswynd as a suitable spouse to Tharon. "I surely hope that her womb is still viable." He chuckled and gazed toward Roswynd as he continued his rant. "What of her looks? Have they gone old?"

"No!"

All at once everyone turned in Roswynd's direction after her outburst. She didn't care that it was she who bit Saxon's bait. She'd had enough of his foolery. With both hands, she clutched the hood and, as she removed it, said, "My beauty has grown more radiant, King Saxon." Her voice didn't waver even a tiny bit, but rather confidence poured from her. If there was one topic on which all previous suitors had remarked, it was her distinct beauty. Even though she was on horseback, traveling, and wearing trousers, she had ensured that her hair was brushed and braided, her face highlighted with a hint of makeup, and her ears and chest accented by her jewelry. From the long silence and drawn-out stares, she knew she had won against King Saxon's accusation.

But most importantly, Roswynd had won over Tharon.

For the first time, Tharon made a noise that bordered on pleasure and satisfaction. She had shifted one step, as if she might attempt to go to Roswynd. But she held her ground and locked eyes with Roswynd now that the hood no longer divided them. A gasp stirred in Roswynd's throat once Tharon's orange eyes held her mismatched ones. As a pup, Roswynd was fascinated with the fiery orange of Tharon's eyes, having never met anyone else with such an unusual color. However, now Tharon's right eye was hazy enough to indicate blindness or partial blindness. There was no doubt it occurred during the war, if the vertical scar from her brow to her right cheek was any indicator.

"As for her womb, Roswynd's mother continues to go through heats, even at her age." Garrett skated around the topic of Roswynd's heats, which were suppressed by medication. Most Alphas were against Omegas using suppressants, citing their troublesome nature in regard to damage to an Omega's fertility. Alphas were more accepting of an herbal contraceptive taken the morning after sex. In Roswynd's opinion, it was her own damn choice.

Like Roswynd and Tharon, Saxon continued a staredown with Garrett, who remained unfazed and waited for the younger king to make a decision about Roswynd. After a rumble, Saxon turned to his sister and said, "In the end, it is up to my sister to make this decision."

Tharon broke the battle of wills between her and Roswynd, then met her brother's piercing gaze. She appeared unaffected by Saxon and remained quiet, perhaps thinking or warring with herself. Somehow the idea that it was Tharon's decision seemed like a joke to Roswynd. But still, she grew edgy and shifted in the saddle while waiting for Tharon to make a choice.

The decision seemed minuscule, but it was deafening and final—Tharon simply nodded at Saxon.

Again, Roswynd gripped the saddle horn to hold herself up on Dragonfly. Her hammering heart slammed against her chest, and a few white spots dotted her vision. She lowered her head and took several deep breaths.

"Well, then, we have a wedding to plan for!" Saxon grinned from ear to ear, again the sole person in the entire region who was perhaps having a good day. "How exciting!" He clapped Tharon on the back, then chuckled and said, "I am to have a niece or nephew soon." His last remark rang in Roswynd's ears, over and over. Saxon was right. Roswynd would give birth to pups, who would tie her even closer to the House of Blakesley, forever.

"My princess," a knight said in a soft voice. He started to reach out but restrained himself.

Roswynd halted him with a harsh stare, then noticed Tharon's returned attention. She swallowed and weighed whether she could handle staying through the rest of the meeting, which would consist of arrangements. They were important details, but her mind was gone at the moment. Her stomach was churning, wanting to revolt at the pending future ahead of her. Within a month or less, she would be wed off to her former best friend, who had become a hated enemy to Roswynd's family.

Soon Roswynd would be wife to the one person who had betrayed her so deeply.

Chapter 3

Date: 09 Sunstone 811G
(About 15 Years Ago)

Roswynd popped out of her bedroom, left the door wide open, ignored the guard on duty, and barreled down the hallway to the guest wing. Behind her, a leg from a pair of trousers flapped. Due to her riding boots, her steps were loud and echoey as she sprinted to her best friend's room. She skidded to a stop by the door, grappling with the metal handle. "Tharon!" Not bothering to knock, she charged into the room and said, "It is sunny, which means we can ride!" Day after day, she had waited for the weather to turn so she could show Tharon how to horseback ride. Now the day was finally here.

Tharon jolted upright in her bed from the sudden commotion and fanfare. "Ros!" She had a sour look and worked her fingers through her messy hair. "It is far too early." The sun had started to shine through the half-covered window.

"No, it is first light." Roswynd slammed the door shut, further jarring Tharon. She bounced across the room and hopped on top of the bed with great ease. Her effortless movements stirred Tharon's attention. With a grin, she held out her legs to show off her fitted trousers and boots.

Rolling to her side, Tharon gawked at the masculine attire on her best friend. She leaned farther toward the edge, clinging to the blankets. Tharon nearly rolled off but caught herself.

Roswynd giggled and kicked her legs in the air as if she were swimming. "Are you fond of them? I love them." She smiled when bright orange eyes turned to her in awe and wonder. "They make it much easier to ride."

Tharon was tongue-tied and stared back at her friend. Her gaze traveled up the length of Roswynd's form, settling on the tunic, which was also for males. Her bewilderment was adorable, making Roswynd's heart melt more.

"Since we are going to ride together, you will need the proper attire too." Roswynd swung around the special items in her arm and placed them in the small space between her and Tharon.

For a minute Tharon studied the folded pair of dark trousers on top of a pale green tunic. She reached out and fingered the material. She was mesmerized by the special clothing that was made for her. Her bright orange eyes cut up to Roswynd, pinning her.

"I have boots for you, too, but they are back in my room." Roswynd's face hurt from her smile, but it started to crack when Tharon withdrew her hand.

"Ros, I cannot wear these." Tharon shoved the blanket and furs that covered her body, then climbed out of bed on the other side.

"Pardon?" Roswynd twisted around in Tharon's direction. "I can show you how to put them on. It is actually simpler than a dress." But Tharon's headshake ended her rambling. She frowned and realized that it wasn't a matter of figuring out how to put on the clothes, but a matter of being allowed to wear them.

"I will wear one of my old dresses," Tharon said as she went to her wooden trunk at the foot of her bed. She lifted the lid and started to pick through the clothing until Roswynd came to her side.

"Why will you not wear the trousers?" Roswynd looked from Tharon's stern features to the feminine items inside the trunk. "The dresses make it difficult. You will have to ride sidesaddle, which I do not wish to teach you."

"I am not a male," Tharon said. Over the past couple of years, she had grown bigger and taller than Roswynd. But right now, she appeared smaller and hunched over in her nightgown.

Roswynd's features became grim, then her voice was rough. "I am not a male, but I am wearing the trousers." She held out her arms and asked, "Do I look like a male in this?"

Tharon fidgeted with the lid and whispered, "Yes, a little."

Roswynd never faulted her friend for being honest, but the truth brought a sting to her eyes. She felt heat in her face and looked away, then took a step back. Many others talked about how she started wearing trousers after her first riding lesson this summer. Even her brother made fun of her, but he stopped after she wrestled him a few times for the stupid remarks. But to now have her best friend make the same claim, it lanced her. She started to leave, yet a strong hand snared her.

"But you look beautiful in them." Tharon waited until Roswynd faced her, then spoke again but in a timid voice. "I-I cannot… I will not look…"

Roswynd dropped her shoulders and neared her friend again. The earlier ache grew stronger and twisted around her heart, but for Tharon this time. She snaked her arms around Tharon's larger form and drew her into a hug.

With Roswynd pressed against her, Tharon rested their heads together and whispered, "If my father were to find out that I wore such attire…"

"But he is not here," Roswynd responded in a gentle voice. She used her delicate pheromones to ease the distress coming off Tharon. "And we are not in Earna or Wulfbite where people will see you in them." Closing her eyes, she listened to Tharon's heartbeat slowing. They were on her family's estate in the Icecrown Forest, far from prying eyes in the capital.

"What about your brother?" Tharon nuzzled her friend's hair, drinking in her delicate scent. Her breathing had evened out again, signaling her calmer state.

Roswynd chuckled and replied, "Do not worry about that lovable idiot." She lifted her head, breaking their contact, and then she met Tharon's bright orange eyes, which held a hint of worry. Her need to banish Tharon's fears was large. "By the bones of Gyldr, I will beat any of my siblings who tease you for wearing them."

Tharon held her next breath and gawked for the second time at her friend. "Ros, you cannot curse in such a way." Her eyes cut to the closed door, as if expecting someone to burst in and reprimand Roswynd for cussing. To use Gyldr's name in such a way was of the highest sin.

Roswynd folded her arms now that the hug had ended. She ignored Tharon's warning and asked, "Will you at least try them, please?"

Tharon bit her lip, which meant she was considering the idea. With one more delicate push, Roswynd would have Tharon's agreement.

"I bet you will feel more comfortable down there too." Roswynd pointed at her friend's crotch.

"Ros!" Tharon backed up a step and almost fell into the trunk. Her face was flushed, matching her eyes.

Roswynd folded her arms and shrugged. She was an Omega and Tharon was an Alpha. She overhead her brother and father's conversations about the differences between the two breeds. Even though Tharon looked similar to an Omega, Roswynd was certain not everything was the same. Each year Tharon's scent changed and grew stronger, indicating other developments. Last summer she built up the courage to ask Tharon if she had what the other Alphas had. Tharon was a stuttering mess for about half an hour before Roswynd could coax out the truth. Roswynd had been confused why Tharon wanted to hide it from her, until

Tharon confessed she feared their friendship would come to an end. Roswynd told her nothing could come between them, not even a stick.

Regaining her bearings, Tharon peered into the trunk and frowned at the feminine attire that mocked her. A displeased rumble started low in her chest the longer she stared at them.

Roswynd sniffed her friend's agitated scent and decided to push fate. She stomped over to the bed, scooped up the clothes, and held them out to Tharon. "Please? For me?" For a moment, the clothes remained in limbo, but then Tharon took them. As Tharon walked behind the tall panels, she said, "I can help if you need a hand."

"I will be fine." Tharon moved behind the wooden panels for a few minutes, then re-emerged in the new attire. The color in her cheeks revealed her uncertainty about wearing masculine clothing for the first time.

Roswynd contained her giddy laugh, not wanting to make her friend any more uncomfortable. She held back her grin, almost. Crossing the short distance, she grabbed the hem of the tunic and pulled it out from the trousers. "You will want this out to protect your skin. I have a belt in my room to keep it in place."

"I look silly," Tharon said.

"No." Roswynd finished adjusting the shirt and trousers. "You look ready for your first riding lesson." She crinkled her nose and whispered, "Almost. We are missing your boots."

Tharon lifted her arms and studied the outfit, then met Roswynd's grinning face. "You had this all fitted for me?"

"It is a little big, but it will last longer, then." Roswynd met Tharon's admiring gaze and smiled now. "Come along." She took a larger hand into her own. "Let us get your boots before your feet get chilled on this floor." Together, they hurried to Roswynd's room and put on the socks and boots. Then she brushed and braided Tharon's hair so it would be out of the way. The last touch was the leather belt, which was simple but effective after she wrapped it twice around Tharon's waist.

On their way out of Frostwood Manor, several guards nodded at them, but Myla Arrington spotted them first and followed them out to the stable. Roswynd tried in vain to shake her little sister.

"You cannot come," Roswynd said. "You are too small." Her four-year-old sister teared up, prompting a sigh from Roswynd. She knelt down so they were at eye level. "I am going to teach Tharon how to ride today. I cannot hold on to you and teach Tharon at the same time."

"But you said I could go on the horsey with you," Myla whispered and bowed her head.

"How about tomorrow?" Roswynd asked, praying her sister agreed rather than cry to their parents.

Tharon stood next to the entrance of the stable, but she joined them and knelt next to Roswynd and Myla. "We can all go tomorrow." She smiled big when Myla turned to her. "You can ride my horse while I walk." She ignored

Roswynd's narrowed gaze. "Perhaps we can have dinner too."

Myla's eyes grew as large as plates. "Can we?" She turned to her big sister.

Roswynd contained a grouse knowing it would shatter Myla's hope. Whenever Tharon visited, Roswynd wanted her friend to herself, but Myla was growing fond of Tharon. Sometimes Roswynd caught Myla following them around the estate; Myla was fascinated with Tharon. "Yes, we can have a nice dinner."

Myla pumped her tiny fists into the air and stomped her feet against the ground. "I cannot wait!"

Tharon chuckled and said, "Me too." She then pulled on her tunic and asked, "Do I look silly in this, Myla?"

Roswynd rolled her eyes, but she was curious about Myla's opinion. At her sister's tender age, she would be honest rather than tease or be cruel.

Myla shook her head and put her hands behind her back, rocking on her shoes. "I think you look handsome."

"Thank you, Myla." Tharon beamed and looked over at Roswynd, who sighed with extra dramatics.

"But I think you look silly," Myla said to Roswynd and giggled.

Roswynd responded with a playful snarl. Selwyn's teasing was starting to transfer to Myla. She shook her head and pointed a finger at her younger sister. "Do not be a brat like your brother, or we are not going tomorrow."

Myla pouted, then jumped into her sister's arms for a quick hug.

After a huff Roswynd returned the affection and kissed Myla's temple. She stood, then shooed off Myla so she could begin the horseback lesson. Once Myla was gone, she took her friend into the stable and said, "First, we have to find the right horse for you."

The riding lesson had turned into an all-day task. Roswynd learned that Tharon was timid with horses. She was unsure why until Tharon mentioned the uncertainty about what a horse might do. But as the day wore on, Tharon became more comfortable with the horse they'd chosen for her. The horse, named Snowball for his white color, was calm, patient, and old. He was also rather comfortable, in Roswynd's opinion.

Tharon quickly learned the different parts of the horse tack, the mechanics of posting, and the proper way to control the horse. They rode at a walk and trot, saving a canter and gallop for later. By midafternoon, the lesson turned into a trail ride around the estate. It was the perfect summer day.

"Do you like it?" Roswynd asked as they rode side by side on a wider portion of the trail. From Tharon's tight features, she could read the answer already.

"Yes." Tharon adjusted in the saddle, having done it more often than Roswynd. "It is tiring though."

"It becomes easier the more you practice."

"Then it will be a long time before it becomes easy for me," Tharon murmured. Her eyes scanned the forest around them.

Roswynd frowned and toyed with the reins. When Tharon returned to Wulfbite, she wouldn't ride, much less mention she had ridden a horse while in the Kingdom of Wyndfeld. It circled back to Tharon's father, who was strict, especially with Tharon. "Why will he not let you ride? What harm can it cause?"

Tharon glanced at Roswynd and sighed. "He is not like your father."

Roswynd nibbled on her lip and shook her head. "It seems so strange. Your father is an Omega, yet he acts like an Alpha." From Tharon's silence, she sensed that her words needled her friend. "I am sorry, Tharon." She nudged her horse closer and touched Tharon's thigh.

"It is fine." Tharon offered a smile, but it was broken. She returned to viewing the beautiful scenery around them. The trees and grass were silky green, the plant life vibrant and happy. Yellow, orange, and white flowers dotted the woods, adding a trace of color.

"Do you wish to take a break?" Roswynd indicated a spot to their left. "If we follow that tiny path, it will take us to the stream." After Tharon's nod, she led the way and dismounted first once they arrived at the creek. She walked toward Tharon, who was climbing down next. Pretending to brush her hands clean on her trousers, Roswynd stayed, ready to assist Tharon if she had a problem.

Tharon groaned from the obvious soreness and pressed a hand against the saddle. She straightened when Roswynd touched her back. "It does not bother you?"

"No, not anymore." Roswynd pulled the reins over the head of Tharon's horse and walked both animals to the stream. She let them drink and returned to her best friend.

Tharon took a seat on a nearby boulder and stretched her legs. "The trousers do make it easier to ride."

Roswynd chuckled and slid onto the large rock next to her best friend. "I fancy them." She ran her hands over her thighs, admiring the clothing. "I have three pairs now."

Tharon snorted low, shook her head, and touched her own trousers. "Perhaps you can wear a set at the next Howling Eagle for the formal ball." She laughed when Roswynd slapped her on the side.

"No one would dance with me." Roswynd leaned her head against Tharon's shoulder and closed her eyes. Like every year, she pictured being able to dance with Tharon at the ball, rather than one of the male Betas or occasional Alpha from the various noble families in the kingdom. Last year she danced with Tharon's brother, Saxon, but it had triggered something in Tharon. After the dance Tharon had been moody and growly, even blocking Saxon from Roswynd for the rest of the night. Roswynd didn't stop Tharon's attempts to keep Saxon away because she never felt comfortable with him. Plus, a tiny, deep part of her liked Tharon's protective nature flaring up, even if it was confusing and silly.

"I would dance with you," Tharon said after a minute.

Roswynd smiled and threaded her arm through Tharon's warmer one. "What if I wore my trousers and boots after mucking the horse stall?"

Tharon chuckled and flashed a playful grin. "I would still dance with you, but with a nosegay or two." She grinned at Roswynd's offended look, but then they laughed together.

"I would need a few myself," Roswynd said after they quieted. She rested her head against Tharon's shoulder and watched the horses munch on bits of grass. It was going to make the horses' bits gross to clean later, but she didn't have the heart to stop them. "Do you mind if we walk back?" They had enough time to walk rather than ride if they left now.

"No. Are you ready?" Tharon was most likely happy to walk and stretch out her legs.

Roswynd stifled a yawn, tempted to stay and nap, but it was getting late. After hopping off the boulder, she collected the horses and handed one set of reins to Tharon. "Thank you for riding with me."

Tharon smiled and canted her head. "Thank you for teaching me. I am afraid I will forget some of it by next summer."

"I will show you again." Roswynd walked closer. Their two horses were in tow behind them, but they had to stagger themselves along the tight path. Once on the trail, she and Tharon walked together again. Roswynd bumped their shoulders together before she slid her fingers through Tharon's hand. "One day we will dance together at the ball." Her mind had wandered back to their earlier conversation.

Tharon considered it, then smiled and squeezed their hands together. "I am certain we will."

* * *

Date: 09 Sunstone 826G
(Present Day)

Roswynd took another measured breath. She continued to hold out her arms while her friend Gleda added the embellishments to her sapphire dress. Off to the right, Myla sat at the vanity table and had organized the few pieces of jewelry from their mother, who was the one person missing. She'd given Myla specific family jewelry to attach to Roswynd's wedding dress. Roswynd could have pressed her mother to join them in the room for the preparations, but she refused to distress her mother any further. Since Edeva's death, Layla had become a shadow of her former self.

The room was otherwise quiet, everyone in a somber mood. Within an hour, Roswynd was expected to trade vows with Tharon at a special location. She had no idea where, only that Tharon had given specific instructions to Roswynd's father.

Yesterday the House of Arrington had traveled from Earna to Leeward, which was still under the control of the Kingdom of White Sommer. They had been welcomed by King Saxon, who explained that Tharon was busy with preparations for the wedding. Roswynd and her family were given comfortable accommodations at Proudpeak Hall, located in the northeastern part of the town. After years of staying at the estate when they traveled between kingdoms, the Arringtons were quite familiar with it.

A fortnight ago, Roswynd had gone from being a freewoman to being promised to Tharon. Soon her father would give her hand to Tharon, who would become her spouse and Alpha. As a pup, she had dreamed of this day. But with it upon her, she now dreaded it. Her pounding heart was burning and cracking into shards. Once the wedding was complete, she needed to focus and keep her promise to her father. Her heartbreak was nothing compared to what could happen if Tharon and Saxon conquered the Kingdom of Wyndfeld.

Not wanting to dwell on her pending future, Roswynd decided to have Gleda distract her with the latest gossip. "Have you heard any more about Princess Kinsey from the Kingdom of Tharnstone?"

Gleda paused and sighed for dramatic effect. "No, I have not heard anything new." She continued her work while discussing the most recent scandal among the kingdoms. "She has a few months remaining before she gives birth. They say she is due at the end of Gyldan or the beginning of White Wulf."

Roswynd recalled the gossip about Princess Kinsey, who was around five years younger than Roswynd. "A baby for the new year," she murmured. "What of the Alpha who impregnated her?"

"Nothing. They say it was a slave who was set free," Gleda replied. "Byron will bring more news after his next trip to Tharnstone."

"Her father is a horrible king," Myla spoke up from her spot. "Grandmother used to visit Tharnstone and always said he would be horrible."

Roswynd seconded her sister's assessment. "I still can hardly believe King Wymarc forced his own daughter to become pregnant. If I were in her position, I would consider running away, especially to protect my pup."

Gleda bobbed her head. "You want to know what I think will happen?" Her grin was big and playful. "I think Princess Kinsey will run away and find the Alpha who impregnated her. I bet they fall in love. There is gossip that the Alpha is a degen."

"She-Alpha," Roswynd corrected and cringed at the harshness in her tone, noticing Gleda's wince.

"S-Sorry," Gleda murmured as she moved behind Roswynd to finish the last half of the buttons.

"Thank you," Roswynd murmured and took a deep breath, calming her reaction to hearing the awful slur. She'd beaten up a few people in her teens when they referred to Tharon as a degenerate. The slur always made every muscle in her body curl up with rage, but she was grateful Gleda apologized.

"I hope that happens," Myla said. "I hope that Princess Kinsey finds her Alpha, falls in love, and begins a family."

"Would it not be simply scandalous for a princess to be mated to a slave?" Even though it was speculation, Gleda had a dreamy voice. "Perhaps one day we will find out," she added and came around to Roswynd's front. "There now."

She took a step to the side, allowing the full-length mirror to show off Roswynd.

The deep sapphire gown reached her ankles and had a soft shine from the combination of silk and velvet. The main part of the dress was velvet, but the silk floral overlay was attached on the front of the dress and the sleeves. Under her breasts, a golden flower pattern began, flowed over her stomach, and fanned out past her hips to her ankles. A golden girdle belt hung loosely around her waist, and the long cord reached her knees. The dress's rich color enhanced her blue eye, and the golden flowers highlighted the amber of her other eye.

"Your beauty enhances the dress so well," Gleda whispered next to her and smiled. Her opinion could be biased, but Roswynd agreed that the gown did her justice.

Roswynd returned the smile, but it was halfhearted. "Thank you." She peered down at their interlocked hands and studied the wedding ring on Gleda's finger. "How have you done it?" Like Roswynd, Gleda had been promised to a suitor of nobility. Gleda and her husband were not royalty, but they both were nobles. Byron's family was much older than Gleda's, which had come from another kingdom a few generations ago.

"Communication and time," Gleda replied. She and her husband were married six years ago, but the first three years were similar to a friendship before they fell in love. Roswynd admired their commitment to each other despite the hurdles and arguments they went through in the beginning. "But every couple is different."

Roswynd agreed with her friend. Her own marriage was to be a political statement, a new union between the two kingdoms. However, it was a ploy, because both sides distrusted the other. She doubted that communication would help, not when it would be fraught with lies. As far as time, Roswynd was certain that time would start a countdown, not progress, upon the completion of the wedding ceremony.

"You will find your way," Gleda whispered while she checked Roswynd's braids. "It may not seem like much, but at least you know who you are marrying."

Roswynd huffed and held Gleda's concerned features. "I hardly do." On the carriage ride from the capital to Leeward, they had discussed the arrangement that Roswynd was bound to after today. Part of the new agreement between the kingdoms was that Roswynd and Tharon were required to spend equal time in both kingdoms' capitals throughout the year. They would make public appearances as a couple to ensure soldiers, nobles, and peasants saw the peace between the kingdoms as secure. The thought of returning to Wulfbite, the capital of the Kingdom of White Sommer, turned her stomach in every direction. On one hand, she missed Wulfbite and wanted to visit the city again. However, Roswynd was viewed as the enemy, a villain, who wronged the House of Blakesley. But if Tharon was going to honor their marriage agreement, then Roswynd must do the same.

Gleda held her smile and confidence in her voice. "You may find remnants of your friend still left under all the dark armor."

"And if I do not?" Roswynd asked and sensed Myla's stare from across the room.

"Then you will learn anew." Gleda kissed her friend's cheek. "Meanwhile, you have me and Myla. Thankfully you are spending the first part of your kingdoms' tour in Wyndfeld."

Roswynd nodded, then gazed over at her sister, who had damp cheeks. She had tried to have Myla stay with their mother, but her sister requested to be with her for the ceremony preparations. Ever since the arrangement was made, Myla remained at Roswynd's side day in and day out, as if Roswynd were being shipped off forever. With a forced smile, she asked, "Are you ready for me, Myla?" She received a nod, so she and Gleda went over, hand in hand.

Myla stood from the stool next to the table where she'd placed a few items for Roswynd. She picked up the bracelet first and put it around her sister's right wrist. One by one, the jewelry was hooked and placed on Roswynd's body. Each piece was special and had a long history with one of her parents' families. Roswynd's favorite was the golden eagle necklace that rested firmly against her exposed neck, above the dress's low, scooped neckline.

"You are ready now," Gleda said and squeezed Roswynd's hand. Her announcement triggered Myla, who broke into a sob.

"No, no." Roswynd collected her sister into a hug, holding her close. "It is all right, Myla." She fluttered her eyelids, warding off her own tears. "This is a happy occasion." But no one believed her words—already the first lie of many.

"No, it is not." Myla tightened her arms and said, "You should not be forced to marry Tharon."

"I do not have to," Roswynd said, "but I wish to." Again, another deception, but it was less heavy because of the temporary good it would bring to the Kingdom of Wyndfeld. She lifted Myla's head off her chest and wiped the tears dry. She smiled, but her lips quivered while she spoke. "Everything will work out, you will see."

"What if—" Myla was hushed by Roswynd. With their foreheads joined, Myla started to calm, thanks to Roswynd's warm pheromones and strong presence. From childhood, Myla had shadowed her older sister, even though she was far more cautious and shier. Over the years, their bond had grown, and Roswynd was grateful when Myla spent time with her, especially after Tharon's betrayal.

A firm knock at the door caused the three females to jump, then Myla gasped and touched her chest. Roswynd kissed her sister's temple before she separated and went to the door. Through a cracked opening, she confirmed that it was her father.

Garrett entered the room and greeted them. He was dressed in his finest attire, which consisted of darker blues and a brown leather tunic. His golden circlet crown shone in the morning sunlight coming in from the windows. On his left side, he carried a ceremonial sword, which could still be used in battle if necessary. Garrett looked to Gleda and Myla and said, "Selwyn is waiting to take you both to the ceremony location."

Gleda collected Myla's hand but placed a kiss on Roswynd's cheek and whispered a word of affection. She guided Myla from the room, closing the door on their way.

"You look beautiful, Roswynd." Garrett beamed, a proud Alpha. But then his enthusiasm slipped in a heartbeat.

"Thank you, Father." Roswynd swallowed against the forming lump in her throat. She refused to shatter into pieces in front of anyone, not today or tonight. Tomorrow she would find time alone to wallow in her misery for an hour or two, then repack her woes in her head and move forward. "When do we leave for the ceremony?"

"Shortly." Garrett reached inside his cloak that rested on his shoulders. "I have a gift for you. It is not your actual wedding gift, but it is important." He retrieved the item and held it in his palm, presenting it to Roswynd.

Roswynd ran her fingertips along the black handle, then picked up the weapon. She had handled plenty of blades in her life, but they were for skinning animals and butchering meat. This was a dagger designed to slice into a person, even kill them. With shaky hands, she yanked the blade from the tight sheath and revealed the reflective surface.

"I thought it wise for you to carry one now. I know many of your clothes have pockets sewn in them." Garrett clasped his hands in front of him. "I wish this was not something I felt necessary to give you on your wedding day." His lips downturned the longer he stared at the blade. "I have wished, prayed, and begged the Divine to give you an Alpha. But this was not what I meant for you."

Roswynd's eyes fluttered for a moment after his speech. She took a deep breath and inhaled the bitterness of his scent, causing her Omega to whine in protest. Her body responded by releasing calming pheromones. Why did everyone in her family have to fall apart now while she had to stay together? With more force than necessary, she drove the blade into the sheath, then tested its smaller size. It was the right length for her dress's pocket. "Thank you, Father." She lifted her eyes to him and said, "I hope I do not have to use it, but I feel better carrying it."

Garrett gave a firm nod, then asked, "Are you ready?"

"Yes. Has everyone else left?" From the quietness of the halls, Roswynd assumed that her family had left for the ceremony location.

"Yes. Now it is our time." Garrett held out his hand, a final chance to decline the wedding. But Roswynd didn't falter and gripped his hand with strength. Together, they departed the room and walked the empty halls of the large home. Outside, a dozen guards and Donnchad waited for them, and there were as many horses but no carriage, thankfully. From an early age, she hated carriages and their confining spaces. However, most brides were brought in by lavish carriages.

Roswynd frowned and peered up at her father, baffled by the arrangement. "How are we being transported there?" She thought the ceremony location was outside the town, but it could be within walking distance from Proudpeak Hall.

"By horse." Garrett indicated the black horse in the center of all the white ones.

Frowning, Roswynd studied the saddled horse in the middle, held onto by a guard. Next to its side were steps. The horse was rather familiar, especially as they walked closer to it. Roswynd was certain that it was the horse Tharon rode two weeks ago.

Garrett released his daughter's hand, then climbed the steps and mounted the horse. He shifted as far back as possible in the saddle and signaled for Roswynd to join him.

Roswynd followed and the guard on her left minded her footing. She noted there was no saddle horn, but she was still forced to ride sidesaddle and relied on her father's support. The guard then handed the reins to Garrett while everyone mounted their own horses.

Donnchad called the orders to ride to the ceremony location. He took the lead, followed by two guards on either side of him. Garrett was next, and the rest of the soldiers flanked him. The procession departed the grounds of Proudpeak Hall, then the town's limits, following to Fringe Road. The road carried them higher and provided a gorgeous view of the landscape around Leeward. They turned left onto a pass, which required them to go single file.

As they traveled the pass, it widened and flattened until a sprawling plateau started before them. Donnchad and the two other guards parted to the sides and allowed Garrett and Roswynd to take the lead. Ahead of them, a talkative crowd was gathered, but the din faded away upon their approach. A moment later, welcoming music drifted on the cool mountain breezes.

Garrett tugged on the reins several steps short of the gathering. He remained still in the saddle and kept his arm snug against Roswynd's waist. Around them the guards halted their horses in a U-shaped formation. Donnchad ordered the guards to dismount in unison.

Roswynd clenched her jaw and blinked away the fresh burn. She found herself leaning into her father's comforting and strong presence. After so many years of arguments about marriage, she was being wed to the one person she had once loved as a pup and now despised as an adult. The single being who was worse in her mind was King Saxon; he'd wrought havoc in everyone's lives.

A guard from the crowd marched toward the father and daughter. In his hand, he carried a set of steps, which he placed on the left side of the horse, then he stood at attention behind the steps.

"I must dismount first, then you have to wait for me to help you," Garrett whispered in her ear. "Then I will walk you to the ceremonial spot where Tharon awaits you."

Roswynd dipped her head in understanding and withdrew from her father. She kept her back straight and watched her father dismount, walk around the horse, and stand near the guard at the base of the steps. No one obstructed the view of Roswynd, who slid toward the top step. Once her flats met the step, she walked down each one and took her father's offered hand. They faced the crowd, hand in hand, and started the slow journey toward Roswynd's new life. The music intensified and the people's faces became distinct. Some were familiar, such as nobles. There were several strangers, but their darker furs indicated they were from the Kingdom of White Sommer.

As Roswynd and her father neared the crowd, the people parted to the left and right, creating a path for them. After a brief pause, Garrett continued their procession down the makeshift aisle that peeled open for them. Near the end, Roswynd's relatives and family greeted her. Layla offered a soft smile while her two young sons waved and Selwyn nodded. Her aunts and uncles were standing deeper in the crowd to the left.

But on the right, Roswynd recognized Tharon's extended family members, such as aunts, uncles, and cousins. As they followed the aisle, she spotted Tharon's twin sisters, Daisy and Holly, then a boy around the age of five, pressed into a female's front. He had to be Radford, Tharon's half brother, and she was certain the female behind him was his mother, Queen Melanie, the late King Eustace's second wife. Rumors circulated that she had pursued King Eustace before Queen Edeva's body had cooled. From Queen Melanie's frigid stare, Roswynd understood why the rumors might hold truth.

Turning her attention forward, Roswynd watched the last few people step aside for them. Her heart had been steadily pounding, but now a buzz filled her ears. She faltered a step, too entangled by the view before her.

The plateau continued for another two or three hundred steps, ending before the glorious White Razor Mountains. The snowy ridgeline ran from the right, heading north, then bowed and went left to the northwest. Below the dusty white peaks began the green wave of trees that swept down to the valley. High above, full clouds traveled the skyline, heading west at a carefree pace.

The view had stolen Roswynd's strength, until she focused on the three individuals who waited for her. At the center was a stranger dressed in formal attire. He was Leeward's constable and would administer the wedding. To his left was Tharon, who stood in refined but black leather, cloth, and metal. Even her black boots shone in the sunlight. It seemed as if she wore no jewelry, standard for knights. However, the pair of black stud earrings caught Roswynd's attention. They were familiar, and then it dawned on her that the earrings had belonged to Tharon's mother, Queen Edeva. The one item to break up Tharon's dark aurora was the sapphire-blue girdle lashed across her waist. She carried one sword this time and no other weapons. Often her midnight-colored hair was untamed like a wolf's pelt, but today it was held back by tight and neat braids on the sides of her head.

Tharon Blakesley was undeniably handsome.

Roswynd swallowed against her body's natural reaction to the power coiled inside Tharon. She took a steady breath, grateful her father had paused with her. When they continued forward, she turned her attention to King Saxon, who was next to Tharon. His smug face stabbed her body's earlier excitement over Tharon's overwhelming presence. Good. Focus on him, she told herself.

"Stand in front of Tharon," Garrett murmured near his daughter's ear. They had discussed the general flow of the ceremony, but Roswynd was in a stupor at the moment. They squeezed hands, and then Garrett guided his daughter to her spot.

Roswynd released his hand, then faced Tharon for the first time in ten years. The hum in her ears returned, but it grew deafening and weakened her knees. A gentle hand pressed against the small of her back, and she closed her eyes for a second. Her father's constant assurance grounded her when she needed it most. She thanked him with a brief glance, then concentrated on the start of the ceremony, using King Saxon's irritating presence to focus her on the present.

The constable signaled the musicians and the song ended on an abrupt note. Clearing his throat, the constable straightened his back and reached deep in his gut for his voice. "Today we are gathered here to witness the union of this Alpha and this Omega. Who here has brought this Omega?" He turned to Garrett and waited for his response.

"I, King Garrett Arrington of the Kingdom of Wyndfeld, have brought my daughter, Princess Roswynd Arrington, here today for this union." Garrett held his chest high, and his strong voice boomed across the plateau.

The constable nodded, then directed his attention toward Tharon and Saxon. "And who here has brought this Alpha?"

Saxon shifted closer to Tharon but faced the people. "I, King Saxon Blakesley of the Kingdom of White Sommer, have brought my sister, Prince Tharon Blakesley, here today for this union." Unlike Garrett, his voice fell flat, which triggered a faint rumble from Tharon. But it was enough for the constable.

Roswynd bit back a smirk at Saxon's weaker display and watched him return to his spot at Tharon's shoulder. Ever since they were young, she had disliked him for his cruel tricks and antics. Several times she had wrestled with him, and there was always mutual venom in their kicks and punches. In the background, she heard the constable speaking, but Saxon was eating away at her interests until Tharon took a deliberate step in front of her brother. Roswynd cut her gaze up to Tharon, who now commanded her full attention.

If Tharon was annoyed by Roswynd, her features didn't show it, nor did her orange eyes. Or rather her one orange eye and the hazy one. Roswynd clenched her hands in front of her the longer Tharon's stare bore into her. But then Tharon gave Roswynd a subtle lift of her chin, toward the constable.

"Princess Roswynd," the constable whispered in a stern tone followed by a rumble.

Roswynd blinked, ending the spell between her and Tharon. She looked to the constable and said, "Yes, sorry."

"Please listen and answer," the constable ordered and cleared his throat, then began asking the sacred promise of the union. "Princess Roswynd Arrington, will thou have this

Alpha to be thy wedded wife, will thou love her, and honor her, keep her and guard her, in health and in sickness, as a spouse should another spouse, and forsaking all others on account of her, keep thee only unto her, so long as you both shall live?"

Roswynd clenched her teeth as the sacred promise was asked of her—was asked of her to be made to Tharon. Her heart slammed against her convulsing chest. An old but sharp memory of another similar promise sliced through her, burning into her very bones. Their first promise to each other had meant nothing. Now she was expected to make a new one that would turn the remaining fragments—all that was left of her heart after the first promise was broken—into ash.

"My princess," the constable murmured, prompting her to speak before the ceremony unraveled before all.

Through scorching tears, Roswynd gave Tharon a bitter stare, and her voice trembled with the two final words. "I will." She took a breath after her promise was sealed, before her tears dried from the rage boiling under her skin. Her voice, her promise, and her tears had no visible effect on Tharon, who remained cold and continued to command Roswynd's attention.

The constable nodded, then turned to Tharon and asked her for the same promise for Roswynd. He waited for Tharon's response, like everyone else at the ceremony.

Tharon never broke her gaze with Roswynd as she gave her new promise. "I will," she declared with thunder that caused several males, both Beta and Alpha, to whine.

Her answer held no fracture or brokenness as Roswynd's had, but it was binding and tight.

To Roswynd, it was almost believable—almost.

Pleased, the constable continued the ceremony. "Now an exchange of rings."

Roswynd faltered at the mention of a ring. Nothing was said of a wedding ring or any symbol of their marriage. The past two weeks, known as Driwice and Tharnwice, had sped past, but she wasn't so out of touch to have missed this piece of the ceremony. Did he say "rings," though? She was almost certain he'd used the plural version of the word. She had no ring to give to Tharon. However, the constable held out his open palm, revealing a ring that was far too large for Roswynd.

"Please, take her hands," the constable told Roswynd.

Once more, panic spiked inside Roswynd, but she shoved it down before it turned her into an idiot again. She took a deep breath and accepted their marital fate. Reaching across the space, her small hands hooked Tharon's larger ones, which were warmer. A few calluses brushed against Roswynd's palm.

"Now, your vows," the constable ordered.

Roswynd swallowed, then gazed into orange eyes framed by dark hair and said, "I, Princess Roswynd Arrington, take this Alpha as mine, to have and to hold from this day forward." She paused, freed a hand, and took the golden fede wedding ring. With her thumb she brushed the two interlocking hands, which reminded her of all the times they held hands as pups. Roswynd refocused on Tharon and placed the ring at the start of her right middle finger. As she slid it into place, she peered up at Tharon and said, "With this ring, I vow to shelter you, cherish you, and care for you until the end of our days."

Once the ring settled into place, Tharon curled her hand around Roswynd's own. Without any prompt from the constable, she declared her vow, but this time her voice was softer, as if only meant for Roswynd. "I, Prince Tharon Blakesley, take this Omega as mine, to have and to hold from this day forward." She released one hand, then plucked another golden ring from the constable's hand. It was distinct and different from Tharon's wedding ring, but it was still simple in design. Tharon held it at the front of Roswynd's right middle finger, bent closer to Roswynd, and said, "Through this ring, I swear fidelity to you. I vow through light and darkness that I will shelter you, cherish you, and care for you until the end of our days." She moved the ring into place, sealing their vows to each other.

Roswynd closed her eyes as the ring's new weight rested heavy on her hand. She opened her eyes as a tear fell, striking her flushed cheek. She lowered her gaze to their locked hands that now carried wedding rings. Then she noticed how stark white her knuckles were from her grip on Tharon's hands. But Tharon returned the pressure with firmness rather than force.

The constable straightened his back and bellowed his great announcement. "Now dearly beloved, I present to you Tharon and Roswynd, the Alpha and the Omega." The crowd responded with a great cheer that echoed across the plateau.

Roswynd still clutched Tharon's strong hands that anchored her in this twisted and most confused moment of her life. These were the hands that had taken lives, had taken pieces of her kingdom, and had taken a promise from her. Now Roswynd was bound to them until the end of her days.

Chapter 4

Tharon was lost in Roswynd's beautiful mismatched but puffy eyes until the crowd's cheering pierced their tiny world. She rumbled and looked at the people's faces, recalling that she was the prince of White Sommer and the lord commander. The all-too-brief ceremony for her and Roswynd was over, and it was time to present their union to the kingdoms. She returned to Roswynd and noted her disjointed motions. With ease Tharon took command of the situation, rather accustomed to the attention compared to when she was young.

After separating one of their hands, Tharon took the first step until she sensed Roswynd's difficulty moving forward. She pivoted, released her other hand, and placed it at the small of Roswynd's back, much as Garrett had done. Now it was Tharon's duty as Roswynd's Alpha.

Roswynd was charged by the subtle touch and shot a glare at Tharon for the unwanted assistance. She stepped out of the touch and moved toward the makeshift aisle with Tharon at her side.

Undeterred by Roswynd's adolescent show, Tharon recaptured her wife's hand and guided her through the tide of people. As they walked together, she controlled her breathing for the first time since the ceremony began. Their promises and vows were complete, sealed before the old and new gods. Even though Roswynd was the enemy, her Alpha swelled proudly in her chest because this Omega was meant to be hers. For days on end, Tharon had warred with her Alpha's burning need to stake a claim on Roswynd from the moment it was announced that she was to wed Roswynd over Myla. After that morning in the field a fortnight ago, her Alpha had paced relentlessly in her chest, waiting for this moment.

Now they were required to celebrate the union back in Leeward. Tharon could give a damn about celebrating it in front of everyone. Yes, she wanted to declare her union in public, but to celebrate it with strangers, who were groveling and snapping for attention, was tiresome to her. With a huff, she reminded herself that she had to meet her brother's expectations.

Stealing a glance at Roswynd, Tharon saw the resignation on her face. Even as an adult, Roswynd was easy to read and hadn't learned a thing about self-control. Tharon wasn't surprised, considering Roswynd's explosive nature. Even from a league away, she could see Roswynd's emotions like a storm rolling over the landscape.

Ahead, Tharon spotted her horse and the Wyndfeld guard straightening upon their arrival. She released Roswynd's hand at the base of the steps, and instead chose to walk around to the other side of the horse. She leaped into the saddle with clean, fluid motion, then scooted back for Roswynd.

With a scowl Roswynd ascended the steps, clearly wanting to refuse help. But the dress made it impossible. She settled into the saddle, albeit with a ramrod-straight back.

Tharon wanted to roll her eyes, but Saxon's voice distracted her. He was announcing the celebration back at Leeward, but Tharon didn't give a damn to listen to it. Right now, she needed space and distance from the people, so she clicked her tongue once and turned her horse around toward the pass.

Roswynd was unprepared for the sudden turn and snatched Tharon's shoulder, then shot her a pointed look for not giving a warning. Tharon simply ignored it and continued the trot down the pass. Once they were at Fringe Road, she guided her horse, Obsidian, farther up the road rather than down.

"Where are we traveling to?" Roswynd asked with enough sharpness to cut stone.

Tharon didn't answer with words but turned off the road onto another pass that was smaller and overlooked the lower one and the plateau. At a gentle pace, they rode the pass and had a few glimpses of the departing crowd below them. She released a sigh and admired the view, ignoring Roswynd's displeased features.

Last week she had spent most of a day searching for the perfect location for the wedding ceremony. Saxon had suggested the wedding be held in Leeward, but Tharon wanted nothing to do with mixing her wedding with her conquest. The White Razor Mountains were breathtaking, if not dangerous. They were an immovable force that could take and give life, land that could not be controlled by mortals. As a pup she had enjoyed traveling through them and seeing what nature had hiding behind rocks, in the lakes, in the streams, and behind trees. From Roswynd's earlier reaction, she had chosen well, and it pleased her Alpha even more.

Right now, however, Roswynd was anything but thrilled by their situation. Wave after wave of heated, angry pheromones poured off her and assaulted Tharon's control. She struggled not to respond to it with her own scent, knowing she could overpower Roswynd in a heartbeat. Since becoming lord commander, no one could contest her, including her brother.

After another minute, Tharon tugged on Obsidian's reins until they ceased moving near a ledge that overlooked the White Razor Mountains. Back to her left was the ceremony spot, which was empty of people other than the last Wyndfeld guards. She and Roswynd remained, together again, until their deaths.

Tharon nudged Obsidian to the right, allowing Roswynd a better view from the sidesaddle position. With her head turned, she gazed upon the lands that sliced up toward the skies, closer to many of the gods. She breathed in the fresh air, but it was tainted with Roswynd's lashing pheromones. Tharon controlled the growl deep in her chest and did her best to ignore Roswynd, but it was simply a matter of time before her new wife erupted on her.

Roswynd stared at the landscape or perhaps into it. She sat stiff in Tharon's arms, searching for personal space that wasn't there. She shifted for the hundredth time, then a low growl broke free from her. "It has been ten fucking years. Will you continue to not speak to me even now?"

Tharon didn't reward Roswynd with a reaction or even a glance. Her Alpha was smug at Roswynd's use of foul language. After years in the army, she could spew dirtier curses that would make even Roswynd gasp. She took in a measured breath before replying. "I will speak only when you are ready to listen." Anticipating Roswynd's reaction, she halted her wife from sliding off the horse and escaping.

With a hiss Roswynd attempt to shove off Tharon's arm locked around her waist, but she was the softer breed between them. She gave up and tilted her head back, breathing heavy, as though prepared to scream out every drop of rage, yet nothing came free.

Tharon then noticed Roswynd's fingertips grazed a spot on her dress, near her hip. Through the fabric, she picked out the faint outline of something long, hidden under the layers. Her gut reaction was to seize the weapon, certainly a blade. But after a steady breath, she let the response fade to the background. She considered the reasons why Roswynd had it, then decided to let her keep it. If Roswynd needed it to feel safe and secure, then Tharon could respect that desire.

However, if it were used against her in the future, she promised herself she would break it. The compromise soothed the darkness nipping at the edges of her self-control. Tharon relaxed her arm after Roswynd withdrew her fingers from the hidden blade.

Roswynd lowered her head, and her swallow was audible. Her eyes were glassy, and her bottom lip quivered. After a huff, she closed her eyes.

Tharon steadied Obsidian's antsy movements. Her horse wasn't accustomed to such volatile emotions from a rider. She didn't want their wedding day to end with her wife being thrown from a horse, over the side of the pass. Although, Roswynd may have found the ending ideal after vowing herself to Tharon. With a rumble, Tharon concluded that her attempt at a peaceful break between today's events was futile. She tugged on the left rein and started the ride back to Leeward for the celebration. Thankfully Obsidian's motions were a familiar comfort, even easing Roswynd's stiff posture a degree.

The journey back to Leeward was long and the silence was painful, at least according to Roswynd's features. Tharon kept a show of indifference and concentrated on steering Obsidian. On occasion, Obsidian's steps caused Roswynd to press closer to Tharon. It was too close, however, even for her. Roswynd's hip rocked against Tharon's crotch, rubbing her cock hard. Several times she was forced to tamp down a groan or snarl of pleasure.

Her last good fuck had been with the two female Betas the night that Saxon announced the cease-fire and political marriage. Now that she had pledged her fidelity to Roswynd, who loathed her existence, Tharon could transform into a virgin before Roswynd would sleep with her. After tonight's celebration, the custom was for a married couple to mate, bonding them even deeper. Tharon's Alpha howled at the idea of making Roswynd her mate after years of wasting energy on worthless female Betas. She clenched her teeth and caged her Alpha's lusty demands.

Ahead, Leeward came into view. The celebrations had already begun throughout the town. As of tomorrow, Leeward, along with other conquered lands that Tharon had taken for her brother, would be returned to the Kingdom of Wyndfeld. She gave a low snarl at the thought but cut herself short when Roswynd pulled away from her.

Roswynd gave her a sideways glance but remained silent, nostrils flared and jaw clenched hard. She was picking up Tharon's increased Alpha pheromones and fighting the effects of them.

Tharon took a deep breath and cooled her temper before she imposed herself on Roswynd. They were enemies, but both were forced into this marriage by their families' games. The marriage would provide Tharon access to Wyndfeld again; it was then that she could truly end the war. Afterward she could walk away from it all with Roswynd at her side… or over her shoulder, whichever Roswynd chose. Sudden cheers carried from Chesford Manor, which was near the center of the town. At one time, prior to the town growing around it, the manor had been the focal point of the area. The manor home had been offered as a residence to

Tharon after she conquered Leeward. As the lord commander, it was her innate right to claim the spoils from war, which included properties, weapons, horses, supplies, and even people. However, Tharon never had a greedy heart and preferred a simpler lifestyle, like her tent, books, and weapons. But tonight would be different.

Nobles outside the manor's gardens called for them, while their kings and queens waited by the open gate to the gardens. Tharon halted Obsidian near the gate, kicked out her boots from the stirrups, and dismounted with grace. Facing Roswynd, she offered her help, a must due to Obsidian's height. As Roswynd pushed off from the saddle, Tharon hooked her wife's hips, caught her, and settled her onto the ground. She remained focused on Roswynd, who didn't break their physical contact, for once. Tharon stole her chance and fixed a few stray light-blond strands of Roswynd's hair. Her delicate touch lured in Roswynd until reality seemed to reassert itself.

Roswynd pulled away and stepped out of the embrace, then headed toward her father and mother with Tharon at her side. However, seeing Saxon and Melanie standing next to her parents, Roswynd hesitated and stared at the four rulers.

Tharon sniffed out her wife's irritation with both Saxon and Melanie. It brought out a rumble in her, but it wasn't meant for Roswynd. Her brother and Roswynd butted heads as pups, and it seemed as if they would continue to do so as adults. And Melanie was as friendly as a starved wolf on a frozen winter day. Over the years Tharon had learned how to dismiss Melanie, and now she would need to teach Roswynd how to do the same.

At the ceremony Tharon had learned that Roswynd tolerated holding hands. Now, she threaded her longer fingers through Roswynd's smaller ones and brought her forward to meet their waiting family. The sooner they started the celebration, the sooner they could retire to their room for the night.

With a forced smile, King Garrett congratulated them first. He shook arms with Tharon, then hugged his daughter, whispering something in her ear. Tharon received a cautious hug from Queen Layla, a dramatic arm shake from Saxon, and a limp hug from Melanie. She noticed that Roswynd refused to hug Saxon but received a kiss to the cheek. Tharon pictured Roswynd later tonight scrubbing that side of her face.

"We have food, wine, and music ready," Saxon said, a proud smile plastered on his face. "Shall we begin?"

"Lead the way, brother." Tharon held out her hand toward the gate, allowing him to be the host. Multiple times she had expressed her disinterest in the celebration, but Saxon insisted on checking every box for the wedding. It had to be authentic for both kingdoms' people to believe it. Saxon also pointed out that the wedding was being paid for by the House of Arrington, and he wanted to take full advantage of it.

Saxon passed through the gate first and remained on the main path that led to the front of the manor house. His movements caused the crowd to cheer and clap for the newlyweds.

Tharon followed him and ignored the people, finding it easy to do. However, Roswynd brushed against her and stole Tharon's attention. Her wife may be a royal, but she never liked the attention it brought upon her. She and Roswynd shared their mutual dislike as pups and seemed to do so as adults. Roswynd's stressed pheromones rallied Tharon's Alpha, prompting her to place a hand between Roswynd's shoulder blades. She expected rejection, similar to what happened at the ceremony. Instead Roswynd pressed closer to her.

Saxon climbed the marble steps to the open doors, then waited in the foyer for everyone to catch up. He hooked his hands in his big leather belt, gloating at the married couple.

Roswynd rumbled, no doubt in response to Saxon's arrogant stance. Once they passed the open doors, she put space between herself and Tharon. They continued through Chesford Manor, which was several hundred years old. The halls even smelled old, but it was hard to ignore the carpenters' craftsmanship. Its art and decor captivated Roswynd the entire way to the ballroom. As pups, the Arringtons often stayed at Proudpeak Hall while Tharon's family would overnight in Chesford Manor. They had to split their families between the two estates when they traveled together for the Howling Eagle Festival.

As they approached a pair of open doors, cheerful music poured out of the square ballroom and into the hallway. The room inside was washed in afternoon sunlight from the tall windows that almost touched the ceiling. Long tables followed along the walls, leaving the center open for music, dancing, and gathering. Saxon took them to the middle table, which was the focal point of the grand room. Hundreds of summer flower arrangements were placed on every table, but the most beautiful arrangements were located on the table set for the new couple and their families.

Saxon announced the seating arrangements for the guests, ranking the nobles by class before departing the area in search of someone or something.

Tharon clasped Roswynd's hand and cut between an opening in the tables. Behind them, Roswynd's parents followed along with other family members.

"Your brother is in fine form," Roswynd remarked in a quiet voice. "At least he can host well."

Tharon grunted at the sassy remark, but she agreed with Roswynd. Parties and celebration went against Tharon's nature, unlike Saxon's. Tharon's one exception had been the Howling Eagle Festival, which the kingdoms had hosted in her youth. Roswynd loved the festival and it bled over into Tharon.

Once at the central table, Tharon pulled out Roswynd's chair and waited for her to take her seat. For a moment Roswynd stood there, regarded Tharon, and parted her lips with what might be a scathing comment on the tip of her tongue. Tharon waited with trained patience and a hint of admiration for Roswynd's courage. Everyone in both kingdoms crumbled under Tharon's authority. Tharon knew her wife was making a choice to accept or decline Tharon's politeness.

Roswynd swept up the back of her gown as she took the offered seat. After Roswynd readjusted her gown, Tharon helped scoot the chair under the table. Roswynd turned her head sidelong and whispered, "Thank you, my prince."

Tharon let her hands fall away from Roswynd's chair. Her mind was assaulted by locked-up memories from her youth, when Roswynd had said the same words to her fourteen years ago. Chesford Manor's ballroom flickered back to the grand ballroom in Earna, but faded away again. Tharon took a deep breath, fighting off the happy memories that she once shared with Roswynd. Those days were far gone, drowned in blood by her position as a knight and lord commander.

Pulling out her seat, Tharon sat down next to her wife and ignored the cautious glance from Roswynd. Perhaps their earlier standoff over Tharon pulling out Roswynd's chair wasn't about authority. Was the ballroom triggering Roswynd's memories from the Howling Eagle Festival too?

To Roswynd's left, King Garrett sat after assisting his wife into her chair. His posture mimicked Roswynd's stiffness. They were far too alike in many ways, Tharon concluded. But Roswynd was a physical duplicate of her mother, who had aged with a wealth of beauty. According to Arrington family lore, Roswynd's spirit and different-colored eyes came from her maternal grandmother. Tharon had once met Roswynd's paternal grandparents, but never Queen Layla's family, who lived afar.

"Everything is in order," Saxon said upon his arrival, loud as ever.

Tharon rumbled and waited until he was seated to her right. "Do not drag out the celebration," she warned him in a stern but low voice. She sensed Roswynd was keen on their conversation.

"Eager to get on with your night, sister?" Saxon asked, smirking at her.

Tharon's responding snarl was cut off by the arrival of their identical twin sisters. They rushed to Tharon and congratulated her. She received affectionate kisses to her cheek and temple from Daisy and Holly. Their warm smiles staved her annoyance with Saxon. "Thank you," she said to them. "You both look beautiful."

Daisy wore a fern-green gown made mostly from silk. A white girdle belt hung around her waist. Her hair was curlier than normal, and she was already flushed in the cheeks.

Holly had on a similar dress but in buttery yellow. She also wore a surcoat and mantle, allowing her braids to fall around her face.

Daisy crept around Tharon's chair and said, "Hello, Roswynd."

Tharon heard the inviting warmth in Daisy's voice. Her sisters were closer to Myla's age and had been infatuated with Roswynd as Myla was with Tharon. Roswynd's adventurous spirit had a way of rubbing off on other Omegas.

"Daisy," Roswynd said with wonder. She pushed her seat out and embraced Daisy in a fierce hug.

Tharon caught pieces of the happy reunion between Roswynd and the twins. But she smelled her brother's annoyance about the exchange, so she pinned him with a dark glare, ceasing his attempt to separate the three.

Roswynd withdrew from Holly but held her shoulders. "You both look so wonderful."

"Are you still riding?" Daisy asked, holding Roswynd's hand.

"Of course I am." Roswynd's voice was cheerful while she talked with the twins.

"When you come to Wulfbite, can you teach us?" Holly asked and grabbed Roswynd's hand. "We wish to learn from another Omega."

Roswynd opened her mouth, but Saxon cut into the conversation. "Please sit, ladies."

Tharon flashed her canines at Saxon, warning him again. Her hand curled into a fist under the table when the excited air behind her immediately deflated. Their twin sisters lived dull, quiet lives, which was mostly Saxon's doing. He kept them under lock and key in their castle. She and Saxon had many fights over the necessity of exposing their sisters to new experiences in life. In the end, Tharon was often forced to respect Saxon's decisions because he was king.

Holly and Daisy exchanged quick hugs with Roswynd, and Daisy whispered something in Roswynd's ear. Roswynd returned to her seat, taking Tharon's assistance to scoot in the chair.

"They are adults now," Roswynd said in a soft voice, meant for Tharon's ear.

Tharon tilted her head toward Roswynd, revealing her hazy right eye. She gave a barest of nods after she considered the heaviness of Roswynd's assessment. It meant her twin sisters needed to marry soon; they would be taken from her, and she would be left with Saxon and her five-year-old half brother Radford.

Roswynd looked away from Tharon and chewed on her bottom lip. Again, her scent shifted and hinted at frustration or anger due to Tharon's continued silence. As pups, they shared everything, but that was then, before the murder of Tharon's mother.

Tharon pushed aside her bleak thoughts, not wanting them to sour the evening. The celebration launched with merriment after everyone was seated in the ballroom. Saxon attempted a moving speech and emphasized that the marriage was the start of a new beginning for the two kingdoms. Many of the nobles appeared to accept the new direction and cheered for the changes. But Tharon could tell that the members of the House of Arrington did not believe Saxon's promises. If she were an Arrington, she wouldn't have bought into it either.

The food and drinks were brought out, first to the royal families. Their table was served a large deer roast, cut and shared between them. Tharon had hunted and killed the deer yesterday morning, per tradition, to provide for her new wife and family. For an instant, she considered whether

Roswynd would question who provided the deer. If nothing else, Roswynd was enjoying the fruits of Tharon's hunt.

The ballroom was alive with chatter, upbeat music, and laughter. The delicious food was plentiful and washed down easily with wine and port. Eventually sweet breads were brought out for dessert, but Tharon declined such treats. Roswynd indulged in a few slices and gave Tharon a curious glance. At one time, Tharon could eat an entire loaf of sweet bread—that was, until she became a squire as a teenager.

Several times throughout the meal, Tharon caught Roswynd studying the wedding ring on her finger. Roswynd would spin it, then run her nail over the intricate details etched into the simple band. Tharon had the specific posy ring made for Roswynd. A nature scene on the outside of the band included a hunting wolf, an escaping rabbit, grasses, a fern, and the rising sun. The band's inside had an inscription from their shared past. Tharon doubted that Roswynd was aware of the inscription, but in time she would learn.

By sunset the guests were slouched in their seats with round bellies. The somber mood from this afternoon's ceremony was gone, replaced by a contentment and perhaps a tiny bit of hope for the future. After the meal, the music style shifted, signaling the next stage of the evening.

Tharon groused at the requirement to dance. If nothing else, her dance partner wasn't new to her, and they were no strangers to public dancing. If she completed the dance, she would have an excuse to leave the celebration.

Before Saxon could prod her, Tharon rose from the seat, faced her wife, and held out her hand.

Roswynd lifted an eyebrow at the silent offer. A question echoed in her mismatched eyes, but Tharon waited for her. Finally, her small hand slid into Tharon's calloused palm and they departed the table. Several family members gawked at the newlyweds willing to dance together despite the circumstances of the marriage.

Tharon brought them to the center of the empty space and aligned herself in proper fashion. Again, she offered herself as a dance partner to Roswynd, who eyed her. Dancing was a special act of intimacy between the two dance partners. Roswynd's refusal or acceptance would send a clear message to their kingdoms. For the barest of moments, Tharon teetered on a mental ledge that left her with a chill she hadn't felt since her first battle as a knight.

Roswynd nodded, stepped forward, and fitted herself against Tharon with familiarity, even though their last dance together was a lifetime ago. She was breathing hard, and her hand was clammy in Tharon's heated one.

Tharon adjusted her arm around Roswynd's waist, then checked that Roswynd was ready to begin. At a slow pace, she took the initial steps and eased them into the first dance of the night. The initial attempt was sloppy, but Tharon persisted until Roswynd relaxed against her. Within moments they were moving with fluid grace as if the last ten years of strife meant nothing. Earlier this week, she had taken half a day to refresh her dancing skills after so long. She refused to embarrass herself or her wife in front of their family or the nobles.

Roswynd matched Tharon's gaze, never stealing looks at the guests. It was an old habit between them from the dances they shared at the Howling Eagle Festival. If they paid attention solely to each other, then the rest of the world disappeared. The ease at which they both slipped into the habit stirred warmth in Tharon's chest.

"Are we ever going to speak?" Roswynd asked in a gentle voice.

Tharon turned them and restarted the steps, still holding eye contact. Similar to Roswynd's tone, she responded with care rather than her usual coldness. "As I said before, when you are ready to listen." Even with the sharpness restrained from her words, Roswynd still bristled in reaction, which caused Tharon to sigh.

"I listen," Roswynd snapped. Her hazel eye burned with fire, in stark contrast to her icy blue one.

Tharon found that she missed that rare ability of Roswynd's mismatched eyes. She worked to steady her breathing rather than be roped into Roswynd's childish temper. With a tilt of her head, she posed, "If that is true, then tell me how my wedding vows differed from yours?" For the first time, their eye contact was broken, by Roswynd. They both had their answer.

Roswynd continued staring at the people around them, features grim, and she whispered, "You have become insufferable."

This time Tharon failed to hold back her reaction. The throaty chuckle came free, then her lips curled into a dark smile. She held her tongue and felt Roswynd try to create space between their bodies, but Tharon denied her. With a rumble, she pulled them together, even closer, and used her pheromones to squash Roswynd's rebellious scent. Roswynd was hers finally, whether it was perfect or full of flaws. They were married to each other until the end of their days.

Clenching her teeth, Roswynd held herself together and finished the last part of the dance with her wife. Once the music paused, people gathered and set up for a line dance, one local to their region. Roswynd separated from Tharon but fell in line with the other dancers.

Tharon was curious that Roswynd decided to continue dancing. After weighing whether to depart and return to the table, Tharon joined the same line as Roswynd. They stood next to each other and waited for the musicians to begin the music.

"Roswynd," Myla called as she hurried to her sister's side, barely in time. She had a bright smile and went out of her way to avoid Tharon on the other side of Roswynd.

"Do you remember this dance?" Roswynd asked her sister.

Tharon recalled that Myla was the least apt at dancing among the Arringtons. From the color on Myla's cheeks, it might still be the case.

"No, I will need your help, please." Myla's confession deepened the blush. She remained close to her sister for help.

"It is about to start," Roswynd warned, her smile shifting into a grin. All at once, the lines of dancers clapped, turned to their left, and walked four steps forward, then pivoted to their right.

Tharon kept pace with ease, also studying Roswynd's movements for assistance. The line dance was known as the Summer Blossom, often said to celebrate the season and bring crop wealth to the local farmers.

Myla missed several steps for the first minute, causing Roswynd to giggle. But her persistence paid off, and she managed to stay within her dancing box as the lines of dancers moved with the music.

After another round of claps, Tharon pivoted and slid to her right, in Roswynd's direction. She caught Roswynd staring at her with a faint grin. Roswynd probably expected Tharon to be less graceful or forget the moves, but becoming a knight had trained her to be hyperaware of her body's exact movements. And if Roswynd was inclined to dance longer, then Tharon would follow her lead.

The Summer Blossom continued for another minute, then ended with everyone cheering and calling for recommendations on a new dance. The musicians took a prompt for a court dance, which was more formal, requiring curtsies and bows. People started to pair off one by one. Myla looked relieved when her younger brother, Archibold, raced over to her.

Roswynd chuckled at her siblings, then she faced Tharon and curtsied as tradition called for. When she straightened, Tharon accepted by bowing to her. The court dance, known as the White Wind, was a special one to their two kingdoms. There were many tales about its origin, but it started generations ago and continued to be honored at every event.

Like the other dancers, Tharon and Roswynd closed the gap but remained one step from each other. Tharon bowed and offered her hand, continuing the role of the male. Roswynd curtsied in kindness, then placed her palm flat on top of Tharon's; they held their loose arms behind their backs. Together, they glided forward with the other dancers, never breaking their hand contact in midair.

"Your technique has improved," Roswynd said in a quiet voice so the others couldn't hear her.

Tharon flashed a toothy smile, but she remained focused on the dance. Her Alpha lathered in the compliment, causing her chest to puff up. At the end of their glide, she rolled onto her tiptoes and spun on them to face the direction they started from. Their contact broke for a beat before their arms swung out from their backs and their hands joined in the air. Together, she and Roswynd hopped forward once, then started gliding on their feet again.

Roswynd's features were bright and joyous for the first time tonight. Her wife's happiness infected Tharon. But it would be short-lived for them both once the dancing ended and the ugliness of their fate stabbed them again. For now Tharon allowed herself to entertain the escape.

Exhausted by the tenth straight dance, Roswynd broke away despite her sister's protests. She freed herself from Myla's insistence and said she wanted to rest and drink.

She parted ways but slowed upon seeing Tharon waiting for her.

Once Roswynd was close enough, Tharon smelled the anxiousness building in Roswynd's scent. They had danced quite a bit, but Tharon reserved the right to end their night in the ballroom at any point. She was the Alpha, and tradition required that she mate with her wife before sunrise. When Roswynd passed her without acknowledgment, Tharon grinned and followed in her wife's wake of wild pheromones. Her mouth watered and her teeth felt sharper than normal, indicating her desire to mate her Omega.

At the table Tharon made sure to pull out Roswynd's seat again, then sat next to her. This time, she sat less dignified, legs parted, and hand resting on her thigh, near her crotch. No one else was around them except a few extended family members several seats away on either end of the long table. They were half-drunk and chatting among each other.

Roswynd snuck a glance at Tharon from the corner of her eye. Her breathing was still elevated, even though they were resting from the dancing. She swallowed larger mouthfuls of wine compared to her sips earlier tonight.

Tharon smirked at Roswynd's uneasiness about tonight. An old, devilish fragment of herself resurfaced the more she smelled Roswynd's heightened apprehension. How many times had Roswynd teased her, played tricks on her, or won a game by cheating when they were pups? Tharon took a long draw from her mug, then returned it to the table with enough force to make Roswynd jump. With a hungry smile, she turned in the chair until she faced Roswynd. Her legs were still spread and she leaned into her prey, who tilted away from her. Tharon warned her with a low growl.

Roswynd stilled her motions. But her nails dug into the table as her pheromones crumbled under Tharon's much stronger ones. She was on the verge of panting.

Endless rumors circulated about Tharon's sexual exploits, including idiotic false ones about her raping. The thought of rape caused Tharon to see red. After becoming lord commander, she made it an army law that rape was punishable by castration or even death. The first year she had sentenced several of her own soldiers and knights to death, and the message became clear. Saxon had snapped and howled at her for enacting the law that wasted soldiers, but she threatened him back. Regardless of her zero tolerance, the enemy loved to make up gross accusations about her and her soldiers.

Tharon was confident that Roswynd was aware of the stories, including the darker ones. For a while she had attempted to crush the stories, but tonight they might serve a purpose. Her predatory smile spread wider as her plan took hold. She continued to inhale Roswynd's sweet scent despite it being marred by distress. To see Roswynd shudder under her was exquisite.

Roswynd remained motionless, leaving her head turned away from Tharon. It was a submissive position that was unlike her, at least when they were young. But in those days, neither of them had grown fully into their natures as an Alpha or Omega. They both reached puberty separate of each other, never having to contend with the new dynamics, until now.

Gripping the back of Roswynd's chair, Tharon dipped her head until her lips were near Roswynd's ear. She was close to her wife's neck, where her scent was the strongest. It was intoxicating and so much better than a Beta's scent. Tharon could feel her Alpha pacing inside her, going mad to claim Roswynd's body. Even taking a taste might be enough, if…

Someone cleared their throat behind Tharon. Saxon's unwanted scent invaded her nose and triggered a growl deep in her chest. Roswynd responded with a broken whimper that further infuriated Tharon. She withdrew from Roswynd, stood, and faced her brother.

"I see you both are catching up after many long years apart." Saxon had a smug smile, and his brown eyes glowed with merriment.

Roswynd was indeed panting and remained seated while Tharon shielded her from Saxon.

Tharon curled her hands into fists at her side and leashed her inner Alpha before it bested her. If they made a scene here, then all the nobles would gossip about the power struggle between her and Saxon. With a rumble, she said, "Yes, we are going to retire for the night."

Saxon chuckled and beamed at Tharon. "I certainly understand."

Tharon touched Roswynd's shoulder and willed her to rise so they could leave before she did anything stupid with her brother. She was grateful that Roswynd interpreted her touch and stood. At least their past afforded them silent communication that took new couples years to learn, if ever.

"By the way, Roswynd, I did not have a chance to thank you for marrying my sister."

Tharon ground her teeth and considered his angle.

"I am proud of her accomplishments in life, but I was so afraid she would end up alone, being the type of Alpha that she is." Saxon had a stern look, but a glint entered his eyes. His remark was a backward poke at Tharon being a degenerate, without using the term. "Now, I can rest easy knowing she has her Omega, finally."

Tharon raised her left arm until it was hooked by Roswynd's hand. She faltered and peered downward at Roswynd, who was focused on Saxon.

"Yes, I could not have imagined myself with anyone but Tharon." Roswynd flashed him a smile, while her eyes swirled with outrage. Even though she was trying to barb Saxon back, there was truth under her words that echoed their past promise to each other. "Everyone else is simply a lesser Alpha than Tharon." The following silence grew thick with warring Alpha pheromones.

Tharon didn't need Roswynd fighting her battles or inciting Saxon even more. As pups, Roswynd stood up to Saxon and attempted to outmaneuver him, like a game. Such games were far more dangerous now that Saxon was a grown Alpha and the king. Regardless, Tharon's first duty was now to her wife, not her king. When Saxon shifted forward, closer to Roswynd, Tharon blocked him and bared her teeth, warning him and reminding him.

Saxon took two steps back after a beat, then blew out a breath that ended the pissing match. "Well, I would hate to delay your night together."

Roswynd slid her hand down Tharon's sleeve, then threaded their fingers together. "I am ready," she said.

Tharon squeezed the smaller hand locked in hers. "Goodnight, brother." She nudged Roswynd behind her in silent order to leave. Not waiting for her brother's response, she followed Roswynd's lead and started through the ballroom. But through the din of music, Saxon hollered one last dig that several guests heard.

"Now, make me prouder and give me a nephew or a niece!"

Chapter 5

Roswynd departed the ballroom with fire in her step, boiling over from Saxon's final farewell. Like a pup, she wanted to kick and punch him for being a bastard. He was worse now as an adult. On top of it, she was certain her reaction was heightened by Tharon's own lashing pheromones. From Tharon's scent, she sensed that Tharon was quite agitated by Saxon's taunts, especially about impregnating Roswynd. It was another secretive jab at Tharon's breed as a She-Alpha, who couldn't impregnate until she was rutting. At least, that was the rumor about She-Alphas, similar to He-Omegas being unable to become pregnant outside of their heats.

"Clearly your brother is still a dick," Roswynd said, venom lacing every word. For once she wasn't bothered by Tharon's lack of response, knowing it would simply work her up more. But Tharon's silence was telling.

Once upon a time, Tharon had attempted to be the mediator between Roswynd and Saxon. But one day it had shifted after Saxon had taken a joke too far. Roswynd had been visiting Tharon in White Sommer for a fortnight before the hunts and the Howling Eagle Festival. A disagreement between Saxon and Roswynd ended with Roswynd locked inside a wardrobe for half an hour before Tharon rescued her. After that day, Tharon went from mediating them to protecting Roswynd, similar to this evening. Old habits seemed to still be buried in Tharon.

As the distance grew between them and the ballroom, Tharon's pheromones waned until they were normal again. She turned at the staircase not far from the foyer, which was lit by a few lamps.

Roswynd went up first with her wife on her heels. They were nearing their room, and her stomach pitched. She paused at the top of the stairs. The hallway only went to the right, but her feet felt lined with iron. She started to pant again. Then Tharon was against her back, waiting for her to go. There was no escape from her pending night with her wife.

Even a step down, Tharon was still taller than Roswynd. She bowed her head closer to Roswynd's neck, breathed in her scent, and rumbled low.

Roswynd closed her eyes and fisted her hands at her side, resolving herself to her fate. She had agreed, she had taken vows, and she thought she had prepared herself for this night. She was wrong. With a deep breath, she moved forward, but the hallway felt like a death sentence. She had dreamed of being with Tharon, but not like this. Never like this. Her stomach revolted again, making her stop. Roswynd turned and faced her wife, who glowed in the lamplight. She almost reached out, but her hand hung in the space between them. "Tharon, please. I-I ca—"

Tharon growled, invaded Roswynd's space, bent over, and hooked her arm around Roswynd's waist. With ease she lifted and tossed Roswynd over her shoulder. Her right arm locked across the back of Roswynd's thighs, keeping her from kicking. But Roswynd landed a solid punch to Tharon's midback, earning a grunt and an amused laugh.

At first Roswynd was shocked by Tharon manhandling her, and she was furious with herself because it thrilled the Omega inside her. She clawed into the leather of Tharon's jerkin and gave a low cry, but no one was going to help her. She was Tharon's spouse now and obligated to appease her. Roswynd loathed the gross rumors that Tharon was a rapist and didn't believe them. She held hope that Tharon wouldn't force her to have sex. However, if Tharon became a squire at a young age and was slowly indoctrinated into the rape culture of the army, then Tharon's young mind might have been warped to believe it was acceptable. Soldiers and knights may have even told Tharon that being a real Alpha meant dominating and taking Omegas against their will.

"Please do not do this!" But Roswynd's plea fell on deaf ears. She heard a bedroom door open, and they entered into the darkness. The door shut before the click of the lock echoed in Roswynd's ears. No, no, no! This cannot be happening! Her ears rang with panic, but she couldn't get free. Inside the room everything smelled of Tharon and overwhelmed Roswynd's senses. She whined in confusion and curled her fists into the leather jerkin.

Tharon's boot steps boomed against the wood floor. Her hold on Roswynd never faltered and her rumbles had grown deeper. She came to a stop, then placed a hand against Roswynd's lower back. She lifted Roswynd off her shoulder, tearing her from the jerkin.

Roswynd kicked once and rammed her foot into Tharon's lower gut.

With a snarl, Tharon tossed her wife into the darkness.

Squealing, Roswynd landed back first into a rather soft bed, but she scrambled backward in hopes to escape somehow. She hardly made it anywhere before Tharon pounced her. Panting and shaking, she gripped the fur under her and gazed up into piercing orange eyes that hovered in the moonlight streaming in from the window behind them.

Tharon was growling again, her lips peeled back to reveal her canines. It was almost as if the tall tales about her being a werewolf were true.

The dangerous, fiery orbs were so close to Roswynd's face. Sharp white teeth continued to glint in warning. But Tharon's smile wasn't cruel or malicious—it held a hint of amusement. Roswynd gasped at first, but Tharon's wonderful scent enveloped her, making her dizzy. She released an uncontrolled moan that caused Tharon to grin like a wolf. Roswynd's body was betraying her at every turn. Already the wetness between her thighs was chaffing her some. Even if her body found her aggressive Alpha thrilling, her mind and certainly her heart didn't agree.

"Please, Tharon, do not do this." Roswynd wished she could reach Tharon, find any scrap of her best friend left. How could they once have been so close, ripped apart by their families' war, and now forced into marriage and sex? This couldn't happen between them. "I know we are married, and you have every right to take me. But please not like this." She sensed two hands pressing into the furs near her shoulders, then watched Tharon bow her head near Roswynd's temple.

Tharon was breathing her in, drowning in her Omega scent. Tharon's rumble deepened to a new octave that sent sparks flying up Roswynd's spine. There was no denying that their attraction was mutual.

Roswynd started to shake her head, but her Omega instincts forced her to turn her head to one side, bearing her neck to her Alpha. She whimpered at what was to come next for her. Already the tears that had formed in her eyes were rolling from the corners and down her temples. "Please," she murmured.

Lifting her head, Tharon stared at Roswynd in the moonlight. She moved a hand and with the most delicate touch, began wiping the dampness from the side of Roswynd's face. "One day you will be asking me to take you," she whispered, turned Roswynd's head, and dried the other temple, then withdrew her hand. It left Roswynd's cheeks even more flushed than earlier. Like a ghost, Tharon was gone from the bed but moving in the darkness.

Roswynd panted and drank in Tharon's fading scent, part of her wanting it to come back. She closed her eyes and listened to her wife's movements. What did this mean? Then she caught a throaty but distinct chuckle that took Roswynd back many, many years ago. Roswynd's eyes flew open, and she bolted upright and growled low. Did Tharon play a prank on her? Did she find the whole damn situation amusing?

"It has been a long day. I suggest you rest," Tharon said from somewhere in the blackness. She spoke as if the earlier prank never happened, as if they were having a casual discussion.

Roswynd covered her pounding heart and glared in Tharon's general direction. "You were simply toying with me?" she asked, ice back in her voice. The sound of wood being tossed echoed in the room. "By the Divine," she whispered after her mind ran through what happened between them after they left the celebration. She was unsure who to be infuriated with more: herself for falling for it or Tharon for taking it so far and making her a begging fool. A few sparks flashed in the room, then small flames started to lap underneath a short pile of wood. As Tharon's profile formed in the growing firelight, Roswynd looked over her shoulder at her wife and whispered, "You have turned into your brother."

Tharon's lips curled back in a silent sneer, but it was the only indicator that she didn't like Roswynd's accusation. She huffed and continued to stare into the fireplace in front of her. Her damaged eye was silvery above the firelight.

Roswynd swallowed and scanned the room, searching for her possessions. Earlier today the Wyndfeld guards had moved her things from Proudpeak Hall to the manor. Once enough light built up, she located the trunk off to the right. She slid off the bed and tested her legs, which were shaky— but not enough to stop her. Searching through the trunk, she found her sleeping attire and was grateful that there was a wooden divider in the room.

With her sleepwear in hand, she ducked behind the wooden curtains and hung the nightgown. She slipped off the flats, and the cool floor started goosebumps up her legs. But already the fireplace was taking off the evening chill. Summer weather in their region was pleasant during the day, but often chilly at night.

Roswynd reached behind but faltered once a slight problem occurred to her. The damn gown required someone to release the tiny buttons that ran from the back of her neck down to her lower back. Often, she could undo her dresses alone, but the wedding dress was far more intricate with its tiny velvet-covered buttons. Tilting her head back, Roswynd gulped several deep breaths and braced herself to ask for help.

"Tharon, I need help undoing my dress." At first there was no movement or response in the room. I am not asking again. I will tear off the dress otherwise. Roswynd waited another beat, then reached behind her neck, but boot steps neared the divider.

In the flickering light, Tharon emerged and waited at the end of the divider, silently offering her assistance. Her orange eyes were searching while her features were neutral.

Roswynd swallowed, approached her wife, turned, and offered her back with all the countless buttons. With her hair pulled aside, she held her breath at first, unsure how to handle the strange moment that echoed their past. She shoved away the fond memory, not wanting to associate it with this bad night.

Tharon worked the first button, then moved onto the next one. She was careful and slow, freeing each button with precision. There was mostly silence between them, except for Tharon's faint rumble that carried an unusual note to it.

Roswynd couldn't place it, but sensed it was acceptable. She shut her eyes when the dress's backing spread open, exposing her tan skin to both the air and Tharon's gaze. The touches to her back were light and tender, opposite of what a knight would be in battle. About midway down, she started breathing a little harder, but she tried to ignore how the closeness and intimacy of the moment affected her body. Even though she struggled to keep from giving Tharon the wrong signals, her pheromones were betraying her.

Tharon finished the last buttons, then removed her hands and said, "You will take the bed." Then she was gone.

Roswynd stood there, bent forward, and back exposed to the chilly air. She stared toward the open window and the moonlight that poured over half of the bed. There was a single bed. *Are we sleeping separate too?* Stilling her thoughts, she focused on changing into her bedwear and hung her gown on one of the panels' hooks. Her thoughts about the bizarre start to their marriage could wait until tomorrow, along with the dagger. Her father's gift was for protection. Especially from Tharon. But Roswynd had given her vows to Tharon, who had vowed equally to Roswynd. At the celebration, Tharon had shielded her from Saxon without hesitation. Regardless of Tharon's cruel prank tonight, Roswynd knew she was still safe from threats. She didn't need the dagger in bed with her.

Roswynd removed her family jewelry, which needed to be returned to her mother. She placed the pieces on the small table to her right. After a shaky breath, Roswynd left the divided space and went into the small attached room. There was enough firelight to find her way in the room. First she relieved herself, then poured water into the washbasin, soaped her hands and face, and washed up. Upon reentering the bedroom, she found Tharon seated in an armchair in front of the fire.

Tharon didn't acknowledge her and stared into the fire. A strange expression was on her face, but it vanished when she seemed to sense Roswynd's gaze.

Without speaking Roswynd passed by and crawled into the empty bed. Goosebumps formed all over her skin as she slid between the cool sheets. She curled up in a ball on one side and gazed out the window at the moon. Occasionally the fire crackled or popped and startled Roswynd; she couldn't release the tension from her body.

The silence was slicing her open. She didn't understand why Tharon was so withdrawn and hadn't expected that to be a part of their relationship now. They used to discuss many topics, late into the night. It wasn't unusual for them to fall asleep next to each other after a full day of playing, hunting, or riding. But now, Tharon barely spoke to her, and it was also difficult to read Tharon. This new Tharon was confusing and maddening.

Her first day as a married Omega was anything but what she pictured a week ago. The wedding ceremony itself had been beautiful in front of the White Razor Mountains. Even riding to the ceremony by horseback was unexpected and exactly what she would have wanted. Had Tharon planned it on purpose? Then there was her wedding ring, which she was able to look at during the party. The band-style ring was something she would have selected herself. At a glance it appeared plain, but its fine details were striking, reflecting Roswynd's fondness for nature. Again, had Tharon gone to extra lengths for her? Her father had mentioned that Tharon organized everything.

Ten years ago Roswynd's best friend betrayed her, threw away their friendship, and broke her in half. Their families became enemies over a horrible, tragic death spun in lies. Roswynd's family were not murderers. But the House of Blakesley refused to believe them and had sought revenge ever since. Now she was forced to marry Tharon in hopes her father could secure peace, once and for all.

However, Roswynd wondered how much she was truly forced into marrying Tharon. As a young teen, she had daydreams about wedding Tharon and despised the idea that someone else might take her best friend. The idea that a teenaged Tharon could have been married off to some distant prince had made Roswynd sick. If it had been Myla to marry Tharon today, Roswynd might have lost her mind. She might have even gained the courage to contest it at the ceremony.

At the celebration tonight, Roswynd was able to forget that she and Tharon were enemies. The food, drink, and dancing felt similar to the Howling Eagle Festival, when they were young and carefree, with nothing between them. The festival had been filled with merriment and love, and tonight's celebration had come close to the old days, until Saxon reminded them of their obligations. And at that they had failed.

Roswynd clenched her body tighter, imagined what she and Tharon were supposed to be doing right now. She should be writhing under Tharon, experiencing sex for the first time, and maybe connecting with Tharon on a new level. But instead, she was alone in the bed while Tharon sat in silence by the fire. Roswynd screwed her eyes shut against the building pressure against her chest. She could still fix tonight if she went to Tharon and asked. That was what Tharon said earlier. Yet, Roswynd's heart and very spirit were torn in half, not wanting to share her body with the person who had turned her back on her.

Her entire world was now fucking chaos and forever heartache.

Hot tears crept out of the corner of her eyes and fell from her face, causing her to curl inward until her back hurt. She dragged the second pillow over and bit into it, keeping her sobs at bay. Years ago she had learned to live on without Tharon. She believed she had moved on, but she was wrong. Today had been a raging storm that left everything a muddy mess in her head and heart.

All she ever wanted was her best friend returned to her. She wanted her Tharon returned to her.

* * *

Date: 07 Wyndenn 812G
(About 14 Years Ago)

Roswynd's creaky bedroom door opened, announcing the arrival of her best friend. She hurried around the wooden divider next to the wardrobe. "Tharon, oh thank the Divine. Can you please help with my gown?"

Tharon picked up the sides of her dress and hurried across the room. "We have to go soon, Ros. We are going to be late."

"I am aware!" Roswynd danced on her tiptoes, turned her back to Tharon, and clenched her hands. "There are too many buttons for me. Mother is busy chasing after my little brothers. I do not know where Myla is. Please, Tharon."

"Be still." Tharon touched her friend's back and steadied her. "It will only take a minute." Already her nimble fingers worked the buttons that followed down Roswynd's spine. "I love your gown."

Roswynd beamed and peered over her shoulder at her best friend. "Yours is beautiful too. The golds and browns bring out the orange in your eyes so well."

"Thank you," Tharon murmured in a shy voice. She hastened to finish the buttons, but there were many of them.

"Do you want to go riding tomorrow?" Roswynd asked, already knowing the answer. Over a year ago, she had started teaching Tharon how to horseback ride. In time she discovered that Tharon not only enjoyed the riding, but also wearing the appropriate attire, like the trousers. They hadn't ridden in snow yet, but tomorrow they would try. Roswynd looked forward to spending the day together, alone. After tonight they'd spent a full four weeks together with their families, between the Howling Eagle Festival and the earlier hunts for the House of Blakesley in Wulfbite. She was ready to be alone with Tharon before the Blakesley family returned to White Sommer next week.

"As long as I can sleep in," Tharon replied in jest.

Roswynd chuckled but nodded and said, "You can sleep in, a little." She vibrated with energy. Tonight's formal ball was the last event of the festival and was her absolute favorite because of the hours of endless dancing.

"We must go," Tharon said, grabbing her friend's hand and tugging her to the door.

"Wait!" Roswynd pulled away, back toward her bedroom. "I must retrieve my shoes!"

Tharon grumbled but let go and waited in the doorway. "Hurry, Ros." She rested her hands on her hips and started to rumble the longer Roswynd took to get her footwear.

"I am coming!" Roswynd retrieved her shoes from the wardrobe, carrying them in her right hand. She stretched out her other hand, which Tharon caught, then burst through the doorway dragging Tharon with her. "We mustn't be late!"

Tharon growled at being yanked away but managed to close the bedroom door. She stumbled twice, then caught up to Roswynd's pace. Together, they ran hand in hand toward the ballroom at the other end of the castle. Even at a sprint, it would take them a good minute to get there, now longer due to the crowd.

The halls seemed endless and the staircases steeper than normal, now that crowds of people spread throughout the castle. Roswynd dodged around nobles and servants, giggling several times. Tharon kept pace with her and on occasion used her larger body to block someone from running into Roswynd. Gasping for air, they arrived at the hallway that led to the ballroom. Music and cheer bellowed out from the open doors.

Roswynd dropped her flats to the floor and hastened to put them on, still holding on to Tharon. "I can hardly wait!"

Grinning from ear to ear, Tharon hooked her arm behind Roswynd's back, then guided them both down the hall. They steered around chatty nobles and servants, who raised their eyebrows at the princesses. Everyone was waiting to be welcomed into the ballroom by the two royal families.

"I see your father," Tharon said, pointing at King Garrett by the door.

"Where is your father?" Roswynd asked with a tiny frown. "He should be here too." She and Tharon slipped past a noble couple with six pups. One of the girls Roswynd had met several times and formed a friendship with. Her name was Gleda, and she had a sparkling personality that Roswynd enjoyed. As they passed Gleda, Roswynd waved at her and gave a smile.

Gleda returned it and mouthed that she would visit with Roswynd later.

"Father, where is King Eustace?" Roswynd asked after she and Tharon made it through the entrance. She clung to his surcoat.

"Roswynd." Garrett smiled and placed a hand on her shoulder. "He went to fetch Queen Edeva." He then shifted his attention to Tharon, and his smile grew impossibly larger. "You both are stunning."

"Thank you, Father."

"Thank you, sir."

Roswynd glanced at Tharon and giggled at how Tharon swelled with pride, like an adult Alpha. It was improper for princesses to bask outright in compliments, but Alphas were expected to do it. Omegas were reserved creatures, well, except for Roswynd at times.

"Please stand with the rest of the family while we wait for the king and queen," Garrett told them, indicating the other members from the Houses. Ever since the first Howling Eagle Festival, all the members from the House of Arrington and House of Blakesley stood together near the entrance of the ballroom and greeted their guests into the ball. This important tradition would take over an hour to complete, but it forged lasting relationships between the royal families and the noble families.

"Yes, Father." Roswynd squeezed Tharon's hand, and they left Garrett's side. They were forced to separate, though, once they neared the other family members. The two Houses created two equal lines with each family member standing in line by age. The House of Arrington and the House of Blakesley mirrored each other. As the procession of people began entering the ballroom, each family member greeted the guests and welcomed them to the grand ball.

Roswynd's mother stood proudly at the center of the line, where her father, King Garrett, would join her to the left. Opposite them would be King Eustace and Queen Edeva. To the right of Roswynd's mother stood Roswynd's older brother, Selwyn, who was mirrored on the opposite side by Tharon, the eldest of King Eustace and Queen Edeva. Roswynd took her place next to Selwyn, straightened her back, and folded her hands in front of her body. Across from her, she beamed at Tharon, who winked back. To Tharon's left was Saxon, who kept poking at Tharon's side to annoy her. After him were Daisy and Holly, the identical twins. The twin sisters always took cues from their older sister, learning from her.

Roswynd's sister Myla stood next to her. Like the Blakesley twins, Myla looked up to her older sister, especially during the ceremonial greeting. Myla was shy and after twenty minutes, she would be against Roswynd's side but still welcoming guests. Sometimes Myla would take it upon herself to hush their two little brothers, Archibold and Josse. Their youngest sibling, Josse, was a toddler and avoided reprimand of his fair share of antics, at least until their father corrected him.

King Eustace arrived with his usual fanfare. Queen Edeva was at his side, calming him with ease. She received a kiss to the cheek from Garrett, then Eustace traded a brief hug with Garrett. Edeva went over to Roswynd's mother next.

"You are gorgeous, Layla." Edeva was all smiles and exchanged a hug with Layla. She was tall for an Omega, even having height over Eustace, who was an Omega too. Her hair was black as a moonless night and her eyes warm as fire. "I am sorry we are late."

Layla hushed her and said, "We have not been waiting long." She and Edeva held hands and their exchange of comforting pheromones seemed to settle both families. Everyone was anxious to greet their guests into the formal ball for the Howling Eagle Festival. After tonight's event, the festival ended and the hunts started for the House of Arrington. Even though they were exciting and important, the four weeks of hunts, traveling, and festivities had exhausted the family members. However, there was still another week of hunts left.

"It has been a long month," Edeva said, then sighed with weariness. Dark circles showed under her eyes, but she continued to radiate energy.

"Tomorrow we will rest," Layla insisted, and both Omegas traded reassuring smiles.

Edeva kissed Layla on the cheek and murmured something in her ear. She then went over to the line for the

House of Blakesley, next to her husband, and threaded her fingers with Eustace's.

Roswynd peered around her brother and mother, listening to her father give the order to the servants to allow the guests to begin entry. Once the musicians on stage started to play, the light from the lamps was turned up and caused all the overhead crystals to sparkle. Garrett left the doors and took his wife's side. With a deep breath, Roswynd prepared for the long first hour. But her reward was hours of magical dancing and food, including sweet breads. She planned to dance until her feet fell off.

Across from her Tharon smiled, but it slipped into a reserved countenance as the first guests started to block their view from one another. On occasion they would sneak glances at each other between people's shoulders and heads. Roswynd could tell that her best friend was wearing down from all the socializing, but she swore to reenergize Tharon after the welcoming procession was done.

As the nobles spread out and filled the ballroom, drinks and appetizers were handed out. Different groups of guests lumped together throughout the room, chatting and laughing. The merriment was infectious and brought great happiness to both kingdoms. Beyond the castle, the people celebrated with dance, bards' stories, and free wine and food supplied by the royals.

Finishing her last welcome to a guest, Roswynd broke the House of Arrington line and dashed over to her best friend. She hooked Tharon's arm with her own, about to race off.

"Where might you two be going?" Edeva asked them.

Roswynd glanced at Tharon, whose face was flushed. She sniffed out Tharon's strange guilt, but Roswynd beamed at Edeva. "To see what appetizers are being served." She prayed that Edeva believed her, especially after last year. Her own guilt bubbled up to the surface.

Edeva eyed them as though they were troublemakers; then her serious expression cracked with a grin. "Stay far from the wine. You recall what happened last year?"

The redness in Tharon's cheeks spread down to her neck. "Yes, Mother." Last year, she and Roswynd had snuck a goblet of wine each. Shortly after, Saxon had asked Roswynd to dance with him. It was the first time he had ever asked her, finding the courage to do so despite Tharon's glares. Roswynd had no reason to decline even though she wished to.

While Saxon and Roswynd shared a couples dance, Tharon watched with a stormy expression. After it was over, Roswynd curtsied to him and took leave, returning to Tharon's side. Saxon had followed and attempted to request another couples dance, but Tharon blocked him, which triggered the physical fight. What started as a few growls escalated into a wrestling match in the ballroom that turned everyone's heads. Eustace and Edeva had been mortified and punished both Saxon and Tharon for days.

Edeva nodded at Tharon's agreement, then moved closer and drew her into a one-armed hug. She nuzzled Tharon's temple and whispered, "Stay clear of your brother tonight."

Tharon nodded and stole a glance at Roswynd, who shuffled on her feet. Roswynd was uncomfortable hearing the tender exchange between them, but she also loved Edeva like a second mother.

"My little Alpha," Edeva murmured and kissed Tharon's temple. "One day soon, you will be another's Alpha."

"Mother," Tharon complained, but she returned the hug and melted into Edeva's affection.

"But you will always be my little Alpha." Edeva continued rubbing her nose and brow against Tharon's temple, spreading some of her scent.

Tharon flushed and whined in protest, but never broke the contact.

Edeva chuckled, then straightened and looked over at Roswynd, holding out her other arm. Roswynd didn't hesitate to take the invite and curled up against Edeva and Tharon, loving the closeness. The festival's demands had been strenuous, taking their toll on both families. The brief moment of shared affection was welcoming, and Roswynd soaked in every morsel of it, breathing in both Edeva's comforting Omega pheromones and Tharon's warm ones.

After a deep breath, Edeva kissed Roswynd's head and said, "Enjoy your evening together." She pulled away from them and returned to Eustace.

Tharon rumbled with contentment, then opened her eyes and smiled at Roswynd. "Ready?"

"Yes!" Roswynd hooked her friend's wrist and dragged them away to find food. It wasn't long before they were sharing a small plate of finger food. Roswynd moaned after every bite, causing Tharon to laugh. Shouldered together, they talked about everyone's attire, pointing out some of the sillier outfits. There were several gorgeous gowns that Roswynd swooned over, but then they focused on the males. Roswynd pointed out a few male Betas' attire that she thought were handsome but would look even better on Tharon.

Tharon snorted and argued that she would never be allowed to wear such attire. They could sneak off in trousers, tunics, and boots for their horseback riding adventures. But wearing something like the males, full-time, would end with Tharon suffering a severe punishment from her father.

"Well, when you are older, you can wear whatever you wish," Roswynd said, then popped a piece of garlicky shrimp into her mouth. "What can your father do to halt you then?" she asked between bites, covering her mouth.

"I am uncertain, Ros." Tharon shook her head and studied the nobles gathered about the ballroom. "Even if my father said it was fine, it is not appropriate for princesses to wear trousers in public."

Roswynd rolled her eyes and said, "But you are an Alpha." She plucked another shrimp from their shared plate that Tharon held between them. "You could do both. Besides, who came up with these silly rules?"

"They have been around since the sacrifice of Glydr," Tharon replied.

"Then you are saying Glydr created these ridiculous rules?" Roswynd asked, then wiped her mouth with a small linen napkin.

"Glydr was a dragon," Tharon said, as if either of them needed a reminder. "Why would she have anything to do with it?"

Roswynd giggled and grinned at her best friend. "Exactly. Glydr gave us this world without rules or restrictions. So who has the right to say what an Omega or Alpha can or cannot do?" She sighed at Tharon's big frown and touched Tharon's hip. "I am sorry."

"Do not apologize." Tharon nudged Roswynd with the plate, offering the last shrimp.

Roswynd snatched it and popped the whole thing into her mouth rather than eating it in three bites. The action was utterly improper, but no one was paying them any mind. The garlic and butter shrimp were one of her favorite dishes.

"Roswynd," Garrett said from behind his daughter, who jumped in response.

Roswynd's eyes grew larger than the sun and looked at Tharon for help. She didn't turn around and struggled to hastily chew up the large shrimp without choking on it.

"Hello, King Garrett." Tharon smiled at him and stepped up to Roswynd's side, trying to delay him from seeing his daughter's mouthful. "We have been enjoying the appetizers."

Roswynd rolled her eyes at Tharon's indiscreet abilities, but so far she could sense her father wasn't put off by Roswynd ignoring him, at the moment.

"I am sure."

"We have tried the fish, the saufes, and now the shrimp." Tharon had her hands behind her back and rocked on her feet. Her smile was bright, to the point it appeared forced.

"Yes, Roswynd greatly favors the shrimp."

Roswynd swallowed the seafood after getting it small enough, then spun around and dabbed her mouth clean. "Hello, Father. How is the ball so far?"

Garrett lifted an eyebrow, then rumbled and studied his daughter for a long moment. "It is going well." He looked between the princesses and asked, "How are you enjoying yourselves?"

"It is wonderful," Tharon replied, her smile normal now. "Do you agree, Ros?" She placed the dirty plate on the small standing table against the wall. A servant would come by later and collect it, but they would reuse their silver cups, which had their House emblems etched on them.

Roswynd nodded and mirrored her friend's smile. "I am excited for the dancing later."

Garrett chuckled and cupped his daughter's cheek. "Soon. Have you both decided who you will dance with tonight?"

Roswynd pursed her lips and delayed her response, sensing Tharon's displeasure in the topic. They always danced together during the line and court dances. But the couples dances were another matter and certainly forbidden for them to enjoy together. "I am unsure, Father," Roswynd replied.

"Perhaps Byron from the House of Blackburn?" Garrett suggested, then looked to Tharon. "I have heard that Leith from the House of Preas has spoken of you."

This time, Roswynd frowned at the news that a noble was interested in Tharon. Byron was rather harmless. His family were wealthy merchants who traveled by land and sea, making their fortunes. They kept ships at the major port in Wyndfeld. However, the House of Preas was an old family that some believed were direct descendants from the Ancient Ones. The Preas family were said to own some of the oldest books in Gyldren history, dating back to before the sacrifice of Glydr.

"We will consider it, sir," Tharon said, holding her smile even though there was nothing in her eyes to suggest excitement about the news.

Garrett was pleased, then shifted closer to the princesses. "I do have a few thoughts about the week of Furywice."

Roswynd looked to her best friend, who gave her a soft shrug. She narrowed her eyes back at her father, hoping this didn't mean she'd be separated from Tharon. Once the House of Blakesley returned to their kingdom, it would be two or three months before she saw Tharon again. They would write letters back and forth, but it didn't compare to being together.

"As you both are aware, this week our Houses will have the second hunts for our families." Garrett smiled, his scent strong with excitement about whatever idea he had in mind. "I thought perhaps since you both have learned to ride that you would like to join us this year. You both are old enough now."

Roswynd was well schooled to be a proper princess, but in that moment, it all went out the window. Her jaw fell, then she squealed loud enough to draw attention. She leaped into her father's arms and tried to squeeze him to death.

Garrett laughed and returned the brutal hug. Once he set his daughter down, he lost his smile to Tharon's uneasiness. "Tharon?"

Roswynd looked to her best friend and touched Tharon's arm, which was stiff. She wanted to hug Tharon and chase off whatever was bothering her best friend. This was an exciting occasion to go out on the hunts. Not all princesses were allowed to go, only select ones who the males thought could handle being in the outdoors, riding, and helping to prepare the kills for winter storage.

"I am sorry, sir, but I cannot join." Tharon's eyes brimmed, while she tangled her fingers together in front of her. "My father—"

"Agreed that it was an excellent idea," Garrett finished, tone firm.

"Pardon?" Tharon asked. Her voice had cracked, and she stared in doubt at Garrett.

"Yes." Garrett lifted his chest high and said, "I spoke to your father shortly ago. He agreed with me that you joining the hunt would be wise." He then leaned over, closer to Tharon. "Between us, you will make an excellent tracker with how well you are able to locate my daughter."

Roswynd giggled at Tharon's awed expression and still hadn't removed her hand.

"I would be honored to join," Tharon said. She was trembling some but held herself together otherwise. "Thank you, sir."

Garrett nodded and straightened, addressing both princesses. "You are welcomed to join us one day or all seven days. You will both be with my pack."

"Yes, Father." Roswynd couldn't care less which pack she was assigned to, as long as she and Tharon were together. She fought to keep her exhilaration under control, but it was hard.

Garrett developed a slight frown and said, "I am uncertain whether your father will be accompanying us this year, Tharon. He has been a little under the weather." It was no secret that two days ago, Eustace was low on energy and grumpy, but Roswynd had heard he was a little ill and would be fine soon. "Well then, you can both discuss it tonight and give me your answer tomorrow," Garrett said and bowed to them in polite fashion. After he received curtsies back, he left them to enjoy the ball.

Roswynd waited until her father was out of earshot before she grabbed Tharon's hands. "Can you believe this? We are going on the hunt!" She had wanted to for years and had hoped that learning horseback riding would prove to their fathers that they could handle it. "I am ecstatic!"

Tharon had a huge smile and clenched Roswynd's hands. She was more reserved, but there was no mistaking the fire in her eyes. "We have to go on a ride tomorrow so I can practice."

"We will. Do not fret." Roswynd squealed again, but quieter, and hugged Tharon, who spun them around in a circle. Once her feet touched the floor again, she said, "I must have more shrimp!"

Tharon laughed, took her friend's hand, and pulled her in the direction of the food tables. Roswynd made sure to grab their cups for a refill of cider. They loaded two clean plates with finger food, found a quiet spot, and chatted about the hunt. They were so engrossed in the discussion that they missed the first few dances, which never happened to Roswynd.

But as the evening wore on, Roswynd and Tharon joined the dancing. They took occasional breaks for drinks or more food, especially when the sweet breads arrived in the ballroom. Roswynd loved the honey bread with walnuts, while Tharon's favorite was always the spice bread. Eventually the line and court dances were broken up by couples dances. Each time, they attempted to escape the crowd and hide, not wanting to be asked by any males.

Once Roswynd had to dance with her father, which brought her under the light, triggering Byron to locate her. With her father near, she had to accept Byron's offer. As he swept her around the ballroom, Roswynd spotted Tharon, who was glowering as she had last year. Roswynd did her best to roll her eyes or give a bored look to Tharon, in hopes it would soothe her Alpha nature. Lately, Roswynd noticed Tharon acting more Alpha than princess, especially around males. A fortnight ago, Tharon had turned eleven, which meant her developing Alpha would rear up in the coming years. Even though King Eustace tried to tame Tharon's Alpha, Roswynd was certain it would all come undone one day.

After the dance with Byron ended, Roswynd thanked him and hurried off with an excuse that she needed to relieve herself. She'd gone earlier, but wanted to find Tharon, who was fending off Leith from the House of Preas. A sudden snarl jumped from Roswynd's lips, causing a few nobles to cast a glance at her. Roswynd flushed and hurried after Tharon, intercepting the pair.

"Tharon!" Roswynd grabbed her best friend's arm. "I require your help again." She pretended to notice Leith for the first time and forced a smile. "Oh, hello, Leith."

"Hello, Princess Roswynd." Leith bowed and scowled some when Roswynd didn't give him a curtsy in return.

"My apologies for interrupting," Roswynd said and sidled up to Tharon, who was eyeing her, "but I need Princess Tharon." She looked to her friend and said, "It is an emergency of sorts." She gave Leith a bashful look. "Something only us females understand."

"Oh." Leith shuffled on his feet, looking between them. "Well, perhaps after you are finished, we could dance?" he asked Tharon.

"Yes," Roswynd answered for her friend. "We shan't be long." She squeezed Tharon's arm and prayed her friend understood the silent hint. But instead, Tharon gave her a strange look, so Roswynd tugged on her arm. "We have to hurry. Come along."

Tharon didn't contest her friend's demands and left their silver cups on the table to her left.

"My apologies again, Leith, but we will return shortly." Roswynd offered a final smile before she hauled Tharon away from the trap. There was no way in Gyldr's name she was going to watch her best friend dance with that idiot, especially a couples dance. Next, Leith would try to kiss Tharon. Roswynd could almost spit on the floor at the idea. Gross!

"Ros, what is happening?" Tharon asked, then tripped over her feet because Roswynd was pulling her so hard. They had already put a lot of space and people between them and Leith.

"I am saving you, idiot." Roswynd was halted when Tharon dug in her heels. She sighed and turned to her friend. They were surrounded by chatting groups of nobles, who paid them little attention.

"I was fine." But Tharon sniffed out Roswynd's upset hidden under the bravado. She sighed and pulled Roswynd into her arms. "I would have refused to dance with him."

"You would have had to," Roswynd murmured into Tharon's neck. "Princesses have so few reasons to deny someone." She peered up at her best friend and said, "That is why we must stay together."

Tharon brushed a loose strand from Roswynd's face. "We will always stay together." She scanned around them, then her attention centered on something. Roswynd followed her line of sight but was unsure what caught Tharon's eye. "Come along," Tharon said, taking Roswynd's hand. Together, they weaved in and out of people, passing the dance area, and snuck over to the sealed doors for the balcony. It was close to the stage where the second group of musicians was playing for the audience. The current song, a line dance, was coming to an end.

"Where are we going?" Roswynd asked, unsure about Tharon's idea.

Tharon played with the glass doors' latch between the heavy curtains. She freed it, then nudged open the left door. "Follow me." She and Roswynd snuck out onto the large balcony coated in fresh snow.

Roswynd shivered and crossed her arms, then looked over at Tharon. "It is a little cold."

"You will adjust." Tharon grinned and left the door cracked open, which allowed the music to filter out onto the balcony. She tamped down the snow.

Tharon was right about Roswynd adjusting to the cold. She was raised in one of the coldest regions. Even the first month of summer could bring snow to Tharon's kingdom. But still, Roswynd was curious why they were out here. "Tharon, what are you doing?"

Tharon had finished her task on the balcony, then turned to her best friend. "Making a dance floor."

Roswynd's features twisted and furrowed until a new song started in the ballroom. She peered over her shoulder at the parted door and sighed at the music meant for couples.

Roswynd didn't want to go back in now and worry that she or Tharon might be asked to dance by a male.

"May I have this dance, Princess Roswynd?" Tharon asked, standing in the center of the snowy balcony. She was basked in silver light from the moon and the reflective snow.

Roswynd stared in awe, before her mind caught up to the question. "Y-Yes." Without hesitation, she curtsied to Tharon, not thinking twice about their dancing roles.

Tharon accepted the response by performing a bow as best as possible with a dress. She held out her hand next, waiting for Roswynd to join her. Her smile spread wider as Roswynd's petite hand slid into hers.

Roswynd giggled and took her position against Tharon. "Are we truly going to dance together, like a couple?"

"Yes, of course." Tharon adjusted her arm around Roswynd's waist, tightened their hands, and then started the dance, finding flow with the music.

Roswynd gazed up into Tharon's majestic eyes as she was swept around the balcony. They moved so well together and fit together even better. The balcony was nowhere near as large as the dance floor in the ballroom, but it was enough that they could dance across the snow that kicked up and swirled around them in the gentle breeze.

Tharon led as a male would in the dance. She had the most gorgeous smile and rumbled in pleasure like the Alpha she was meant to be. Halfway through the song, she lowered her head until their foreheads met. Their interlocking bodies continued to glide over the snow as if magic were still real in their world. Their shared warmth chased away the cold of winter and wind.

"I want to dance with you every festival," Roswynd whispered and breathed in Tharon's wonderful scent that was familiar and safe.

Tharon's eyes matched the harvest sunsets in their region, full of joy and promise. "Every festival?"

"Yes," Roswynd replied with insistence. "Until the end of our days."

For a moment, Tharon's eyes fluttered, then remained open, revealing some sorrow. "I wish we could, but…" Her unfinished words were heartache to both of them.

Roswynd clenched Tharon's hand more and rasped. "I do not understand why not. You are an Alpha and I am an Omega."

"But I am not like the other Alphas," Tharon whispered, guiding them back to the right corner of the balcony, before they had to spin.

"Thank the Divine." Roswynd grinned, turned with Tharon, and continued the dance moves toward the center of the balcony.

Tharon rumbled and said, "I am serious, Ros. Two princesses cannot dance together at the ball." She broke their forehead contact and gestured toward the open door. "At least in there."

Roswynd chewed on her bottom lip but thought about the problem. She sighed when Tharon's forehead returned to hers. Shortly, the music would end for the couples dance, and she didn't want their dance to end on a sour note. "Well, you are an Alpha, so by right you could be a prince, then you could be my prince at the ball, and we could always dance together."

Tharon's smile was unexpected, but it warmed Roswynd more than anything. Tharon moved her head and nuzzled Roswynd's temple and whispered, "I would love to be your prince at the ball, if you can be my princess."

Roswynd purred for the first time. The little Omega inside her felt strong and certain, telling her this moment with Tharon was all she needed to be happy, today and all the tomorrows. She held on to it. "You already are mine, Tharon."

Chapter 6

Date: 15 Sunstone 826G
(Present Day)

Roswynd sighed and lowered the book to her lap, then looked to the bedroom window. From the movement of the sunlight on the bed, she predicted less than an hour had passed. The wedding ceremony had been six days ago, and since then Roswynd had grown bored. Her family had returned to Earna while she remained in Leeward, not that she had to. Tharon had given her the option to travel with her family back to Earna, and then Tharon would follow a week later. As lord commander, Tharon had many duties to attend to in Leeward and needed to assist Saxon with the return of the conquered lands to Wyndfeld.

After five days of sitting and reading or walking the town, Roswynd was beginning to regret her decision to remain in Leeward. She had hoped to spend time with Tharon and forge better communication, or any communication at this point. But Tharon spent sunup to sundown with the army and Saxon. They shared supper but always with Saxon and a few important knights in the dining hall. At night Tharon sat in the armchair by the lit fireplace and read late. Roswynd read, too, but went to bed alone. She had no idea how Tharon could sleep in the armchair. Most mornings Tharon was gone before daybreak, except for today. Roswynd had been up first and covered Tharon with a fur, finding the room rather chilly.

This morning Roswynd walked around the town and visited the market, which was busy despite it being kept in strict order by the soldiers of the Kingdom of White Sommer. She'd learned that a large unit from their army was camped out about a five-minute walk to the west of the town. Roswynd had considered going out there but thought better of it.

Wandering back to Chesford Manor, Roswynd returned to their empty room and rekindled the fire. Tharon must have left at least an hour ago. She sat by the fire and tried to read and busy her mind, but the book wasn't holding her attention. Dropping the book to the short table in front of her, she stared at the fire and considered other options. Perhaps she would venture out to the White Sommer encampment. Tharon would be there and might show her around or ignore her. Regardless, it was worth an attempt.

Roswynd smothered the fire and decided to change into trousers, a tunic, a girdle, and boots, as the encampment was outside of town. Dresses, flats, and mud turned into a disastrous mix. The camp was probably a bit of a mess, like most of them. Hesitating at the door, Roswynd went back and retrieved a cape, hoping it would soften her masculine attire. She had been wearing dresses since her wedding day. She was unsure how Tharon would feel about her outfit, even though they both wore such clothing as pups.

Tying off the maroon cape, she departed the room but faltered due to the strange looks from the two knights in the hallway. The day after her wedding, she had been assigned two White Sommer knights to guard her when Tharon wasn't with her. Roswynd argued that guards weren't necessary, but Tharon ignored her.

The two knights exchanged looks after Roswynd emerged from the room. They held their tongues and straightened. As Alphas they seemed proud to be knights guarding their lord commander's spouse.

Roswynd hated having them.

After rolling her eyes, Roswynd breezed past them and adjusted the cloak on her shoulders. Behind her, the knights remained steadfast and continued to shadow her as they had this morning, and yesterday, and all the days since the wedding.

Her wife truly had a control problem. Roswynd hadn't decided whether the knights also had a secret duty to ensure she didn't snoop into White Sommer affairs. She was about to test that theory by going out to the encampment. If the knights halted her, then she would have her answer.

After leaving Chesford Manor, Roswynd headed west through town and found the worn path between the town and the encampment. As she predicted, it was muddy after the storm two days ago. She soon smelled the campfires and spotted the tops of hundreds of tents. Her stomach knotted up, but she continued toward the camp. Her guards made no attempts to stop her, other than to walk closer to her.

Roswynd had seen one or two encampments in her time. Depending on the army, the layouts could differ, but usually the army's leader was located in the center. A few soldiers with crossbows were leaving the camp, heading in her direction. They eyed her until the two knights warned them with a look.

One crossbowman flushed and said, "Welcome, Princess Roswynd." His comrades gave curt nods and continued on their way.

Roswynd paused by the first tent and scanned the area, taking in everything. The camp was well organized with straightaways to make it easy to navigate. The grounds were neat and tidy, few items sitting outside of the tents. Campfires were built between every six tents and not all of them were burning. In the distance, horses whined from a corral. Farther away, the whistle of arrows and metal striking metal caught her ear. Roswynd watched two chatting officers walk past.

"Would either one of you know where Prince Tharon may be?" Roswynd asked her two guards.

The knights looked at each other, then one stepped closer and said, "Follow me." He led the way while the other knight remained behind Roswynd. The walk took a minute or two, but they came to a double tent that otherwise looked the same as all the rest. The leading knight paused by the flap and said, "Wait here." He vanished inside but everything was quiet.

Roswynd assumed it was Tharon's tent, especially since it was close to the center but offset to the southwestern corner. It was for safety purposes. If the unit was attacked, Tharon could flee to the southwest where the corral of horses waited for her.

The knight returned and said, "You may enter and wait inside." He rested a hand on his sword hilt. "One of us will retrieve the lord commander for you."

Roswynd frowned at being sequestered to the tent. However, the tent was Tharon's, which meant it might have personal effects that would help her learn more about her wife. She was about to go inside but paused and asked, "What are your names?"

The quieter knight groused, but replied, "Murray." He was young and handsome with traditional dark, curly hair indicative of people from the southern kingdoms. His beard was neat and tidy while his eyes were a warm brown similar to his skin tone.

"I am Pòl, my princess," the friendly knight said. He was a hair taller than Murray, stockier too, and had straight hair that reached his shoulders. His older features indicated that he was perhaps in his late forties. "Please wait inside." Pòl then departed on his mission to retrieve the lord commander.

Roswynd flashed a smile at Murray, but he shifted and turned his back to the tent's entrance. She chuckled and slipped into the tent, taking in everything. It was undoubtedly Tharon's space. Her scent had been strong in their shared room back at Chesford Manor. But in the tent, it enveloped Roswynd and reeled her deeper into it.

The main tent was large and contained a sitting area to the left with four armchairs. Nearby was a firepit built underneath the tentpole opening at the top of the tent for the smoke to escape. Next to the fire ring was a long, rectangular table that could hold about six Alphas. On the right side of the tent was a rack with eight different swords, two of them wooden. A closed trunk with leather strapping was next to that, then a tall, square table was placed to the far right.

Roswynd went to the tall table after noting a map on it. The map was of the eastern section of White Sommer and the western section of Wyndfeld, the mutual lands that touched each other along the borders. There were many white marks to indicate the areas White Sommer had either conquered or lost over the years. The most recent mark was on Leeward, and there was a circle around Duskgard Keep. The map indicated Tharon's intent to march up Fringe Road, take out the defenses on the road, and then knock on Earna's front door. With enough time and resources, Tharon would accomplish it. That idea alone left a heavy weight in Roswynd's stomach.

Extracting herself from the map's madness, she walked around the tent, then slipped into the smaller, attached tent. It was set up for sleeping, including a bed low to the ground, a changing area with another trunk, and a washbasin. Roswynd was drawn toward the bed without realizing it. Her wife's scent was the strongest here, to the point that her Omega wanted to crawl into it and roll in the intoxicating scent. But the longer she inhaled Tharon's smell, she began to detect fainter notes tangled with Tharon's scent.

They were female Betas' scents.

Roswynd growled without restraint. Not only were they female Betas, but the scents indicated arousal. Tharon had fucked two female Betas here, she was certain of it. Her nostrils flared and her skin itched in response to the turmoil in her. The one saving grace was that the scents were rather aged, at least two weeks. Within another week, they would fade to nothing.

Regardless, Roswynd needed air. She hastened from the bedding tent, returning to the main tent. She slowed beside the long table but realized her mistake too late. The damn table carried one of the same Beta scents, along the edge. Again, Roswynd snarled and backed up from the table, picturing Tharon fucking a female on it. She should not have come here.

Forcing herself away, Roswynd went over to the weapons rack and berated herself for being stupid. She could still leave, and at least one of her guards would be with her. In truth, she wanted to be alone again but not locked up in the room back at Chesford Manor. She preferred the outdoors no matter the time of year. In the past few days she had wanted to saddle Dragonfly and go for a ride, but Tharon had forbidden her without reason. The knights were instructed to keep her away from the stable at Chesford Manor, where Dragonfly was kept.

After several gulps of air, Roswynd went to the open trunk inside the tent and spotted all the books inside it. They were well organized with their spines facing up, making it easy to read the titles. The books were close to the deep trunk's edge, indicating that there had to be at least one layer, if not two more underneath. Too compelling to ignore, she knelt down in front of the trunk and studied the title of each book; there were so many. But certain ones caught her attention.

One leather-bound book was rather thick, painted gold, and worn from use. On the spine, it read The Ages Before Gyldr, which meant it had to be a history book about the Ancient Ones, before Gyldr sacrificed herself. After her sacrifice, a new age had begun, and the world was healed and gifted to the survivors. Those who blossomed from the great sacrifice were known as the Heirs, and they became the Alphas, Betas, and Omegas of today. There were thousands of stories about the Ancient Ones, magical beings who had once lived on their planet. It was rather mysterious, but many believed the Ancient Ones had magic and practiced dricraft. Today, some believed that remnants of magic still existed in their world, but it was all conjecture. Both priests and historians believed all magic died with Gyldr, while scholars argued that fragments of it remained on the planet. There were even people who attempted to perform dricraft, but no one had proven that magic still existed.

With a sigh, Roswynd continued studying the other books. Another book next to The Ages Before Gyldr was worn from use too. The title was hard to understand at first, but Roswynd was certain it was called The History of Our Ten Months. Roswynd found that fascinating. Like others, she'd been taught about each of her world's ten months, but she didn't know the history behind them. Based on the thickness of the book she held in her hand, it seemed the ten names of the months was a lengthy discussion.

A third book located near the center had a fun title. Roswynd lifted the old book up a little, tilted it, and murmured, "The Songs of Rasa Fire-Eye." The dark red leather of the front cover had a hand-drawn image of an orc. At least, the creature appeared to be an orc with orange eyes that reminded Roswynd of her wife. She couldn't make out the entire illustration, but it was obvious the orc was a female warrior.

Returning the book, Roswynd ran her fingers along the spines and skimmed the other titles until a new one called to her. She gasped and whispered, "No." She peered over her shoulder to confirm she was still alone, then carefully wiggled out the thick book, turned it over, and stared at the symbol burned into the front. She brushed her palm over it, feeling the dark lines pressed into the leather.

Roswynd opened the book, flipped past the first blank page to the second, which had very dark handwritten words on it. The page itself was made from animal hide, meant to last centuries or longer. But the words themselves were in a tongue that she had never seen and doubted Tharon could read. Or can she? Why else would she have it?

On the next page, the foreign writing continued in earnest, leaving barely any white space, except between the letters. On the page after that was a hand-drawn illustration of a plant of some type. Unable to read it, Roswynd closed the cover and stared at the front again. "It is an ancient spell tome. Where did she locate this? How did she procure it?" Her mind raced at the possibilities of why Tharon owned such a rare book.

Noise outside the tent interrupted Roswynd's thoughts. She returned the thick tome, stood, and searched for the location of the voices. Roswynd crossed the distance to the corner of the sitting area and made out the deep and familiar voices of Tharon and Saxon. She canted her head and concentrated on their conversation.

"Selwyn Arrington is expected here tomorrow to begin the transition of the lands," Saxon said. "Our mines in the northeastern region will finally be returned to us."

"I would have recaptured them in the spring," Tharon responded in a gruff voice.

Saxon chuckled and patted Tharon. "You have more important concerns now." After a pause, he asked, "You travel to Earna on the fifteenth?"

"Yes."

"Excellent."

"Lord Commander, I am sorry to interrupt you and King Saxon." It was Roswynd's guard, Pòl, who had left to find Tharon. He must have made a huge loop simply to return here.

"Pòl, why are you not with my wife?" Tharon asked in a growly tone and further demanded, "Is she all right?"

"Yes, my prince." Pòl hesitated, then said, "Princess Roswynd is here, in your tent. She wished to see you."

Tharon rumbled, then there was brief movement before Saxon chuckled. "And how does your new marriage fare, Tharon?" Saxon asked. "I have yet to hear cries of passion." After a pause, he chuckled again and added, "Or pain."

Tharon warned him with a low snarl. "It is not your concern, Saxon."

"But it is my concern." After a few soft movements, Saxon said, "Use your little Alpha to coax her into a heat, knot her, and be done with this game." There was a low growl, but Saxon kept talking. "Knowing Roswynd Arrington, she may be taking a suppressant, so keep a watchful eye on her."

Tharon was still growling, the sound becoming distinct to Roswynd's ears. "My wife is not your concern, Saxon. If you press me further, I will handle this situation my way."

Saxon chuckled but fell quiet under Tharon's continued growl. He sighed and said, "Go to your wife and do not forget everything I have given you."

Roswynd was breathing hard, on the brink of marching out there and punching Saxon. She heard movements and assumed they were done speaking. She skated around the armchairs and moved away from the corner of the tent. What in Gyldr's bones should she be doing in here anyway? Her eyes settled on the swords, so she rushed over to them, tempted fate, and lifted one. Roswynd grunted at its weight but managed it with two hands and pretended to find it interesting. Behind her, she heard the tent flap fly open and felt Tharon's presence wash over her.

Tharon rumbled and neared her wife, watching her hold the sword. At first her features were stony, but a glint of amusement shone in her eyes.

Roswynd looked from the burly sword to her wife and said, "I think I need a more petite sword." She flushed and attempted to return the sword but almost dropped it on her foot. She yelped when Tharon grabbed it before it was too late and placed it on the rack again. "Thanks."

Tharon chuffed in response and continued to watch her wife with mild curiosity. Her unspoken question lingered in her eyes. She wanted to know why Roswynd was here.

Moving to the other end of the rack, Roswynd stretched up and fingered the soft fletching of arrows in a quiver that hung on the side. "I have always wanted to learn how to shoot, but Father still...," she murmured, then sighed, lowered her arm, and turned to Tharon, who was tracking her eyes up and down Roswynd's length. The masculine attire hadn't gone unnoticed by Tharon after all.

Tharon had both swords on her hips again. She folded her arms, causing her thick biceps to stand out against her beige tunic underneath her black jerkin. After a beat, Roswynd realized Tharon's tunic was made of a special material called dracin, which came from dragon beetles in the south. When the material was woven together, it created a strong bond that could resist a slash of a blade or a puncture of an arrow. Selwyn told her the expensive tunics were called softshield tunics, and usually the wealthiest of nobles or royals could afford them.

Roswynd cleared her throat, doing her best to ignore her body's natural reaction to Tharon's Alpha stance. "I would truly enjoy a ride. I have been cooped up in that godsforsaken manor for five days now." She already sensed Tharon's answer and said, "Please, Tharon."

"No." Tharon lowered her arms and walked to the tent flap until Roswynd blocked her path.

"Do you even remember my name?" Roswynd asked, heat rising in her cheeks. It had been over ten years since she last heard her name fall from Tharon's lips. "You have not spoken it once since we have been reunited."

Tharon regarded Roswynd, then growled and said, "I know your name." She sidestepped her wife and ordered the two knights to enter. "Take my wife back to Leeward. I will return this evening."

Roswynd ground her teeth as she crossed the distance and didn't look at Tharon, much less speak to her. In her head, she was counting numbers to keep herself from exploding on Tharon in front of the knights. They could have arguments but not in front of others, especially those Tharon commanded. Well, that was assuming Tharon would speak to her enough to even have an argument.

The knights departed next and remained at her side, helping her leave the camp.

Roswynd didn't bother to look back at her wife, who was absolutely infuriating and pushing Roswynd to her limits.

She stomped all the way back to Leeward with boiling waves rolling off her. The two knights gave her space.

Outside the garden's gate, Roswynd studied the front of Chesford Manor. She didn't want to go back in there again, even if they'd be leaving for Earna in two days. A horseback ride would help a lot, especially since the cloudy weather to the east indicated that there might be more rain tomorrow. As she passed the gate, she considered how she could rid of the knights long enough for a ride.

The inside of Chesford Manor was quiet other than the sounds of the staff cleaning, doing chores, and preparing supper. Roswynd stood in the foyer for a moment after a thought occurred to her. She placed her hand against her stomach and started for the kitchen. Once down the hallway that led to the kitchen, she paused and pivoted toward her two shadows. "I am going to pick up food from the kitchen. Would either of you enjoy a bite?" She hoped they would remain in the hall and wait for her.

Murray grunted and remained silent.

Pòl looked from his partner to Roswynd and replied, "No, thank you, my princess."

Roswynd nodded and smiled at the pair of idiots. "I shall not be long." She found it strange that Pòl used the term "my princess," but she had heard it a few times since marrying Tharon. By royal law, she was a princess to both White Sommer and Wyndfeld now. Slipping into the busy kitchen, she danced around two servants, who greeted her with curious smiles.

"May I help you, Princess Roswynd?" a third servant asked after she cleaned her hands on an apron.

"Yes, are there a couple of apples that I may have?" Roswynd followed the servant to the pantry. "Also, perhaps a small loaf of bread, if you can spare it."

"Of course, my princess." The servant retrieved the three items and handed them to Roswynd. "Is there anything else?"

"Actually, yes. Is there a backdoor here?" Roswynd asked, knowing most manor kitchens had outdoor access to the back of a house. She smiled when the servant nodded at her. "Excellent. Can you show me?" She followed the servant and grinned at the door. "Oh. If two White Sommer knights happen to ask for me, please tell them I went to the market."

"Of course, my princess." The servant closed the door after Roswynd hurried out of the manor.

Roswynd glanced about the area and pinpointed her location. It was the back part of the house, which meant she wasn't far from the stable. With a grin, she spotted the structure off to her right. She hurried across the plush yard and slowed when a stable attendant came out with straw in his hair. "Hello, sir."

"Hello, Princess Roswynd. Have you come to ride your horse finally? He has been rather lively for the past few days." The male was an old Beta and rather cheerful.

Roswynd had met him once the other day when she was allowed to visit Dragonfly. "Yes. I hope that is agreeable?"

"Of course." The Beta walked into the stable and continued to chat. "I will gather your tack. Do you require your saddlebags as well?"

"Please. I have a few items to take with me." Roswynd indicated the food, which the Beta took and promised to put in the bags for her.

Roswynd went to Dragonfly's stall and giggled at his happy whine. "I missed you, too, my sweet horse." She petted him and slipped into the stall. Next to Dragonfly was the black horse from the wedding ceremony. The Beta returned with the tack, which she put on quickly.

"Are you looking for a trail?" the Beta asked. "I can make a suggestion."

"That would be wonderful. Anything on the east or south end of the town?" Roswynd didn't want to go anywhere near the encampment and raise an alarm. Or for that matter, have Tharon catch her scent on the breeze. Omegas and Alphas had strong noses compared to Betas, but Tharon's seemed extra sensitive.

"Yes, if you go across town, take Golden Wheat Road, and you will spot a trail in the woods to your right." The Beta had a thoughtful look and said, "I believe it is about a three- or five-minute walk once you are out of town. The trail goes to a pond, turns, and returns to Golden Wheat Road. You make a left on Golden Wheat Road to return to Leeward."

Roswynd was done tacking Dragonfly in record time and said, "Thank you, sir." She guided her horse out of the stall when the Beta opened it. "I will return in a few hours."

If the knights or even Tharon started to look for her, at least the Beta had an idea. Once outside, she mounted her horse, straightened out her cape, and adjusted the reins in her hands.

"Enjoy your ride, my princess."

Roswynd tapped Dragonfly's sides and hurried off at a trot, wanting to get away from Chesford Manor before it was too late. She was forced to slow down in the streets because of the people. There were several White Sommer soldiers, so she raised her hood to hide her distinct hair. Few people knew her face, but her hair coloring was an Arrington feature. Her eyes were also distinct, even a piece of legend. However, being high up on Dragonfly afforded her enough separation that no one would notice them.

Taking the north road out of town, Roswynd guided Dragonfly around the town rather than going into the market area, in case her guards were there. She spotted Golden Wheat Road after a few minutes and turned onto it, letting out a big sigh. She was relieved to get away from the town, the manor, and even Tharon for a while.

She understood it was risky to go riding alone, but Roswynd needed space and some time to think. Her life had been turned upside down earlier this week. Even though she was with Tharon, she felt even more alone and isolated now than she had in the ten years they'd been apart from each other. Wiping her eyes, Roswynd spotted the trail's entrance. It was wide enough for two horses, and the brush appeared maintained by the locals. It was peaceful and nice, especially through the woods. Birds sang around her, and squirrels and rabbits scampered across the trail. Dragonfly almost stomped on one silly squirrel.

Looking to the sky, Roswynd checked the sun's location to confirm she was on track with time. Puffy clouds filled the vibrant blue sky. It reminded her of her wedding day on the plateau in the White Razor Mountains. She thought back on the ceremony, churning over all the tiny details she hadn't had time to focus on then. She struggled to remember Tharon's vows; she had assumed they were the same as hers. However, Tharon pointed out otherwise, and Roswynd hadn't stopped thinking about it since the celebration.

On top of that knowledge, she discovered that Tharon had a decent collection of books, several having to do with the history of their world. The spell tome was the most fascinating one, at least on the top layer of books. Roswynd wanted to know if Tharon could read it, or if she knew someone who could. The language was bold and strong, like an Alpha.

Her adventure out to the encampment had been worth her while. She learned more about her wife today than she had all week. The conversation between Tharon and Saxon was also of interest. Did Tharon have an idea that Roswynd had heard the conversation? She suspected not since they continued to talk after Pòl announced Roswynd's presence in the tent; it all could have been a ploy, but Roswynd doubted it.

Saxon was still an asshole, if not a bigger one now. When they were young, he picked on Tharon because she was a female Alpha, who grew slower than he did. As their early teens neared, Roswynd recalled Tharon starting to match Saxon's height and weight. Over the years, Saxon also targeted Roswynd, and she later came to realize his behavior stemmed from jealousy. He loathed Tharon and Roswynd's friendship and made attempts to drive a wedge between them. Today, it seemed to still be the case, except now it was a dangerous game.

Roswynd rumbled at this idea of jealousy. Saxon and Tharon were family and had the same goal: to bring down the Kingdom of Wyndfeld. But if Saxon was threatened by Roswynd's presence, then something was off. If Tharon had married Myla, the game's landscape would be very different. Then why did Saxon allow Tharon to wed Roswynd if it endangered their plans? Her best guess was that Tharon simply couldn't say no to having Roswynd, as Roswynd's father predicted. And Tharon was the lord commander, the pin, of Saxon's army.

With a sigh, Roswynd rubbed her brow and pushed the hood off her head. She needed a rest, and the pond ahead was a peaceful spot. The location was infinitely pretty, and the fallen tree next to the pond was a perfect place to sit. Dismounting, she walked Dragonfly the rest of the way, then allowed him to enjoy the grass and water. She grabbed the two apples from the saddlebag, sat down, and started to slice them with the dagger from her pocket, tossing most of the slices to Dragonfly.

Roswynd smiled at her horse enjoying the sweet treat, then studied the quiet pond until the sounds of galloping hoofbeats caught her ear. She frowned, stood, and turned toward the approaching rider. The black horse was distinctive and caused her stomach to pitch. Roswynd groaned when she saw the rider's rather aggravated expression—Tharon might murder her and bury her body out here. She hastened to sheathe and hide the dagger before it was too late.

Tharon slowed the horse, then yanked his reins once she was off the trail and near Roswynd. She kicked out both feet from the stirrups, swung a leg over, and dropped to the ground.

Roswynd was unsure what to expect from her wife, who was a trained knight, able to kill and flatten people with one hand. This would be her first lesson in defying Tharon and suffering the consequences, whether they were verbal, physical, or some other form of punishment. However, she didn't expect Tharon to begin speaking to her now, but she had thought she would have more time to prepare for the confrontation.

Leaving the black horse, Tharon's dark expression locked on Roswynd. As she came closer, the beads of sweat were noticeable on her brow. Had Tharon been running? She looked as energized as she was furious.

In the past Roswynd had angered Tharon over silly things, but they always talked through it. Tharon never harmed her once in all their youth, not like Saxon. But right now, she wasn't so sure and took one step back. She held up a hand as if it would hold Tharon back, then dove into an apology first. "I am sorry, but I had to get out of there for a little while."

Tharon snarled, bared her teeth, and fisted her hand while her other hand remained on a sword hilt. She stayed two steps from Roswynd and loomed over her. "Listen to me very carefully."

Roswynd lowered her hand, swallowed, and nodded. "I am listening," she said and went quiet to show her interest.

"You are now married to the lord commander of the White Sommer Army. You are still a princess of Wyndfeld." Tharon took another step and narrowed her eyes at Roswynd. "You are a very valuable prize to an enemy."

Roswynd glanced away but nodded her understanding, knowing Tharon had a point.

Tharon closed the last gap between them and whispered, "Also, these lands are in turmoil due to the war and strife. Bandits and thieves are everywhere, until these lands are secured again." She flashed her teeth and asked, "Must I lock you in our room until we depart for Earna?"

Roswynd sighed and shook her head. "No." She flexed her hand, itching to touch Tharon. In the past, she would hold Tharon during arguments, using it to calm them both. To not do it now was hurting her, but she had no idea what was acceptable to her wife.

After a huff, Tharon nodded once, went around Roswynd, and took a seat on the log. She stretched out her legs and stared at the pond.

Roswynd released the breath she'd held for a while. She was trembling and needed to sit too, but first, she grabbed the bread from the saddlebags. Breakfast had been light, and she couldn't stomach supper last night with Saxon.

Then she skipped dinner today. Sitting in the same spot as before, she played with the short loaf and glanced at Tharon seated on the other end.

They were two years apart in age, but somehow Tharon seemed much older than her. Roswynd contributed it to Tharon's years in the army, experiences on the battlefield, and general travel on the road. Tharon had to grow up faster than Roswynd, who spent the last ten years sheltered in Earna.

With a sigh Roswynd broke the bread in half and offered a piece to her wife as another form of apology. She expected to be disregarded, but instead Tharon took it after a beat.

Tharon sniffed the bread once, then tore a smaller piece off and tried it.

Roswynd popped a bite into her mouth too. It was a honey wheat, which Tharon used to enjoy. She'd had no idea what type of bread she'd received from the kitchen servant. But she was especially glad as she watched Tharon continue to eat it. After they were done, she brushed her hands clean and went to Dragonfly. It was time to go back to Leeward.

Tharon followed suit and mounted her horse with little effort. She waited on the trail for Roswynd, who joined her after walking Dragonfly up to the trail. Roswynd hopped into the saddle and prepared to go to the left toward Leeward, except Tharon went right. For a beat, Roswynd sat motionless, befuddled by Tharon's decision to continue the trail ride. Not about to question anything, she tapped Dragonfly's sides and caught up to Tharon.

The trail continued for another two leagues, winding its way through the woods and fields before it returned to Golden Wheat Road. They approached the roadside and studied both directions, then checked the sun.

"I believe it is this way," Roswynd whispered and directed Dragonfly to the left. Tharon returned to her side and seemed on high alert. Roswynd assumed being on a major road, rather than tucked away in the woodland, made Tharon more cautious. Clearing her throat, she said, "Thank you for riding with me."

Tharon looked at her and held her gaze for a moment before she returned her focus to the road. On the trail, her pheromones had gone from wired to calm and now they were strong again. When they turned a bend, Tharon slowed her horse and stretched out her arm toward Roswynd. Ahead of them was a long, straight stretch of road.

"What is it?" Roswynd asked, not seeing anything in front or behind them.

Tharon's chest vibrated with a low sound. She dismounted and took the horse's reins over his head. Leading the way by foot, she kept a hand on her sword and was sniffing the air.

Roswynd twisted the reins around her fingers, unsure what Tharon sensed on the road or around them. She had no idea, but she trusted Tharon's sharp instincts. After another minute of slow walking, she heard it—voices and laughter. Ahead of them were three needle-sized bodies walking their horses. "Tharon?"

"Stay on the horse." Tharon took a few steps forward and watched the three people. She growled low, pivoted, and said, "If I go down, ride into the woods and take the trail back to Leeward."

"If you go down?" Roswynd fought the rise of dread and said, "I am not going without you." She fingered the dagger in her pocket.

Tharon bared her teeth at her wife and snapped, "Listen to me." She faced the three people, released the reins, and checked her swords, making sure they were loose in the sheaths.

Roswynd shifted in the saddle and glanced at the three travelers, who were looking less friendly the closer they approached. If she and Tharon rode off, the three males might give chase. Such a scenario seemed possible once it was clear they were thieves.

The trepidation inside Roswynd gripped her. She had traveled in her kingdom and in the Kingdom of White Sommer, participated in hunts, watched knights practice with swords, and wrestled with siblings. Never once had she been in the middle of an actual fight, until now. Her natural instinct was to flee, but it was clear her wife's natural instinct was to walk toward the danger.

Roswynd was not leaving Tharon.

From atop Dragonfly, Roswynd could see the thieves closing in on them. She had no skills as a fighter and had been educated only on how to skin and butcher dead animals. She was shaking, exposed, and useless before the thieves. Tharon was her sole protector.

"Well, hello there," a thief said once in earshot. He eyed Tharon and Roswynd with obvious interest. Seeing Tharon and Roswynd riding horses as females perhaps confused him. "Where are you… lasses headed?" His two comrades chuckled.

Tharon remained silent and stayed between them and Roswynd.

The same thief huffed and said, "Three against one are nasty odds, lass." He fingered his sword, which had no sheath and dangled from a leather strap around his waist. "Even if you are…" He paused, sniffed the air, and said, "You are an Alpha with two swords." A dose of wonder or respect lingered in his voice.

"She is a mute," another thief remarked. He had a sword, too, but it was in a scabbard. "Maybe they cut out her tongue when they blinded her."

Roswynd parted her lips, about to speak to her wife, but thought better of it. She didn't want to be a distraction to Tharon, who reminded Roswynd of a black wolf arching its back, baring its teeth, and preparing to attack.

"What about the other one on the horse?" the third thief asked and retrieved a decent-sized battle-ax. He had a rather hairy chest peeking through his tunic, making Roswynd nauseous.

The first thief leaned toward him and ordered, "You can handle her, and we will take care of the degen."

Roswynd shifted in the saddle, torn between using Dragonfly as a shield and getting off the horse with her dagger. But Tharon had demanded she stay on the horse. She tracked the hairy thief's every movement as he crossed in front of the two swordsmen. He stole glances at Tharon but continued to gaze in Roswynd's direction.

"Come off the horse, little Omega," the hairy thief said, giving a toothless smile. He was diagonal to Tharon and gave her a wide berth. He began to lower the ax in his hand as he neared Roswynd's horse.

Dragonfly responded with a high-pitched whine and stomped his hoof, but Roswynd controlled him. She allowed her horse to back up a step, sharing in his panic. Her eyes cut to Tharon, who hadn't moved a muscle and looked like a statue. She opened her mouth to yell and wake up Tharon, but the two swordsmen were closing in on her. The air was roiling with aggressive, thick pheromones to the point that Roswynd would have choked if they weren't outside. Then something snapped like a thunderstorm sending down its first bolt of lightning.

In a blink, the hairy thief was clutching a dagger sticking out of his throat. Blood poured from the wound, over his fingers, and down his neck into his dirty tunic. He dropped the ax and latched onto the dagger's handle, but it was too late. Falling to his knees, he gurgled nonsense.

Roswynd gave a shocked scream and struggled to control Dragonfly, who reared up. The sounds of metal clashing against metal rang out, followed by yells. By the time Roswynd settled Dragonfly again, a wrenching scream came from one of the thieves.

The first thief was bent over, holding his stomach and using his sword as a cane. Blood coated his arm and soaked into his tunic. He went onto one knee, peering down at his gut.

Turning her eyes away from the gory sight, Roswynd looked to the left of the road to see Tharon exchanging blows with the last thief, who looked overwhelmed by the assault. With two swords in hand, Tharon parried and attacked with ease, then blocked the thief's one swing. She'd crossed her swords to hold back his blade, then slammed her boot into his chest. Tharon growled and chased after him when he darted to his right.

Again, the thief tried to break her defenses, but Tharon's next strike was hard enough to knock the sword from his hand. She thrust her right sword, plunging it deep into his gut. He gasped out in shock and clung to the blade in his stomach.

For good measure, Tharon twisted the sword before she extracted it. With one glinting sword and one red sword, she walked over to the first thief, who was on his knees.

The thief raised his sword in a weak attempt to keep her away. Tharon kicked the flat of his blade, sending it flying and skidding against the road. Drawing her arm out, she extended her sword to the right and sliced into the thief's neck.

Roswynd gasped and clawed the saddle horn as the thief's head separated from his body, and with such momentum from Tharon's blade, it rolled along Golden Wheat Road. She sat unmoving, other than the frantic rise and fall of her chest, and stared at the carnage on the road. All three thieves were dead in less than ten minutes. Blood was everywhere around the lifeless bodies. Tharon had done it all without hesitation or a second thought.

Tharon walked over to the hairy thief and tapped his head with her boot tip to confirm that he was dead. She knelt and extracted her dagger that she'd thrown out of nowhere to kill him before he could touch Roswynd.

"I..." Roswynd looked from dead body to dead body, then saw the blank eyes that stared lifelessly in her direction. Her stomach pitched hard. Scrambling, Roswynd hurried from the saddle and nearly fell off her horse. To her right, she had level view of the hairy thief, whose blood was pooled all over the road. She groaned, halfway stood, and stumbled off the road, needing to get away from the slaughter.

Roswynd made it down the incline a few steps, then collapsed to her knees and hands. Her revolting stomach clenched hard, then sent up what little contents were in it. Roswynd heaved a few times while tears streaked her face. Behind her she sensed Tharon's presence, but she fixated on the three dead males. Her stomach tried again to send up more vomit, but she was empty.

Her entire body felt clammy, her heart palpitated, and the ground felt as though it were shaking when she took two steps to get away from the foul smell under her. She caught herself on a tree trunk, rolled her back against it, and slid to the ground into the tall grass. Between the incline and the grass, her view of the road was blocked. With her head against the tree, she gulped air and closed her eyes until the image of the dead males invaded her mind. She whined and opened her eyes to find Tharon knelt in front of her.

Tharon was calm but worry shone in her eyes. She held out an uncorked waterskin to Roswynd, who took it with a shaky hand.

Roswynd filled her mouth, rinsed, and spit it out, then repeated. She wiped her forehead with her other hand and whispered, "I have never seen…" Shaking her head, she returned the waterskin, then noticed Tharon offered her a few dried mint leaves. She laughed despite the situation, but plucked them from the large, callused palm. The same hand that had taken three males' lives within minutes. For a moment she chewed on the mint, which was a small reminder of Tharon's cleanliness. As pups, Tharon had no qualms about being in dirt, mud, food, or whatever else, but she insisted on being clean once done.

Tharon remained resting on her haunches in front of Roswynd. With a tilt of her head, she asked, "Will your horse come if you call for him?"

Roswynd glanced at Dragonfly, who stood several steps behind Tharon. She nodded, unsure why Tharon was asking her.

After a rumble, Tharon shifted closer.

Roswynd thought it was time to go, yet she couldn't stand. She was weakened from her body's reaction to the fight and her mind's desperate attempts to grasp what had happened so suddenly. Slouching against the tree again, she whined in protest, yet didn't want to show her weakness to Tharon; she stiffened when Tharon knelt closer into her personal space.

Tharon reached for Roswynd, getting one arm under both her knees then her other behind Roswynd's back. She pulled her away from the tree, stood, and adjusted her. Cradling her, Tharon continued into the woods until the ground leveled out again.

"Wait. Where are we going?" Roswynd twisted her head to the left, worried about leaving their horses.

"Around," Tharon said with a rough timber. She held Roswynd close and took a few deep inhales, seeming to drink in her scent. Turning, she went back up to the road, then gave a short but sharp whistle. Tharon kept her back to the slaughter behind them so that Roswynd didn't have to see it again. The black horse trotted down the road without hesitation.

Roswynd was prepared to get down and call Dragonfly, but Tharon restrained her. A few furrows pulled together across her brow, she withheld her question and waited for Tharon to voice her plan.

This time, Tharon's whistle was low and long, and it finished louder. Her horse huffed once, then lowered to the ground on his belly and waited for her.

"Wow," Roswynd whispered, looking from the resting horse to her wife. "You must show me how to teach Dragonfly to do that." She was placed in the saddle, legs on either side, and handed the reins. Tharon climbed into the saddle behind her and slipped her boots into the stirrups.

Tharon repeated the special whistle, causing the horse to rise. "Call your horse," she ordered.

Roswynd cleared her throat, whistled a specific way, and called, "Dragonfly!" She heard him trotting up to them. "What about the other horses and the…" Shaking her head, she pushed aside her unfinished question that caused her stomach to churn again. She didn't want to know.

Tharon clicked her tongue once at Dragonfly, who came closer, especially when Roswynd reached for him. Tharon grabbed Dragonfly's reins and tied it off the rear of the black horse's saddle. She then took the reins from Roswynd and tapped her horse's sides.

Roswynd clung to the saddle horn and leaned forward, trying to give Tharon space. After a few minutes, Tharon growled above her, halted the horses, and snaked an arm around Roswynd's waist. She pulled them together and even pressed her hand flat against the underside of Roswynd's breasts.

Closing her eyes, Roswynd fought with her accelerated breathing while Tharon rumbled near her ear. They were safe, at least she hoped they didn't run into any more trouble. After Tharon's display of prowess as a warrior, Roswynd felt secure. She allowed her body to relax into Tharon's bigger form. That seemed to appease Tharon, who signaled the horses to continue toward Leeward. This time, their bodies moved in unison with the sway of the horse.

Gazing about the world again, Roswynd noticed her heart had slowed down, but her muscles were still weak. She was grateful she didn't have to ride Dragonfly right now, even though Tharon might think her weak for it. Tharon was confident, strong, and a force of power as a knight. The tall tales about the Black Wulf were not so tall. They were rather realistic.

The rest of the ride to Leeward was quiet and uneventful, at least on the road. Roswynd's mind was overwhelmed by a landslide of memories, sounds, and smells from the fight. The mint had helped, but she thought she tasted blood, or the coppery scent was stuck in her nose. There had been so much blood, and their screams still echoed in her head.

Tharon gave a throaty sound and pushed her palm firmer against the underside of Roswynd's chest. The pressure forced Roswynd to take deeper breaths. Tharon's Alpha pheromones were swirling around Roswynd, trying to soothe her.

Roswynd gave a soft whine and frowned at her body's natural response. She bit her lip and closed her eyes again, but the bloody images came back. Her eyes flew open, and she peered down at her hand clawing into the saddle horn.

Today was a disaster. Roswynd had wished to go for a horseback ride to clear her head. But now three males were dead, albeit thieves. If she had been smarter and less childish, if she had listened to Tharon, then none of this would have happened. Tears formed at the corner of her eyes.

Besides the males' death, she had put Tharon in danger. She had forced Tharon to protect her. Tharon, the lord commander, who was nothing like the sweet and gentle princess from their childhood. Roswynd had no idea whether any of her best friend was left inside this new Tharon. She had no idea how to reconcile the two people.

What was Roswynd supposed to do now?

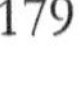

Chapter 7

Tharon left her wife in their bedroom after making sure she was comfortable. She promised to return soon with supper for them to share in their room rather than eat with Saxon. Last night Roswynd had played with her food in the dining room. According to the two guards, Roswynd hadn't eaten breakfast, and if she'd had anything midday, it was back on the side of the road.

Coming down to the second floor, Tharon went out the main door of the manor and located the two knights who were assigned to Roswynd. Their scents told Tharon they were prepared to be punished for losing track of Roswynd. She couldn't place the full blame on them, as her wife had outsmarted them. Beneath the mountain of frustration, she admired Roswynd's sneakiness, and now that her wife was safely back in their room, Tharon could see her own faults as well.

First, she should have forewarned Roswynd's knights before assigning them. After all, Tharon had grown up with

Roswynd, who enjoyed bending or breaking rules when they were pups. One particularly fun pastime was sneaking around the guards. Second, she made the mistake of not clarifying to Roswynd why the knights were necessary. Roswynd wasn't one for long periods of indoor spaces, especially small ones. She probably took the guards as a sign of distrust rather than protection. Right now, the surrounding lands were far too unsafe compared to the secure lands in Earna.

"Lord Commander," Pòl said and bowed. "Is Princess Roswynd well?" He had a thin frown and shifted on his boots. His care for Roswynd was genuine and touched Tharon. They had known each other for many years, before, during, and now after the war. She trusted no one more than Pòl to protect her wife.

"Yes." Tharon waited for the two knights to straighten, then said, "She is resting now." She paused when a servant in the garden passed them and continued to the rear of the manor. "I will allow this to pass, but in the future do not let her out of your sight. My wife is extremely clever."

"Yes, Lord Commander. She is very clever," Pòl said with a frown. He seemed prepared to return to his duty of guarding her. "She is truly an Arrington."

Tharon huffed and agreed with her knight. "I will remain with her for the evening." She looked from Pòl to Murray, who was always quiet. "There are three dead thieves on Golden Wheat Road about a league and a half away. Take six or eight men with you, dispose of the bodies, and collect their horses if they are still there."

"Yes, Lord Commander. Should we both go?" Murray asked.

Tharon nodded, then dismissed them for today; they would begin their guard duty tomorrow at first light. She returned to the manor and went to the kitchen for food. One of the servants gave her several light items to start and promised that someone would bring entrées and more drinks soon. Tharon headed back to the room and considered whether to tell Saxon that they wouldn't be joining him.

Fuck him, she told herself. Tharon entered the darkening room and saw Roswynd sitting in front of the unlit fireplace. She seemed to be staring at nothing, lost in this afternoon's events. With a huff, she placed the small tray on the table between the armchairs, closer to Roswynd, in silent offer. Tharon went to the fireplace and loaded it with fresh wood, then worked to light it. The warm glow was inviting, yet it didn't seem to interest Roswynd.

Tharon left for the washroom, grousing to herself. She went to the washbasin and started cleaning up after today's failure. This was exactly what she expected to happen but not this soon. When she and Roswynd rode on horseback after the wedding ceremony, she'd sensed that Roswynd was holding on to the belief that Tharon was the same childhood best friend, but that weak pup was buried years ago alongside her mother. After her mother's murder, Tharon became a squire in hopes to be a part of the army that would destroy her enemies. She'd endured having her face buried in the mud under a knight's boot early on in her quest. Because she was a degenerate Alpha, she had to learn faster, fight harder, and kill quicker than all of them. Being the princess of the Kingdom of White Sommer made it worse, despite her father almost disowning her.

Today as the lord commander, Tharon was not a princess nor Roswynd's best friend. Those facets of who she'd been were long torn away. Now Roswynd had a glimpse at the real Tharon, and she hadn't liked what she saw. Tharon was doing her best to shield Roswynd from the reality, which included not speaking. If they started to talk, then Roswynd would question, dig, and pursue every tiny corner of Tharon, and Roswynd wouldn't like what she found.

Besides, a connection meant heartbreak for Roswynd again. Tharon wasn't an idiot and was well aware of Roswynd's buried anger about the betrayal to their friendship pact. Under Roswynd's soft layers, there was a hard and ugly ball of rage waiting to free itself. If they reconnected, this time Tharon would crush Roswynd's spirit, once she and Saxon finished their plans to take down Wyndfeld. It was simpler to hold Roswynd at arm's length, keep her safe, and carry her off after the House of Arrington fell. Tharon could survive Roswynd hating her, but Tharon would break if Roswynd died.

Tharon finished washing her arms and face, grabbed the towel, and dried off. She returned the hand towel, but slowed seeing the wedding band on her finger. The two interlocking hands were an ancient symbol of love and faith. Turning over her hand, she stared at the old diagonal scar across her palm, running from the upper right, under her index finger, down to the left corner. She traced it with her finger, like so many other times in the past. She growled and shook out her right hand, then went into the bedroom.

Roswynd hadn't moved or eaten any food. The glass of water looked untouched too. She was still staring at the fire or into it. Nothing in her face showed recognition. It was as though she was in the room physically but no longer present.

Tharon frowned and considered what to do about Roswynd eating tonight. Her wife was unintentionally starving herself. A knock at the door caught Tharon's attention. She instructed the servant to place the tray on the bed, then reclosed the door after she left. Glancing over at Roswynd's unmoving form, she made her decision to resolve the eating issue.

Going to the bed's nightstand, Tharon unlashed her sword belt, propped the weapons against the small table, then looked over the hot food. There were items that Roswynd would like, at least she had when they were pups. She went behind the divider, removed her jerkin and tunic; both needed the blood cleaned off. Going to her trunk at the other end of the divider, she retrieved a clean tunic, pulled it on, and tucked in the front half.

Tharon returned to the sitting area and stepped in front of Roswynd, who stirred for the first time. Without warning, she pulled her wife out of the armchair, lifted her, and carried her to the bed.

"What are you doing?" Roswynd latched on to the front of Tharon's fresh tunic.

Remaining silent, Tharon placed her wife on the side of the bed, using one hand to keep her there. Roswynd released her tunic and peered up with concern in her eyes. Tharon rumbled in response, then sat down behind Roswynd with her one leg bent. She picked up Roswynd again and settled her wife into her lap so that their bodies were pressed together.

Roswynd started breathing harder, but not in panic. She remained stiff against Tharon yet made no attempt to leave.

Tharon grabbed the tray with two plates on it and dragged it closer to them. She picked up a chicken thigh and tore a piece of the meat free. With glistening meat between her fingers, she brought it near Roswynd's lips.

Roswynd went even stiffer. She latched on to Tharon's forearm and gave a small whine of protest, then peered up with hooded eyes.

Lowering her head, Tharon pressed her nose into the side of Roswynd's head, near her ear. "You have not been eating. I need you to eat." She could force Roswynd into eating, but she wanted Roswynd to agree and accept Tharon's care. Raising her head, she caught the hint of surprise in Roswynd's mismatched eyes. *Yes, I pay attention to you*, she told her wife mentally.

Roswynd squeezed Tharon's arm and nodded. She accepted the first morsel given to her. As Tharon gave her more of the chicken, Roswynd started to relax into her wife's embrace.

What they were doing was considered appalling for a royal or even a noble. They were both giving into their base instincts as an Alpha and Omega, by one feeding the other. Tharon didn't give a damn so long as her wife was eating again. If it took using her Alpha to appeal to Roswynd's Omega, then she would do it. In truth, Tharon was enjoying this intimacy and closeness with Roswynd. They had never given in this deeply to their natures, but they both seemed to need it.

Forgetting her place in the world, Tharon pressed her left hand against her wife's upper stomach, the same spot as when they rode back to Leeward together. She kept her head close to Roswynd's, rumbling in pleasure and breathing in her scent. After the chicken was done, she picked up the spoon and scooped up some rice, which would fill Roswynd's empty belly.

Each passing minute, Roswynd leaned deeper into Tharon and basked in the tenderness. The food and the closeness were bringing her back to life.

Tharon's Alpha swelled inside her chest and made her dizzy with delight. She hadn't rumbled this long or deep in ages, if ever. Her Omega was being so good to Tharon, eating for her and drawing on Tharon's care. This was what she was made to do, take care of her Omega. This is what she vowed to do.

Roswynd kept a hand over Tharon's left forearm, down by her stomach. Her touch was light, but always there. Her other hand had slipped behind and tangled into the waistband at Tharon's hip. At one point, she halted Tharon's arm and said, "You must eat too."

Tharon smiled into Roswynd's hair and promised, "After you finish." Her voice was rough and thick, resonating from her Alpha.

Roswynd continued to eat anything Tharon gave her. Near the end, Tharon offered her the bread, but she whimpered from the familiar honey wheat smell, having thrown up the bread this afternoon.

Tharon touched it to her nose and huffed in agreement, then tossed the bread back to the one empty plate. She encircled Roswynd with both arms and kept her flush against her body. Her head was still swirling with Alpha tendencies, not ready to let go. Somewhere deep inside, she told herself this was dangerous for them both. But Roswynd needed the tenderness and security after what happened on the road. Her Alpha wanted to show she wasn't all claws and fangs.

The longer they remained so close, the more Tharon started to lose control. Her head was muddled from Roswynd's sweet, tender scent. Right now, Roswynd was so pliant and willing to please her Alpha. Tharon could smell it and could easily turn Roswynd onto her back. Then Tharon could climb on top of her, taste her all night, and finally take her. Her skin began to itch. Her cock had hardened a while ago, but it was now a bit painful.

Roswynd gave a throaty whine, so animallike and needy. She reached up with one hand and tangled her fingers into Tharon's hair. "I-I..." Whatever she was feeling was trapped inside her, but her scent twisted with confusion, causing Tharon to straighten some.

Tharon started to withdraw as her mind cleared a little. She needed to eat, then maybe handle her hard-on later tonight after Roswynd fell asleep.

"Stay," Roswynd whispered. "Please, Tharon."

After a deep breath, Tharon settled back into her spot and tightened her arms again. Within seconds the thrum in her chest returned and relaxed Roswynd once more. They sat, quiet and content while their pheromones remained calmer.

At some point, Roswynd started to rub her face against Tharon's chest. The affectionate motions were scent marking, and Tharon was unsure if Roswynd realized she was doing it. Eventually Roswynd leaned her forehead against Tharon's bicep. All her upper weight rested on Tharon. "I am so tired," she murmured and fought a yawn.

With a sigh, Tharon untangled herself and encouraged Roswynd to get up. She stood and took the tray of food, still sensing her Alpha's warm pride in taking care of her Omega.

Roswynd slid off the bed and dragged her fingers through her hair while she headed to the dividers. Her movements were soft and slow.

Tharon set the tray on the table next to the other one, then put two pieces of wood in the fire. She sat in her usual armchair and took the remaining plate of food. Everything was cold, but it didn't bother her. Many of her meals in the army were cold and tasteless. The meals from the manor's kitchen were a huge improvement, even when cold.

Roswynd went from the divider into the washroom and returned after a few minutes. She approached Tharon, who had her hands full with the plate and fork. Roswynd hooked her arms across Tharon's shoulders in a light hug, pressed her forehead against Tharon's temple, and whispered, "Thank you."

Tharon should have growled at her wife for the random affection, to keep her from doing it again. But Roswynd was already gone and so was the moment. Tharon huffed, but Roswynd's scent lingered in her nose. She listened to Roswynd turning off the lamps, getting into bed, and settling under the blankets and furs. It wasn't long before Roswynd was asleep, but it wouldn't last. Tharon was sure of it.

For now, Tharon had her personal time to sort out this evening's events. She berated herself for getting too close to Roswynd and letting out her Alpha; her iron grip had loosened. But the way Roswynd responded to her was beautiful.

After finishing the meal, Tharon stacked the plates and stepped out of the room with them, setting them on the floor in the hallway for a servant. She grabbed her sheathed swords and returned to the armchair. Tonight she would sleep on the floor. The Divine knew her back needed to be realigned after falling asleep in the armchair one too many nights.

She went to her trunk and retrieved a book from the bottom. The book was titled *The War of 312G*, which had been a long, grueling war between all the kingdoms. Hundreds of thousands of lives were lost in the fifteen-year-long war. Many scholars believed that was the century that decimated the Alpha and Omega population, which was still recovering today. What piqued Tharon's interest the most about the war was a naval captain, a She-Alpha famous for her sieges on port cities. Tharon was inept at sea since her kingdom was landlocked, but the Kingdom of Wyndfeld had a major port city that had always held her interest.

Tharon dove into the book, losing herself in the two-hundred-year-old history. The dying fire forced her to put the book down, realizing at least an hour had passed. Perhaps it was closer to two hours. She set the book on the table and picked up the folded fur that Roswynd had covered her with this morning. She spread it out on the floor in front of the fireplace to pad her back. It was more comfortable than what Tharon was used to as a squire.

Seated back in the armchair, Tharon considered her wife while she waited for the fire to die. Today's events had drained Roswynd, and the lack of food hadn't helped. She would continue to monitor Roswynd's health, but returning to Earna would be good for her. Being restrained to Leeward made Roswynd tense and antsy, feelings Tharon could relate to, as she was accustomed to traveling, training, and riding, especially between the battlefields. Once she and Saxon took down the House of Arrington, Tharon would be empty-handed. What did knights do without a war?

"Thar…," Roswynd whimpered, turned, and muttered nonsense.

Tharon remained motionless, listening to her wife's erratic breathing. She turned her head to the side and groused as the nightmare continued to take hold of her wife. This was to be expected after what happened on Golden Wheat Road.

Roswynd whined, then gave a sharp cry before sitting up, shoving off the blankets and furs. "Tharon!"

Tharon growled and bolted from the armchair. Her large emerging presence from the darkened room caused Roswynd to call her name again. She crossed the distance in a few wide steps, then latched on to her wife's trembling shoulders.

Roswynd touched Tharon's right cheek near her scar and whispered, "You are safe."

Tharon frowned and assumed that the nightmare was about her fighting the thieves again but losing this time. She rumbled and kept her hands on Roswynd's trembling shoulders.

Roswynd hung her head and took a few steady breaths. Her eyes were squeezed shut. "You killed those males." She drew up her legs to her chest and whispered, "You killed them so quickly, like it was natural." Peering up, she revealed her blue and hazel eyes, which glistened in the fading firelight. "Who are you? Is there anything of my best friend left?" Roswynd asked in a lost voice, her gaze searching Tharon's features.

Tharon held the stare and allowed Roswynd to look for her answer. She was no longer Roswynd's best friend or a princess. Then a slow, wolfish smile spread across Tharon's lips. Releasing her wife, she cupped Roswynd's chin for a moment and traced her thumb over Roswynd's bottom lip. *The thieves were not the nightmare. I am.*

Roswynd swallowed but didn't break the eye contact or bare her neck to Tharon. She was far too brave for her own good.

With a soft growl, Tharon latched on to Roswynd's hips and pushed her back under the blankets. She pulled the blankets and furs back over Roswynd, then returned to the armchair and waited for her to fall asleep again, which didn't take long. When there were embers in the fireplace, Tharon laid down on the fur with her sheathed swords above her head. Tomorrow she and Saxon were meeting with Selwyn to discuss the transition of lands. From that point, Saxon would handle everything while Tharon went to Earna as required by the marriage arrangement.

Tharon woke before dawn and felt more rested than she had after the last few nights in the armchair. Roswynd was still asleep, so Tharon collected her bloody clothes, a fresh set of clothes, and her swords, then went in search of a servant. One of them emerged from downstairs and organized to have a bath filled with hot water. She also handed over her bloody clothes to be cleaned and ready by tomorrow before she left.

Once the hot bath was ready, Tharon instructed the servant to prep water for another one so that Roswynd could bathe after her. Alone in the bathing room, Tharon locked the door, stripped down, and undid the hair braids on either side of her head. The water was plenty warm and loosened Tharon's muscles. Even though she had wiped her arms, hands, face, and neck last night after the fight, she still felt filthy from fighting the damn thieves. They had been dirty, unkempt, and in poor health.

She scrubbed every part of her body with vigor and washed her hair twice. After she was done, she rested against the tub and noted the change of light from the window to her right. With her half-blind eye, she was forced to turn her head more to the right to check the early sunlight from the window. Roswynd would wake soon and may search for her.

After the nightmare, Roswynd had slept in peace and would hopefully be rested this morning. Tharon weighed getting out of the tub and getting ready for her day, but her mind kept slipping back to last night on the bed. Her Alpha had loved caring for Roswynd, and it left a craving in her. Thanks to the memories, her cock had stiffened.

"Why did I vow fidelity?" Tharon whispered to herself, then growled low. She slipped her hand around the firm shaft, feeling its girth. She had sworn fidelity to Roswynd and would do it again, even though Roswynd had missed that piece of her vows. Even if she hadn't promised fidelity, the silly female Betas were nothing compared to Roswynd.

With a grunt, Tharon started to pump her cock. There wasn't much time, but she had enough to jerk off and not be a growly dickhead all day. She tightened her hand and clenched her teeth to hold back the noises. The very tip was exposed out of the water, revealing the angry redness. As she worked the hard length, she pictured Roswynd here with her, her scent all around her, and her unusual, wild eyes burning into Tharon. She groaned and rolled her head back as the buildup started to peak. Heat burned low in her gut, then it rushed up her spine as the climax hit her.

Snarling, Tharon gripped the tub with her free hand. Inside her, the hungry Alpha wanted to get out of the tub, go to the bedroom, and claim Roswynd. She took deep breaths and soothed the demands roiling inside her. Her cock was still hard, but she would learn to live with it. At least her trousers were leather and hid her arousal well.

Releasing the plug, Tharon climbed out of the tub, dried herself, and started to dress. She growled at forcing herself into her leather trousers—Roswynd might be the one to kill Tharon in the end. Of course, Roswynd had little to no idea how much she affected Tharon. According to King Garrett, Roswynd was still a virgin and had heats. However, Tharon agreed with Saxon that Roswynd was taking a suppressant. After being so close to Roswynd, Tharon had picked out a foreign hint in her scent. It wasn't that it wasn't natural, but it wasn't natural to Roswynd. She also noticed Roswynd's sense of smell was weaker than it should be for an Omega. There could be other side effects, like a weakened sense of taste, cramps, and spells of light-headedness. Tharon was keeping an eye on Roswynd.

Inside the bedroom, Roswynd sat upright and glanced at Tharon, who was now clean and dressed for the day. She started to climb out of bed but paused when Tharon spoke. "A servant is drawing a bath for you." Tharon straightened out her belt so that the swords sat at the correct spots on her hips. "Selwyn will be here in about an hour."

"I forgot he was coming." Roswynd had a sleepy expression, still not quite awake. "When do we leave tomorrow?" she asked, voice hinting at her enthusiasm to go.

"In the morning." Tharon crossed the space between them and stood in front of her wife. "Are we clear about your guards now?"

Roswynd nodded and replied, "Yes."

Tharon watched her wife's expression, confirming the agreement was true. She backed off a step and said, "I will wait for you in the dining room. Saxon will not be there." Without another word, she departed, went to the kitchen, and prompted the staff to start breakfast for them. Later in the dining hall, their meal was quiet but not uncomfortable compared to prior ones. It helped that Saxon was at the camp, handling the soldiers.

After breakfast, Roswynd's guards arrived and announced that Selwyn was in the front gardens. Tharon noticed Roswynd's bright expression and escorted her to see her brother, who was walking through the garden.

"Good morning," Selwyn greeted with a slight smile but held concern in his eyes for Roswynd. He pulled her into a hug and whispered something in her ear, to which she nodded back.

Tharon waited until they parted, then she held arms with Selwyn. She and Selwyn were close in age, separated by a few months. They were both the eldest of their siblings and held the most responsibilities. When young, she never had qualms with Selwyn, finding him upfront but quiet. He would make a good Alpha to an Omega one day.

However, Selwyn was less successful than Tharon. In recent years, he'd become a lord of a northern region along the coast. He trained under a knight, but not as rigorously as Tharon had. They never met on the battlefield. Tharon assumed Garrett was shielding his heir. A year ago Tharon had clashed swords with the Wyndfeld's lord commander and killed him on the battlefield. He had been strong at one time but had grown weak and old, losing his backbone years ago. Tharon had done Wyndfeld a favor by killing him. But Tharon always wondered why Selwyn didn't take the position, and why Garrett filled in the gaps himself.

"King Saxon is waiting in the camp. I will be waiting there as well, if you wish to visit with your sister first." Tharon felt Roswynd's piercing gaze, but she ignored it.

"Yes, thank you. I will not be long," Selwyn said, rocking back on his boots. He seemed unsure about the unexpected offer to visit with his sister, but he was clearly pleased.

Tharon nodded, then left them to talk with each other. Their time together would give Tharon a chance to speak with Saxon, who angered her yesterday. She went to the encampment and located her brother alone in her tent. Swallowing a growl, she neared her brother and said, "Selwyn will be here soon."

"Yes, we are expecting him." Saxon was studying the map, arms folded, and he held a curious expression. "How many of our mines do they control again?"

Tharon almost rolled her eyes and replied, "Six gold mines and one stone quarry."

"That is right," Saxon murmured. "Having the gold mines will help us greatly. We will be able to rebuild the army." He pivoted toward Tharon and asked, "Are you prepared to return to Earna for the first time in ten years?"

"Yes." Tharon folded her arms and waited for Saxon's real speech.

"I expect you to learn as much as you can before your return to Wulfbite." Saxon rumbled and tilted his head. "I want to know who Myla Arrington is being wed to, which might tell us who Garret is seeking military help from. The girl used to follow you and Roswynd everywhere, so I am certain you can manage to regain her trust."

Tharon grunted and said, "I will find out. I hope to learn more about Earna's defenses."

"Do not forget Stormbreaker Landing," Saxon said. "It is one of your stops. The port could benefit us greatly when we attack Earna." After Tharon's nod, he shifted closer and grabbed her shoulder with a firm grip. "Do not forget what the House of Arrington owes us. And do *not* let Roswynd Arrington into your head."

"She is merely a means to an end," Tharon said.

Saxon patted Tharon's cheek and whispered, "Do not let it be your end, sister."

Tharon flashed her teeth; her Alpha was loose in her head and chest. She snared Saxon's arm, spun him, and shoved him to the floor. Kneeling, she pinned her knee to his chest and a had dagger at his throat. She snarled at him and continued to apply more of her weight to him.

"Tharon—"

"Be silent and listen." Tharon pushed the blade against his throat, forcing him to be quiet. "Do *not* threaten me again." She leaned over him and gazed into his dull eyes. "Or I will uncrown you."

Saxon snarled and grabbled with Tharon's wrist, but she was stronger than he was. "Then what? You will make Radford king? He is a child with diluted Blakesley blood."

Tharon narrowed her eyes and enjoyed Saxon wriggling under her. It had been too long since she last put him in his place. She'd been gone from Wulfbite for too long. "Perhaps I should." She flashed her canines as her pheromones started to crush Saxon. "Now, bear your neck to me." With a menacing smile, she whispered, "*Little* Alpha."

Saxon started shaking underneath Tharon, trying to resist her dominance. He growled and raked his nails down her arm, but his head was turning anyway.

With deep satisfaction, Tharon watched her brother begin to twist his head in submission. Once his neck was offered to her, she basked in his inferiority. She brought her face closer to his, breathed in his weaker scent, and continued displaying her canines at him. "You may be the king, but *I* am the Alpha." From Saxon's hiss, she knew he hated that fact.

Saxon remained silent and bared his neck until Tharon rose, releasing him.

"Get up." Tharon kicked his leg. "Selwyn will be here any moment." She crossed to the other side of the tent, needing the space from her brother. They had many arguments over their lifetime, and whenever there had been one too many, Tharon knocked her brother back down. She tired of the constant rounds with him, but Tharon was responsible for keeping him in check. As king, Saxon had to uphold an image so that their people were happy and loyal. She didn't want her kingdom to become like the Kingdom of Tharnstone, ruled by a heavy and cruel hand.

After Saxon straightened himself, Selwyn arrived, and they went on with the meeting. Several hours passed before the meeting ended, then Selwyn was shown a room at Proudpeak Hall. He would remain in Leeward for nearly a fortnight, helping with the transition of lands between the kingdoms. Saxon handled introducing Selwyn to a few important officers from the encampment.

Tharon was relieved to be alone and spent time composing a message to her second-in-command, Lord Erland, who was handling the southeastern sector of Wyndfeld. The lands were mostly farmland, but there was a major city in the region. If not for Saxon's plans, Erland would have taken the city by the end of the year. While in Earna, Tharon had every intent of staying in communication with Erland. She wanted him to expand the camp at a fortress along the border to Wyndfeld. Erland didn't need to be at the fortress to have the construction done. No, she wanted Erland to remain in Wulfbite and watch over her little brother.

After finishing her letter, Tharon had it sent out with three soldiers. She then met with her officer in charge of escorting her and Roswynd to Earna. A unit of a hundred cavlarymen would ride to Earna, then return to Leeward. Tharon would be the sole person from White Sommer in Earna. Saxon argued with Garrett that Tharon should be allowed a dozen White Sommer guards, but Tharon disagreed because guards meant distrust. People had to believe that the political marriage meant something for the future.

Besides, Tharon was daring Garrett to make an attempt on her life.

* * *

Tharon held her horse's reins in her left hand and hooked her right hand in the collar of her leather cuirass. She studied the first fort along Fringe Road. It was an older one, but it was still used and manned by two hundred Wyndfeld soldiers. The fort was known as Duskgard Keep, as it was built into a cliffside on the western side of the White Razor Mountains. In the evenings it was the last fort to see sunshine before the end of the day.

Several Wyndfeld soldiers stood at attention as the unit of White Sommer soldiers rode past them. Tharon exchanged a wave with the captain of the fort but said nothing. If it weren't for the cease-fire, she would be here with her army, decimating the fort and killing the captain.

Already the temperature had dropped since they started the ride up Fringe Road. By the time they made it to the great plateau, some of the soldiers would want their cloaks and capes. Tharon remained at the front of the unit leading them. Roswynd rode her horse but was secured in the middle with her two guards. Tharon did her best not to steal glances at her wife, not wanting to show her hand to her men.

Yesterday Tharon had spent the last few hours of daylight with Roswynd. They went to the market together and checked the shops. When they were little, Roswynd rarely bought items from the merchants and that was still true today. But Roswynd did enjoy looking at the different things for sale, especially unusual clothing. As sunset approached they had supper at the local tavern rather than with Saxon. Their evening together held so few words, yet it still had been nice, a complete contrast to the day before. Tharon concluded that Roswynd had adjusted to their silence rather than pushing and demanding Tharon to talk. Somehow the silence had become comfortable for them.

When they made it to the great plateau, Tharon left a high-ranking knight in charge of leading the unit. She nudged Obsidian off to the side and allowed the unit to pass her until Roswynd was close enough.

Roswynd greeted Tharon with a slight smile and made room on the cobblestone road for Tharon to ride next to her. Behind her were the two knights, Pòl and Murray.

Tharon appreciated the welcome and urged her horse to match Dragonfly's pace. They rode side by side, enjoying each other's presence. Checking their location, she estimated they had at least half an hour before they passed Fort

Snowfalcon, which was the halfway point between either side of the great plateau.

Roswynd shifted in her saddle and adjusted the heavy cloak that held back the cool mountain air. She canted her head and asked, "What is his name?"

Tharon patted her horse's neck and considered whether to answer. It would be these tiny questions from Roswynd that led to bigger things. Roswynd was testing her, seeing if she could toe the door open any wider. Over the past week, Tharon observed Roswynd finding her comfort level with their relationship. But the bloody fight on Golden Wheat Road had shaken her, leaving a dark impression deep in her mind. Tharon herself struggled with her own desires about that incident. She was a knight designed to win and kill. Yet after it was all done, what was left for her other than blood on her hands?

After such a long silence, Roswynd returned her focus to the journey and observed the beautiful landscape. The cool air was freeing, and the mountains were raw with wonder. Roswynd was comfortable in it, a creature of nature.

"Obsidian."

Blinking, Roswynd centered all her attention on Tharon and seemed to fight a smile. "Fitting."

Tharon didn't comment back and kept her gaze straight ahead. Again, they rode in silence for a while until Roswynd broke it once more.

"I remembered your vows." Roswynd played with the reins, then peered over at her wife. "I remember how they differ from mine." Her blue eye was bright, matching the sky above them, while her hazel eye contrasted with warmth.

"Then tell me," Tharon said, challenging her.

Roswyn started to play with her wedding ring, turning it with her thumb. "You vowed fidelity to me." She took a deep breath, then her pheromones shifted with her mood. "You vowed through light and darkness to me." Lifting her head, she stared forward, and a few tears fell to her cheeks. "You promised me that last time."

Tharon noticed that Roswynd was rubbing the inside of her right palm with her other hand. She frowned and fisted her right hand, holding back the need to massage her own palm. "This time will be different."

For once, it was Roswynd who said nothing. At first she didn't discredit or challenge Tharon's words, but her pungent scent said she didn't believe Tharon. Her breathing had accelerated, then calmed again after a while. She glanced over at Tharon and whispered, "We both know what is going to happen this time." Her eyes held challenge, warning Tharon that she was well aware of the game behind their marriage.

Tharon nudged Obsidian closer to Roswynd, leaned toward her, and whispered, "I *will* honor my vows. Will you?" Her fierceness startled Roswynd. Tharon was satisfied that she had made her point. She might tear down the Kingdom of Wyndfeld, but she would make damn sure Roswynd survived it. Roswynd was hers now, as it should have been years ago.

Nothing was taking Roswynd from her now.

Chapter 8

Date: 17 Sunstone 814G
(About 12 Years Ago)

"Steady," Garrett whispered and kept a light touch on Tharon's leg. His breaths were short, and his gaze fixed on the deer in front of them.

Tharon had an arrow drawn and trained on the buck. If she waited long enough, the deer would turn and bare his chest to her. With one arrow, she could bring down the buck and possibly claim the title for the largest deer killed on their hunting trip. Roswynd would be proud of her.

The buck lifted his head and flicked his ears. Behind him were three does that continued to move between the trees. A distant sound made one doe jump, while the others lifted their heads. The buck took a few steps.

Garrett double-tapped Tharon's leg in a hidden signal.

Tharon drew the arrow back a bit farther and checked her aim. With a deep breath, she released the arrow and heard it sail past the brush and sink hard into the buck's chest. Dropping her bow, she launched out of the brush with a long blade in hand.

The does had sprinted off, but the buck stumbled several times until Tharon drove her blade into its chest, near the arrow. The buck toppled to the ground, huffing and kicking while his blood coated the brown leaves.

Backing up, Tharon sensed Garrett beside her, and he held her shoulder.

"That is a fine kill," Garrett said, beaming at her skill. "I will be surprised if anyone else is able to match or beat his size."

Tharon watched the life fade from the deer, which was her second kill since Garrett started teaching her to hunt. Two winters ago she and Roswynd had gone on their first hunting trip with Garrett's pack. That year, Tharon wasn't able to hunt, being so young and new. She and Roswynd had learned how to set up camp, start fires, and gut an animal. Garrett had also taught both princesses how to track. Tharon was more apt at it than Roswynd, but they both helped each other.

Last winter's hunting trip was different. Garrett had shown Tharon how to use a bow and arrow for the first time. Roswynd wasn't allowed to use any weapon, other than the knives to gut and skin the kills. At first Roswynd didn't seem to mind the change, but after the hunt was done, Tharon noticed a difference. Roswynd had been grumpy and finally admitted to wanting to learn how to shoot arrows, but not for hunting. Tharon had considered showing the basics to her best friend but feared angering Garrett and being uninvited from future hunts.

Before her return trip home to Wulfbite, Garrett had gifted Tharon a bow and a dozen arrows. He instructed Tharon to practice alone in the woods at her home, and she was welcomed to practice anytime she was in Earna. Tharon spent the whole year mastering the bow and arrow, preparing for this winter's hunt. Her hard work was paying off. Two days ago she killed a doe and today a large buck that might win her the competition between the pack members.

From Garrett's inflated chest, Tharon could tell that he was proud of her. When they returned to the camp with her prize, everyone clapped her on the back before they weighed the buck. So far Tharon had the largest kill of the hunt, but there was one day left of hunting.

Two males helped lower the buck after they weighed it, then dragged it away for processing. Next to Tharon stood her best friend, who was shaking her head.

"How did you and Father manage to drag it back?"

Tharon lifted her arm next to Roswynd and flexed her muscle. "This is how."

Roswynd laughed and slapped her friend's bicep, which had grown after a summer of archery. She turned to Tharon, smiled, and said, "I am proud of you."

Tharon let the compliment wash over her. Without restraint, she lifted her chest and rumbled like a growing Alpha. "I have worked all summer."

Roswynd's smile widened, and she slipped her arms around Tharon's neck. "I know. You are becoming a great hunter, my prince." She glanced about the camp, making certain no one else was around them. "Next year, maybe you will have the most kills and the biggest one."

Tharon grinned and lowered her head closer. "I will try." She didn't want to inflate her own ego, not when she had so much to learn.

"Are you headed back out again?"

Tharon shook her head. "It is getting late." She touched Roswynd's jacket, which was the clean one that she wore after she was done processing the deer. "I wanted to spend time with you before supper."

Roswynd brightened and giggled. "Do you want to go for a walk?"

Tharon nodded, then said, "Let me put away my bow." She started to leave, but Roswynd grabbed her wrist.

"Keep it." Roswynd had flushed cheeks and said, "I like it on you." After Tharon nodded, she went in search of her father and told him they were going for a walk. Together, Roswynd and Tharon left the campsite and followed the sun, making it easy to find their way back. The woods were blanketed in snow that reached halfway up their calves. Once far enough from the camp, they held hands and Tharon regaled Roswynd with her story about tracking, hunting, and killing the buck.

Roswynd was amazed by Tharon's natural ability to track and hunt. Tharon was aware that Selwyn had a more difficult time with it. Saxon had little interest in it but still went on the hunting trips. Roswynd insisted that her father took the most pride in Tharon's hunting skills.

"How many deer did we bring in today?" Tharon asked when they arrived at a resting spot. With her gloved hands, she started to clear snow off a rock for them. "Do you want a fire?"

Roswynd bit her lip and flushed.

Tharon knew what Roswynd wanted instead of a fire, so she chuckled, sat on the boulder, and patted her lap. In a heartbeat, Roswynd was snuggled into her for warmth and affection.

"There were five today, including yours. It will be a busy morning tomorrow," Roswynd said. She and two males were in charge of butchering the deer so that the meat could be sent back to Earna for storage. "I am glad my father is teaching you how to hunt." She pulled at Tharon's fur coat, then looped her arms around Tharon's neck. Under her words was bitter hurt because she was excluded from learning how to shoot arrows.

"Ros, I will teach you how to shoot," Tharon whispered.

"I know you would if I asked you." Roswynd leaned her head against her friend's shoulder. "But I will not ask you."

Tharon swallowed and leaned her head against Roswynd, thinking about her friend's distress. If Roswynd wanted to learn something, she hated being told that a princess or an Omega wasn't allowed to. With horseback riding, Roswynd had been forbidden a number of times until Garrett gave into her demands. But the riding seemed to be the limit of Garrett's good graces for his daughter. It left

Tharon wondering why Garrett believed it was acceptable for Tharon to learn how to hunt.

"But I mean it that I am glad he is teaching you, Tharon." Roswynd lifted her head and revealed the glisten in her eyes. "You deserve to do this, and I know you love it."

"I do." Tharon adjusted her arms around Roswynd's waist, drawing her closer. "I do not understand why your father is teaching me. Or why my father is accepting of it."

"Perhaps my father convinced your father that you should learn."

"But why?" Tharon asked, searching Roswynd's eyes for the answer.

"Because you are an Alpha." Roswynd removed her gloves and cupped Tharon's face, which warmed under the soft touch. "Also, perhaps my father knew you would have a gift for it. I mean Selwyn struggles to track himself much less a deer." She and Tharon traded a laugh. "Father takes great pride in teaching you. I think he is happy to be teaching an Alpha who succeeds at being a hunter."

Tharon bowed her head, still in thought about Roswynd's opinion. She closed her eyes and rubbed her cheek into Roswynd's hand. Last summer she had started the habit of rubbing her cheek into Roswynd's neck, stomach, or head. It was comforting and left her scent on Roswynd.

"And most of all, you are family, Tharon," Roswynd whispered and smiled when Tharon looked at her again. "You are another daughter to my parents."

Tharon crinkled her nose and said, "I do not wish to be your sister."

Roswynd laughed and tickled Tharon's side, earning a playful growl. "You are not my sister, idiot. You are my prince."

Tharon blushed at her friend's claim on her. After their first couples dance two years ago, Roswynd referred to Tharon as her prince, which excited and confused Tharon. The first few times Roswynd called her a prince, she felt conflicted by the title change, but she was an Alpha. Each summer, she grew taller and bigger, starting to catch up with her younger brother. In the last two years, she was feeling less like a princess too. After spending all summer learning how to shoot, she realized she was more comfortable being called a prince than a princess. But only Roswynd called her a prince; she was still a princess to the rest of the world. At least she could count on Roswynd to understand and accept her. That had to be enough.

"Does it still bother you that I call you 'prince' or 'my prince'?" Roswynd asked, probably noticing Tharon's distant look.

"No." Tharon smiled because Roswynd always checked on her. "I prefer it."

Roswynd's different-colored eyes shone in the late sunlight. "I am glad." She brushed her fingers along Tharon's face, tracing her jaw. "One day you can tell people to call you Prince Tharon, if you wish."

Tharon shook her head and argued, "I cannot. What if I am married to a prince?" She puffed up her chest and pretended to have a deeper voice. "It cannot be Prince Tharon and Prince Charming." With a frown, she moved her hand to Roswynd's thigh, which was warm from the heavy trousers.

Roswynd rolled her eyes and asked, "What if it is Prince Tharon and Princess Gorgeous?"

Tharon snorted low and lifted an eyebrow at her friend. "I will not be allowed to marry a princess."

"Why?" Roswynd asked and started playing with her friend's hair at the back of her head. "You are an Alpha who should be with an Omega."

"My Omega father is with another Omega."

Roswynd frowned and remained quiet for a minute. She shook her head and said, "It must be difficult for him."

Tharon scowled at her friend, unsure what she meant. "My parents love each other, Ros." A threatening growl came out at the end, by accident.

Roswynd went still but then squeezed the back of Tharon's neck. "I am sorry. I did not mean to infer they do not love each other. I simply meant it must be difficult for two Omega breeds to be together." As she and Tharon aged, they were learning more about their nature as an Omega and Alpha. Under the common law of nature, it was common for an Alpha and Omega to mate rather than two Alphas or two Omegas. Roswynd trembled once and whispered, "I am sorry, Tharon."

Tharon tightened both arms around her friend. "I am sorry too. I did not mean to growl at you." Roswynd tucked her face into Tharon's neck and whined low. She hushed Roswynd and apologized again. Over the past six months, Tharon's growls had changed, at least when she wasn't playing around with Roswynd. Sometimes her growls came out with a force that caused Roswynd to back down in a heartbeat. She regretted it each time but hadn't found a way to control it better.

Roswynd took a deep breath and murmured, "It is all right." She fisted her hand in Tharon's fur coat and said, "When you do that, I feel myself crumble."

Tharon jerked back, cupped Roswynd's chin, and lifted her head. "I would never hurt you, Ros. I promise."

"I know." Roswynd offered a soothing smile, then lowered her head and exhaled. "You are going to be fourteen next year. You will start to change a lot more soon." She shook her head and murmured, "Then they are going to separate us."

"*No!*" Tharon snarled again, with even more heat. Roswynd whined louder, halting Tharon's rising aggression. She took a few deep breaths, which formed white clouds above their heads. "No one can separate us," she said in a calmer voice, but it was too late. Roswynd was crying in her arms. "Ros," she whispered, whining herself.

Roswynd whimpered and buried deeper into Tharon. She cried for several minutes but eventually allowed Tharon to wipe her face. After a deep breath, she whispered, "I am sorry. I am confusing our conversations."

Tharon nuzzled Roswynd and whispered, "I am sorry I am reacting so poorly." She inhaled Roswynd's scent, which chased off her rise of aggression. "But I do promise that no one can separate us." She tilted up Roswynd's head until their gazes met. "Do you believe me?"

Roswynd nodded and rested her forehead against Tharon's own. "I do, my prince."

Tharon smiled and tightened her arms around her friend, keeping her close. They remained quiet, snuggling, and enjoying each other's company until the sun hugged the horizon. She peered over at the setting sun and sighed at the fact that they needed to return to camp. Whenever they were around other people, they did their best to be less affectionate with each other. Tharon doubted they would be scolded, much. However, they were getting older and receiving lessons on public etiquette about what kinds of touches were appropriate and even about kissing.

"I guess we should go back," Roswynd murmured. She turned her head toward the sun too. "They will be serving supper soon."

"I am hungry," Tharon whispered, then a slow grin spread across her features.

Roswynd laughed, straightened, and patted her friend's belly. "You eat twice what I can."

"I am growing," Tharon said, in a fake defensive tone. In the past year, her appetite had doubled to the point that she often carried snacks with her.

Roswynd slid off her friend's lap, took a step back, and offered her hand. After she helped Tharon stand, she teased, "Into the Black Wulf."

Tharon rolled her eyes, adjusted the bow on her back, and started the walk back to camp. "Saxon will be the Black Wulf." Their family name, Blakesley, meant "Black Wulf" and each generation one Alpha was seen as the Black Wulf. She and Saxon were the only two Alphas in their generation, but Tharon's makeup as a degenerate Alpha stole the title from her. By default, the honor would be given to her brother. Saxon was intelligent and clever, but he was a terrible hunter in Tharon's opinion.

Roswynd shook her head and argued, "It is not like an actual crown that goes from hand to hand. The Black Wulf title has to be earned and bestowed on the Alpha." She paused and hooked her arm through Tharon's arm. "At least, that is what you told me."

"It is true, but since I am a degenerate Alpha and we have no other Alpha brother, then it will go to him."

"I hate that word," Roswynd whispered.

"Degenerate?" Tharon asked and frowned when Roswynd nodded at her. "But that is what I am, Ros."

"No, you are an Alpha." Roswynd's brow knitted together. "Do you even know what degenerate means? I looked it up in the library. It means you are below normal and of poor quality." She came to a sudden stop and freed her arm, forcing Tharon to do the same. She faced her friend and said, "They call you a degenerate Alpha, but it is you making the kills, not Saxon or even Selwyn. You are the Alpha making the contributions to our food stock so that we can survive the winter."

Tharon shifted from foot to foot, unsure how to handle Roswynd's convictions.

Roswynd huffed and whispered, "They are the degenerates." She fisted her hands at her sides and her eyes filled with fire and ice. "I *hate* that word." She stomped off, continuing to the camp.

Tharon stood there with her mouth hanging open, unsure what happened a moment ago. Many times in the past, her friend had been annoyed or frustrated about certain situations or people. But this was something new and bigger, truly personal. After her stupor faded, a gentle warmth spread through her chest because Roswynd cared so much for her. Sometimes she wondered if Roswynd understood her better than she understood herself.

"Ros!" Tharon chased after her friend, then slid on the snow once she was close enough. She grabbed her friend's wrists and halted her, a goofy smile on her face.

"What are you smiling about?" Roswynd asked, glowering and red in the cheeks.

"Thank you." Tharon's appreciation undid Roswynd's anger, and they both stood in silence for a moment. "Thank you for defending me."

Roswynd released a heavy breath that formed in the air between them. "S-Sorry. I truly detest that word. You are many things, but you are not that, ever." She frowned and said, "I have known you all my life, and I would know if you were below normal."

"Would you tell me if I am ever below normal or poor quality?" Tharon asked, a grin tugging at her lips.

Roswynd snorted and said, "Do I not tell you when you are being an idiot?"

"Well, yes." Tharon held out her hand and waited for Roswynd to take it. "But poor quality is different. Something more permanent, perhaps."

Roswynd shook her head, clasped their gloved hands, and continued the walk to camp. "If you knock your head enough times, you could become a permanent idiot."

Tharon laughed and admired her friend's softened profile. Their joking had helped ease Roswynd, but Tharon knew that the degenerate topic was now a sensitive subject. Tharon questioned whether or not she, too, should be defensive about the label. She set it aside and focused on the last few minutes of her walk with Roswynd. "I hope to not become a permanent idiot. You may disown me then."

Roswynd chuckled, bumped their shoulders, and said, "You would still be my idiot, even then."

With a laugh, Tharon smiled, leaned over, and kissed Roswynd's head. "Better to be someone's idiot than no one's intellect." She traded a grin with Roswynd. The rest of their walk continued in silence, then they separated when they smelled the campfires. At the camp, several hunters were already eating while someone was dishing out the soup, bread, and cheeses.

Tharon nudged Roswynd to go first, then she followed in line next. After she received a full bowl and spoon, she followed Roswynd to a comfortable spot in front of one of the campfires. But she hesitated when Garrett headed for them. He had a strange look that concerned her.

"There you both are." Garrett was a little winded, but he knelt down in front of them.

"Sorry, Father. We were on a walk."

Garrett shook his head, then said, "I am sorry to inform you both that I must leave tonight and return to Earna." His attention shifted to Tharon, then he touched her knee. "Your father is not well."

"Is he hurt?" Tharon asked, preparing to rise and go to him. Her father was with another pack hunting farther north while they were at the southern end, to the west of the city.

"No, he is fine." Garrett gave a gentle smile and said, "I promise."

"Is he sick again?" Roswynd asked, her own worry evident in her features. "Will he be all right?"

"Of course." Garrett's smile was bigger, but his eyes held something else in them. "I am taking him back to Earna tonight so that he can rest. He will be fine in a couple of days. I promise."

"I should join you," Tharon said.

"No, Tharon." Garrett squeezed her knee and said, "Your father would be upset if you left the hunt early. He would want you to stay and so would I." He leaned in closer and whispered, "Frankly, you are one of the top hunters here. It would be a disservice to our people if you left the hunt early."

Tharon fidgeted and weighed what she should do. Her father often didn't feel well. It was normal for it to happen around this time each year, then sometimes in the summer he had a relapse. The illness never seemed any worse than the previous time.

"It is only one more day," Roswynd said to Tharon. "Then perhaps we can leave tomorrow evening, instead of staying to break down camp the next day."

Garrett nodded at Roswynd and turned back to Tharon. "Roswynd has an excellent idea."

Tharon bit her lip and glanced at her friend, whom she trusted more than anyone else in her life. Her silent question showed in her features as she looked to Roswynd for help. Was she being selfish for staying when her father wasn't well? She was the eldest and therefore responsible for her siblings and mother when her father was ill. But Garrett and Layla had always cared for Tharon's father for as long as she could recall.

Roswynd smiled at Tharon and nodded at her.

"I agree," Tharon whispered and focused on Garrett again. "But you will send word if he worsens?"

"Yes, of course." Garrett's smile hadn't broken, then he promised, "Your father will be fine."

Tharon nodded and said, "Thank you, sir." She was less uneasy; she trusted Garrett to continue taking care of her father even though she was growing older. One day it would be her responsibility to handle her father's illnesses. She was certain Saxon wasn't up to it.

Garrett started to rise but leaned forward and kissed Tharon's temple. "Try to rest tonight and not worry." He stood to his full stature and promised, "I will see you both tomorrow."

"Be safe, Father." Roswynd received a kiss from him, too, then watched him go before she spoke to Tharon. "He will be all right. He always recovers."

"What if he does not one day?" Tharon asked, voice low and uncertain.

Roswynd hooked her arm across Tharon's shoulders and replied, "Your Father is a strong male."

Tharon was quiet as she considered her father over the years. He was a degenerate Omega, but also the king of White Sommer. She admired his strength to run a kingdom despite being a degenerate breed. Like previous illnesses, he would recover from this. "Yes, you are right. He is one of the strongest I know."

Roswynd touched her friend's leg and said, "Like you."

* * *

Date: 15 Sunstone 826G
(Present Day)

Tharon scanned each and every face as she led the unit down Gyldr Street, the main street that ended at Skye Hunter Castle, which was located in the northern corner of Earna. After all these years, she hadn't forgotten the way to the castle. The city wasn't much different other than the occasional new building. However, the people were not as happy as she remembered from her youth, prior to the war. In her youth, her family was always so well received when they marched through the streets to Skye Hunter Castle. But not now. They cast glares and hisses in her direction, but she ignored it all.

Ahead the city's inner wall came into view, marking the closeness of the castle. Wyndfeld guards manned the stone gatehouse and stepped forward as Tharon neared them. She itched to touch one of her sword hilts, but instead she tightened her hand on the reins. If their cease-fire were to last, she had to play the peaceful knight now.

"Ho there," a guard called.

Tharon signaled for the unit to halt, then she urged Obsidian a few steps closer. "I am Prince Tharon, wife of Princess Roswynd."

The guard glanced past Tharon before he nodded and focused on Tharon again. "Yes, you are expected here. You and Princess Roswynd are welcome to pass the inner wall, but not your men."

"I understand." Tharon twisted in her saddle and ordered her high-ranking knight to come to her side. "You are to return to Leeward."

"Are you certain, Lord Commander?" Hywel asked, uneasy pheromones pouring from him.

"Yes." Tharon received a nod from him before he returned to his unit. She looked to the Wyndfeld guard and said, "We have brought a few personal belongings on a cart."

"We will have them brought to Skye Hunter Castle," the guard said, then commanded another guard to handle it. "You and Princess Roswynd will follow me once your unit has departed the area."

It took several minutes for the entire unit to turn itself around in the street. Roswynd's two guards brought her to Tharon, then bid farewell. The cart that was hauled by a mule was left near them.

"I might actually miss those two," Roswynd murmured, watching her two guards depart with the unit.

Tharon canted her head, weighing whether or not Roswynd was serious. There was a hint of teasing in her voice, but Tharon sensed it was mostly truth. She could understand why Roswynd was naturally drawn to Pòl. She was pleased that they were getting along well. Tharon had planned to assign him and Murray to Roswynd in Wulfbite, and Roswynd's acceptance of them was a relief.

"Follow me," the same guard ordered. He and two others joined him in guiding the married couple to Skye Hunter Castle.

Tharon noted two male Betas had hitched up a mule to their cart. She tapped Obsidian's sides and rode alongside Roswynd into the open gatehouse. When she entered the stone gatehouse, she glanced upward and noted the seven murder holes overhead. When she was young, she thought they were holes for letting light shine in. After she became a knight, she learned they were for defense: shooting arrows, dropping rocks, pouring boiling water or tar, and a number of other nasty things.

After they exited the gatehouse, she counted the turrets on the inner wall and noted the guards were still as well armored as they were ten years ago. The outer bailey was busy with guards moving about from the stable and the barracks, yet it was still lush and green, other than a few walking paths to the stable and barracks. They continued on the cobble street that passed the buildings, then they went through a smaller wall that had a simple iron gate, which was open.

After the secondary gate, Tharon noted that the kitchen building and the kitchen's vegetable gardens were to her left. Near the kitchen was another similar building but it was meant for housing guests if the keep was overfilled at any time, or if there were unwanted guests, who didn't belong in the keep. On the right was a much larger garden for the keep, for the guests to enjoy. She had spent many hours talking and playing in the garden with Roswynd. Between the guesthouse and the keep was an old family cemetery for the House of Arrington. Up ahead stood the keep itself, still as towering, imposing, and impressive as it was years ago. At the top, a bronze statue of a great eagle in flight was mounted to a rod, which was connected to a bronze line that ran to the ground. The statue served as a symbol, and it also protected the castle from lightning strikes in the springtime. In front of them, King Garrett and Queen Layla waited.

Roswynd smiled upon seeing her parents, kicked out her feet from the stirrups, and hopped off Dragonfly. "Hello, Father and Mother." She brought the reins over her horse's head, then handed them to the guard and thanked him.

Tharon was slow to dismount but followed her wife's lead. She gave the reins to another guard, who left with Obsidian. Once her horse was gone, she neared the reunited family and waited for their acknowledgment. Even though she was an adult, a knight, and the lord commander, she felt small again, but she forced it aside.

"Welcome, Prince Tharon," Garrett said, then held his hand in offer.

Tharon stepped forward and held hands for a moment. She shifted her attention to Roswynd's mother, who had always been quieter than Garrett, except when she and Tharon's mother had been together.

Layla offered a proper curtsy with her dress and said, "Welcome back, Prince Tharon." She appeared indifferent, but her voice held a small quiver.

"Thank you," Tharon said to them both, then noted the servants were taking her and Roswynd's belongings into the keep. At least she wasn't being assigned a room in the unwanted house.

Roswynd cleared her throat and said, "I thought I would show Tharon around before supper."

"You will find not much has changed," Garrett said, then he looked at Roswynd. "Did you see your brother?"

"Yes. He was well." Roswynd hooked her hands in front of her body, as she was taught at a young age. "How long will he be gone for?"

"No longer than a fortnight," Garrett replied.

Roswynd nodded and glanced at Tharon, then back to her parents. "We shall see you in the dining hall."

"Yes, of course," Garrett said. He touched his wife on the back but mentioned, "Your sister may be about."

"What of Archibold and Josse?" Roswynd asked.

Garrett smiled and replied, "They are practicing their riding skills."

Roswynd gave a half snort but nodded and said farewell. She led the way to the guesthouse and blew out a breath after a minute. "Like Father said, very little has changed here." She shouldered the front door open and said, "We have been busy for the past ten years."

Tharon narrowed her eyes but didn't take the bait. She followed her wife into the guesthouse, finding it the same other than fresh paint on the walls. They came to the door at the south end of the house, departed the house, and were now facing the building dedicated to the kitchen. Again, she followed Roswynd into the kitchen and was introduced to the head cook, then a few other important servants. The other, smaller buildings behind the kitchen included the buttery, pantry, larder, spicery, and chandlery. On the other side of the small wall were the storerooms that included a few cellars. Very little had changed other than the equipment inside each building.

They arrived at the stable after going around the barracks. Tharon considered whether they were skipping the barracks because they were concerned about Tharon's intent. She made no comment and decided it mattered little to her. There were plenty of occasions in the past where she'd explored the barracks with Roswynd. Once in the stable, Roswynd indicated their two horses in side-by-side stalls.

"Deri is still the groom of the stable," Roswynd said.

Tharon nodded, remembering Deri, who took over as the groom when Tharon was about ten. He was a nice Beta and he adored Roswynd.

Roswynd patted Dragonfly, nodded toward Obsidian, and said, "And here is your horse, in case you need a speedy getaway one night."

Again, Tharon narrowed her eyes at her wife and struggled to remain silent after the latest jab. Her continued quietness seemed to irritate Roswynd, who was looking for a reaction. *Will I need a speedy getaway?*

Roswynd returned to Dragonfly, smiled at him and whispered, "I will bring you apples tomorrow." She guided Tharon out of the stable, then headed back to the inner bailey and went to the large family garden. The garden was beautiful this time of the year, but within the next two months it would die off. Roswynd wandered to the bench closest to the main wall.

Tharon watched her wife sit, but she remained standing for the moment. She studied the curly willow behind the bench, recalling its much smaller size from years ago. In the late afternoon sun, it was beautiful and radiant, leaves painted in soft oranges. Gradually her attention turned to the keep, which towered high above the main wall at the south end. The entire castle's lands were oval-shaped, with the keep located in the southeastern part. There was no other gate to the south, but Tharon was certain there was a second secretive passage for the family. Something she was never privy to, being a Blakesley.

"It must be strange to be here again," Roswynd said.

Tharon was studying the windows and balconies along the keep's eastern side. One of them was Roswynd's room, at least when they were young. But Roswynd's soft whispers pierced her focus on the keep.

"Especially after everything you have done."

Tharon lowered her eyes to Roswynd and rumbled in silent response. She attempted to dissect Roswynd's remark, to know whether there was a hidden agenda in it. As a pup Roswynd was never the one to say anything shallow or without meaning. Taking a seat beside her wife, Tharon said, "I was mistaken in thinking we found common ground yesterday evening." Their trip to the market and tavern had been comfortable, or so she had wrongly assumed.

"Truly?" Roswynd asked, then huffed and stared at Tharon. "You may have changed and become a stranger, but I am the same, having only grown older." She gave a bitter smile and whispered, "Do you think my silence is a positive sign?"

Tharon watched Roswynd's features and became entangled in Roswynd's different-colored eyes. It was true that Roswynd's quietness meant a nasty storm was brewing inside her; she should have recalled that. This afternoon they'd shared a tense exchange about the wedding vows and now this conversation. After the wedding they had been at odds, then days later things seemed to even out, and now they were trading barbs again. It felt like a ride on a bucking, moody horse itching to toss Tharon.

Roswynd shook her head and stood from the bench. "Why do I bother?" She continued through the garden, following the U-shaped path.

Tharon watched Roswynd's departure and considered her angle. Perhaps Roswynd was foolish enough to believe they would reconnect as though they were best friends again. Or was Roswynd attempting to play Tharon, gain her trust, and learn what Saxon was planning for Wyndfeld? But Tharon was no better. There was a secretive part of her that wanted Roswynd's blind trust, even after Wyndfeld was defeated. It was a ridiculous notion because the defeat of Wyndfeld would leave Roswynd broken. Tharon could live with damaged because damaged could still work, just like her.

Tharon took wide strides until she met Roswynd's side by the entrance to the keep. In uncomfortable silence, they entered the keep, and went to the second floor and into the eastern wing. Their bedroom was Roswynd's bedroom that she'd had since youth. The furniture and decor were different, but it was the same space.

"I am going to change before supper," Roswynd said and started turning on a few lamps. She moved about the room in relative silence while Tharon checked through her contents in the trunk, confirming no one inspected her belongings. She had expected it and thought it was strange they hadn't done so. Her current book was pressed against a stack of tied letters. She fingered the letters but took the book to a seat in the sitting area, needing to read before she faced the House of Arrington at supper.

After changing from her riding attire into a dress, Roswynd had left for the garderobe but returned a few minutes later, ready to go. She waited at their bedroom door for Tharon, who was changing out of her tunic into a nicer one and pairing it with her black leather jerkin. Roswynd had a strange look that Tharon couldn't quite place, but she wasn't about to ask.

They left the room, returned to the first floor, and went to the great dining hall, which was busy with a few staff members eating in the back. Several of them greeted and congratulated Roswynd, but few made eye contact with Tharon. In the main part of the hall, they sat down at the head table.

Garrett was seated in his usual spot at the head of the table and to his right was Layla. Often Selwyn sat to Garrett's left, then each pup of age went down either side of the table. But tonight Roswynd took Selwyn's spot with Tharon next to her. Across from them were Myla, Archibold, and Josse. The brothers were giggling and chatting about their riding lesson. Myla was reserved and refused to look at Tharon.

Servants arrived with food and drink for everyone, and two of them took care of adding wood to the firepit located in the center of the dining hall.

"Have you settled in, Tharon?" Garrett asked after he passed the meat platter to Roswynd.

"Yes, thank you." Tharon decided simple, short answers were the best option while she was in Wyndfeld. She worked to keep her Alpha under control, which was a challenge. She was accustomed to having full authority in her position as Lord Commander, but here she was below the king. She had reverted to being a prince.

"Excellent." Garrett was passing platters and filling his plate. "I thought perhaps tomorrow would be a perfect day to explore Earna." He smiled first at Roswynd, who lifted an eyebrow at him. "As agreed, we want our kingdoms to see that while our unity might be a little fragile right now, it is real."

Roswynd held her tongue but gave a faint nod.

"Agreed," Tharon said after she passed a bowl full of brown rice over to Josse.

Garrett nodded, then centered his attention onto Roswynd. "Do you not think so, Roswynd?"

"Yes, of course, Father." Roswynd offered him a slight smile. "Tharon and I can go to the market."

"You will take a few guards," Garrett said and was pleased when Roswynd nodded. He started eating but asked, "I take it you did not have trouble traveling here?"

Roswynd didn't answer and focused on her meal, which was a small serving. She seemed inclined to allow Tharon to handle the inquiries. But whether she was defaulting to Tharon's status as an Alpha in their relationship or simply disinterested in it, Tharon was unsure.

"We had no trouble," Tharon replied, then she pressed her right leg against Roswynd's thigh. In their youth, they used the touches as a silent request to ask whether the other was okay. The person receiving the contact was expected to respond with one push back as a "yes" or two pushes as a "no."

However, Roswynd ignored the contact and continued eating small bites of her food.

"Good," Garrett said. "The day after, we will journey to Stormbreaker Landing and spend the day there."

Tharon considered the plans and looked forward to seeing the port city again after so long. She'd been there two or three times as a pup but never appreciated it.

"I am sure Tharon would enjoy a ride on a ship," Roswynd said, her voice was upbeat, but Tharon knew it was fake. In fact, Roswynd was taunting Tharon with the prospect of being out on the water. Tharon had a slight aversion to water ever since childhood, but she would go swimming in a stream or lake at times with Roswynd, who loved swimming in the summer.

Garrett cleared his throat and looked between the two. "Well, I am afraid we will not have time, if we are to return home the same day."

"Pity," Roswynd muttered under her breath.

"That is understandable," Tharon said, fighting to keep an edge out of her voice. She was on the verge of growling at her wife. Roswynd used to tease Tharon in a good-natured way. But tonight Roswynd was being spiteful. If it continued Tharon was unsure how much longer she could restrain her Alpha before it responded to Roswynd's flippant taunts.

"Well, good, then that is settled." Garrett nodded, then shifted his attention to his two young Alpha sons.

Tharon was grateful that Garrett struck up a conversation with the other family members. She took a few deep breaths to calm herself, but Roswynd's defiant scent lingered under her nose. How she wanted to use her own pheromones to overpower Roswynd's childish mood, but it would be noticed by everyone else. Now that they were in Earna, it seemed that Roswynd was feeling more comfortable and inclined to push Tharon's limits.

After supper Tharon walked with Roswynd back to the bedroom on the second floor. As the room grew closer, her inner Alpha started to uncoil inside her chest. They would be in a private space in a moment, and she had to strike hard before Roswynd's childish antics grew worse.

Roswynd entered the bedroom first and searched for a lamp, which she lit with ease. She placed the lamp in the center of the table in the sitting area, then turned but ran into Tharon.

With a growl, Tharon grabbed her wife's hips and pushed her back toward the table.

"Tharon!" Roswynd yelped when she was lifted, then shoved onto the end of the table. She gasped and latched on to Tharon's biceps. "What are—"

"*Listen* well to me," Tharon said, baring her teeth and demanding Roswynd's submission. Her thick pheromones rolled off her in waves, making Roswynd whine and turn her head. "Are you listening?"

Roswynd tightened her fingers against Tharon's arms, nodded, and kept her head turned in submission.

"Your childish mood swings might work in Earna, but do you truly wish to start a fucking pissing match with my Alpha?" Tharon bent over, closer to her wife's face. She breathed in Roswynd's rising scent, which was harsh with fear, but also threaded with arousal. *So, my wife does like roughness.* "Because in Wulfbite, it will be only me standing between you and my people."

Roswynd closed her eyes and her jaw was locked, but after a beat, she whispered, "I understand."

Tharon recalled the last time Roswynd said the same words, by the pond outside Leeward. But now they were hollow and eerie with something Tharon couldn't place. Her Alpha retracted in response, uneasy about it. "Good." When Roswynd opened her mismatched eyes, Tharon saw the same emptiness in them matching Roswynd's voice.

Even though their conversation was finished, it felt incomplete and wrong. Tharon struggled with herself and whether to further the discussion. Even though she had Roswynd's agreement, she was losing something else. However, she needed Roswynd to understand that when they went to Wulfbite, her people would not take kindly to a member from the House of Arrington. Tharon would protect her at every turn, but if Roswynd was battling with Tharon, then it would make the situation worse. They needed to get along enough to show a unified front.

"I wish to visit with my sister tonight," Roswynd said and kept her gaze to the left, away from Tharon.

Tharon rumbled at Roswynd's continued submissive nature and the unspoken request to see Myla. She realized they kept ahold of each other despite the argument. "You do not require my permission." She lifted her wife off the table and placed her back on her feet. She broke their contact, then went over to her closed trunk and opened it. She listened to Roswynd going to the door and said nothing.

Roswynd stood by the door for a moment, then spoke in a soft voice. "I will return in an hour or so." She left without another word, closing the door behind her.

Tharon sighed after her wife left. She confirmed that her wedding gift for Roswynd was still in the trunk, fingering the wood frame of it. She had planned to give it to Roswynd tonight, but it wasn't the right time. Perhaps tomorrow morning they would be in a better place.

Closing the trunk, Tharon returned to her book that sat on the table next to the lamp. She took it to a wing chair, placed it there, and took care of lighting a fire in the fireplace. As she did so, she considered Roswynd's attitude today. Tharon was certain they'd made some headway over the past week, but it shifted after the events on Golden Wheat Road.

At first Roswynd acted familiar with Tharon, as if they were best friends again. It was natural to fall back into old habits. However, the incident with the thieves had altered their dynamics. Tharon was certain that Roswynd had realized that the old Tharon was gone. Roswynd's nightmare was perhaps the war within her, and Roswynd realizing the truth about their situation.

The truth was that the new Tharon, the Black Wulf, was a creature not capable of being loved.

Chapter 9

Roswynd took deep breaths on her walk to her sister's room, then quickly stopped and tested a door to an empty, dark guestroom. She slipped into it before a guard noticed her, closed the door, and pressed her back against it. A few tears slipped free, but she covered her face and held back the sobs. Her mind rehashed the earlier argument with her wife.

Again, Tharon had manhandled her, forcing her onto the table and imposing herself on Roswynd. She hated how her body responded to the physical excitement of it even when they were heading for an argument. The entire time she had gripped Tharon's biceps, needing any kind of physical contact similar to when they were pups in a fight. Tharon's brief lecture about getting along replayed in her head.

Tharon was right, again. They needed to get along on some level rather than butt heads, especially when they were in Wulfbite in a month. Tharon spoke of the White Sommer citizens, but behind that issue was Saxon. Roswynd was used to standing her ground against Saxon, but he was the king now and far stronger than she was. She hated to admit that it was Tharon's presence that kept him at bay. She wanted to handle Saxon on her own, yet she was foolish to keep jabbing Tharon, who would be her protector in Wulfbite.

However, Roswynd was failing to control her cold attitude toward Tharon after what happened on Golden Wheat Road. Tharon had protected her from the thieves and cared for her after they returned to Chesford Manor. In the morning, when Roswynd had a clearer mind, she had come to grips with the ugly truth about Tharon. Roswynd's best friend was gone.

Many years ago Roswynd had "buried" her best friend after Tharon broke their friendship pact. At the time, she had accepted that she may never see Tharon again to heal their friendship, their promises, and their hearts. Having been suddenly forced to marry had set Roswynd on a course to see if there was anything left of her best friend inside the tall, dark, and menacing Alpha. The incident on Golden Wheat Road was a slap to her face.

Her Tharon was gone.

Now Roswynd was faced with having to bury her best friend all over again. Her chest constricted, heavy with the consuming rage inside her. She wanted to hate Tharon for doing this to her. She hated herself for ever having hope that her best friend lived inside that brute. To make it worse, Tharon was handsome, strong, and all Alpha, stirring Roswynd's Omega in response.

With a growl, Roswynd crumpled to the floor and furiously wiped the tears, but they kept coming one after another. "I hate you for this," she whispered to no one. "I hate that you broke our first vows. I hate that you gave us new ones. And I *hate* that you took my best friend from me." She fisted her hands, wishing she could pound them into Tharon right now.

Propping up her legs, she lowered her head to her knees and didn't care if her dress was stained with tears. Roswynd wanted to forget her past with Tharon, make it all disappear. Except maybe keep the good memories, which were most of them. Her tears welled up again and the crushing pressure in her chest started once more.

In the past Tharon had been so loving and tender with Roswynd. They talked about everything and anything. They shared stories and read stories. They snuggled with each other, often falling asleep in the same bed. They played night and day when they were together. When they were apart, they wrote letters back and forth until they could see each other. Every memory was so precious to Roswynd, but each one felt like a tiny needle pricking her heart. When she gazed upon Tharon now, those needles were pushed deeper.

Taking several deep breaths, Roswynd fought to control her wild emotions that were spiraling her into oblivion. She needed to be stronger and to focus on her kingdom. She was letting her past feelings beat her. If Tharon and Saxon were planning to defeat Wyndfeld, then Roswynd needed to find out what they were going to do. Roswynd was certain the political marriage was a lie to gain access to Wyndfeld again.

Roswynd took a deep breath, lifted her head, and rested her chin on her knees. "She is not your best friend anymore. She is your enemy," she whispered to herself. After taking several deep breaths, she wiped her cheeks one last time, stood, and left the guestroom.

Roswynd knocked on her sister's door firmly in control of her emotions. Myla ushered her into the room and gave her a long hug. She melted into the affection that she'd needed for days. She kissed her sister's temple and whispered, "It is good to see you again."

Myla held her sister's head for a beat, then asked, "Do you want to lie on my bed?"

Roswynd nodded and they both hopped up onto the tall bed. Roswynd rolled onto her back on one side while Myla rested next to her.

"Are you all right, Roswynd?" Myla turned her head to her sister and bit her bottom lip.

"I am fine." Roswynd refused to worry her sister more than she had already. "It is not easy." She sighed and placed her hands on her stomach, which had a small ache. Above her, she watched the shadows of light from the fireplace dance on the bed's beige canopy. "She is nothing like she was when we were young."

"I know." Myla fiddled with the girdle around her waist, rolling it. "Did she hurt you the first night?"

Roswynd's eyelashes fluttered a few times, but she whispered, "No, nothing like that." In fact, she had failed one of the major duties as an Omega wife. On top of it, the suppressant she took each month would make it more difficult, but Roswynd would not become pregnant by Tharon, not when her marriage was based on lies. "Nothing happened that night or any night since."

Myla released a soft breath.

"Please do not tell Father or Mother or—"

"I will not tell anyone," Myla said and grabbed her sister's hand next to her. "I thought for sure after all the rumors about her…" She couldn't finish the thought aloud.

"I know." Roswynd frowned and considered the rumors about Tharon being a rapist, which had sounded far-fetched to her. At least, the old Tharon would never stand for such a vile act, much less perform it. "I do not believe they are true."

Myla released a heavy breath, nodded, and whispered, "Perhaps you are right." She was quiet for a minute, then said, "I thought the wedding ceremony was pretty."

"It was," Roswynd whispered, smiling with bitterness.

"Can I see your wedding ring?" Myla asked in a meek voice.

Freeing her hand, Roswynd pulled the golden band free, then placed it in Myla's palm. She glanced at it while Myla looked over it with a curious eye.

"It is so beautiful. I love the wolf hunting the rabbit," Myla said and ran her thumb along the tiny images etched into the band. "Did you notice what it says on the inside?"

"What?" Roswynd rolled toward her sister and narrowed her gaze at the strange lettering on the inside of the band. "I-I do not know." She retrieved the wedding band and brought it closer to her face, tilting it so the fire's light caught the inside of the band. The inscription simply read *'Until the End of Our Days.'* They were the exact words they promised each other as friends and again as spouses.

"Did you know it was there?" Myla asked, continuing to study the band as Roswynd turned it.

"No," Roswynd murmured. Tharon had put it on her finger at the ceremony, and she hadn't removed it since that day.

"That is very romantic," Myla whispered in a breathless tone.

Roswynd rumbled low and considered why Tharon had chosen the inscription. The words had once meant the world to her. Perhaps they still meant something to Tharon, but she banished that idea from her mind. She slid the wedding band back on her right hand's middle finger and admired the nature scene on it. If only she had received the wedding band for love rather than politics, then it would have been perfect.

"It is a very pretty ring." Myla smiled and added, "It reminds me of you."

Spinning the band on her finger, Roswynd whispered, "It was… unexpected." She turned onto her back again and lowered her hands to her belly but kept playing with the ring.

"Tharon has a ring too?" Myla asked.

Roswynd sighed and nodded. "It is a fede ring."

"Oh." Myla chewed on her lip, then turned her head in Roswynd's direction. "Why do you think she picked the rings?"

"It is part of the act, Myla. It means nothing," Roswynd replied in a quiet voice.

Myla didn't say anything for a minute, then touched her sister's shoulder and asked, "But what if it does mean something? Tharon used to—"

"She has changed, Myla." Roswynd met her sister's gaze, then frowned. "It is merely an attempt to trick me into trusting her."

Myla gently pulled on the sleeve of Roswynd's dress, seeming to gather her thoughts. After a sigh, she asked, "But what if it does mean something? It all seems rather elaborate and not only the wedding rings, but the ceremony location, how you came in by horse, how she matched the color of your gown, the couples dance, and not forcing you on the first night." She peered up at Roswynd, who continued to stare at the canopy. "What if there is still a part of her that cares for you?"

Roswynd rumbled, buying time so she could fight off the burn behind her eyes. She wasn't going to cry in front of her sister, not over Tharon. "I do not think that is possible."

Myla sighed and was silent, but there was an unspoken persistence humming from her. Roswynd knew her sister wanted to argue she was wrong, that maybe there was a spark of hope worth chasing when it came to Tharon. Roswynd understood why Tharon was no longer the person she'd known. If someone had murdered Roswynd's mother, she too would spiral into anger and darkness, hunting for vengeance at any cost. That was the one sliver of Roswynd that connected with this new Tharon, even though Edeva wasn't murdered by the House of Arrington. No one in her family would poison Edeva, certainly not Roswynd's parents, who'd loved Edeva.

"Father said you are going to the port the day after tomorrow?" Myla asked, smiling some. "I would love to go to Stormbreaker Landing."

"Perhaps you can," Roswynd said, considering the idea and whether she could convince their father.

"I have studies with my tutor," Myla replied. "It has been so long since I left Earna, even for a day."

"I will talk to Father," Roswynd promised and held her sister's hand. They spent the rest of the evening discussing the future, especially the return of the lands from the Kingdom of White Sommer. Everything was changing quickly. Myla then mentioned that Prince Drust was to visit when Roswynd and Tharon were in White Sommer. Roswynd was disappointed to not meet Prince Drust, but their father didn't want Tharon to learn of the possible marriage that would benefit Wyndfeld.

After an hour, Roswynd was feeling sleepy and left after kissing and hugging her sister goodnight. She returned to her bedroom and found Tharon reading in front of the fireplace. *I guess she still does love to read*, she realized as she went to the privacy area behind the dividing panels. After changing, she washed up and retired to her bed without speaking to Tharon. Exhaustion claimed her within minutes and one bad dream bothered her through the night. It was the same one about Tharon, who conquered the Kingdom of Wyndfeld, sentenced Roswynd's family to death, and became the lord of Wyndfeld under Saxon's rule. All the while Roswynd was unable to halt any of it or save her family.

At dawn, soft movement stirred Roswynd from her sleep. She peeked out from the blankets and spotted Tharon coming out from behind the panels; she was fully dressed and attaching her sword belt. In the past, Tharon preferred to sleep in later than Roswynd; however, that no longer seemed to be the case. With a soft groan, Roswynd started her day, going behind the panel to put on a simple dress, as they would be walking around Earna. Perhaps afterward she could go for a horseback ride.

After dressing, Roswynd went into the washroom, cleaned her face, and brushed her teeth. Compared to yesterday, she was in a better mood and felt prepared to face her people in the city. The people were sure to be a mixture of leery and snide about their former enemy being at Roswynd's side. Upon exiting the washroom, she found Tharon seated on the end of the table and waiting for Roswynd. In direct contrast, Tharon's boots easily touched the floor while Roswynd's feet had dangled off the table last night. It was a stark reminder of Tharon's sheer size as an Alpha.

Roswynd took a moment to admire Tharon and felt a soft throb between her legs. Tharon was truly handsome. Her leather trousers were black, as usual, and tight, hugging her muscular curves. Her two swords hung from each one of her hips. Her tunic was white and stood out against her black leather jerkin. She wore Edeva's stud earrings, which matched her attire. Tharon's black, thick hair was down, but a single braid started at her right temple and went to the back of her head.

As Roswynd stood there, she became lost in the fiery-orange glow of Tharon's eyes, especially the left one. The hazy eye was still alive but was milky orange from the blindness. Roswynd found it attractive regardless and wanted to know what happened. She suspected Tharon would ignore her inquiry, considering it had taken a week simply to learn the name of Tharon's horse.

Then Roswynd noticed next to Tharon's legs was a long item wrapped in cloth and tied off at each end. Tharon's beckoning expression brought her over to her wife. Roswynd watched her place the item across her lap. "What is that?"

Tharon ran a hand down the length of the hidden object and replied, "It is your wedding gift."

"Gift?" Roswynd shook her head as a furrow drew across her brow. She cut her attention from the item to her wife's neutral features. "I…" She faltered and tried to grasp why she was receiving a wedding gift, or even what it could be. It was common for brides to receive a wedding gift from their new spouses, but it wasn't required. On occasion the bride would give a gift as well, yet that was even more uncommon. The thought to refuse the gift crossed her mind until the barest hint of excitement shone in Tharon's eyes.

Tharon raised the gift in silent offer, allowing Roswynd the chance to decline or accept it.

Roswynd clenched the long girdle around her waist and stared at the gift for a moment. Her heart jumped in her chest, and her hand trembled a little. Her curiosity was piqued by the object tucked under the folded layers, and it won her over. She lifted her hand, hesitated, and studied Tharon's features, which remained calm. There was a faint tug of a smile or grin at the corner of Tharon's lips.

Taking a deep breath, Roswynd let go of her caution and touched the twine that held the fabric in place. She untied it, then pushed it and the cloth out of the way, revealing strange long wooden objects. Several frantic heartbeats passed before she pieced together what the gift was. Her head jerked up, and she stumbled over her question. "Um… a bow?"

Tharon pulled the cloth away from the bow, which was split into two pieces. She kept one portion in her left hand while the other half was nestled in her right palm. Her body language remained open as she presented the gift.

Roswynd shook her head and took one step back, as if the weapon were aimed at her. "I-I cannot. Father would be so cross with me." She stared at the bow as though it were a sin.

With a huff, Tharon said, "He is no longer your Alpha."

Roswynd's attention jerked back to Tharon, whose simple reminder crushed her anxious thoughts. She was at a loss and looked again from Tharon to the weapon. Since her youth she had wanted to learn how to shoot, not to hunt or kill but to learn a new skill, increase her arm strength, and test her eyesight. At the Howling Eagle Festival, she was enthralled by the archery competitions and always thought Tharon should compete in them. She also wanted to compete in them, but her father rejected every single one of her attempts to reason with him.

With a deep breath, Roswynd came closer again and touched the grip area, then peered up at Tharon. "Are you going to teach me?" If Tharon declined to help her, she was uncertain that she would still want to learn.

Tharon frowned and replied, "Yes, of course." Her chest puffed up and a thrum started deep in her.

Roswynd tried hiding her grin, but it came loose. Her Omega savored how Tharon's Alpha responded to the need to teach Roswynd. She traced her fingers over the lower limb, which was separated from the rest of the bow. That was rather strange to her. "Why is it broken in half? How can I use it?"

Tharon raised the pieces vertically and held out the upper limb, which appeared to have one piece with the grip. "Hold this." Once Roswynd wrapped her hand around the grip, Tharon slid the lower limb into a hidden recess on the underside of the grip. "The lower limb fits into this slot here." She turned Roswynd's hands to show her the underside. "Once it is strung, it cannot separate."

"Oh." Roswynd's eyes were big as she pulled the lower limb free, reinserted it, and tried it all over again. "That is amazing. Is this new?"

"Mmmm." Tharon stood from the table and headed to her trunk, opening it, and searching for something. "It was a new design about two or three years ago. It makes a bow more portable."

"Or easier to hide," Roswynd murmured, looking over the weapon. Did Tharon pick this type of bow on purpose so that Roswynd could tuck it away from prying eyes? She focused on Tharon, who returned with a few items in her hands.

Tharon placed the items on the table, then took the bow from Roswynd. One item was a string, which Tharon picked up and hooked on the lower limb. With quick finesse, she used her leg to lock the bow in place, bent the recurve bow, and strung the upper limb. Picking up the bow, she offered it to Roswynd.

Staring in wonder, Roswynd received the weapon and looked it over from end to end. She tested the grip with both hands, deciding it was meant for her left hand.

"There is another feature on the bow." Tharon picked up the last item from the table and touched the bow, near her wife's hand. She tilted the weapon and indicated the tiny hole in the grip. "This tray fits in there." The tiny item was a flat piece of wood with a plug end. Tharon slid the plug part into the hole, then twisted it until the tray was parallel with the grip.

"What does it do?"

Tharon lifted the bow vertically in Roswynd's hand again and indicated the new add-on in the grip. "It is for beginners. You rest the arrow's shaft on this while you nock and draw the arrow, align your sight, and release."

Roswynd gave a soft sound of recognition and studied the tiny ledge that was large enough for an arrow shaft to sit on. "That is clever." She looked up at Tharon. "Then I can remove it later as I become better?"

Tharon nodded and replied, "It will take time for your upper body to adjust to drawing a bow, so this will help."

"But you did not have something like that on your bow when you were learning?" Roswynd caught Tharon's headshake. She studied the bow in more detail and marveled at it, running her hand along the limbs, grip, and string. Of all the gifts for her, she would have never guessed a bow as a wedding gift. Tharon did have a point—her father had no say in the matter now that Tharon was her Alpha. Her stomach fluttered in excitement at the prospect of finally learning archery after so long.

"Then you accept my gift?" Tharon asked.

Roswynd lowered the weapon and studied it for a minute. In their youth, she had wanted to learn archery, and even more so after Garrett taught Tharon. Roswynd knew Tharon had been well aware of her interest, and Tharon would have taught her in secret. However, Roswynd refused to allow her best friend to teach her and incite Garrett's wrath. As adults, Tharon was gifting her a beautiful bow and archery lessons. For a moment, she could sense her best friend peeking at her through the layers of the lord commander.

If she took the gift, then she was indicating to Tharon that she accepted their tumultuous relationship. Part of her considered refusing it rather than mislead Tharon and even herself. But, within the last few minutes, Tharon had spoken to her more than any other time. Somehow the bow was connecting them. The gift was a weapon that Tharon was an expert at as a hunter, and Tharon could teach her. Even though it could promote a new facet to their relationship, it was also something from their past. As the air thickened with their entangled pheromones, Roswynd weighed the outcome of accepting the gift and lessons.

Perhaps if I try, then she will find her way back to me, Roswynd thought, then steadied her hopes. She blinked away the initial onset of tears and took a deep breath. Meeting Tharon's expectant gaze, she whispered, "Yes." If they had been pups, they would have been giddy together, exchanging hugs and laughing with excitement about archery. Instead, Tharon was calm and she nodded, but her pheromones softened, the one indication she might have been tense. "Thank you, Tharon."

Again, Tharon's scent changed and became gentler. "You are welcome." She reclaimed the bow and undid the string to break it back down.

Roswynd took the two pieces and smiled at how compact it was. "Perhaps I should hide it under my mattress, so no one finds it." Some part of her was worried that her father would learn about it. He would one day, but right now they had too many concerns to be arguing over archery. Besides, Tharon, her Alpha, said it was acceptable. Rushing to her bed, she lifted the mattress and placed it on the bedframe under it.

Tharon waited by the door and said, "We will purchase arrows today while we are at the market."

Roswynd hurried over to her wife and asked, "Does that mean we can start this afternoon?" She struggled to hide her enthusiasm, but it was impossible. Her words tumbled out in a higher pitch, edging on a squeal.

Rumbling, Tharon grabbed the door ring, nodded, and opened the door.

Clenching her hands, Roswynd held back her desire to hug Tharon as if they were best friends again. Still, her smile didn't break as she left the room with her wife. They went to the dining hall, had a silent breakfast together, and departed the keep before anyone saw them. Outside, the warm sun welcomed them into the beautiful day.

"We should go to the barracks first," Roswynd said. Her father required that they take a guard detail with them. Few people, if any, were fond of those from White Sommer, especially Prince Tharon. It stirred an anxious note in her scent that she hoped Tharon didn't notice.

Guards came and went, changing their shifts. Roswynd was on her way to find Sir Donnchad, the captain. Tharon was on her heels, acting like a protective Alpha around all the males at the barracks. Roswynd groaned at how her Omega loved the attention. *I need to get a grip on myself.*

Knocking on the open door to Donnchad's office, Roswynd smiled at him. "Good morning, Sir Donnchad."

"Good morning, my princess." Donnchad had been speaking to a subordinate guard next to him. "Your father mentioned that you and Prince Tharon would be visiting the city today. How many guards would you like to accompany you?"

Roswynd paused and waited to see if Tharon would answer for her. After a moment, Roswynd replied, "Six or eight, if you can spare them."

"Eight then," Donnchad agreed, then nodded at the guard next to him. "I have already assigned Flann to be in charge."

Flann bowed to Roswynd and said, "It is an honor, my princess."

Roswynd chuckled at his formality. She had met Flann numerous times in the past. He was favored by Donnchad. "Do not be silly, Flann." With a smile she looked to Donnchad and said, "Thank you. We will not be all day."

With Flann in the lead, they went outside and waited for the guards to assemble. Roswynd requested that Flann have the guards remain a certain distance from her and Tharon so they could somewhat enjoy their stroll through the market. She was also concerned with Tharon's response. If she felt threatened by the guards' close proximity, then the mood would pass on to Roswynd. For now Tharon was in a reasonable mood.

Once past the castle grounds and outside the secured location, Roswynd sensed Tharon's hackles rising. She rested a hand on a sword hilt and was scanning people's faces. Her pheromones were stronger, almost acting as a buffer between them and the rest of the world.

Roswynd's reaction to her protective wife was confusing. Tharon was ever the Alpha, guarding her Omega from trouble, which kept her Omega preening, but Roswynd did not appreciate the spiteful expressions her people sent in Tharon's direction. They loathed Tharon for her family's betrayal to the Kingdom of Wyndfeld, even if they were in a cease-fire now. Both Houses blamed the other for the war that should never have been. Even though the political marriage provided temporary peace, it left swelling guilt inside Roswynd. Somehow she felt like the betrayer now, marrying someone from the House of Blakesley. A slight whine freed itself from her, leaving her blushing because Tharon heard it.

Tharon gave Roswynd a questioning look, but Roswynd shook her head. She cleared her throat and said, "The market is this way." It was silly to mention the way to the market because Tharon probably recalled it quite well. Roswynd was trying to keep her mind off today's strange start.

The market was busy with a mixture of locals and merchants from different areas of the kingdom. Wonderful food smells comingled with awful smells like rotting fruit. Several times Roswynd caught whispers about her and Tharon, and some pointed in their direction. She found herself walking closer to Tharon, who welcomed it.

"Oh sweet, beautiful Princess Roswynd," a merchant called from the left. He waved her over and used his big smile to reel her into his stall.

Roswynd chuckled, recognizing her favorite stall in the market. "Hello, Ewan." She went to his stand, which was full of baked goods. "How are you today?"

"I am well, my princess." Ewan was a male Beta with a warm smile. "Congratulations to you and Princess Tharon on your wedding."

"Prince Tharon," Roswynd corrected without thought. Beside her, Tharon gave her a curious glance, but she didn't meet it. Her need to uphold Tharon's title change came naturally to her.

Ewan bent forward and said, "My apologies." He turned his brilliant smile onto Tharon and said, "Welcome back to Earna, Prince Tharon."

Tharon gave a slight nod.

"Is your business well?" Roswynd asked.

"Fabulous." Ewan hooked his fingers in his soiled apron around his waist.

"Ewan is the best baker in Earna," Roswynd told her wife and peered up at her. "Even better than the one in Skye Hunter Castle." She chuckled at Tharon's raised eyebrow, then turned a grin onto Ewan. "If only I could convince my father to hire you."

Ewan waved her off, but he lifted his chest anyway. "Your beauty and my baked goods could conquer Gyldren, my princess."

Roswynd snickered at his flattery and folded her arms. Tharon's rumbling was broken by a low but amused snort. Looking up at her wife, she swatted Tharon's stomach and asked, "You do not believe Ewan?" For a moment, she reverted to her younger self and teased Tharon, who wore a slight grin.

The faint upturn of Tharon's lips spread wider into a wolfish grin. "If this is true, then all I need now is to win over Ewan so that I may become the King of Gyldren."

"And all that takes is endless flour, my handsome prince," Ewan said, then wiggled his eyebrows.

Roswynd tensed at Ewan's attempt to coax Tharon further into the playful moment. Much to her surprise, Tharon bantered back without hesitation.

"I will work on that," Tharon promised.

Ewan beamed and glanced once at Roswynd before he said, "Enough about my spectacular baked goods. I asked you over so I could give you both a gift." He hurried to the other end of his stall.

"Ewan, we need nothing," Roswynd called to him.

"You were married." Ewan returned with a rectangular object wrapped in cloth. "To each other no less, after so long."

Roswynd fought to hide her dismay after Ewan's keen observation. She forced a smile while he opened the item to reveal a sweet bread. "Oh my gods!" Latching on to Ewan's forearm, she asked, "Is that honey pem nut bread?"

Ewan chuckled and presented the bread to Roswynd. "Yes. I made it fresh this morning."

Roswynd bounced once on her feet and asked, "How did you get pem nut this time of the year?"

"I may have been saving it," Ewan said and winked at her. He folded it back up while he spoke. "I suppose you wish to take it now?"

Roswynd covered her racing heart and felt her mouth water at the thought of honey pem nut bread. "Are you certain, Ewan? I would be happy to pay—"

"Nonsense." Ewan tied the covered bread with twine, then placed it in front of her. "It is a wedding gift for you both." Again, he puffed up his chest.

Roswynd turned to her wife and said, "Ewan's honey pem nut bread is magical. I have tried to get the recipe, but Ewan refuses to share it."

Tharon had a slight smile and said, "Thank you for your kindness."

Ewan handed the bread to Tharon, perhaps assuming the Alpha would be in charge of it. "It is my honor."

Roswynd grabbed Ewan's wrist, pulled him across the table, and kissed him on the cheek. "Thank you so much." She released him and promised, "We will enjoy every bite."

Ewan had a dark flush across his cheeks. "Yes, I know." He winked at Roswynd.

"Thank you again, Ewan. We will visit soon." Roswynd exchanged a final farewell with him, then returned to the market street. The guards followed them at a distant pace.

Tharon kept the bread tucked in her left arm while her right hand returned to her sword hilt.

Roswynd was amazed by Ewan's thoughtfulness, but more touched by how he included Tharon in the discussion. Ewan didn't shy away from Tharon, who was intimidating from head to toe. Nor did he treat her with disrespect for being the lord commander of White Sommer. She found the entire moment strange, as if they had wed for love rather than a political statement.

As they rounded a corner to another section of the market, Roswynd slowed upon seeing a familiar figure. She chuckled and hurried off with a few wide steps, which startled Tharon. She came up behind a woman, grabbed her sides, and tickled her.

"My word!" The female raised a hand to slap at the touch but pulled up short and laughed. "Roswynd!"

Roswynd laughed and hugged her friend Gleda. "It is great to see you."

Gleda was all smiles and held Roswynd's shoulders. "Out for a stroll?"

Roswynd indicated to Tharon, who stood a couple of steps behind her. She leaned in and whispered, "Yes, Tharon and I are doing our unity march through the city."

Gleda snorted but nodded her understanding before she looked at Tharon. "Hello, Tharon. You are looking ever like the dapper Alpha prince."

Roswynd swallowed at Gleda's frank attitude, praying it didn't clash with Tharon's Alpha. In their childhood, Tharon liked Gleda well enough, but after Tharon broke the friendship pact, Gleda cursed Tharon up and down. With them being out in public, Gleda had no restraints and no fear of Tharon scorning her. As long as Gleda didn't call Tharon a degenerate, they would all be safe.

"It has been a long time, Gleda," Tharon said, keeping a considerably even tone.

"Pity it was not longer," Gleda said, then looked to Roswynd as if dismissing Tharon. "We will have to catch up later when you have time."

Roswynd fidgeted and tried not to look at Tharon, who was probably irritated with Gleda's remark. She touched her friend's arm and said, "We will. Perhaps breakfast in a few days." Releasing Gleda, she shifted closer to Tharon in hopes to make a silent stand against Gleda's earlier comment.

Gleda narrowed her eyes but sighed and nodded. "Of course. That would be lovely." She slipped in for another quick hug. In Roswynd's ear, she whispered, "Be safe with her."

Roswynd rumbled and kissed Gleda's cheek. Her friend was concerned about her well-being after learning many of the details about the arranged marriage. They said good-bye, then Roswynd and Tharon continued through the city.

Roswynd remained by Tharon's side, reinforcing the message that they were married and a tentative peace was real. They didn't speak but instead gazed about the market. People moved out of their way, especially due to Tharon's sheer presence. Roswynd exchanged smiles or waves with a few familiar merchants; then they went down a side street.

"The guild shop is this way," Roswynd said. "At least, I am fairly certain."

Tharon rumbled and eyed a few people sitting on steps in the tight street. She glanced over her shoulder and confirmed the guards' presence.

"There it is." Roswynd pointed at a sign with an arrow sticking out of an apple. Below the image was the shop's name, the Archery Guild of Earna. Coming to the closed door, she faltered and stared at the storefront. It seemed strange to go into an archery store after being restricted from learning the skill for so long. She gazed toward the guards, who spread out in the street and waited for them.

Tharon stood behind Roswynd and said, "They will think it is for me."

Roswynd glanced at her wife, then nodded and went into the storefront. Inside the shop, two male Betas greeted them and gave curious looks, especially in Tharon's direction. But they seemed to ascertain that Roswynd and Tharon were at least nobility. Their attire wasn't that of commoners.

Roswynd drifted to the left where there were different arrows on display with arrow-filled buckets below them. "Is there a certain kind we need?"

Tharon handed Roswynd the bread, then looked over the arrows and touched the fletching on a few of them.

Roswynd tucked the bread against her arm, waited, and watched Tharon inspect them. The quiet moment gave her a chance to reflect on the wedding gift waiting for her back in her room. The gift hadn't quite registered yet. Or maybe she wasn't ready to accept that Tharon picked out a wedding gift that she knew would mean something to Roswynd. Similar to the wedding ceremony, Roswynd didn't grasp why Tharon was doing thoughtful and even sweet gestures. She froze after it occurred to her that the gestures were sweet, once she wiped away the political burden of the marriage.

What in Gyldr's name is she planning? Am I silly for trying to reach her? Roswynd was torn between believing Tharon's gestures were honest and true or if they held an ulterior motive. Teaching Roswynd archery served no real purpose. In fact, the bow was a weapon that could be used against Tharon. Instead the one explanation that made the most sense was that Tharon wished to fulfill one of Roswynd's dreams. However, she reminded herself to remain suspicious, even though Tharon's gift sparked hope in her. She needed to keep her guard up and find a balance between finding her best friend and watching her enemy.

Tharon returned to Roswynd's side and held out a sheaf of arrows. She held up the pointed end and said, "These arrowheads are for training. It has one pointed tip and no other sharp edges."

Roswynd nodded and asked, "How many are there?"

"Arrows are sold in sheaves, so twenty-four to a sheaf," Tharon replied and lowered the bundle. She headed toward one of the shop owners and said, "We are also looking for a quiver."

Roswynd remained in front of the arrow wall, studying the different arrowheads, shafts, and fletching. She could guess which ones were better and best for hunting or piercing armor. She went to the far back wall that had bows hanging on it. Many of them were plain and simple compared to hers. Perhaps three met the same craftsmanship as hers, at least from her point of view.

Tharon traded a few words with one of the owners. He disappeared into the back, then returned with two items and gave them to Tharon, who came over to her wife. Roswynd touched the two quivers and pursed her lips.

"This one is a back quiver," Tharon said and held it higher. "It is not quite as common, but if you are wearing a dress then it may be easier."

Roswynd glanced at the two male Betas, who were looking at them and listening to the conversation. They were intrigued by her and Tharon. Perhaps they were even taking bets on whether she and Tharon were royalty rather than nobility.

Tharon picked up on Roswynd's concern, so she pivoted and bared her teeth at them. Her pheromones thickened and filled the shop in a heartbeat, chasing the two males into the back. After a chuff, she refocused on the quivers. "This is a belt quiver, but it can be changed to a back quiver." She indicated the rings that could convert it from one setup to another.

"Should I go with that?" Roswynd asked, keeping her voice even. Tharon's earlier display of dominance sent a shiver racing down her spine, then it had settled lower in her gut and left a burn between her legs. The experience was strange but not all bad. She distracted herself and touched the convertible quiver.

Tharon nodded.

"All right," Roswynd murmured, then reached in her dress's pocket to produce a coin purse.

Tharon put both quivers in one hand and pushed Roswynd's purse away in silent order. She went to the counter where she placed the bundle of arrows and one quiver while putting aside the other. Calling to the shop owners, she straightened even taller and eyed the bravest Beta to barter with her.

Roswynd remained to the side, observing and smirking. Tharon used to hate haggling, but her skills at it had improved a great deal. She was impressed that Tharon was able to get the price down by ten kents. After the items were paid for, they returned to the waiting guards outside. Tharon placed the arrows into the quiver, then slung the quiver over her shoulder.

Leaning in closer, Roswynd asked, "Time to shoot?" The prospect of going back to the castle, putting on riding clothes, and sneaking off with her new bow and Tharon was putting fire in her steps. She warned herself about getting too comfortable with Tharon, but then thought maybe it was acceptable, at least for this afternoon.

Tharon huffed and replied, "If you can string your bow first."

Chapter 10

Roswynd snarled and fought against the bow, which continued to resist her with ease. "Fuck!" For the past twenty minutes, Tharon had stood there and watched her wife struggle with stringing the bow. With a harsh growl, Roswynd released the string, but held the bow against her thigh and gazed up at the sky. She coached herself to not throw the bow across the clearing. Finally, she turned to her wife, who had a stoic face but an amused glint in her orange eyes. "You are laughing at me."

"I am not." Tharon had her arms folded, causing her biceps to bulge against her tunic.

"Not out loud, but on the inside you are." Roswynd took a deep breath and peered down at the bow. At least one of them was getting joy out of the first archery lesson. It was midafternoon, and they'd left the castle grounds about an hour ago on their horses. At first Roswynd thought they would go to their old overlook, but instead Tharon suggested the fallen tower due north of Earna.

After a deep breath, Roswynd made another attempt to hook the hemp string to the upper limb. Her arms ached from the challenge she was losing repeatedly. She paused and moved the bow between her knees, trying a different position. Before she could start, Tharon grabbed her hands.

"Do not do that." Tharon sighed and took the bow, holding it underneath the grip so the lower limb stayed in place. "Hold it for a moment." She returned the weapon to Roswynd, then crossed over to Obsidian. After freeing her recurve bow, Tharon returned to Roswynd's side and unstrung the bow in the blink of an eye. "You are not positioning the bow between your legs correctly." With one leg, she stepped through the bow. "Like this, then brace the lower limb against the outside of your foot."

Roswynd shifted closer to her wife's side and mirrored the position.

"Before you try to string it again," Tharon said, "you want to pull down on the highest point of the upper limb." She lowered her hand to the middle of the limb. "If you try too low, then the resistance is too great."

Grabbing the higher end of the upper limb, Roswynd noticed how the give increased.

"As you start to bend the bow," Tharon instructed, "you will feel the bow press into the back of your left thigh." She demonstrated stringing her larger bow at a much slower speed for Roswynd.

Mimicking her wife, Roswynd kept the string taut and near the upper limb, which she started to pull down. The tip was much closer to the string's loop this time; Roswynd needed a little more umph.

Tharon reached out, but then closed her hand and said, "Put some shoulder into it. You are almost there."

Roswynd bared down on the upper limb, which bent lower for her. Finally, she hooked the string around the groove. "Yes!" She stepped out of the strung bow and raised it up. "I am never unstringing you again!"

Tharon snorted and shook her head, then returned to her horse. "It will get easier after a hundred times."

"You kid." But Roswynd sensed it was true. She moaned and wiped the sweat from her forehead. "It would be impossible to string this if I had a dress on."

"Not impossible but difficult." Tharon came back with the quiver filled with arrows. "I have done it."

Roswynd went wide-eyed and gazed up at her wife. "When we were pups?" She noticed how her reference to their shared childhood caused Tharon to withdraw. With a frown, she touched the colorful fletching on the arrows. Not wanting to ruin the afternoon, she asked, "So how do I shoot an arrow?" She hoped the question redirected Tharon's thoughts.

"This way." Tharon lifted the quiver over her shoulder, held it there, and carried her bow on her way to the tower.

Roswynd passed Dragonfly and patted him on the shoulder. "My sweet horse," she murmured to him. Dragonfly looked up at her and whined in response, then returned to eating grass.

They came around to the east side of the fallen tower where the entrance had once been. Alongside it was a dilapidated building that had served as quarters for the guards who were stationed here. The structure was made from wooden logs and was starting to rot away after decades of neglect.

"We will use the quarters as our target."

"That is a big target," Roswynd whispered and tilted her head.

Tharon grunted and gave the quiver to Roswynd but took out one arrow. She went to the building's single front door, which was half hanging from its hinges. After pressing her back to the building, she walked one foot in front of the other while counting numbers under her breath. At twenty paces she stopped, then dragged the arrowhead through the dirt, making a line. She took more steps and repeated the process four more times.

"Come stand here," Tharon ordered, indicating the line closest to the building.

Roswynd decided to put on the quiver, slinging it across her back. It was the first time she'd worn it, and she fiddled with the strap.

Tharon put the arrow back in the quiver, groused, and helped Roswynd adjust the strap to the correct length. "On the back of the quiver there are two straps to carry your bow with."

"Oh." Roswynd attempted to peer around her back and chuckled at her mistake. "That is clever."

"First, we will work on your stance," Tharon said, then stepped up to the line. With the bow in her left hand, she positioned her feet and said, "Mimic me."

"Right," Roswynd muttered and studied her wife's stance. Unlike Tharon, she pulled on the string even though she had no arrow.

"Do not release the string without an arrow." Tharon lowered her bow and narrowed her eyes at Roswynd. "You do not want to shoot dry. It is bad for the string."

Roswynd blushed at her mistake and gently returned the string, then let go of it. "Sorry," she murmured, but held her position otherwise.

Tharon walked around her wife, slow and deliberate. She kicked out Roswynd's right boot to widen her stance a little more. "Turn." Grabbing Roswynd's hips, she adjusted Roswynd's position. "Higher here." She raised Roswynd's left arm, which had the bow.

Roswynd was certain her heart was the loudest war drum in all Gyldren. Their bodies were so close and Tharon's scent was alluring. A moan almost broke free, but she bit her lip in time.

"Draw the string back as far as you can," Tharon ordered. She remained behind Roswynd with her hands resting on Roswynd's petite hips. "But do not release it."

Roswynd cleared her throat, grabbed the string, and pulled it back as far as possible. "How is that?" She felt the strain in her arm and shoulders within a few heartbeats, and she fought to not show it. Worse was how Tharon's closeness was affecting her, making her legs weak and mind muddled with forbidden images of Tharon touching her.

"Good." Tharon glanced at Roswynd's fingers on the string and said, "You can use two or three fingers. You will figure out what feels natural once you start releasing arrows." After Roswynd's faint nod, Tharon smirked and leaned in closer to her wife, bending over some. "How much longer can you last?" she whispered in Roswynd's ear.

Roswynd choked on the question's double entendre, then the string slipped from her fingers. "Shit! Tharon!" She elbowed Tharon right in the stomach, swung around, and said, "Do not be a dick!"

Tharon rubbed her abdomen and stepped back after the retribution for her tease. She eyed Roswynd and bared her teeth.

With a blush, Roswynd held out her free hand and said, "S-Sorry. You caught me…" The heat in her cheeks spread across her face and down her neck. *Oh sweet Divine, is she going to kill me now?*

Tharon smirked and said, "Let us try nocking an arrow." She retook her earlier spot next to Roswynd, grabbed two arrows, and gave one to her wife. "When you nock an arrow, you want to point the arrowhead toward the ground. You do not want to accidently release it and hurt someone." Tharon nocked her arrow, keeping the bow pointed low.

Roswynd was familiar with nocking the arrow from watching Tharon when they were young.

"Remember you have that shelf to balance the front of the arrow shaft," Tharon said.

Nodding, Roswynd rested the shaft on the shelf and continued pointing the arrowhead at the ground.

"I am going to turn this way so you can see my stance better." Tharon rotated until she was turned a hundred eighty degrees from Roswynd. From this angle, it was easier for Roswynd to take in Tharon's form. "I use two fingers. One above the nock and one below." She drew the arrow back and held her position, ready to release. "The arrow's nock should be close to your cheek or mouth area." She didn't release the arrow but allowed the string to go back. "Your turn, but do not release the arrow."

Roswynd nodded, lifted her arms, and drew the string back with the arrow nocked in place.

"Lift your right arm higher." Tharon placed her bow on the ground, then adjusted Roswynd's form again. "A nice *T* stance." She took one step back and nodded at Roswynd. "Good. Now loosen the arrow."

Roswynd did so and wondered if she'd ever get a chance to shoot one. It was making her somewhat antsy, but she respected Tharon's teaching style. Plus, Tharon was speaking more than any previous time, which warmed Roswynd. She wished every conversation between them were like this.

"Before you shoot your first arrow, there is one more thing." Tharon came to Roswynd's left side. "Give me the arrow." After she received it, she tucked it under her arm and said, "Draw again."

Roswynd lifted the bow, drew the string, and set her stance. With Tharon so close again, her breathing quickened, but she remained focused on her sight through the grip.

"When you release the arrow, the string will come back, and it can scrape the inside of your left forearm." Tharon touched the area on Roswynd's arm, which was covered in her tunic's sleeve. "Right in here. After about six shots, you will have a nice bruise."

"I remember that on your arm," Roswynd whispered. That was early on, and then the bruises faded and never occurred again. "How did you stop it?"

"It is how you hold the bow. You have to twist your left arm out." Tharon held out her hand and said, "Let me see your bow." Handing over the bow, Tharon raised it and drew the string. "This is how you are holding it right now." She twisted her left arm to demonstrate how it should look when Roswynd held it. "This is the safe way to hold it."

Roswynd received the weapon back and attempted the new adjustment. "It feels strange."

"For a while you will have to remind yourself to do it until it becomes second nature. If you forget, the bow string will remind you." Tharon grinned, took a step back, and held out the arrow. "Shoot your first arrow."

Grinning, Roswynd took the arrow, nocked it, raised the bow, and drew the string back. "Does it matter where I aim?"

"Try releasing it first, then we will work on sight." Tharon folded her arms and watched Roswynd, but taunted, "It is an entire building anyway."

Roswynd rolled her eyes, then focused on the fallen structure in front of her. She wasn't sure what she was waiting for, since all she needed to do was release the arrow. After a deep breath, she allowed her fingers to roll, then the string snapped forward and sent the arrow flying toward the building. "Shit!" she yelped when the string swiped the inside of her arm.

Tharon lifted an eyebrow and took a hesitant step toward her wife. Her earlier grin was replaced with a worried frown.

"That stings so bad." Roswynd blinked away the burning tears, then pulled up the sleeve to reveal the rash forming over her skin. She blew out a strained breath and shook her arm again.

Tharon shifted closer and studied Roswynd's arm without touching her. She rumbled, then pointed at the building.

Roswynd followed her wife's direction, then her jaw went loose. The arrow had embedded itself directly in front of them, sticking out from one of the logs to the left of the front door. She flushed at her small accomplishment.

"Good start," Tharon praised. "Now the fun part."

"Which is?" Roswynd watched her wife, who went around her to pick up the bow.

"Practice, practice, practice." Tharon extracted two arrows from the quiver and handed one to Roswynd. She ordered Roswynd to nock and draw the new arrow. This time she reminded Roswynd to mind her left arm. Together they started shooting arrows at the building until all of them were spent. Once the quiver was empty, Tharon showed Roswynd how to collect the arrows from their target without damaging the arrowheads.

They practiced two more rounds before Tharon backed them up to the next line, putting more distance between them and the structure. The first round at the new line didn't go as well as the first three rounds at the closest line. Tharon proceeded to explain aiming, giving Roswynd pointers on how to hit her mark.

Roswynd counted that merely six of her arrows actually hit the general area she was aiming for. After releasing the last arrow, she noticed the shaking in her arms and shoulders. She peered back at the next two lines that Tharon had made in the ground for her and grumbled at herself.

Tharon rested the lower limb of her bow on the ground and studied Roswynd. "Perhaps it is time for a break."

"I can do another round." Roswynd kept her chin up, not letting her wife see her tiredness.

Tharon nodded and joined Roswynd in collecting the twenty-four arrows. So far they hadn't lost any, but that was due to the sheer size of their target. Back at the second line, Roswynd nocked her first arrow and continued her practice. Tharon shot a few arrows but left most to Roswynd.

When Roswynd released the ninth arrow, her aim was the worst yet. The arrow went way off target and buzzed through an already broken window, going inside the building. She groaned and rubbed her damp forehead.

"You are getting tired," Tharon said. "Your aim is not going to improve at this point."

Roswynd agreed with Tharon, but she wasn't ready to stop until her quiver was empty. She reached for another arrow and focused again on her gigantic target.

Tharon remained quiet and watched Roswynd, then glanced a few times at the spots where the arrow struck the structure. Eight of them bounced off and landed in the ground. It was the largest amount so far that hadn't sunk into the building.

Roswynd aimed the last arrow, lining it up with the front door as a pseudofocused target. She released the arrow, which sailed through the air and dug between two boards in the door. She sighed, and relief flooded her body after completing the last round.

Leaving her bow on the ground, Tharon followed Roswynd to the building and started retrieving the arrows.

"I will get the one inside," Roswynd said after she extracted the one from the door. She shoved the door open, entered, and went to her left, but she was forced to hop over debris and junk. The arrow was nestled into the wall opposite the window. After freeing it she noticed a stench that drew her attention to the left. Up against the wall, a dark, sunken face stared back at her.

A scream erupted from Roswynd, echoing through the fallen structure. She scrambled toward the front door, tripping on rubble and almost collapsing until a strong arm hooked her.

Tharon pointed her sword toward the corpse pinned to the wall while she drew Roswynd against her. She growled low, sheathed her sword, and assisted Roswynd out of the building. Once outside, Roswynd gulped fresh air and leaned heavily into Tharon, waiting to see if her stomach would revolt. Tharon rumbled, then picked up Roswynd into her arms and cradled her. She took Roswynd back to their horses and set her on a large rock. Roswynd almost whined at the loss of Tharon's closeness.

"Wait here. I will retrieve our belongings."

Roswynd nodded and continued to take deep breaths. In her right hand, she clutched the arrow from inside the structure. She slipped it into the quiver with the other one. When Tharon returned, she lifted her head and asked, "How long do you think he has been dead?"

"At least a week," Tharon replied. "He was murdered, if the iron blade sticking out of his stomach is anything to go by." She loaded the arrows into the quiver.

Roswynd groaned and leaned forward after propping up her legs. "I have seen one too many bodies this month," she muttered, then cringed at her mistake.

Tharon rumbled but went to their horses and lashed down the bows. She returned with a waterskin and handed it to Roswynd.

"Thanks." Roswynd took a few mouthfuls, then returned it.

Tharon drank some as well and remained quiet, standing near Roswynd. She was staring toward the forgotten tower and appeared deep in thought. Going back to

Obsidian, she retrieved the wrapped sweet bread from Ewan and brought it to Roswynd.

Roswynd shook her head before Tharon could open the bread. "I am not hungry."

Pausing, Tharon narrowed her eyes and said, "You have not eaten since breakfast." She set the covered bread down next to Roswynd. "The archery weakened you sooner than it should have."

With a sigh Roswynd pointed toward the tower. "I cannot exactly eat after what I saw in there." It was a lie, though. Her faint nausea was gone, but she didn't care to eat. The suspicious look on Tharon's face was a bad sign. She lowered her gaze, hoping that Tharon didn't sniff out her fib.

Tharon's chest shook with a discontented sound. She came closer, hopped onto the rock, and took a seat behind Roswynd. First, she removed the quiver and dropped it to the ground, then lifted Roswynd onto her left thigh somewhat similar to the night after the incident on Golden Wheat Road.

"Tharon, I am not a damn pup." Roswynd pushed against her wife's legs, desperate to break their contact. But she was still weak from the archery, and Tharon's strong scent was invading her senses. She whimpered and slumped against Tharon's larger body. Again, her heart thundered in her chest until she allowed herself to relax into Tharon, who was rumbling near her ear.

Tharon kept her arm behind Roswynd's back and pressed her other hand flat against her wife's stomach for another minute. Her pheromones further calmed and coaxed

Roswynd. Tharon picked up the bread, placed it in Roswynd's lap, and opened it. A dagger appeared in Tharon's hand, and she sliced a few pieces.

Similar to last time, Roswynd latched onto Tharon's wrist when the morsel of bread was brought toward her mouth. She told herself to fight harder, to not get entangled in Tharon's care, or let herself enjoy it. But again, she failed to stay in control of the situation. Her hand fell away and she allowed Tharon to feed her. The bread's honey filled her mouth, then the nutty flavor took over. A soft moan escaped her from the wonderful taste; her stomach growled in agreement.

Leaning in closer, Tharon nuzzled Roswynd's temple and grinned. "You have always been a bad liar." She picked up another piece and brought it to Roswynd again.

Roswynd frowned at the truth and sighed, knowing she had lost this round. She accepted the bread and enjoyed the mouthful. The honey pem nut was her most favorite flavor. "We are not supposed to do this." She indicated their current situation. As royalty they were trained to hold themselves to a higher standard than the peasants, who would slip into their primal instincts. In truth Roswynd believed it was a bunch of horseshit, but her tutors had hammered it into her regardless.

Tharon chuckled in her wife's ear and whispered, "They can fucking suck my cock."

"Tharon!" Roswynd turned bright red, from the tips of her ears down to her chest, at the crude remark. She squirmed in Tharon's lap at the mention of a certain part of her wife's anatomy. Now it seemed like a bad idea to get Tharon to talk to her, if this was the kind of response she would receive back. From the smugness on Tharon's face, she suspected the comment was meant to get a rise out of Roswynd.

With another chunk of bread in hand, Tharon offered more to her wife but didn't push it.

Roswynd took a deep breath and glanced sidelong at Tharon, who was stoic again, as if the earlier conversation hadn't happened. With a sigh, she took the offering and enjoyed it rather than thinking about how they were going against royal traditions. *When have we ever cared about those, or about what people think?*

At some point Tharon had slipped a hand under Roswynd's tunic, and she now was massaging Roswynd's lower back. Roswynd couldn't help melting deeper into Tharon and savoring all the attention. For ten years, she was starved of Tharon's touch and comfort. They were supposed to be enemies, but they were married, and Roswynd didn't smell any deceit in Tharon's current actions. Each time Tharon lifted a piece, the golden fede ring shone in the afternoon sunlight, reminding Roswynd of their vows to each other.

Roswynd ate about half the loaf, but a partial slice rested on the cloth. "You have not had any." She received a soft rumble, making her frown. "I noticed you did not eat any sweet breads at our wedding celebration. You used to eat them all the time when…" Her rambling tapered off, then she frowned at the bread in her lap. But Tharon hadn't stopped rubbing her lower back, indicating that maybe it was safe. Roswynd couldn't eat the half slice, but she didn't want to waste any. Taking a risk, she broke the partial slice into two pieces and picked up one.

With a bright orange eye and a hazy one, Tharon stared into Roswynd, then her lips curled back a little, showing some of her canines. At first she appeared threatening, but her pheromones were still inviting and warm, keeping Roswynd calm.

"Please," Roswynd whispered and waited for Tharon's decision. To her delight, Tharon leaned in to accept the food. Roswynd hummed and slipped the piece into Tharon's mouth, then soft lips covered her fingertips. A sharp gasp escaped Roswynd, and she moaned when Tharon's tongue brushed her fingers.

Tharon withdrew and ate the morsel but never broke their eye contact.

Roswynd panted some and clawed her nails into Tharon's hip. Her face was on fire, but it was so hard to tell herself it was wrong. She wanted to feel it all again, to ensure it was real. She needed the memory seared in her mind. Picking up the last piece, she tempted fate and hoped Tharon would do it again.

This time Tharon had a wolfish smile and remained still, toying with Roswynd, who was holding her breath. After a long moment, Tharon rumbled and leaned in to accept the offer. Going even slower, she took the bread, then licked one of Roswynd's fingers before sucking on her thumb.

"By Divine," Roswynd murmured, struggling with the onslaught of sensations coursing through her body. A strange but strong throb started between her legs. Then as Tharon's lips pulled away from her thumb, she moaned and found herself wanting to lean in to kiss Tharon after so many long years. To have their lips touch again. To reconnect with Tharon. And Roswynd needed to know how the sweet bread tasted on Tharon's tongue. Somehow, she found herself closer, her lips caressing Tharon's silky ones. *Your Tharon is dead*, a voice whispered in her head and caused fear to jab her in the chest, crush the air in her lungs, and send her tumbling out of Tharon's lap.

With a soft cry, Roswynd hit the ground on her ass and crawled backward until she had some distance from her wife. She was panting and shaking after nearly giving into her desires. The bread had fallen to the grass, too, but it was still in one chunk.

For once, Tharon had a distraught look, then her lips pulled into a frown. Her eyes were stormy and dark from her heightened arousal. Her strong pheromones swirled around Roswynd, jerking at her senses. After a deep breath, Tharon stood, then picked up Roswynd and placed her on the rock. Without a word, she took the bread, cloth, and quiver, and walked away with them.

Roswynd groaned and rubbed her face, which hurt from the furrow across her brow. "Damn it," she muttered to herself. After several deep breaths, she gazed over at Tharon, who mounted Obsidian. *Is she leaving without me?*

Tharon remained poised in the saddle and stared toward Roswynd. She said nothing but seemed to be waiting. It was time to leave and go back to Skye Hunter Castle.

Roswynd slid off the rock and went to her horse without looking at Tharon. She put the reins over Dragonfly's head, then went to the saddle and grabbed the horn. For a moment she stood there and considered what happened on the rock. "I am an idiot," she said under her breath. Shaking her head, Roswynd hauled herself into the saddle, ready for the ride back. It was going to be a tense ride to Skye Hunter Castle.

* * *

Supper with Roswynd's family was similar to the night before. Garrett asked about their stroll through the city. Then they discussed the day trip to Stormbreaker Landing and the plans afterward, which included going to the other two major cities on the east side of the White Razor Mountains. Roswynd noticed that Myla flashed her questioning looks, reminding her that she had to ask their father about Myla coming with them tomorrow.

Her two brothers, Archibold and Josse, left early. Both were tired from their studies with their tutors. Toward the end of supper, Myla opened the door of opportunity further by asking her mother to play draughts in the ladies' chamber. As she left with their mother, Myla gave her sister a final pointed look.

Roswynd sighed and waited until her father was finished speaking to Tharon. She sipped on her cup of water and put together her arguments about why Myla should join them tomorrow.

"Yes, about five days in Montisgard," Garrett agreed with Tharon.

Catching the brief silence, Roswynd jumped into the conversation and said, "About tomorrow's trip to Stormbreaker Landing…" She smiled when her father shifted his attention to her. "I was thinking it would be good for Myla to join us."

"Myla?" Garrett frowned and studied his daughter, gauging her angle. "Did she put you up to this?"

"Father, I need little assistance in coming up with ideas." Roswynd hoped her playful smile won her some credit, but she doubted it. She went serious and said, "I feel it would be good for her to leave the castle and see Stormbreaker Landing."

"She is to spend the day with her tutor tomorrow," Garrett said, eyeing his daughter.

"Oh." Roswynd pursed her lips, shrugged, and said, "She would learn more from the experience than she could from a book about our great seaport." Beside her, Tharon was studying her too.

But then Tharon turned to Garrett and said, "The experience and salt air would benefit Myla. Has she been there before?"

Garrett rubbed his chin and studied the pair, then murmured, "No."

Tharon nodded and said, "Then the experience would benefit her. Now that our war has ceased, it is far safer."

Roswynd hadn't expected Tharon's help and wondered about it. Why was Tharon persistent about seeing Myla join them? Did Tharon have a strange, devious plan for Myla? If that was true, Roswynd could not imagine what. However, when they were young, Tharon often encouraged Myla to join her and Roswynd on trips to the market, on horseback rides, and on nature walks. Perhaps it was an old habit returning?

"I suppose we can take more guards and the carriage," Garrett murmured, then nodded. "I will ask her tonight."

"Thank you, Father. I am certain she will be excited to join us." Roswynd suspected her father wasn't averse to riding in the carriage with Myla rather than on horseback. The journey to Stormbreaker Landing would take about two hours one way. In some regards, Roswynd was looking forward to the journey and the visit to the seaport. The horseback ride would be nice, and dinner in Stormbreaker Landing would mean shrimp.

"Well then, I shall retire for the night after I see your sister. We have an early day tomorrow." Garrett said goodnight to them and left through the side door.

Roswynd stood from her chair and waited for Tharon to join her. They returned to their room in silence. Roswynd struggled with whether or not to thank Tharon for the help with convincing her father about Myla. A part of her still believed Tharon had a hidden agenda, so in the end, Roswynd said nothing.

Their quietness was deafening at times. After their return from the archery lesson, neither of them spoke while they cleaned up and prepared for supper. Roswynd had changed back into the dress from this morning, then waited for Tharon to accompany her to the dining hall. The strain between them had been almost tangible. Even now, it felt like little pinpricks all over Roswynd's body.

Once in their room, Roswynd escaped to the balcony, relieved to have some fresh air, even if the night was growing chilly. She leaned against the stone handrail, then looked toward the south. The city's larger streets were glowing from the overhead lamps that the city guard had lit an hour ago. Already the days were getting shorter, signaling the nearness of harvest and winter. Sunstone was considered the last month of summer and a time for the weakening of daylight.

With a sigh, Roswynd turned her head to the left and gazed up the length of the tall keep. Warm light from one of the other balconies shone through the windows. That particular balcony was attached to her father's office. With a frown, she muttered, "So much for turning in early." He might be meeting with Donnchad about the trip tomorrow, especially if Myla agreed to go. There was no doubt Myla would have agreed, as it was her hope to see Stormbreaker Landing too.

Straight ahead toward the eastern horizon, the moon showed more of its ring. It wouldn't be long before the next full moon, when the ring would be complete. In the deep winter months, the winter lights known as Gyldr's light reflected in the night sky. A few times she and Tharon had danced on the ballroom's balcony under Gyldr's light. Each one of their couples dances was more special than the previous, which left Roswynd with bittersweet memories.

Today turned into another distressing memory after Roswynd almost kissed Tharon. The archery lesson had gone so well and helped Tharon open up a little. Since seeing each other again, Tharon had kept up her guard around Roswynd. She refused to speak Roswynd's name, as if speaking it would shatter a barrier. Even though they weren't talking about their complicated past, they had at least been communicating about something and taken a step forward, only for Roswynd to destroy it in a few moments, reverting it back to edgy silence.

The almost-kiss itself was the ugliest, most difficult piece. They had been in an intimate embrace to begin with, close and feeding each other. In that moment Tharon was being an Alpha, but the tender half that few Alphas showed to people. In Tharon's Alpha mind, she was caring for her Omega by having her eat. Roswynd had taken advantage of Tharon's trust by almost kissing her, but then she recoiled out of fear. There was no doubt that Roswynd's scent had broadcasted her dread about sharing a kiss with the enemy. But Tharon was her wife and had been her best friend— someone she'd once loved deeply. Admittedly, in her heart she knew she still loved Tharon.

With a groan, Roswynd rubbed her face and noticed the onset of a mild headache. Her mind wouldn't stop replaying the brief but painful distraught on Tharon's face. *She wanted that kiss as much as I did.*

But it was far too late.

"What am I doing?" she muttered to herself as tears welled in her eyes. Nothing was making sense anymore. Her heart jerked her in one direction while her mind pulled her in another. Roswynd started breathing hard and clutched her head. A scream built up in her chest, then clawed in her throat. All the noise in her head ate away at her self-control as the scream pushed farther up inside her. But then a familiar, strong scent wrapped around her and calmed her mind. Taking deep breaths, Roswynd allowed the Alpha pheromones to soothe her before peering over her shoulder.

Tharon brought a cloak to Roswynd and placed it over her shoulders without a word, then headed back to the room until Roswynd called her name. She stopped in the center of the balcony, her back to Roswynd.

"I am sorry for what I did," Roswynd said, voice rough with emotions. She adjusted the cloak over her shoulders and held on to it at her sides. "Everything between us is confusing and complicated." Closing her eyes, she whispered, "You will hardly speak to me, and all I want to do is fix what happened to us." She opened her eyes again, staring at Tharon's back and willing her to open up. Again, the tears started, but she blinked them away. Her voice had grown shaky but no weaker. "Do you not wish to fix this?" She clenched her lip so hard that a coppery taste filled her mouth. If her plea failed to turn Tharon, there was no hope or even purpose. When Tharon faced her, she trembled and twisted the cloak through her fingers.

Tharon closed the space and studied Roswynd's features that glowed under the half-moon. She slipped an arm around Roswynd's waist and drew their bodies together. "We are wives now." Lifting her hand, she cupped Roswynd's chin and tilted up her head a little more. "We could be lovers." She grazed her thumb across Roswynd's lower lip, grinning at Roswynd's small hitch of breath. Her thumb rested against the bleeding spot. "Even mates."

Roswynd was gasping for air while Tharon whispered soft truths to her. The idea that they could be lovers caused a flutter deep in her belly, then the throb returned between her legs. Her heart swelled at the promises, until Tharon's grin fell away.

"But we can never be friends again after all that has happened," Tharon added. She wiped the blood off Roswynd's lip and smeared it across her fingers. The moon gave her orange eyes a silver glow as she bowed her head closer. "The sooner you can accept that, the easier this will be for you."

"N-No." Roswynd shook her head and pushed against Tharon, who tightened her arm. Tharon couldn't mean such words or believe that they would never be friends again. It was *wrong*. "N-No, no!" She gritted her teeth, trying to hold back the tears. They fell without permission and scorched her flushed cheeks. "No! Please, Tharon!" She threw a fist into Tharon's chest as desperation took hold of her. "Please! We have to fix this!" Another fist landed, but into Tharon's side.

With a grunt, Tharon took it, then growled and latched on to Roswynd's wrists.

"Tharon, please *listen* to me!" Roswynd was growing louder. Her voice was probably carrying across the castle grounds and perhaps stirring the guards. She didn't care because she had to get through to Tharon. "I kn-know we can fix this." She felt her insides cracking and sharp blades cutting through her.

Tharon simply rumbled. She bent her knees, grabbed Roswynd around her waist, and lifted her.

"No!" Roswynd's cry was ignored as Tharon hefted her over her shoulder similar to their wedding night. They were headed back into the bedroom, away from prying ears. "Tharon, *please*," she implored again, tears coating her face. How could Tharon believe they couldn't fix their friendship? Resolve their past? They had *always* worked through their differences.

Tharon closed the balcony door with her foot and shoulder, then took Roswynd to the bed. The fireplace was the sole light in the room.

Roswynd tried to wiggle free, but her wife was far stronger. She cried out and clawed at Tharon's black jerkin, then slammed her knee into Tharon's upper stomach.

With a low growl, Tharon lifted Roswynd off and placed her on the bed. She moved fast and crawled over Roswynd, who nailed her with another punch but to the jaw.

Roswynd stiffened and gasped after hitting her wife by mistake. Flaming orange eyes recentered on her, and she whined in worry. "Please," she repeated in a shaky voice. "We can fix this. All of this."

Tharon bared her teeth and dragged Roswynd to the center of the bed, remaining over her. "No, it is done."

Roswynd shook her head and latched onto Tharon's shoulder. "You do not believe that." The speed of her heart was wild and yet crushing her. The earlier scream bubbled in her chest again, needing to be set free. But she still tried to fight it, all of it. "Please, Tharon, I *miss* my best friend." The tears turned into sobs. "W-We made promises t-to each other." Her head hurt so bad and the agony was piercing her, going deeper the more Tharon resisted her. "Y-You promised me!"

Tharon pinned Roswynd with her body. Using her right hand, she covered most of Roswynd's mouth and whispered, "Scream for me."

Somehow the demand freed the overwhelming scream buried in Roswynd's chest. The powerful cry was muffled by the scarred palm that had sealed their friendship pact so long ago. Roswynd buried her nails into Tharon's shoulder while her other hand wrestled against Tharon's hand over her mouth. Her face was on fire, wet, and hurting from the surge of rage. How could Tharon *not* need to fix their past? They had traded vows as friends.

Bowing her head closer to Roswynd, Tharon murmured, "That is it. Let it out." She moved part of her hand out of the way, letting Roswynd gasp for air. But the next violent scream she caught with her palm again. "Give me all your anger." Another one of Roswynd's knees landed on her, close to her crotch. She grunted, then growled and closed her eyes.

Roswynd wrenched on Tharon's wrist, but she was far too weak. She wriggled and screamed again, but it was covered like the last ones. As it died on her lips, Tharon moved her hand out of the way, and she gulped the fresh air. "Please, Tharon," she whispered between whimpers, clinging to the last shred of her dying hope.

Tharon sighed and ran her thumb across Roswynd's lips. "No. There is no returning to the past." She held Roswynd's gaze, showing the hollowness in her eyes.

Closing her own eyes, Roswynd arched back and her body pressed tighter against Tharon. Yet another cry burst from her lips and again was squashed by Tharon's hand.

"It will become easier," Tharon said in a firm but distant voice, then took a few deep breaths herself.

Roswynd collapsed to the bed after the fury faded from her. Her mouth was freed, allowing her to gasp. She was spent, every last piece of her. She moaned in anguish and shook her head. "*Tharon*," she whispered and cupped her wife's flushed cheeks. Without thought or reason, Roswynd pulled Tharon down; their lips brushed together, so faint and delicate.

Tharon rumbled and waited for Roswynd's decision.

Pulling back a fraction, Roswynd faltered but then drove up and crashed their lips together. She pushed harder, forcing her tongue into Tharon's mouth. They groaned together, then their tongues fought and caressed until they were both left breathless. Roswynd was panting and clinging to Tharon, her cheeks still damp. Now she felt utterly drained of life.

With a sigh Tharon lowered her body, balancing her weight, and started to cocoon Roswynd from the harsh new reality, seeming weary from Roswynd's angry release. She dropped the side of her head next to Roswynd's and closed her eyes.

Roswynd hooked her arms around Tharon, the lord commander of White Sommer and the Black Wulf. Not Tharon, her best friend. No, this was her wife, the only part that she was allowed to have now. Perhaps it was easier to let go rather than fight anymore. Wars were so exhausting and left everyone dead.

With each slowing heartbeat, Roswynd's eyelids drooped lower. She relaxed her head against Tharon's temple and mumbled something incoherent. But it seemed as if Tharon understood whatever it might have been because she heard Tharon's last promise before she fell asleep.

"You do not need to fix us for us to work."

Chapter 11

Date: 35 White Wulf 815G
(About 11 Years Ago)

Tharon dismounted from the horse and went over to her friend, who was getting off her horse too. She helped Roswynd to the ground and smiled at her.

"Are you having a nice day?" Roswynd asked, mirroring her best friend's warm spirit.

"It is perfect." Tharon admired the sunny hue of Roswynd's hazel eye and the vibrant sapphire of the other one. Her chest was filled with joy and contentment after this week's merriment at the Howling Eagle Festival. Last night their two families had traveled from Wulfbite to Leeward, spent the night at Proudpeak Hall, and then arrived at Earna this morning. The second half of the festival was in full swing when they rode into the city.

The sun was low in the western horizon, close to touching the White Razor Mountains. Roswynd had suggested they steal away for a horseback ride and take a break from the festival. No one would miss them. Besides, it was Tharon's fourteenth birthday, and spending alone time with Roswynd was her most favorite gift.

"I love your birthday," Roswynd said, grinning now.

"Only because it means yours is tomorrow," Tharon teased, then drew Roswynd into her arms. She rumbled low and nuzzled into Roswynd's neck, which was a bit furry from the heavy cloak.

Roswynd chuckled and tangled a gloved hand in Tharon's braided hair. "Well, that is true too. Perhaps this year Father will finally give me a horse!" She earned a soft laugh from Tharon.

"Come along." Tharon separated but took Roswynd's hand into hers. Together, they walked up the incline to their favorite spot in front of the waterfall. The tree that they often climbed was covered in snow and ice, but they had somewhere else to sit in the winter months. "Would you like a fire?"

Roswynd nodded and brushed against Tharon as they neared the two tree stumps. They brushed the snow off the stumps and removed the snow from the fire ring, which they borrowed from Skye Hunter Castle. Tucked behind a boulder was a pile of firewood and kindling that stayed dry thanks to a canvas tarp. After a few minutes, a small fire was burning in the ring. They sat side by side and admired the frozen waterfall reflecting the sunlight.

"Are you hungry?" Roswynd asked.

"A little," Tharon whispered, blushing because shortly ago they had shared a sweet bread at the festival.

Roswynd giggled and retrieved a snack bar from the inside of her cloak. "Here. I snatched one for you."

"Thank you." Tharon kissed Roswynd's temple and devoured the sweet, nutty treat while humming.

Roswynd shook her head, then leaned against Tharon and hooked her right arm around Tharon's back. "I, um…"

Tharon stiffened and peered down at her friend, who had a soft blush. "What is wrong?"

"Nothing at all," Roswynd replied in a gentle voice. "I simply… I might have bought something for your birthday. Or perhaps it is for my birthday." She fidgeted, and her blush brightened the longer she rambled. "Our birthdays."

Tharon tilted her head to the left and studied her friend's peculiar expression. "What is it?" They never exchanged gifts for their birthdays. At first, they were too young to understand the concept of trading presents between friends. Their parents gave them one or two gifts but nothing else. As they grew older, they agreed spending time alone was the best gift, especially because their birthdays fell in the middle of the busy festival.

Roswynd straightened and fidgeted while she stared at the campfire. "It is silly, I guess."

Tharon shook her head and again asked, "What is it? You know I will not think it is silly."

Brightening some, Roswynd reached into her cloak and pulled out a small satchel that she'd tied to her waist. She opened the satchel and extracted a square wooden box that had a tiny latch on it. On the top, the box had a strange symbol burned into it.

Tharon touched the box's lid, feeling compelled to do so. A soft vibration met her fingertips, but it faded to nothing. She wondered if it had been real.

Roswynd flipped the latch and opened the box. "I bought it from an old lady in the market at Wulfbite. She said they are the Bracelets of Ælfwynn, a goddess from the Ancient Ones' time." She held the two bracelets in her palm. The pair were simple in nature, forged from two ropes of bronze, twisted together into one strand. It appeared that the bracelets had been one single piece at the start of the process, then severed in half and shaped into bracelets. At one end, the bracelets had a tiny hook neck while the other end had a loop clasp.

"They are beautiful," Tharon said and touched one, running her thumb over the twisted braid. "Why are they special?" She sensed how well they had been cared for over the centuries.

"The old lady said that the god Ælfwynn was the goddess of friendship. So these are friendship bracelets." Roswynd reached into the box again and pulled out a long and tattered folded cloth. She opened it and revealed the writing on the thin strip. "It is hard to read, but she explained that there is an accompanying spell."

"Spell?" Tharon frowned, but took the cloth, stretching out her arms and getting the firelight to shine on it. Like Roswynd, she couldn't read much of the wording on the strip, since it was so old. "What is the spell?"

"We make a blood pact," Roswynd replied. "We use this small blade." The bronze blade was sharp on one side and blunt on the other. It looked as though it had been forged from the same piece of bronze as the bracelets. "We cut our palms, tie our hands together with that cloth, put on the bracelets, and make vows of friendship."

"That sounds simple," Tharon murmured and lowered the cloth to her thigh. She picked up a bracelet and studied it from one end to the other. Even though it was bronze, it glowed as brilliantly as gold.

"The old lady also mentioned that after we make the friendship pact to each other, the bracelets' magic would be evoked."

Tharon made a small noise in her throat, then looked at Roswynd. "Evoked?"

Roswynd nodded and replied, "They are enchanted and would allow us to always find each other."

"Oh," Tharon murmured and stared at the Bracelets of Ælfwynn. They were fascinating and ancient, especially if they had such a story behind them. The idea that magic was involved intrigued Tharon even more. Back in the Ancient Ones' time, magic was plentiful and a part of life, practiced as a skill or gift called dricraft. But then it was lost all at once. Today scholars believed that shards of magic still lingered in objects. Was it possible that Roswynd had indeed found jewelry with magic still imbued in them?

"It is silly. S-Sorry," Roswynd muttered and took the bracelets from Tharon's lap. "I should not have—"

"No." Tharon latched onto her friend's wrist. "No, it is not silly, Ros." She covered Roswynd's hand and the bracelets with her other hand. "I was thinking about the possibility that they are magical."

Roswynd shrugged and whispered, "Perhaps they are not, but maybe they are." She peered up and met Tharon's tender gaze. "Regardless, I fancy what they mean."

Tharon smiled and leaned closer to Roswynd. "I do too." She touched their foreheads together and asked, "Do you wish to trade vows with me?"

"Do not be an idiot. Of course I do." Roswynd withdrew her head and looked at Tharon with determination. "You are my best friend and nothing will change that."

Nodding, Tharon squeezed their hands together and said, "Then let us do it." She and Roswynd moved their log stools closer to the campfire. After adding more wood, they took off their gloves and faced each other, thighs locked together.

"I want to clean the blade first," Tharon said and snatched it from the box. With a steady hand, she nudged it into the glowing embers and let it sit there for a minute.

"So we have to cut our palms, tie our hands together, and exchange vows," Roswynd said.

"But when do we put on the bracelets?"

"Oh, wait. We should do that before we tie our hands," Roswynd murmured.

"Or before cutting our palms," Tharon suggested, grinning at her friend's thoughtful look.

"Yes." Roswynd retrieved the bracelets and gave one to Tharon, who placed it in her lap.

Using her glove, Tharon retrieved the bronze blade, which had a slight glow. She pressed it into the snow to cool it off, then wiped it with the inside of her tunic. "We are ready now."

Roswynd nodded and said, "How about we do each step for the other person? I put on your bracelet and you cut my palm."

Tharon chuckled and smirked at her friend. "You simply do not wish to cut your own hand."

Roswynd rolled her eyes, but the flush in her cheeks confirmed it. "I can cut my hand."

"I will do it," Tharon said, then took the bracelet from her knee. "Ready to start?" Roswynd nodded, so she brought the bracelet closer, but hesitated. "Which hand and wrist?"

Roswynd looked between her own hands, then held out her right one. "Our right palms for the blood pact." Then she held out her left arm. "Left wrists for the bracelets."

Tharon wiggled the bracelet's opening past Roswynd's small wrist, turned it, and hooked the clasp into place. She offered her left wrist next.

Roswynd copied her friend's earlier motions and smiled now that they had matching bracelets. "Cut my hand first." She opened her palm, bit her lip, and vibrated her left leg while she waited for it to be done.

Tharon cupped Roswynd's open palm, then brought the glinting blade to the soft skin. "Ready?"

"Do it," Roswynd snapped, then began panting some.

Tharon clenched her bottom lip to hold down a giggle at her friend's nervousness. Roswynd was always a bit squeamish when it came to blood, even the smallest of cuts. Roswynd would rather suffer a hundred broken bones than one laceration, as long as all the blood stayed inside her. Once she'd made a decision about how to do the cut, Tharon was fast and sliced the skin open from below the thumb to the underside of Roswynd's pinky. Roswynd hissed and looked away for a beat. Tharon considered cleaning the blade again, but it made no difference, as their blood would be mixed in a minute.

Roswynd took the blade next, held Tharon's right hand, and pressed the blade into the tender skin. She was breathing even harder now and looked a little pale. With a deep breath, she started slicing the skin open.

"Ros! That is too deep!" Tharon screamed and pretended to be hurt until Roswynd screamed back, then jumped up. "I kid you!" She hopped up and grabbed her friend's arm with her left hand.

"You dick!" Roswynd shoved her friend, then released a huge breath while Tharon cackled. She pointed the bloody tip at Tharon and snapped, "Sit!"

Tharon smirked, then cleared her throat and took her seat again. She held out her palm, which was halfway cut open. The blood was already seeping out, much like on Roswynd's hand.

This time Roswynd went faster and tossed the blade into the snow. A huge gust of air left her, and her shoulders fell.

Tharon squeezed Roswynd's leg, which was between her thighs. "Now we have to tie our hands." She picked up the strip that had landed in the snow when she was tormenting Roswynd.

Nodding, Roswynd refocused on the task. She took Tharon's right hand into her bleeding palm, resting both on Tharon's knee. Together, they slipped the ancient wrap under their joined hands, then managed to tie two knots on the top.

Tharon smiled at the union of their hands and sensed their mixed blood smearing against her skin. She noticed how Roswynd was calmer now that the blood was gone from her view. "Do you know what you are going to say?"

Roswynd nodded and asked, "Can I go first, please?"

For a moment, Tharon was flustered by her friend's enthusiasm, but it kept her warmer than the campfire. "Yes," she agreed in a shy voice.

After another deep breath, Roswynd cleared her throat and started her vows of friendship. "Tharon, I vow to always be your best friend. To always listen to you. To always support you. I will go on any adventure with you, even if it is on a stupid boat." They traded a small laugh, but then Roswynd's eyes glistened in the firelight from pending tears. "I vow that nothing will take you from me." She wiped her damp cheeks.

Tharon let her own tears fall and noticed how hard they were gripping each other's bound hands. After a shaky breath, she locked her gaze with her best friend and promised, "Ros, I vow to always be your best friend. To protect you. To care for you. I will be there when our lives are easy and when they are dark. I promise we will work through any hardships." She leaned closer, held Roswynd's cheek and whispered, "I vow we will always be together." A low, needy whine left Roswynd, but Tharon couldn't pull Roswynd into her lap with their hands tied together.

Roswynd took Tharon's hand off her cheek and laced their fingers together. "Until the end of our days."

"Until the end of our days," Tharon echoed.

A bright flash emitted from the bracelets.

Roswynd jerked back and blinked, staring at the bracelets on their wrists. "Uh, did you see that too?"

"Yes," Tharon whispered. They turned their wrists, but the bracelets simply reflected the firelight rather than flash like a beacon.

Roswynd was awestruck and wide-eyed. "It worked."

Tharon freed her left hand and poked her bracelet, but it still did nothing. "Perhaps it was from the firelight."

"I do not think so," Roswynd said, her voice growing high-pitched. "They truly are enchanted!" She grabbed the collar of Tharon's cloak and yanked her closer. "Do you feel different?"

Tharon snorted and replied, "Yes, I feel as if I can fly."

"Do not be an idiot. I am serious."

Tharon rolled her eyes but still had a grin as she said, "No, I do not feel different. But you said the bracelets will help us find each other."

Roswynd was quiet and staring off in the distance past Tharon. "Perhaps the old lady meant that if we are separated, we can find each other. We will have to test it later."

Tharon chuckled and said, "I am certain we can at the festival this week." She watched Roswynd's mismatched eyes center on her again, then a blush colored Roswynd's pale cheeks. Their faces were very close to each other. Roswynd's stare dropped to Tharon's mouth before lifting up again. "Ros?"

"Is it acceptable if we kiss?" Roswynd whispered. "Not like mates or lovers, but like…" She was flustered and breathing harder.

"Like sisters?" Tharon teased, attempting to lighten the mood.

After releasing Tharon's cloak, Roswynd smacked her on the side, withdrew some, and muttered, "Like princess and prince." Again, her cheeks tinted a little.

Tharon relented her taunting, then grabbed Roswynd by her cloak and pulled her in for a tender kiss. They had no idea what do other than press their lips together. She breathed in Roswynd's sweet vanilla scent and became lost in it. A slight growl started in the back of her throat, but it shifted into a sort of purr. Nothing compared to touching Roswynd, ever.

Roswynd ended the kiss first and smiled at Tharon. Her eyes were misty, but full of life. "Thank you for exchanging vows with me."

Needing to be closer, Tharon undid their tied hands and placed the cloth in the box, near the stained blade. She ignored their sliced hands, which had either dried or frozen blood at this point. She hauled Roswynd off the stool and placed her across her lap.

Roswynd ran her arm across the back of Tharon's shoulders and snuggled into her. She always fit in Tharon's arms well, as though she was made to be there.

Tharon tucked her face into Roswynd's neck and inhaled the honey-vanilla scent. She rumbled for a minute, then whispered, "You and my mother are the two most important people in my life."

"I am aware." Roswynd trembled against Tharon, then wrapped both arms around Tharon's neck. "I love you."

"I love you too," Tharon whispered back without hesitation and nuzzled into Roswynd more. They had never spoken the words, even though their time together always showed it. The sentiment was easy to share, easy to hold, and final. From this day forward, she would do anything she could to keep her vows to Roswynd, especially the part about staying together until the end of their days.

Roswynd released a strained breath after their first exchange of the tender words. She sighed a happy sound and rested her chin on her best friend's head. "Happy birthday, Tharon."

* * *

Date: 17 Sunstone 826G
(Present Day)

"Why can we not go?" Josse complained with a shrill in his voice.

"Because you are too young and stupid," Myla replied, then scurried off when Josse tried to tackle her.

"Stop," Garrett ordered Josse, who groused, then grew red faced when Myla stuck her tongue out at him. Garret turned and missed his daughter's antics but said, "Enter the carriage, Myla."

"Yes, Father." Myla headed to the carriage that had several guards around it.

Tharon shook her head at the siblings, causing her to think of Holly and Daisy. Similar to Josse, Saxon loved to tease the twins, to the point that Tharon had to intervene at times. She crossed the short distance to the front of the stable where Deri brought out her and Roswynd's horses.

Roswynd was checking over Dragonfly's tack. Tharon was about to inspect Obsidian's tack too, but Archibold approached her. She gave him a sideways glance, then started looking over the tack and checking the straps' tightness.

"Can you use both swords?" Archibold asked and point at the weapons sheathed at Tharon's hips.

"Yes," Tharon replied and continued to the front of Obsidian. She sensed the teenager shadowing her.

"At the same time?" Archibold asked again.

Tharon paused and smirked at Roswynd's brother. "Yes." As a pup, she recalled first holding Archibold in her arms about four months after he was born. At the time, she adored his blue eyes, which mirrored Roswynd's icy one.

Archibold shifted closer with a doubtful look.

"Do you require a demonstration?" Tharon asked, reaching for one of the hilts. Her voice grew deeper and held a thunderous warning in it.

Archibold's eyes grew big. He was prepared to back down now, especially when Tharon's lip curled back with a silent snarl.

"Yes!" Josse appeared out of nowhere, jumping and landing beside Archibold. "But first, how many people have you killed with your swords?" He danced from foot to foot.

Tharon's growl lowered, but she was cut off by Roswynd.

"Leave my wife alone, little brothers." Roswynd was in the saddle and urged Dragonfly closer to her brothers. "Or do you truly wish to learn why your sister-in-law is called the Black Wulf?"

Josse opened his mouth to reply, but Tharon cut him off. "I fondly recall having to change your soaker after you drank too much at the Howling Eagle ball. Still having that trouble?" Tharon smirked at Josse, who went bright red at hearing the embarrassing story. It was enough to throw him off and end the conversation. She hopped into the saddle and tapped Obsidian's sides.

Archibold snorted and said, "You used to wet your soaker all the time." He yelped when Josse punched his shoulder.

Roswynd trotted up to Tharon's side, then slowed the horse as they continued to the main gates. "That was rotten," she said and narrowed her eyes, but there was no accusation in her voice.

Tharon shrugged and turned in the saddle when the carriage followed them. Ahead of them a mixed unit of guards and soldiers waited for them. A holler came from one of the officers in the unit, which prompted the soldiers to begin the march for Stormbreaker Landing. The journey to the seaport city would take over two hours, and the sun had peeked over the eastern horizon about ten minutes ago.

Roswynd adjusted the cloak around her shoulders, keeping the morning chill at bay. Her body swayed with Dragonfly's motions. She was gazing ahead and appeared much calmer than she had last night after their argument.

Canting her head, Tharon attempted to study Roswynd from her peripheral view, but it was hard with her half-blind eye. Over the years, she had learned to rely on her other senses to stay aware of her surroundings. However, it didn't change her limited view, especially of Roswynd.

Last night, Tharon had fallen asleep on top of her wife, who was spent from releasing the raw anger that had been burning inside her for years. In that moment, Tharon sympathized because she had been in a similar place after her mother's death. Nothing was fixed, never could be fixed. But at least it made life bearable again. The anger wasn't gone, not truly. Somewhere inside her and Roswynd, their mutual anger sat dormant, warm, and ready to detonate again.

After the fire's light had faded, Tharon crawled off the bed and covered Roswynd with a fur for the night. She forwent the armchair and sat on the floor with her back against the bed. At least the mattress was soft against her upper body after a mentally strenuous day. She had a decent sleep until delicate fingers played with her hair. Tharon had peered up to find Roswynd alert and more stable.

They'd risen before dawn and prepared for their trip to Stormbreaker Landing. Roswynd didn't speak while they readied; she remained quiet at breakfast, and had spoken only moments ago when they were mounting the horses. Her silence was different today. It wasn't withdrawn or riddled with tension, but a reserved peacefulness that wouldn't last forever. At least it was an interlude from the subtle standoff between them.

Once beyond the capital, the soldiers and guards organized around the small convoy and ensured the royals were protected from all sides. A few people chatted on occasion, but the early hour made it difficult to be cheery. At the head of the unit was Donnchad. He seemed to be a rather capable captain of the guard from Tharon's observations. Tharon was always prepared for a fight, between her swords, daggers, and bow. She'd also brought Roswynd's filled quiver and bow, strapping them to the outside of her saddlebags.

The approach of Roswynd's horse interrupted Tharon's thoughts. Turning her head to the right, she stole a glimpse with her good eye at Roswynd's expression. A strong sniff confirmed that Roswynd had something on her mind. A curious hint laced Roswynd's sweet scent. Adjusting the reins, Tharon turned her focus ahead and waited for whatever her wife was thinking.

Roswynd played with the reins and shifted in the saddle before she glanced at Tharon. She bit her bottom lip, then spoke in a quiet voice that Tharon managed to catch. "Is being lovers still an option?"

"Yes," Tharon replied without hesitation. She contained the hungry grin that wanted to break free and pretended her indifference. "Does that interest you?" Roswynd's honest reply mattered to her. There were far too many rumors about Tharon taking advantage of female Betas, raping them, and marking them with a blade. She was unsure which conquests were talked about more: the ones on the battlefield or the ones in the bedroom. Regardless, Roswynd's agreement and trust in the bed was important to Tharon. Their friendship may be forever lost, but a sexual relationship didn't have to follow the same path.

Roswynd didn't reply as quickly and stared at her horse. After a minute, she whispered, "You know the answer."

"Perhaps, but I wish to hear it." Tharon waited and would continue to wait until Roswynd asked her for sex. Since the wedding ceremony, Roswynd's scent often carried arousal brought on by Tharon's closeness or touches. "Tell me your honest answer."

Roswynd worked her bottom lip for a beat, then looked over at her wife. "Yes, it interests me, but I would want to go slow."

Rumbling while thinking, Tharon nodded at Roswynd's concerns and asked, "Have you been with anyone?" Even though her Alpha seethed at the idea, she didn't let it show and remained indifferent. After all, Tharon had slept with many rather than hold out for her one Omega, who she believed would never be hers. She might have had grand plans to one day remove Roswynd from the House of Arrington, protect her from the fall of Wyndfeld, and keep her, but those were barbaric dreams in the dark recesses of her Alpha mind.

"No," Roswynd replied in a meek tone. Her cheeks took on a red tint. They didn't need to discuss the fact that Tharon had past lovers.

Tharon bobbed her head and took a deep breath. "We can start slow when you are ready."

Roswynd wiped one hand at a time on her trousers and said, "And if I wish to stop at any time? Stop all of it."

"Then we stop." Tharon strangled her Alpha's displeasure at the idea of having Roswynd, then having her taken away. A snarl fought its way up her throat, but she strangled it down.

"What if you want a different lover?" Roswynd asked and swallowed loud enough for Tharon to catch it.

"I swore fidelity," Tharon said and met her wife's worried gaze. "It is you or no one."

Roswynd broke the staring match and remained quiet. The silence held an unspoken question until Roswynd was brave enough to risk asking it. "What if I want a different lover?"

"I would kill them."

Roswynd gasped and jerked on Dragonfly's reins by mistake. The horse whinnied at the confusing command and danced on his hooves until Roswynd calmed him. She patted his neck a few times and said, "Sorry, Dragonfly." Sighing, she sat up in the saddle and noticed a few soldiers glancing at her, but they looked away.

Tharon rumbled and waited for more questions. Since childhood, her wife had been inquisitive and pensive, something that Tharon admired about her. As an adult Tharon still respected that characteristic of Roswynd, who was different from most Omegas and other female breeds.

"I-I would like to think more about it," Roswynd said, gaining control of her voice. She straightened her back and gazed down the road known as Gateway to the Sun, due to its eastern and western direction.

Tharon didn't respond, already understanding that Roswynd needed more time. But Roswynd's pheromones had reacted with excitement to their conversation about sex. Tharon tried to not let it go to her head, especially her smaller one, so that the ride didn't get uncomfortable. However, the idea that they might become lovers left her Alpha pacing and hungry. She had waited year after year to have Roswynd wrapped around her cock, calling her name, and pleading for more. If Tharon had to wait a little longer, she would, until she finally had a taste of every curve of Roswynd's soft flesh.

With a deep breath, Tharon redirected her thoughts and adjusted herself in the damn saddle. She peered over her shoulder toward the carriage behind them. Today would require focus and patience. Myla was with them, and it offered an opportunity to find out who Myla was marrying in the near future. Last night at supper, Tharon had been pleased when Garrett agreed to allow Myla to join them. She hoped to have a chance to weasel out the information from Myla, if she could get time alone with her. After all, Myla was naïve and far too sweet.

The seaport itself would reveal its own strategic features, especially for war. Once or twice Saxon had posed the idea of sending soldiers via ship to Stormbreaker Landing, taking the port city, and then marching to Earna. The major hurdle was that White Sommer was landlocked, but a larger fishing village in southeastern Wyndfeld had a port. They could easily take it, purchase warships, hire pirates, and take out Stormbreaker Landing. But they would need to conquer Dragontooth Pass in the southern part of the White Razor Mountains.

Even now the front of Tharon's skull pulsed with a dull ache at the idea of shifting their campaign to southern Wyndfeld, which was farmland and bogs. They'd had enough of that wet, mushy shit for the past ten years. Still, Tharon hadn't ruled out the idea of taking over the water village to the south, especially now that she would have the chance to see Stormbreaker Landing firsthand. If the seaport had significant defenses, then it was off the strategy books.

The rest of the ride to the city was peaceful, other than greeting merchants and travelers on the road. As they neared the outskirts of the seaport, everyone stirred with excitement to take a break and enjoy their visit. The air had a salty note to it and welcomed them to the region. The landscape along the coast was mostly flat except for the more northern reaches where the coastline turned into cliffs that joined the White Razor Mountains.

The gates came into view, which triggered Donnchad to send a rider ahead of them. Last night Garrett had explained that the lord of the seaport was a man named Orton. He would be their guide and host for the day. As expected, Lord Orton was at the gates when they arrived.

Garrett stepped out of the carriage and greeted Orton. He promised introductions later after they had their horses stabled and everyone was ready. Enthused by the visit, Orton directed his visitors into the city. He walked at the front with Donnchad, chatting away.

Roswynd leaned toward her wife and murmured, "And you thought I was unable to be silent." Tharon snorted and gave a pointed look at Roswynd, who was still eyeing Orton. "He could outtalk me," Roswynd declared after another minute of constant chatter from Orton. "Do you think he breathes?"

"Perhaps he has mastered speaking from his mouth and breathing from his nose at the same time," Tharon joked and earned a laugh from Roswynd.

"A sought-after skill," Roswynd bantered back.

"For an auctioneer," Tharon joked without thought. Somehow their conversation and comfort with each other had slipped back to their old ways. She chastised herself for letting her armor down around her wife. Yet Roswynd's playful grin tugged at Tharon's heart.

Roswynd chuckled and traded a grin with Tharon, then straightened in the saddle. The city around them started to capture Roswynd's attention.

Tharon observed the city, too, but she kept a careful eye on their surroundings. Small crowds had gathered at certain intersections to see their king and princesses. Several pointed in Tharon's direction, then whispered among themselves. She disliked tight spaces like streets, but she was certain the guards would handle a situation, if one occurred.

They came to the front gate of an old but beautiful manor that faced to the east. The manor had three floors, making it one of the tallest residential structures in the seaport. At the gate, a groom and other servants took care of the dozen horses.

"Welcome to Seavu Manor," Orton said to his guests after he broke away from Donnchad.

Tharon took her wife's side and folded her arms. She noticed Garrett and Myla joining them as the carriage was led away.

"Thank you, Lord Orton." Garrett adjusted his cape and held out his hand to Roswynd. "This is my eldest daughter, Princess Roswynd."

Orton stepped forward and took Roswynd's hand, kissing it. "A pleasure to see you again, my princess. You were but a toddler when I last saw you." He beamed at her and said, "You have grown into a beautiful Omega."

"Thank you, sir." Roswynd gave a slight bow that was unnecessary but still kind of her. She was smiling, but her pheromones didn't indicate that she was flattered by his compliments.

"This is Prince Tharon Blakesley, Princess Roswynd's wife."

"Ah yes." Orton offered his arm to Tharon and said, "I have heard much about the Black Wulf."

Tharon took his arm, held strong, and kept an even tone. "Pleasure, sir."

"It is mine, Lord Commander." Orton released arms and kept a curious gaze on Tharon until Garrett introduced Myla last. Like Roswynd, he took Myla's hand and kissed it. "You are so young and fair, Princess Myla. I must say that any Alpha will be blessed to have you." He then started to chat with Garrett about today's plans.

Tharon heard Roswynd's low groan and peered down at her.

"This is going to be a long day," Roswynd muttered. "I may have to get drunk to survive it."

Tharon huffed but agreed with her wife's mood. Orton was pleasant, but he was too talkative and was already wearing on her patience.

"First we will take a rest in Seavu Manor before we begin our tour of the city." Orton waved on his guests toward the iron gate.

"Thank you, Orton." Garrett followed first.

Roswynd sighed and glanced in the direction that her horse went earlier. She frowned some until Tharon placed a hand at the small of her back. "Must I go?"

Tharon chuckled and coaxed her wife forward. She planned to take up the rear, protecting Roswynd's back. Not that she expected any trouble on the estate, but it was habit to be prepared for an attack anywhere. With her hand on a sword hilt, she went last, studying the few city guards assigned to the estate's grounds. The male Betas studied them as they passed through the gardens. Roswynd was right; it was going to be a draining visit, but they both had agreed to the political arrangements of their marriage.

Chapter 12

All day Tharon resisted the need to keep a hand on her sword hilt while they toured the port city. Stormbreaker Landing was a significant city, about eighty percent the size of Earna. Similar to the capital, many of the buildings had A-frame roofs to ease the buildup of snow in the winter months. But the buildings in the port city were a combination of stone, log, and thatch while those in Earna were predominantly stone.

Their tour had started in the residential area, which as they traveled transitioned into the government buildings. They spent time at the market next and took dinner at a local tavern that Orton had reserved for them. Roswynd had her fill of shrimp, which was no surprise. For a moment, Tharon thought her wife might make herself sick on them. Tharon lost count at twenty pieces, but she was glad Roswynd was eating more.

After dinner they continued their tour and entered the heart of the city—its port. The port itself was nestled in a crescent-shaped harbor. At some point in time, a major breakwater had been built to better protect the harbor. The breakwater also forced ships to enter the harbor on the north or south end, leaving the middle half blocked off. Now, major construction was being performed on the breakwater to make it taller and wider. In the future it might support one or two defensive towers.

The actual port was divided in half, with the north end reserved for the Wyndfeld fleet and the south end for commercial and private use. They went to the northern half and Orton showed off the inner harbor that was man-made about a century ago. The inner harbor was connected to the main harbor via a gated channel. The inner harbor provided extra protection from winter winds and enemies. At the inner harbor was a circular dock in the center where warships came in to dock by water or be hauled out on a dry dock for work and repairs.

Garrett was rather proud of the inner harbor for the fleet. He boasted that the fleet had a hundred ships with plans for more. The Wyndfeld fleet wasn't as famous as others, but the ships were known for being well-built and strong, especially due to heavy ice in the north. The ships themselves were reinforced with iron ribs and had iron plating on the bow for breaking ice.

As they continued south, they came to the public and private docks for both the commercial industry and a few private, wealthy families. The docks buzzed with activity from the merchants, traders, and fishermen. Again, Orton dove into grand tales about the merchants, including a few battles with pirates.

As Orton blabbered on, Tharon stole an opening to speak to Myla, who was fascinated by one particular ship. The rest of the group had wandered ahead, so entranced by Orton's latest story.

At first Myla was startled by Tharon's presence and reacted by resting a hand against her chest.

"You should be careful," Tharon said. "Sailors are a dangerous lot." She noticed the color in Myla's cheeks.

"S-Sorry." Myla stepped away from the pier that the ship was docked to. She glanced over her shoulder and confirmed that a few guards were with them.

"How do you like the city?" Tharon asked, matching Myla's slow pace.

"It is amazing and so is the food."

Tharon offered a grin and said, "According to your sister, nothing outmatches the shrimp."

Myla crinkled her nose and whispered, "I thought perhaps she would make herself sick at dinner."

"She is an expert seafood eater."

Myla chuckled, peered up at Tharon, and fidgeted for a moment. "It is one of the few things she eats a lot of."

Tharon rumbled in response, then said, "If it had been possible to have shrimp and saufes at our wedding celebration, I would have requested it." In the winter months, it was easier to transport seafood from Stormbreaker Landing, but Sunstone was still too warm, even at night.

"She would have loved that." Myla folded her hands in front of her and studied her family a few hundred paces in front of them.

"Your sister mentioned that you may be wedding soon." Tharon kept her voice calm and even, not wanting to stir Myla's suspicions. But she needed the details soon, before Roswynd or Garrett took notice of them walking alone.

Myla rubbed her hands together and responded with a gentle rumble. "Yes, my father is finalizing the arrangements."

Tharon nodded and tilted her head. "She said his name is Prince..." She rubbed her brow and picked a random, unwed prince she knew of. "Prince Erik, is it not?"

Myla groaned, shook her head, and replied, "Certainly not Prince Erik. He is far too dull and stupid." She blushed, as if embarrassed she said the truth aloud. Clearing her throat, she said, "It is Prince Drust."

"That is right." Tharon had a slight smile and said, "His father is King Morcant of Black Beacon." From her recollection, King Morcant was a widower who had lost his wife to the Ravage Disease when it swept across his kingdom. The kingdom itself was an enormous island known as the Black Beacon Isle. Prince Drust was between sixteen and twenty, Tharon estimated. Drust was well-liked compared to his father.

"Prince Drust is the second eldest," Myla said.

"I have heard several positive remarks about him." Tharon hooked her hands in front of her and considered other details about Drust. "He is close to your age and is kind. He will care for you." She grinned at Myla's flush. "Do you fancy him?"

"I have not met him, but we have exchanged—"

"Myla?" Garrett called, then halted the tour, turned, and waited for them.

Roswynd narrowed her eyes at Tharon and adjusted her cloak to hide her masculine attire. Once Tharon and Myla rejoined them, she took Tharon's side and managed to put space between them and the rest of the group. "What were you speaking to Myla about?"

Tharon saw no need to hide the truth and tilted her head. "We were discussing her future husband, Prince Drust."

Roswynd opened her mouth, but nothing came out after a minute. She huffed and whispered, "I hope you were not manipulating her."

"I was conversing with my sister-in-law," Tharon argued and kept her voice calm rather than bite back. They were playing a delicate game between them and testing each other. Roswynd was intelligent and clever. The House of Arrington was aware that the political marriage might be a ruse and that Saxon was using it to his advantage. Like Garrett, Roswynd probably assumed that Tharon was here to collect strategic information. Of course Garrett couldn't make public claims that the marriage was a ploy, not when both sides needed the cease-fire. However, if Tharon was found guilty of spying, or worse, plotting, then it made matters far more dangerous.

"Do not play coy with me," Roswynd said in a low but dangerous tone. "You are the lord commander of White Sommer before you are a sister-in-law."

Tharon remained quiet and weighed how to handle Roswynd's accurate assessment. She relied on silence rather than lying, but something else compelled her to counter the claim. Meeting Roswynd's gaze, she said, "I am your wife before I am the lord commander of White Sommer."

Roswynd seemed to chew on the statement, then whispered, "We will see." As the tour continued, she remained at Tharon's side the entire time, ensuring that Tharon couldn't corner Myla again. It no longer mattered now that Tharon had the information she needed about the upcoming marriage.

Such a marriage also meant a political alliance between Wyndfeld and Black Beacon, which was a decently sized kingdom with both naval power and an army. The alliance would mean Wyndfeld may have access to more soldiers to help them fight against White Sommer. If that was Garrett's plan, then it was a decent strategy so long as they could wait. Black Beacon would need time to solidify their relations with Wyndfeld, gather their men, and cross the seas. At the moment, the alliance wasn't a threat to White Sommer.

After the tour ended, they returned to Seavu Manor for a brief respite before the journey back to Earna. Once the farewells and pleasantries were over, the royal family started their trip to the capital. The sun was midway, if not a little low in the western horizon.

As they rode Tharon considered what she'd learned about Stormbreaker Landing. The port city was magnificent and large. It wasn't impenetrable, but its defenses were strong. On top of that, Lord Orton was intelligent and had years of experience as a leader. If an attack befell the city, he would have the ability to withstand an enemy. Garrett may have used the tour of Stormbreaker Landing to dissuade Tharon from wanting to attack them there. Rightfully so, Garrett was proud of the city.

If nothing else, Tharon had learned the name of the prince who had Myla's hand in marriage. There was no way she could relay the information to Saxon, so it would have to wait until she and Roswynd went to Wulfbite for a month. At the thought of marriage, she studied the golden fede ring on her right hand. It gleamed in the late sunlight and reminded her of her vows to Roswynd. The marriage vows were important to Tharon, who had every intent of upholding them. However, she suspected Roswynd held a lot of doubt in their exchange of vows, considering the last time they'd exchanged them.

Tharon studied the old scar that Roswynd had made in her right palm when they were young. In the days following their friendship vows, Tharon had picked at the scabbing in her palm and forced a scar to form so that she would forever be reminded of Roswynd. Every day since, the scar had laughed at her because she failed to keep her friendship vows.

Tharon adjusted the reins in her hands and hid her scarred palm. Her thoughts were jumbled by the earlier conversation with Roswynd about being the lord commander versus a wife. Saxon had warned her to not let Roswynd get into her head. Her wife was still part of the House of Arrington, the enemy. Regardless of Roswynd's lack of direct guilt in the murder, Tharon swore on her mother's bones that Garrett would pay with his death. She and Saxon were close, and the right strategic intelligence could change it all. As long as Tharon kept her rage locked up and continued to fake her new life as an in-law, they would defeat Wyndfeld.

Tharon and Roswynd had a few weeks left in Wyndfeld, and she needed to learn more. The best option was to get into Garrett's office on the third floor. She recalled going into Garrett's office with Roswynd many times as a little one. From the balcony she and Roswynd played on, she knew which balcony belonged to his office. She needed to gain access to it one night, and she was certain she knew how but needed to wait for a brighter moon to aid her.

"Are you all right?" Roswynd asked, breaking Tharon's scheming thoughts.

Tharon glanced at her wife, who had been riding next to her. She gave a faint nod in response.

"You were someplace else," Roswynd whispered with a note of concern. She didn't press the matter further but stole a few peeks at Tharon's profile. They slipped into silence again until Roswynd made another attempt. "Will you tell me what happened to your eye?" Her voice was gentle and soft so that the soldiers wouldn't hear her.

Tharon stared ahead and weighed her wife's request. Again, Roswynd was testing Tharon's defenses, trying to determine what could make her open up. The memory of her eye's damage was an unpleasant one, but it had forced her to be a more effective knight. Cocking her head, she studied Roswynd's resigned features. Tharon worked her jaw a few times and then said, "I was attacked by another knight not long after I was knighted by my father." Pòl wanted to protect her at the time, but she handled her own battles.

Roswynd cringed and shook her head. "Why did another knight attack you?"

Tharon smirked and replied, "I told him to suck my cock." She chuckled at Roswynd's appalled look, then said, "He called me a degenerate before that."

Now huffing, Roswynd gave a growly response and said, "I *hate* that word." Her pheromones were wild and fiery, stirring Tharon's Alpha.

Tharon was well aware of Roswynd's disdain for the slur. As a young adult, Tharon grew to loathe the slur too and corrected anyone stupid enough to call her a degenerate. "I did best the other knight, but only after he slashed my face."

Roswynd frowned and displeasure lingered in her scent. "Are you fully or partially blind in your eye?"

Sighing, Tharon checked that none of the soldiers were listening to them. They were marching several paces ahead and behind them. She disliked airing her weaknesses. After shifting in her saddle, she replied, "Partially."

Roswynd nudged Dragonfly closer to Obsidian, squeezed Tharon's knee, and offered her an appreciative smile. Their conversation had clearly meant something to her.

Tharon growled at her wife's affection, not needing it. She turned away, but she didn't push Roswynd's hand off her knee, which lingered there for another minute.

Roswynd straightened and put space between them. "If it is any consolation," she said, "I think the scars are rather dashing."

I have plenty more, Tharon responded in her mind but said nothing aloud. She focused on the ride to Earna rather than on furthering a closeness that Roswynd was relentless to rekindle. They had made some peace last night with the fact that they could never be friends again. However, Tharon wondered how long it would last before Roswynd's hopes came crashing down once more. In time, Roswynd might fully accept their new reality, but it would be a difficult adjustment.

Shortly after sunset, the unit entered the castle grounds and started to break up. Tharon and Roswynd dismounted when Deri came to retrieve their horses. He promised to have their few belongings taken to their room. After sharing some words with Garrett, Tharon guided her tired wife to the keep and helped her to their room.

"Are you hungry?" Tharon asked when they arrived on the second floor.

"I could eat something small."

Tharon rumbled and tilted her head. "The fifty shrimps were not enough?"

Roswynd rolled her eyes and paused by their bedroom door. "I had twenty-six. And as I recall, you ate your fair share of saufes." She ignored Tharon's smirk and opened the door, sighing. "I am exhausted but I need a bath."

Tharon agreed she wanted the same. She took it upon herself to find a servant, who promised to draw up baths and bring food for them. Tharon returned to the bedroom to find Roswynd removing a few layers. They ate first while a tub in the bathing room was being filled with hot water. Roswynd would go first, then probably lie down.

By the time Tharon finished her bath, she discovered her wife had gone to bed. Tharon retired to an armchair in front of the burning fireplace and started to read. A few times she heard Roswynd move under the furs or sigh in frustration.

"Tharon?" Roswynd had shifted and was seated up against the wooden headboard. When Tharon twisted around in the chair, she said, "I cannot sleep, even though it has been a long day."

Tharon sensed something on Roswynd's mind, not the usual things but something specific. She weighed her options and decided to take the bait this time. Rising, she placed the open book on the chair and went over to the bed. Roswynd's scent held a twinge of arousal; now she understood what was keeping Roswynd awake.

Roswynd stared at her lap and played with the blanket under the fur. "I keep thinking about your offer."

Rumbling, Tharon tilted her head in silent interest. All day Roswynd was probably mulling over whether or not to have sex, to take that next step. For Tharon, it was an easy decision because she could dissociate her feelings from sex.

But for Roswynd it would be more complicated, if not impossible. As pups, they never explored that aspect of their relationship, being rather young at the time. They had kissed once, hugged thousands of times, and snuggled at any chance. Now faced with the option to have sex, Tharon respected Roswynd's need to understand the long-term impact.

"I want to try," Roswynd whispered, and soft pink colored her cheeks. "But I know very little about sex." She closed her eyes and toyed with the blanket. "I have studied it in books." She looked over at Tharon and gave a weak laugh. "That sounds silly."

Tharon ignored the jerking of her heart when Roswynd's last words echoed the time they exchanged friendship vows and those not-so-silly bracelets. She focused on the present and recalled that Roswynd was cautious with new things. But once Roswynd grasped the basics, she dove into it. Similar to riding or archery, Roswynd needed information, experience, and time. Tharon had no doubt that Roswynd would be a confident and capable lover.

"The sex in books is written by males, Beta or Alpha." Tharon huffed and shook her head. "It is not to say the information is irrelevant, but it is not accurate for us."

Roswynd lowered her eyes to the blanket and furs again. "I-I did not find any information about female Alphas in the books."

Tharon was intrigued by the idea of Roswynd searching for specific details about her type of breed. She grinned as an idea came to mind. "I can show you and teach you." Her words triggered an interesting shift in Roswynd's pheromones, ones that excited her Alpha.

"S-Such as? And do you mean tonight?"

Chuckling, Tharon slid off the bed and stood, still facing Roswynd. "I can show you my body and explain it to you." Her grin turned a bit wolfish. "I do mean tonight, since you are not so tired after all."

Roswynd's breathing had increased, and based on the scent of her pheromones, she wasn't resisting the idea. "Must I do anything?"

Tharon shook her head and replied, "Nothing that you do not wish to do." She watched Roswynd consider the offer that could change their dynamic forever.

Narrowing her gaze, Roswynd said, "Do not play any stupid jokes on me again." Her warning referred back to their wedding night when Tharon pranked her.

Tharon nodded, then asked, "Then you want me to show you?"

"And explain," Roswynd said, eyeing her wife. Nothing satisfied Roswynd's curious mind like explanations and lessons. She was still breathing faster and responding with sweet, thick pheromones.

After another nod, Tharon started with her boots and socks, having dressed into fresh clothes after her bath. She didn't have on a jerkin but removed her tunic.

"Do you not have any sleepwear?" Roswynd asked.

Tharon snorted and replied, "I sleep naked." She enjoyed the blush on her wife's soft cheeks. With the tunic somewhat folded, she placed it on the floor near the boots. "I am going to add more firewood." She broke away, giving Roswynd the chance to collect herself for the rest of what was to come. If she was truthful with herself, she also needed a minute to prepare for the new direction in her relationship with Roswynd. Once she had Roswynd as a lover, her Alpha would refuse to have anyone else, ever again. The last few years as a knight had given her access to many female Betas, but they were ordinary and plain compared to Roswynd. They were nothing.

After adding wood to the fire, Tharon cleaned off her hands and returned to the side of the bed. Roswynd hadn't moved except to sit in a cross-legged position under the furs. For a moment, Tharon stood near her and allowed the increasing firelight to play off her exposed upper body. She wore a band that supported her breasts, especially during fights.

"You have more scars," Roswynd whispered while her eyes roamed over Tharon's chest and stomach.

Tharon had a variety of scars from different battles. Most were from blades like sword tips or daggers, but others came from arrowheads. Each had a bloody, painful memory tied to them. These days her skin felt like a storybook, albeit a gruesome one. Reaching behind her, Tharon undid the breast wrap and removed it. She grinned when Roswynd squirmed, but Roswynd didn't avert her gaze from Tharon.

Roswynd swallowed and curled her fingers into the top fur. A warm, red hue dusted her cheeks, but she was captivated by Tharon's body. She emitted a strong scent of arousal that called to Tharon.

Above the trousers' waistband, Tharon's stomach muscles clenched and flexed from her increased breathing. It had been ages since a sexual partner made her a little nervous. As a pup, Tharon lacked confidence in her body and its abilities, but that all changed when she went from a squire to a knight. It had to change if she was going to survive the army. She was stronger than most, and her muscular body intimidated everyone. As a teenager, she had been blessed with beauty from both her parents, even if the scar and half blindness marred her features. Although Roswynd wasn't the first to find her hazy, scarred eye handsome.

Once she became a knight, female Betas followed Tharon to her tent without hesitation, and plenty of males, both Beta and Alpha, wanted to try their hand with her. Tharon found males' scents pungent and sometimes repulsive. Only female breeds caught her attention. However, Roswynd was the female Omega she'd been hunting for years, and now she was so close to having her for herself.

Tharon reached for the tie of her leather trousers, undoing the knot and loosening the laced fly. The thickness of her pants kept her cock flush with her thighs, but soon it would be free. From the achiness in her groin, she sensed that she was hard already. Her own pheromones were responding to Roswynd as well.

As she peeled off her trousers, Tharon heard Roswynd's breath hitch. She grinned to herself and removed the trousers, folding them in front of her lower body and blocking Roswynd's view. Turning her back to Roswynd, she went over to the other clothing and placed the trousers on top of the tunic, bending over some. With each movement she made, Tharon could feel Roswynd's stare burning into her skin.

Roswynd wriggled and dragged her fingers through her hair when Tharon straightened and turned toward her again. She cleared her throat and kept her stare above Tharon's shoulders, at least for the most part. Once or twice, her eyes dropped to Tharon's breasts and upper stomach, but they refused to go any lower now that Tharon was free of clothing.

On instinct Tharon almost grabbed her cock, but she instead fisted her hands at her side. With an amused grin, she neared the top of the bed and asked, "Having trouble taking it *all* in?"

Rolling her eyes, Roswynd pretended to be annoyed by the tease's double meaning. "I am perfectly fine."

Tharon chuckled and nodded. "Do you mind if I join you?" She indicated the lower half of the bed.

Roswynd cleared her throat, but her voice was rough when she replied, "No, I do not mind." She shivered after Tharon took a step back from her.

Tharon climbed onto the bed, taking the lower half and lying across it. She decided to give her wife a full show and rolled onto her left side so that they faced each other. With her right leg propped up, her body was on display for Roswynd, who was rather flushed, aroused, and anxious, according to her scent. In response, Tharon rumbled from the mix of emotions and newness.

This time, Roswynd looked toward the fire and plucked at the fur in her lap. Her hand trembled each time she pulled at the blanket. She was breathing heavy, on the verge of panting. After a minute, she muttered, "I do not know what I was thinking." Looking down in her lap, she seemed to be silently berating herself for the whole idea.

Sighing, Tharon propped her head against her hand and arm, then studied Roswynd. She needed to coax Roswynd out of her shell, which meant assuring her. It had been a long time since she'd reassured anyone, let alone Roswynd. Her Alpha despised giving in to tenderness, but with Roswynd she didn't feel the same resistance she did with others. It took her a good minute to struggle through and develop a comforting response to Roswynd's mental chaos.

"You were thinking it would bring us closer." Tharon waited for Roswynd to deny the truth, and when there was no argument, she said, "And you are attracted to me." She paused and studied the returned color in Roswynd's cheeks. "There is nothing wrong with that idea or with being attracted to your wife."

Roswynd peered up at Tharon and asked, "Are you attracted to me?"

"Yes."

Roswynd's eyes went wide at the strong response, but uncertainty lingered in her stare. "I am not..." She shook her head and frowned at the furs again.

Tharon was torn with how to respond to Roswynd's strange lack of confidence. Even with new challenges in life, Roswynd always had her determination to propel her forward and tackle any hurdle. For some reason this was different, and it was tearing Roswynd into pieces. Her Alpha whined in protest, clawing in her chest. The natural need to go to Roswynd and hold her was palpable to the point that Tharon almost hated herself for it. How did Roswynd break down Tharon's years of rigorous training and self-control in a matter of days?

Not quite willing to give in to her Alpha, Tharon at least met halfway and asked, "Do you want to touch me? I will lie on my stomach." She was horrendous at verbalizing comfort, but the physical assurance was a lot easier for her to offer. Roswynd's meek nod pleased her, so she rolled onto her stomach and exposed her back, which was difficult to do. As a knight, she was hypersensitive about what and who was behind her, but she turned her head to the right. Even though her partial blindness disrupted her view, she sensed Roswynd coming to her.

Roswynd settled into a spot next to Tharon's hip and hesitated, but asked, "Does it matter where I touch you?"

"No." Tharon smiled at her wife's concern. She pushed aside her dark hair that had fallen around her face. Peering back, she attempted to see Roswynd, but her wife was a shadow with flickers of color and light from the fireplace. Her entire body jumped and stiffened when Roswynd's hand pressed into her midback. Thanks to her blind eye, she hadn't been ready for the contact, but she settled deeper into the bed and allowed Roswynd to explore her body. Her growing calmness echoed inside of Roswynd, who started to move her hand.

"How did you get so muscular?" Roswynd whispered. "I mean I understand how, but…" She traced a spot with her fingertip, perhaps a scar. "It was not from sweet breads."

Tharon snorted and crossed her arms around her head. "Training," she murmured.

"Did you like being a squire?" Roswynd asked while her hand crept lower, closer to Tharon's ass.

"I hated it." Tharon closed her eyes and soaked in Roswynd's tender caresses. This wasn't what she had planned on them doing right now, but she basked in the contact. No one else would be allowed to touch her like this, ever. Roswynd might argue and even kick or punch at her during a heated argument, but Roswynd wouldn't maliciously hurt her otherwise.

Roswynd paused and asked, "Why?" She traced her fingertips toward Tharon's hip, near a distinct scar from an arrowhead. She paused there, inspecting it with interest.

"I was the king's daughter and a degenerate. They hoped to break me before I was knighted by my father." Tharon huffed and fisted her hands but fought to relax her body again. Her bitter pheromones would simply throw off Roswynd. "My knight was a knowledgeable teacher, even if he could be a knothead."

"Did your father not put a stop to the mistreatment?" Roswynd massaged a spot near Tharon's hip and turned her head toward Tharon's gaze.

Tharon huffed and considered whether to reply beyond that. Her memories as a squire were long shut out from her mind and opening them was unpleasant. Roswynd was curious and had missed out on ten years of Tharon's life. Tharon wanted to keep that piece of her life closed off from Roswynd, but the delicate touches and soft Omega scent was wrapping around her. Letting Roswynd touch her this way might have been a mistake.

"No," Tharon replied, losing the battle to restrain herself. "He did not approve of my squireship or becoming a knight."

"So he simply ignored it," Roswynd summarized aloud and trailed her hand along the side of Tharon's thigh. She sighed low and shook her head. "Your father was a good king." She hesitated, then whispered, "But a poor father to you."

Tharon remained silent and closed her eyes, not wanting to discuss her dead father. Roswynd was well aware of Eustace's shortcomings, which were often compensated for by Tharon's mother, who loved Tharon without a single condition. Now both her parents were gone, and nothing could change the past.

Roswynd was quiet too but enjoyed touching Tharon's thigh, both the back and right side. She pressed the heel of her palm into one of Tharon's muscles, which loosened under her ministrations. "And I thought I was tense." The playfulness was back in her tone.

Groaning, Tharon shifted her head and considered her wife's massaging, which was a turn of events. She rumbled without control and melted under the warm but firm touch against the underside of her shoulder blade. "You do not need to do that."

"Are you sure? After I kicked and punched you like a pup last night?"

Tharon chuckled and closed her eyes, feeling bewitched by Roswynd's touch, closeness, and scent. She moved her arm, reached back, and grasped Roswynd's calf. Even though the nightgown separated their skin, Tharon squeezed the muscular leg in response. Roswynd's calf was well-defined from the years of horseback riding. For a moment, she pictured Roswynd straddling her hips and riding her cock. She pressed her face into the fur under her and muffled a needy groan.

Roswynd paused in her ministrations, then grazed her nails down Tharon's side. Goosebumps followed behind her touch, leaving a trail. "I am ready for you to turn over."

Peering over her shoulder, Tharon attempted to confirm it with a glance, but her blind eye made it impossible to see Roswynd's expression. The shadows played over Roswynd's face, except for the hint of amber and blue from her eyes. "Are you certain?" Earlier Roswynd's tone had been strong, even a bit assertive.

"I am certain." There was no mistaking it this time. Roswynd was ready.

Tharon rolled and shifted until she was on her back, exposing all her skin, scars, and curvy muscles. She heard the slight hitch of Roswynd's breath, but she remained next to her. Without needing to look, she knew her cock was already swollen and at full length. Again, she withheld the urge to tug on it, even though the soft ache was there.

After a minute, Roswynd placed a hand on Tharon's stomach and cupped a muscle. The minor contact kept Roswynd calm. When they'd started this, her motions had been stiff and unnatural, but now she was less startled by what was in front of her. She peered up at Tharon, and they matched stares for a moment. Roswynd seemed to need approval or encouragement to take in all of Tharon's body.

Tharon remained motionless and stretched out across the bed in a vulnerable position so that Roswynd had a sense of control over their situation. She might be the Alpha, but Roswynd's security was important to Tharon. Using her pheromones, Tharon comforted Roswynd and watched how her wife's shoulders dropped little by little. "Am I what you expected and want?"

Roswynd blew out a shaky breath and regarded Tharon before lowering her gaze, taking the invitation to look more. "You are soft like me." Her eyes roamed farther, but her breaths didn't increase until she was near Tharon's waist. "But hard too."

Tharon lifted her head and grinned at Roswynd staring at her cock for the first time. "Hard would be an accurate description."

Clearing her throat, Roswynd met Tharon's gaze and asked, "Is *it* always like that?"

Tharon snorted and lowered back to the fur. "Lately, yes." She smirked at Roswynd's flushed features.

"Does it hurt?"

"It can," Tharon replied. Again, she struggled with the need to massage the strain in her cock. By the end of this lesson, she would need to do something about her sexual needs. Even if it meant going somewhere else to jerk off in private.

After a bit of silence, Roswynd scrunched up her nose, looked from the upright penis to Tharon, and asked, "That is supposed to fit in me?"

Tharon snorted low, then groaned and rubbed her brow. "Those educational books did you no favors, I see." She dropped her hand and chuckled at Roswynd's bashful expression. "Yes, *I* will fit in you."

"I am not so certain," Roswynd argued, staring back at Tharon's cock. "Perhaps I should take measurements."

Tharon sat up onto her elbows and gawked at her wife, who was teasing her. She huffed at Roswynd's smirk and shook her head. But the fact that Roswynd was attempting to make light of their situation meant that she was getting comfortable. In the past, Roswynd never shied from speaking her mind, being upfront, or asking anything. From the gleam in Roswynd's mismatched eyes, she knew the earlier trepidation was gone.

"How will it fit in me?" Roswynd shook her head. Perhaps some part of her did doubt the possibility of the mechanics.

Sighing once, Tharon decided to be blunt. "My *cock*," she emphasized, "will slide inside of you with the right encouragement. Once you are wet enough and excited, it happens naturally."

"I see," Roswynd whispered and frowned a little. "Will it hurt?"

"It usually does the very first time," Tharon answered with honesty, which caught Roswynd's attention. "We will go slowly and carefully until you are comfortable. It will start to feel good to you." She caught the hint of confusion flowing from Roswynd.

Roswynd shook her head and said, "You are supposed to work yourself to an orgasm so that you can fill me with your seed." She withdrew her hand and plucked at her nightgown over her knee.

Tharon chuckled and shook her head, then moved into a seated position. "Whatever you read in those books, remove it from your mind. They are nonsense." She tilted Roswynd's head back and ran her thumb over Roswynd's lips. "We work ourselves into an orgasm, together."

"But I thought…"

"Females orgasm too, not only the males." Tharon indicated her own nude body as an example.

Roswynd blushed but nodded and seemed to accept the new information. "I suppose I have a lot to learn between archery and sex."

Tharon chuckled and pulled against Roswynd's bottom lip some, enjoying the soft wetness there. She could only imagine whether it was anything similar to being inside of Roswynd. Being this close and naked with Roswynd was taxing on her self-control, but she was determined to gain all of Roswynd's trust.

"Can you lie down again?" Roswynd asked in a low but determined voice.

With a wolfish smile, Tharon followed the request and became comfortable on her back again. She tucked her arms under her head, waiting for Roswynd's next question or move.

"Is it all right if I touch you again?" Their sole contact was Roswynd's knees pressed against Tharon's side.

"Yes." Tharon turned her head in Roswynd's direction. "Do you need help?" As with anything new to Roswynd, Tharon had a habit of offering a hand or two, if Roswynd needed it.

"Not yet." Roswynd rested a hand on Tharon's thigh and nibbled on her lip. "I read there is only one position that we are supposed to use during sex."

"The female is on her back and the male on top," Tharon said and rolled her eyes. "There are many other positions and ones a lot more pleasurable."

Roswynd chuckled, and then tsked while her hand crept closer to Tharon's inner thigh. "Sex is about procreation, Tharon. Not pleasure."

Tharon growled low and said, "You will think differently later." She watched the firelight dance on the underside of the canopy and allowed it to distract her, which it did, until Roswynd's hand left her thigh and then a light touch appeared on the underside of her cock. Tharon gritted her teeth and closed her eyes. Even though Roswynd grazed her, it was enough to send her in a mental spiral. She had waited and wanted this for so long. For a second, she was tempted to use her pheromones to overwhelm Roswynd and make her compliant. Once they were slowly fucking, Roswynd would understand the need to be together.

Taking a deep breath, Tharon grappled with her Alpha instincts and glared up at the canopy. If she remained patient and understanding, Roswynd would ask her. She had no fear of rejection, but the wait was eating away at her.

"Are you all right?" Roswynd asked and withdrew her hand.

Tharon growled at the loss of contact but took a heavy breath that helped slow her heart rate. "Yes."

"Is this too much?" Roswynd squeezed her wife's hip and said, "Your scent is confusing me." Her voice wavered for a moment.

"It is not too much." Tharon controlled her breathing and scent before she scared off Roswynd. "I want you to touch me." Roswynd was learning from her and getting comfortable. Tharon wanted that first, and maybe then they would have some fun tonight. Adjusting her mindset, she sat up onto her elbows and offered a smile.

Roswynd returned it, then reached again and brushed her fingertips along the underside of Tharon's cock.

"You do not have to be shy," Tharon encouraged.

Roswynd briefly ducked, but checked with Tharon first before she scooted closer. This time, she pressed more of her hand around the shaft, then rubbed her thumb along some of the length. Her touch remained delicate, but she felt more of the full length. She seemed to be avoiding the head for the moment, exploring the rest. "You once told me that you are similar me."

"Mmmm." Tharon was forced to roll to her left side, putting all her weight on her arm. She grabbed her penis and pushed it flat against her stomach. "Below the base of my cock I have a vaginal opening like female Omegas."

"Oh." Roswynd shifted and pressed her hand against Tharon's thigh, urging her to widen her legs. She leaned closer and rumbled, then jerked her attention toward Tharon. "You do. Does that mean you can get pregnant?"

Tharon chuckled and rolled onto her back but remained upright on her elbows. "Yes, I think so."

"Have you met other female Alphas?" Roswynd asked.

"No, not yet." Tharon directed Roswynd's hand to her cock, then settled back on her elbows. During her time in the White Sommer Army, she learned that it was typical for female Alphas to die of unspoken complications after birth. Tharon suspected the complication was murder. She banished the dark thoughts from her mind and instead focused on Roswynd studying her cock.

This time Roswynd wrapped her hand around the shaft and gripped it with firmness, eliciting a groan from Tharon. Roswynd loosened her grip in seconds, a look of concern on her face.

"It did not hurt," Tharon said.

Roswynd nodded and grinned, realizing what Tharon's response meant. "You are harder than I thought. I can also feel your pulse." Her thumb traced a vein. "Will it hurt if I touch the tip?"

Tharon now understood why her wife was avoiding it. "No, it will not hurt. The head is more sensitive than the shaft."

Roswynd slid her hand up, then rubbed her thumb across the underside of the head. "What is the part of the skin that is moving?" She was blushing again, but still determined to learn everything.

"A foreskin to cover the head when I am not this hard." Tharon shifted, then showed Roswynd how the foreskin moved up some. "If I did not have that, it would be uncomfortable to have the head brushing everything."

Roswynd frowned some, then rumbled and said, "I guess that is like the lips covering my clitoris."

Tharon started to chuckle until Roswynd rubbed the head of her cock. She made a strangled sound, then collapsed into the furs under her. "Fuck."

"Hmmm." Roswynd was excited by Tharon's reaction. Her own scent grew thickly sweet, calling to Tharon's Alpha. "Your slick is clear. The books said it was supposed to be white?" She withdrew her hand and smeared the fluid over her fingers.

Tharon was panting, but managed to speak after a deep breath. "I believe it will be white when I am in a rut." She felt Roswynd's burning stare locked on her now.

"Then that means I can only get pregnant when you are in a rut."

"Yes."

Roswynd snorted and whispered, "That is convenient or inconvenient, depending on how we look at it."

"Perhaps convenient," Tharon replied. *If I can rut*, her mind taunted her, but she pushed aside the ugly thought. She didn't want to ruin their mood again. She sat up and noticed the droplets of slick beading at the tip of her cock. Her arousal was spiking to the point that she couldn't wait any longer. She needed to please herself soon or she would become restless, moody, and overbearing tomorrow. With that in mind, Tharon began to move off the bed until Roswynd halted her.

"Where are you going?"

"To deal with this," Tharon replied and indicated her cock, which was on the verge of hurting. She needed release.

Roswynd held her wife's arm, nails curling into the bicep. "You can do that here." Her cheeks were red, but not with embarrassment this time. She was aroused and giving off pheromones that halted Tharon's escape. "Here on the bed."

Tharon lifted an eyebrow and studied Roswynd in silence. Her Alpha howled at the idea of showing off in front of Roswynd, for Roswynd.

"I-I want to watch," Roswynd whispered.

Tharon didn't need to double-check. The certainty in Roswynd's bright eyes was clear. Tharon grinned at her wife's heightened and hungry curiosity to both watch and learn. This was the side of Roswynd she hoped to bring out to play. "Sometimes I have to go twice."

Roswynd licked her lips, then teased, "You become that hard, huh?"

"I become that hard," Tharon replied, then flashed her canines at her wife. "Especially around a certain Omega."

"Oh, so it is my fault?" Roswynd leaned into Tharon's space and whispered, "If that is true, then I should help, if you are still hard after the first time." She had relinquished her hold, but traced her fingertips along the definition of muscle. "If you would like."

Tharon responded with a soft snarl and whispered, "Yes, I would." She lowered her head closer to Roswynd and breathed in her scent. Without even starting, she knew from both her cock's firmness and the rising excitement from tonight, she would stay hard.

Roswynd shifted, turning to her left some so she had a better view. She kept her hands on Tharon's thigh, always making contact.

Grinning, Tharon tilted back her propped-up leg to open herself more. With her left hand flat against the bed, she used her other hand to massage the shaft a few times. She had pleased herself countless times in the past, but not with an audience. Tharon rather liked it, especially because Roswynd was equally intrigued as she was turned on by the show.

Moving to the tip, Tharon gathered the slick and spread it around the head, then down the shaft. She massaged the shaft more, encouraging more slick to lubricate the full length. Pleased with herself, she started stroking at a steady but slow pace and glanced at Roswynd, who was watching with fascination.

Tharon increased the speed and growled from the heat coiling low in her gut. "Fuck." She tilted her head back, then pictured Roswynd riding her cock again. How she looked forward to that day, knowing it would be even better than her fantasy. She snarled and peered down at her hand jerking and stroking her cock.

Roswynd's nails dug into Tharon's thigh, reminding Tharon that she was there. When Tharon looked over, her breath caught at the hungry glow in Roswynd's eyes and the curl of her lips. There was no doubt that Roswynd wanted her. It tipped Tharon over the edge.

With a soft cry, Tharon climaxed, and slick ran down the underside of her cock. She groaned, then started panting while she smeared the slick all along the swollen length. Once done, she withdrew her hand and demonstrated the continued hardness of her penis. She couldn't help feeling smug, especially because this meant Roswynd would help her jerk off now.

Roswynd responded with a soft rumble and didn't delay keeping her promise. Without any need for discussion, she sat up on her knees, then straddled Tharon's left thigh. With her left hand on Tharon's right knee, Roswynd leaned forward some and wrapped her other hand near the base. She didn't hesitate to mimic Tharon's slow strokes from earlier, seeming to test it.

Tharon grinned and watched for a moment. Her wife was learning, running up and down the full length. "You can grip me harder." She moaned from the increased grip and whispered, "Fuck. This feels so much better when you do it." Tharon twisted her fingers in the fur under her.

"But am I doing it right?" Roswynd asked.

"Yes." Tharon was moaning but managed to say, "To get me off, you stroke faster. When you come up to the head, you can give a gentle pull at times."

"Like this?" Roswynd slid her fist up, then tugged near the top and stroked back down without hesitation.

Tharon stiffened and hissed between her clenched teeth. "Yes." She could tell Roswynd was about to put more effort into the strokes, but she asked, "Do you want to try something before you make me orgasm?"

Roswynd paused at the head and rubbed her thumb around it, earning several moans. "What is it?"

After a few gulps of air, Tharon grabbed Roswynd's hand before she fell apart from the massage to the head of her cock. "Make a fist around the shaft, about here." She guided Roswynd's hand down and waited until Roswynd closed it. "Keep your hand steady, then I am going to move my hips up and down. You can tighten and loosen your grip."

Roswynd gave a sound of agreement, then bit her lip as Tharon adjusted her arms under her body. She gasped from the first thrust.

Tharon savored her wife's small intake of air. She pumped her hips again, still slow, and watched how Roswynd's eyes darkened more. Her wife was enjoying this as much as Tharon was. "Should I stop?"

"No, do not." Roswynd's attention cut to Tharon, pleading with her to keep going.

Tharon wasn't about to deny her. She started pumping her hips at a steady pace, groaning each time Roswynd tightened her grip. For a moment, she dropped her head back while thrusting into Roswynd's fist. But Tharon started watching, needing to remember this moment. Roswynd was determined to get her off and even did small strokes. How Tharon wanted to please Roswynd in return, but she suspected it would be too much right now.

"Can you go faster?" Roswynd asked, a challenge in her voice.

With a growl, Tharon answered back with quicker but shorter thrusts, fucking Roswynd's fist. Her earlier moans turned into grunts and snarls. Roswynd's hand wrapped around her cock was amazing and sent heat roiling through her body. Slick was building up at the head again and leaking down onto Roswynd's hand, making it easier to go harder.

"Tharon," Roswynd demanded between gasps. She seemed unsure what to do next, if anything.

Tharon growled and her cock throbbed with building heat. All her muscles coiled with tension as she reached the edge. "I am c-close." She gritted her teeth and pumped harder while Roswynd added short strokes. "Fuck!" Throwing her head back, she howled low from the orgasm rushing through her. But Roswynd extended it with several firmer strokes to the point that Tharon had to grab her wife's wrist.

Roswynd stilled her motions. Her panting matched Tharon's heavy breaths. For a minute, they both sat there and struggled to regain awareness.

Tharon removed Roswynd's hand from her softened cock but held on and turned to her left side. She kept her leg back since Roswynd continued to straddle her thigh.

Roswynd twined their hands even though the wetness coated her hand some. "That was…"

Smirking, Tharon met her wife's lost gaze and waited to hear what Roswynd thought of it. From Roswynd's aroused look, Tharon knew it was a good experience, which would encourage Roswynd to open up and explore more. "Pleasant?"

Roswynd huffed and gave Tharon a pointed look. "Better than pleasant."

Tharon chuckled, then said, "It gets even better when you are receiving the pleasure." She withdrew her leg from under Roswynd, sat up, and moved into a seated position. "Do you want me to please you tonight?"

Roswynd was quiet and stared at their interlocked hands between their bodies. She turned Tharon's wedding ring to the left and right before she looked up. "I am not ready."

Nodding, Tharon lowered her head and felt compelled to rest her temple against Roswynd's head. She breathed in her wife's distinct scent that called to her. Right now she could wrap her body around Roswynd and hold her, similar to last night, but for different reasons. "I can please you without penetration."

"You can?"

Tharon withdrew and had a bewildered look. "Have you never touched yourself?" She frowned at Roswynd's returned blush and sighed at the lack of experience or real education Roswynd had about her body.

"I did a little the night before our wedding." Roswynd fidgeted with Tharon's wedding ring again. "Gleda suggested it for our wedding night."

Rumbling and considering the tidbit of information, Tharon shook her head and asked, "Did you make yourself orgasm that night?"

Roswynd laughed softly and shook her head. "I touched myself for a few minutes." She shrugged, then looked up at her wife. "How can I orgasm without penetration?"

"I can use my hand or my mouth," Tharon replied and swept back golden strands of Roswynd's hair. "Your clitoris is very sensitive like the head of my cock."

"Oh," Roswynd murmured and considered the new information.

Tharon suspected Roswynd's mind was overwhelmed with ideas and images. It would take at least a day for Roswynd to process the possibilities before she was ready to venture further. However, she wanted to make sure Roswynd didn't need anything from her. "Are you certain I cannot please you?"

Roswynd offered a smile, but it was a little weak. "Not tonight, but thank you. Will you be fine now?"

"Yes." Tharon untangled herself from Roswynd, needing to clean up. "I will return." She went into the washroom and soaked a washcloth in fresh water from the basin. First, she wiped the slick off her cock, then her hands. She tossed the washcloth and dampened a second cloth, then went out to Roswynd. "Let me see your hands."

Roswynd offered them and a smirk played on her lips. "I guess some things have not changed."

Tharon grunted at the remark and finished cleaning her wife's hands. She returned to the washroom, disposing of the cloth in the laundry bin. The fireplace was fading and almost down to glowing embers. She might add wood to it and read before dozing off in an armchair. But first, she went to her clothes on the floor.

"Tharon, you do not have to sleep in a chair or on the floor." Roswynd was seated near the top of the bed and patted the space to her right. "There is plenty of room." She canted her head and studied her wife before adding, "Besides, if we start having sex, we should be able to sleep next to each other."

"I sleep naked," Tharon reminded.

Roswynd shrugged and patted the spot a second time in silent invitation.

Tharon eyed her wife but could tell that Roswynd's offer was firm. She was unsure about sharing such a close space, even though she'd fallen asleep over Roswynd for part of last night. Her Alpha wanted to be near Roswynd tonight, especially after what they shared moments ago. Plus, Roswynd's scent was reeling her in. With a huff, she carried her clothes and boots to the table, placed them there, and collected her swords leaning against the armchair. She left her swords against the wall near the head of the bed on her designated side.

Roswynd scooted under the blanket and furs while her wife climbed onto the bed. But when Tharon didn't get underneath with her, she sighed loud enough to maybe be heard across the castle. "You are so fucking stubborn."

"I can return to my armchair." Tharon settled onto her stomach and pulled out the pillow for her head. She was comfortable like this anyway.

Roswynd sat up again, then fished out a fur from underneath her wife and tossed it over her. "You are being an idiot." She adjusted the fur over Tharon's body before she settled back in the bed again.

"You married the idiot." Tharon grinned in the growing darkness of the room and closed her eyes. For the first time in a while, she felt content; the noise in her head was quiet. Thunder rolled deep in her chest.

"Like I had a choice," Roswynd muttered and rolled onto her side, facing Tharon. Her voice sounded playful at first, but resignation underlined it.

"You *had* a choice," Tharon said, gazing at her wife again. Even in the dimness, she could make out the bronzy eye and the cobalt one peeking back at her. She never forgot how much she loved Roswynd's two different-colored eyes despite the fact they were duller than normal. She still craved looking into them.

"I did," Roswynd whispered.

Tharon was growing sleepy, and Roswynd's beautiful scent was lulling her. Her rumbles shifted into quiet purrs, but she caught Roswynd's final words.

"And I chose you."

Chapter 13

Date: 11 Black Drak 815G
(About 11 Years Ago)

Tharon rolled and unrolled the white girdle that stood out against her mint-green dress. In the past twenty minutes, she had completed sixteen laps around the cloister and even walked through the cloister's fading garden. Everything in the garden was dusted with snow after the first falling last night. She adjusted the cloak around her body but didn't mind the cold today. Not when her mind was burning with thoughts.

Returning to the garden, Tharon cleared the snow from the sundial, then studied the sun's position in the sky. Her father should be finished soon with court and come to her. He had promised this morning that they would speak about what was on Tharon's mind.

Tharon brushed snow off a stone bench beside the sundial and sat. She toyed with the bronze bracelet that Roswynd had given to her on her birthday several months ago. The day after they exchanged their friendship vows, they had tested the bracelets' supposed magic. At the festival,

Tharon had hidden from Roswynd, who used her bracelet to locate Tharon. Much to their surprise and joy, the bracelets had rejoined them even after Tharon tucked herself behind a stall in the bustling market. Roswynd had insisted that the bracelet helped her feel Tharon's presence and it pulled her toward Tharon. Ever since the test, Tharon sensed Roswynd's physical presence in the world and what direction she would have to travel to locate Roswynd. It was a strange but wonderful tug inside of her being.

Often times she found herself tracing one of the braids with her thumb. The new habit comforted her, as if the friendship bracelet reconnected her to Roswynd when they were apart. The evening they had made a blood pact and exchanged friendship vows had changed Tharon. Her vows were on her mind and inspired her to finally speak to her father.

In about two months the Howling Eagle Festival would start, which also meant their birthdays were near. Tharon would turn fifteen and Roswynd would be thirteen. They were both growing older and closer to the age of marriage. Princesses could be wed off between the ages of fourteen and eighteen, depending on a kingdom's needs and the parents' choices. So far, Tharon's father hadn't discussed marriage for Tharon, but it had to be on his mind.

A noise started in the northwestern corner of the cloister, echoing into the garden. Tharon stood and watched as two burly guards escorted her father to the central walkway of the garden. Without delay, Tharon crossed the distance to her father.

"Sorry to keep you waiting, daughter." Eustace smiled at her, but it faltered. "Why did you wait here? It is winter now."

Winter had started this month, but it was still early winter, and nothing compared to the coming months. Tharon was accustomed to the cold and noticed it affected her less in recent years. "I do not mind. It is a beautiful day." The sun was warm like Roswynd's one eye, and the sky crisp blue like Roswynd's other eye. Soon the days would grow cloudy, and constant snowfall would mark the true beginning of winter.

"Well, do you mind going to the solar room? Then we will have dinner with our family."

Tharon nodded and joined her father on the stroll through the castle to the solar room on the second floor. The two guards accompanied them to the red door of the solar room. One went inside first and handled starting a fire for them. Tharon took a seat in front of one of the tall bay windows.

Eustace ordered the guard to close the door on his way out.

"How was court, Father?" Tharon asked once they were alone. She enjoyed court herself, sneaking in sometimes. Saxon joined their father often times, but because he had to as the firstborn male. Saxon preferred to play around the castle grounds, wreaking havoc on the guards.

"It was eventful." Eustace took a seat on the other side of the bay window and folded his hands in his lap. "I passed the new law that forbids anyone from taking advantage of an Omega in heat."

Tharon had a sad smile at the news. The law being passed and enacted meant that Omegas were better protected, but it was disheartening that the law needed to be put in place. It made her think of Roswynd, who was an Omega and would someday soon start to have heats. The idea that an Alpha or a male could take advantage of Roswynd in such a weakened state made her furious. Not only was her best friend an Omega, but so was her father and mother. Tharon steeled her features and said, "That is excellent news, Father."

Eustace nodded and regarded Tharon for a moment. "What did you wish to discuss? You have not seemed yourself since you returned from your visit to Earna last month."

Bowing her head, Tharon realized she had twisted her fingers around the Bracelet of Ælfwynn. She sighed and looked at her father again. "It is what I wish to speak to you about." Pausing, she went over her speech in her head, but it was jumbled now that she was in front of her father. "I-I know I am coming of age. I want to request of you that I be betrothed and wed to Roswynd Arrington." Her father's features tightened, but Tharon pressed on while she could plead her case. "We are close and would make a strong match as spouses. Also, a marriage between an Arrington and a Blakesley would further unify our two kingdoms. Our pup—" She faltered and corrected herself in haste. "I m-mean our children would—"

"Tharon," Eustace cut off and held out a hand. "As much as I respect your passion for this... dream, it cannot be." He returned his hand to his lap. His features were still grim while he cut down Tharon's wishes. "You both are princesses. It would be disastrous to our kingdoms to have two princesses wed. It goes against centuries of royal tradition."

Tharon was prepared for her father's argument and said, "But I am an Alpha and Roswynd is an Omega."

"But you are a female as is Roswynd," Eustace reminded. His voice became firmer the longer the conversation continued. "As a royal, your sex comes before your breed. We are not like the peasants and must hold ourselves to a higher standard." When Tharon's eyes started to burn, he sighed at her and said, "I know it may not be what you wish to hear, but it is what is best for you and Roswynd. You both will each have a prince, who will balance you."

"Roswynd already balances me," Tharon argued with a growl.

Eustace took a deep breath and kept a calm composure, at the moment. His scent hinted that he was close to losing his patience with Tharon. "I thought that too about another at one time, until I met your mother."

Tharon fought against the sting in her eyes and the panic in her chest. "Please, Father. I do not wish to wed a prince, especially another Alpha." The idea of kissing a male Alpha, or more, left her skin crawling and her stomach filled with bile. Within a year or two, Tharon would experience her first rut like other Alphas. She couldn't imagine another rutting Alpha trying to dominate her.

"You may think differently as you grow older and bear children," Eustace said. Even his usage of "children" over "pups" was a stern reminder of his belief that they were above their nature. "And if not, you will learn how much easier your life is when you follow the traditions."

Tharon lowered her head and closed her eyes. Images of being with a male Alpha or Beta bombarded her as her father tried to reason with her. None of it felt right to her. It was unnatural to her. She growled and fisted her hands as she met her father's widening eyes. "No!" Standing, she took a few steps away but turned on her father, who slid off the bay window. "I will wed Roswynd!"

"Tharon," Eustace demanded in a strong voice, "control your Alpha." His pheromones filled the solar room, curling around Tharon. "You must learn to control your breed instincts." Coming closer, he held Tharon in place with stern regard. Even though he was an Omega, his pheromones were more mature and plentiful compared to Tharon's.

Tharon took deep breaths, remembering her lessons. Her father's strong scent also soothed her Alpha and helped her. But still, the tears dampened her cheeks. "I promised her that we would always be together," she whispered, her voice trembling. She met her father's gaze and said, "I thought perhaps you would understand and agree since you have allowed me to ride and hunt."

Eustace neared Tharon and clasped her shoulders. They were about the same height now, but Tharon was bulkier, indicating her nature as an Alpha. "I thought perhaps riding and hunting would give your Alpha an outlet so that you could learn to control it." His eyes were bright and reminded Tharon of amber stones. "I could be wrong. Perhaps the activities are instead encouraging your Alpha." He squeezed her shoulders and scrutinized her.

"I wish to continue hunting and riding," Tharon said. She hadn't expected their conversation to head in this direction. Was she about to lose everything that her Alpha craved to have and hold?

"I will allow you to continue those activities if you promise to never speak of wedding Roswynd Arrington again." Eustace held her gaze, then added, "I will let you have a choice of which prince or noble you can wed once I have located a selection."

Tharon closed her eyes and bowed her head, feeling her chest compressing at the unfair compromise. It was a bribe, an unspoken threat of the consequences should she continue to push the idea of marrying Roswynd. For now, she had to submit and perhaps find another way to be with Roswynd until the end of their days. Her last option was King Garrett, who seemed more open-minded.

"Yes, Father," Tharon murmured and looked at him. He wanted to make sure her eyes matched her verbal agreement.

Eustace smiled some and cupped his daughter's flushed cheeks. "I promise that everything will work out." He kissed her forehead, then whispered, "I care for your well-being greatly, Tharon. One day you may be in my place with a child of your own who requires such care."

Tharon swallowed and gave a faint nod. She caught his underlying meaning. If she ever had a degenerate pup like herself, then she would have to take on the responsibilities of raising a degenerate in a harsh society. But right now, Tharon vowed to her unborn pup or pups that they would have more freedom than she did.

"It is time for dinner." Eustace guided his daughter out of the solar room. As a family, they always shared dinner and discussed the afternoon plans. Supper tended to be optional, but dinner was the most important meal as a family.

After a few deep breaths, Tharon followed her father to the great hall where everyone else waited for them. During the meal, Tharon ate very little and instead played with her friendship bracelet or rubbed at the scar on the inside of her right palm. She wished that Roswynd were here in Wulfbite with her. Her friend's Omega scent would calm her better than her father's. She would be able to snuggle Roswynd and hide away from the stupid world for a bit.

When dinner was over, Tharon vanished to her room before anyone could speak to her. She stepped out onto the gigantic balcony that wrapped around to other rooms. With her cloak still on, Tharon went to her favorite spot in one corner where there was a stone bench. From her higher view, she admired Wulfbite spread out below the castle. Beyond the capital, the woodland was endless and beautiful, providing endless resources to White Sommer's people.

Tharon loved her kingdom as much as she loved Wyndfeld. Closing her eyes, she concentrated on the different sounds coming up from the city—metal tapping, wheels rolling over stone, horses neighing, and people laughing.

Tharon pulled her legs up onto the bench and hugged them to her chest. Her mind drifted back to Roswynd, who meant the most to her, next to her mother. She had promised Roswynd that they would always be together. If they were wed to other royalty or nobility, they would be separated for life. Roswynd could end up on the other side of Gyldren, much to Tharon's horror. Perhaps they could sneak off to the Howling Eagle Festival because of family traditions, but that was assuming their husbands approved of it.

The mere thought of a husband left Tharon huffing and grousing into her dress. She refused to marry a male, even if he could be sweet. Her heart belonged to Roswynd, who could be her perfect mate. The word "mate" made her cringe. It wasn't supposed to be used among royals. Peasants called their partners mates, especially because most peasants couldn't afford a wedding or even pay for the legal marriage documents. Every day lessons about presenting as royalty were squeezed into Tharon's head. She did her best to follow the lessons, but sometimes her Alpha could overrule her, especially when it came to Roswynd.

Tharon was supposed to resist her Alpha, even more so because she was a degenerate one. Over the past two years, Tharon's Alpha had grown stronger and now came to the forefront often. She was told to contain it, to hold it down, and to chain it. If someone asked her how well she was at doing those things, she would have to lie. Her Alpha provided strength and comfort, which couldn't be bad qualities in her opinion. However, a princess was expected to be docile, and seen but not heard.

With a sigh, Tharon considered the major issue in front of her. If her father refused to let her wed Roswynd, she had to find another way. The Howling Eagle Festival was about two months away, and their families would be together. She could talk to King Garrett about marrying Roswynd, and ask him for Roswynd's hand. Garrett respected Tharon, who was becoming an excellent hunter under his tutelage. The hunting had brought them closer, to the point that Tharon truly saw Garrett as another father. Roswynd often said that her parents viewed Tharon as another daughter. If Garrett would agree to such a marriage, then perhaps he could convince Tharon's father.

Yet Tharon was unsure about the plan. Her first attempt already backfired and nearly took away her hunting and riding privileges. She needed a third plan in case Garrett refused her. If she were denied again, then she would have to go against both fathers' wishes and take Roswynd for herself. The thought scared her, but being separated from Roswynd was a far worse fate.

At the right moment next summer, Tharon and Roswynd could ride off from Earna and never return, or only return if their families accepted them together. She was certain Roswynd would agree to the plan. They could save and hide enough coin to buy important items like clothing and supplies. Tharon could build fires and hunt while

Roswynd could gut and skin the animals, then they'd sell the pelts. Thanks to their education, they could find other work. If they hid in another kingdom, Twin Stars, then their families would have a harder time locating them.

The thought that they could forever be considered peasants didn't bother Tharon. She was fond of the idea that they would be mates rather than spouses. Tharon would be free to be an Alpha instead of a princess. Roswynd could ride and wear trousers whenever she pleased. One day they could buy a simple home and have pups, if they wished it.

"Tharon?"

Hearing the gentle voice, Tharon jerked around and studied her mother on the balcony, coming from Tharon's room.

"Do you mind if I join you?" Edeva asked and remained in the doorway between the balcony and bedroom.

Tharon shook her head, unable to refuse her mother anything.

Edeva smiled, slipped into the room, and then returned with a fur around her shoulders. She sat beside Tharon, opened the fur, and silently invited her daughter into her body.

Tharon snuggled in without hesitation and breathed in her mother's loving scent, needing it more than she realized right now.

Edeva kissed her daughter's head, then ran her fingers through Tharon's dark mane of hair. "How are you, my little Alpha?"

Tharon whined at the tender nickname. Her mother was the one person allowed to use the childhood nickname. At times Saxon used it as a slur against her degenerate nature, berating her. They had ended up in several fights over it until Eustace lectured Saxon about never using the nickname again.

"I am fine." Tharon rested her head on her mother's shoulder, then slid an arm around her mother's petite waist.

"You were quiet at dinner and left quickly." Edeva nuzzled her daughter's temple and whispered, "Tell me what is wrong."

Tharon didn't want to involve her mother, but it was impossible to hold back her distress under her mother's concern. "I-I..." She started to gasp and clung to her mother. "I-I tried to talk to Father."

"About?" Edeva continued combing Tharon's hair, but whimpered when Tharon trembled against her. "What is it, Tharon?" She leaned back and wiped the tears from Tharon's face. "Please tell me. It displeases me to see you this way."

Tharon struggled with the pain in her throat and tried to get the words out, even though her mother might be appalled as well by the idea of two princesses wedding. She opened and closed her mouth several times, but only tears escaped her.

Edeva tried to stop her daughter's tears, but her pheromones were doing nothing to calm Tharon. With each passing heartbeat, the distress on her face grew stronger. "Speak to me, Tharon. Does it have to do with Roswynd?"

Hearing her best friend's name broke Tharon into pieces. She nodded and managed to speak between her sobs. "I-I asked Father if I-I could marry Roswynd b-but he said I-I c-cannot marry another princess." She tried to hide her face, not wanting to see her mother's rejection or disdain for the idea. But Edeva refused to let Tharon tuck her head away into the fur.

"It is all right, Tharon." Edeva drew her daughter off the bench and onto her lap. It had been several years since she last held Tharon this way, but their closeness helped them both. "Breathe, my little Alpha." She hugged Tharon against her chest and kissed her temple over and over. She began rocking them, then her soft rumble overtook Tharon's fading sobs.

"Please do not hate me, too, Momma," Tharon whispered and twisted her fingers into her mother's soft dress under her hand.

"I will never hate you." Edeva lifted her head, tilted it, and peered down at Tharon's stricken features. "You are my first born, my daughter, and my little Alpha." She brushed Tharon's hair from her face and whispered, "You are my everything." Her strokes against Tharon's temple helped calm them both. "I love you so very much, Tharon." She kissed her daughter's forehead and rumbled in her ear. "Do not ever again think I could hate you," she whispered to her. "Do you understand?"

Tharon nodded and took several deep breaths that chased off the uncontrolled wildness in her head. The tightness in her chest began to loosen, then her mother's sweet scent took away the last of her doubts.

"And your father does not hate you," Edeva promised. "If that were true, none of us would be here right now." She rested her chin on Tharon's head and the rocking hadn't stopped, both still needing it. "You and your father have a difficult time. You both are alike in certain ways."

Tharon wiped her face and rested the side of her head against her mother's chest, listening to her mother's calm voice. Finally, her heart stopped feeling as though it was going to burst from her chest.

"I am also aware how much you love Roswynd."

Tharon gasped, then stiffened and waited to hear more.

"Roswynd would make an excellent spouse for you one day," Edeva said, her voice a touch proud. "Do you not agree?"

Tharon lifted her head and rose to eye level with her mother. "Yes, but Father said two princesses cannot wed."

Edeva pushed a few stuck strands from Tharon's forehead. "It is a matter of perspective, my little Alpha. You are a princess because we said you are, not because that is who you are."

Tharon stared at her lap and played with a tiny jewel sewn in her mother's dress. She bit her lip and thought about the meaning behind her mother's words. Roswynd often called Tharon "my prince" when they were together. "You mean I could be a prince, if I wanted to be. But the traditions—"

"Are flawed," Edeva cut off. "They are very flawed." She placed her chin back on Tharon's head and resumed the conversation. "I respect what the royal traditions try to do, but they can make some of us unhappy. Some of us who are different."

Tharon closed her eyes and listened, relieved to hear that her mother didn't agree with every tradition. "I am different."

"You are, and I love how different you are," Edeva said, pride coloring her voice. "I think that is why Roswynd takes to you too. Not simply because you are different, but because you treat her differently." She hadn't stopped rocking their bodies. "As an Omega, I wish I had grown up with a friend like you. I am happy you both have each other."

Tharon frowned and whispered, "It will not be for much longer."

"You cannot be so certain." Edeva took a deep breath as the silence stretched on for a minute or two. A contented rumble rolled in her chest and kept Tharon's mind at ease. "Give your father time, Tharon. I believe he will change his mind."

"But what if King Garrett weds off Roswynd before Father can change his mind? If he ever does." Tharon traced the friendship bracelet.

"I suspect King Garrett is not in any rush to promise Roswynd to another."

"But at the ball he always pushes Roswynd to dance with a noble," Tharon said, frowning at the different dance partners Roswynd had at the past few balls.

Edeva chuckled and said, "Yes, well it is important to keep up appearances and set positive examples. But I have a suspicion that Garrett is not so inclined to lose his daughter anytime soon. He is protective of her."

Tharon chewed on her bottom lip and considered her mother's insight about Roswynd's future. She moved her head and peered up into fiery eyes. "Do you think it is possible Father will change his mind?"

"Yes, in time." Edeva pressed her lips to Tharon's forehead and whispered, "I will speak to him as well." She smiled when Tharon's breath hitched, then she said, "Until then, try to enjoy your time with Roswynd and not fret over losing her."

Blushing, Tharon felt caught because her mother understood her so well. She shifted in her mother's lap and muttered, "S-Sorry."

Edeva chuckled, nudged her daughter's temple, and murmured, "I hate seeing you distressed, my little Alpha."

"I-I am sorry," Tharon repeated and sank into her mother's body again. She didn't like worrying her mother, but her father's denial had shattered her dreams. If she lost Roswynd, Tharon would break in half. Somehow Roswynd had become her foundation over the years.

"It is all right." Edeva tightened her arms and brought the fur around them more. She nuzzled into Tharon's temple and whispered, "You and Roswynd will always be together."

* * *

Date: 18 Sunstone 826G

(Present Day)

Roswynd stirred from the early sunlight in her bedroom. She rolled to her side, stretched, and smiled when her vision sharpened on the person next to her on the bed. Yesterday had been a strange occurrence of events. The ride to Stormbreaker Landing had been pleasant, and the tour of the port city was interesting. Roswynd spent most of the day thinking about Tharon's offer for them to become lovers. At first she had been unsure and concerned about what would happen if Tharon was scheming to take down Wyndfeld. And it could still be true. But Roswynd hoped that the good pieces of Tharon remained. She was certain she caught glimpses of those fragments of her old best friend.

Even if Roswynd was wrong, she accepted a different truth that hadn't occurred to her until yesterday. Tharon was the sole person Roswynd ever wanted to share her body with. She didn't discredit the possibility that she may be forced into sex with another. But to have Tharon was Roswynd's ultimate choice. Whatever their future may be, Roswynd had a chance to finally be with Tharon. She prayed the decision wouldn't cost her.

Stretching out her arm, Roswynd rested her fingertips near Tharon's arm but didn't touch her. From what she could tell, it didn't seem as if Tharon moved a single muscle last night. The numerous nights in the armchairs and on the floor may have caught up to Tharon. Plus, her wife appeared much calmer after masturbating.

Roswynd flushed at the memory, then her heart trembled in her chest after a deep breath. Already her palms were damp from her rising body heat. Last night had been exhilarating, new, and fun for Roswynd. She learned several things in a short window, especially about Tharon's body as a female Alpha. The books from the library were limited, and Tharon had a point that males might have a skewed viewpoint.

The sunlight caressed Tharon's body, highlighting her muscular physique. The tanned curves glowed while the fur hid the rest, but Roswynd remembered what she couldn't see at the moment. Tharon was beautiful from head to toe, even more so than when they were young. The scars dotting Tharon's body had intrigued Roswynd last night. She hadn't asked for their histories, but that didn't keep her imagination from painting stories in her head.

But what captivated Roswynd the most was Tharon's cock. There were plenty of drawings in books, artwork, and sculptures depicting naked males and females from each breed, except for female Alphas or male Omegas. Those were rare finds. Last night, Roswynd enjoyed learning firsthand about a female Alpha, especially because it was Tharon.

Even now, Roswynd was a little skeptical that Tharon could fit inside her. Her doubt had humored Tharon, who had far more sexual experience than Roswynd. She hoped Tharon was right about that, and the part about the pain being minimal. It was confusing. She was much smaller in stature than Tharon. As young ones, they were about the same size, then around ten years old, Tharon started to grow up and out at a rapid pace. As an adult, Roswynd could compare Tharon's size to that of a bear or maybe a large wolf. Either way, Roswynd felt tiny next to Tharon, but she'd grown to like the new difference.

Even though Roswynd was smaller, Tharon respected her wishes and gave her control over last night's events. Roswynd found the most power when Tharon was thrusting her cock through Roswynd's fist. If she had changed the pressure, she could control how quickly or slowly Tharon would orgasm. Every one of Tharon's moans was exquisite. Even now, Roswynd struggled with the returning throb between her legs. She had never felt something like this. It was strange but not unwelcomed, even though she was unsure what do about it. Perhaps she had to masturbate like Tharon, though she didn't know what to do.

Tharon's soft movement stirred Roswynd from her thoughts. She found eyes that matched the harvest sunsets staring back at her. Roswynd admired the mild cloudiness of Tharon's right eye, even though part of her missed all the orange color. Stretching out her fingers, Roswynd touched her wife's forearm and curled her fingers around the warm skin.

"Did you sleep well?" Roswynd asked and squeezed the arm under her hand.

"Yes."

Roswynd grinned and teased, "Better than the armchair?"

Tharon huffed, then lifted up and exposed her breasts. She pulled the blankets and furs aside until she had enough room to wrestle Roswynd free of them.

With a low squeal, Roswynd allowed herself to be pulled to Tharon, then she found herself underneath her nude wife. She gasped and covered her pounding chest with one hand, and clutched Tharon's shoulder, dropping her head against the pillow.

Tharon rested most of her weight on her arms and knees while her front pressed into Roswynd. She studied her prize under her and asked, "Did you enjoy last night?"

"Y-Yes," Roswynd replied in a shaky voice and curled her nails into the broad shoulder. "Did you?"

"Yes." Tharon regarded Roswynd in stern silence. Her eyes were blown, losing all the orange. "Would you like to continue later?"

Roswynd nodded, more than sure of herself. She suspected her features showed her confidence because Tharon grinned at her. Pressing her hand harder against her chest, she wished her heart would slow because it sounded like a drum. "Is that acceptable?"

Tharon nodded, then combed back her hair to one side with her fingers. "I am not great at slow, but I will wait."

"I am well aware," Roswynd teased, but her grin slipped the longer Tharon studied her. She cupped both of Tharon's cheeks and whispered, "Thank you for your patience, and for teaching me."

Tharon grunted at the warm appreciation, seeming unsure how to handle it. She rumbled, then lifted her body higher and studied Roswynd trapped under her. The arrangement pleased her, according to the hungry smile on her face. Tharon grasped Roswynd's hip, which was covered by the nightgown.

For a moment, Roswynd was lost in Tharon's gaze and wanted to stay there. She held on to Tharon's shoulders and remained hidden from everything but her wife. Maybe they could forget all the hardships of war, their arranged marriage, and the ugly past. Roswynd started to believe it was possible until someone walked past their closed door. She jumped from the familiar sound of a guard, gripped Tharon harder, and gasped in reaction.

Tharon shielded Roswynd again with her body and growled deep toward the door, as if natural to her. The animalistic growl itself wasn't directed at Roswynd, but it was possessive of her. After the guard's steps faded, Tharon came to her senses and made an attempt to get off Roswynd, but she was pulled back by nimble hands.

"Stay," Roswynd pleaded. For ten years, she was starved of Tharon's touch and comfort. Now an adult Alpha, Tharon had a natural need to claim Roswynd as her own. She and Tharon were supposed to hold back such instincts, but they failed to do so at times.

Settling in again, Tharon enveloped Roswynd with both her body and her heady pheromones that left Roswynd dizzy. She accidently moaned and rocked her hips up, hitting Tharon's stomach area with her pelvis.

Tharon breathed in Roswynd's scent and rumbled low. "You are very aroused."

"Well, I have a big, naked Alpha above me," Roswynd snapped, wishing she had better control of her body. Tharon was powerful and felt sensual against her. How was she supposed to handle the situation? Since the day she first saw Tharon, she was excited by the tall, dark knight, who was once her best friend. After last night, Roswynd was aroused and had no idea what to do.

"Let me please you," Tharon whispered and nuzzled into the side of Roswynd's head.

Roswynd could feel Tharon's grin, but she heard the desperation too. The request was also a plea for Tharon to have some of Roswynd, anything. She groaned and asked, "How?"

"With my mouth," Tharon replied, voice rough now.

"Will it hurt?"

Tharon stiffened when Roswynd ground against her again. "No."

"Will I orgasm?"

Tharon released a strained breath near Roswynd's ear, then gave a short growl. "Yes."

Roswynd turned her head and pushed Tharon's head back until their gazes met. She rubbed her thumb against Tharon's bottom lip, wondering how this mouth could please her.

"You do not have to take off your clothes either," Tharon added. Her blown eyes were big and full of desire. Her lips were curled back, showing off her canines.

Roswynd took a deep breath, then nodded her approval. She gasped when Tharon sat up and removed the fur from her back. It seemed as if Tharon wasn't about to lose out on the invitation to please Roswynd. "What do I have to do?"

"Stay right there is all," Tharon replied as she scooted down farther. "You can tell me to stop if you are ever uncomfortable. Or push my head away."

"Push your head away?" Roswynd asked in confusion. She didn't receive an explanation other than Tharon's smirk. What in Gyldr's name had she agreed to?

Tharon relocated her upper body to the middle half of the bed and rested on her knees.

Roswynd tried to ignore Tharon's cock, which appeared somewhat hard, but nothing like last night. She bit her lip to hold back a whimper. Two strong hands collected the lower half of her nightgown, lifting it up. She trembled but followed the silent instruction to lift her hips, then the sleepwear settled around her waist and left her lower half exposed to Tharon. Her undergarment was truly soaked, confirming Tharon's earlier statement about her arousal. With the nightgown and furs out of the way, her wetness permeated the air around them.

Tharon growled with such ferocity that it caused Roswynd to squirm in place. For an instant, she and Roswynd held gazes, but then Tharon lowered herself and pushed Roswynd's thigh. "Spread your legs open for me."

Unable to form words, Roswynd did as she was told and closed her eyes, tensing at the pending experience. She had no idea what Tharon planned to do to her, but she trusted Tharon to not hurt her. Both excitement and fear swirled deep in her gut as she waited. She stiffened when several fingers hooked her undergarment.

"These will need to come off," Tharon said, then tugged them off Roswynd's waist to the top of her thighs. "In a minute."

Roswynd whined and tried looking down to find Tharon, but her view was blocked by the furs and nightgown. She took deep breaths, pacing her frantic heart. It was impossible once Tharon's hot breath brushed against her inner thighs. Roswynd gasped and clawed the fur under her hands. Before she could muster a word or noise, something warm and firm brushed across her clitoris. Again, a strangled sound started in her throat, then the same soft thing rubbed her clit again. With Tharon's breath grazing her skin near her groin, she realized it was Tharon's tongue touching her.

"Oh g-gods," Roswynd finally managed through a strangled breath. She clenched the furs harder and focused on the feeling of Tharon toying with her sensitive clit. The sensation was light but sent heat roaring through her veins. She wanted to feel more of it. No, she *needed* to feel more of Tharon's tongue. Thankfully, Tharon seemed to notice.

Tharon raised her head and pressed her lips against Roswynd's lower stomach. "Can I remove these?" She tugged on the undergarment.

"Y-Yes, please." Roswynd was panting already and placed a hand on her damp chest. She lifted her ass and allowed Tharon to remove the obtrusive clothing. Their disappearance was perfect and allowed her to squirm with need. "Tharon?"

"Right here." Tharon returned to her earlier spot and kissed the inside of Roswynd's thigh. She then pressed her mouth against Roswynd's exposed sex and ran the flat of her tongue up through the middle, tasting all of Roswynd.

Roswynd gritted her teeth from the amazing feeling of Tharon's tongue brushing across her clit. Lifting her head, she struggled to see Tharon, only finding her head between Roswynd's legs and face buried between her thighs. Roswynd moaned and dropped back to the bed, gasping from another stroke across her throbbing clit. How could it hurt so bad, and Tharon's tongue feel so right?

Tharon slid her hands under Roswynd's ass, cupping both cheeks and lifting some. The extra bit of height encouraged her to give even more. Tharon began sucking on the swollen clit, taking it into her mouth and playing with it.

"Fuck!" Roswynd snared her pillow from her side and half covered her face to muffle her noises. What if one of the guards heard her? Or worse, a family member who might be stopping by to see them? They couldn't enter with the door bolted, but she was being loud. Tharon's mouth felt too damn good.

Shifting some, Tharon swirled her tongue around the needy bud, then pulled it into her mouth again. She increased the pace, eliciting small but muffled cries from her wife. With a rumble, Tharon switched between licking and sucking, working Roswynd into a fever.

Roswynd writhed and moaned while her body curled up from all the increasing heat in her belly. Then she had the urge to grab Tharon, twisting her fingers into black hair. Her wife did not seem to mind and actually rumbled in pleasure. When Tharon returned to licking, Roswynd was compelled to rock her hips and match the tempo. Her needy demands seemed to spur Tharon, who clenched Roswynd's ass harder and sent fire bolting up Roswynd's spine.

Needing air, Roswynd shoved the pillow aside and gulped as Tharon sucked on her clit. Somehow it was a little different, more precise and even a bit rough, but Roswynd loved it. She clenched her teeth and hissed, then ordered, "Do not stop doing that!" Her entire body was ablaze and reaching some breaking point that might be the orgasm that she needed. Her pants were harsh like her slamming heart, but she was almost there.

Tharon then sucked harder and flicked her tongue over the sensitive clit that was swollen past the hood. The single, delicate motion sent an exquisite rush tearing through Roswynd from head to toe. The pillow somewhat muffled her cry before it was too late.

Roswynd was overwhelmed by the heat from the orgasm. It took more than her breath. It took everything from her, but then released her with both pleasure and brief happiness. Tharon had given all of it to her and taken away the maddening need. A few aftershocks raced down her spine, leaving her moaning and reliving the moment. A light kiss to her thigh further calmed her.

Tharon rose and gently pulled the nightgown back into place, covering Roswynd again. She crawled over Roswynd, who closed her trembling legs. Tharon returned to her earlier spot, covering Roswynd and waited for her to process the new experience.

After a murmur, Roswynd hooked her arms around Tharon and held on to her, needing the closeness. She tucked her face into her wife's neck, which was strong with pheromones that comforted her. They traded affectionate rumbles until Tharon broke the silence first.

"So, was it terribly painful?"

Roswynd rolled her eyes and then smacked her wife's bare ass, not thinking about her action. When they were young, it was common for Roswynd to do that when they wrestled or played together.

Tharon responded with a light growl and pressed deeper into Roswynd for a moment.

A blush crossed Roswynd's features. She gripped Tharon's hip and hoped to distract Tharon with a response. "No, it was fair." Her voice was playful and taunted Tharon.

"Fair?" Tharon lifted her head and revealed her dark eyes. "It sounded a lot better than simply fair." She was smug and stared into Roswynd, who squirmed under her.

"I think it would be wise to do it again so I can make a better assessment." Roswynd grinned at Tharon's eyebrow lifting into a perfect arc. "Things became a little fuzzy at the end."

Tharon snorted and grinned at her wife. "I see." She lowered her head again and pressed her nose into Roswynd's neck, breathing her in.

Roswynd closed her eyes and soaked in the attention, but then noticed her own scent lingering around Tharon's mouth. She grinned at the memory of Tharon's tongue worshipping her. Earlier she made light of it because that was easier than trying to grasp the intensity of it. She needed time again and maybe more of Tharon's tongue. A lot more.

After another deep breath, Tharon withdrew from Roswynd and climbed out of bed. She vanished into the washroom and Roswynd heard water being poured into a basin.

She took a moment to collect herself before leaving the bed. They needed to start their day. She wanted to visit Gleda and hoped Tharon would be fine with her leaving for breakfast. After she picked up her discarded undergarment, she went to the wardrobe and selected a buttery-yellow dress for today. She changed behind the divider and listened to Tharon in the other room.

"Tharon, do you mind if I have breakfast with Gleda?" Roswynd asked, turning her head sidelong toward the washroom.

"No." Tharon emerged from the washroom and stood behind Roswynd. She pushed Roswynd's hands away from the few buttons on the dress.

From her peripheral view, Roswynd noted that her wife was nude and unbothered by it. She bit her lip, but it was too late because the slight burn started between her legs again. "We should speak to Father later. Find out what other plans he has for us."

Rumbling, Tharon took care of the last button at the base of Roswynd's neck. "Perhaps a parade of some sort."

Roswynd chuckled, turned, and responded, "Or a formal ball, since that is your favorite." She noticed Tharon had a toothbrush stuck in her mouth. Few people cleaned their teeth, but royals and nobles were known to do it. In her youth, Tharon's routine included using a toothbrush and a pick, and then rinsing with mint-infused water. Roswynd had taken on the same morning ritual. It appeared neither of them had given up the habit in all the years.

"I can escort you to Gleda's," Tharon said.

Roswynd shook her head. "I will take a few guards." She touched Tharon's bare stomach and teased, "Are you going to walk around our room naked all the time now?"

"Does it bother you, Princess?" Tharon asked, voice heavy with her Alpha.

"No." Roswynd grinned at the taunting nickname and murmured, "You have no shame, do you?" She chuckled at Tharon's responding smirk, then said, "You could go to the library to read. Change of scenery at least."

Tharon rumbled, then shrugged and started back to the washroom. Roswynd raised an eyebrow at her wife's nice ass cheeks that ached to be squeezed. *She is going to be the death of me*, she concluded with a worried frown. Roswynd left for the garderobe and returned a few minutes later to find the washroom free. She washed up and brushed her mouth, then rinsed with the minty water she kept tucked on a shelf.

Tharon was fully dressed and seated in front of the rekindled fire. She peered up from her book when Roswynd neared her. "How are your shoulders?" Stretching out her legs, she crossed them at the ankles.

"They are fine now." Roswynd rolled them.

"Good." Tharon returned to the book and muttered, "Archery today, then."

Roswynd smiled at the promise. "I will not be long." She started to the door, but paused with her hand on the bolt. "Oh. Tharon?" Once her wife looked toward her, she said, "In the future, do not jerk off anymore without me." She chuckled at Tharon's gawk, then left before Tharon had a chance to recover.

Yes, I know what you were doing during your baths.

Chapter 14

Gleda sipped from the porcelain cup, then lowered it to the saucer in her hand. "You are eating well for once." She indicated her friend's empty plate. A bowl of fruit for them to share sat to the side, but their plates and bowls were empty otherwise.

Roswynd rested her hands on her stomach and replied, "Yes, the food was very good. Thank you." She shifted back in the chair when a servant came to collect the dirty dishes. For a moment, her attention roamed to the outside world beyond the window next to them. The window was cracked open, allowing a fresh breeze and the sounds of the city to enter the room. Someone was walking past with a horse, and its hooves clopped against the stone street.

"How is Tharon treating you?" Gleda asked after the servant departed with the dishes.

Roswynd was quiet and considered how to explain it to Gleda. She shook her head and met her friend's concerned features. "It is confusing. She does not mistreat me."

"But?" Gleda set her cup and saucer on the table, then plucked a handful of luke berries from the fruit bowl. She popped one of the deep red berries into her mouth and waited for Roswynd to speak her mind.

"Tharon is keeping me at arm's length." Roswynd rested back in the seat. "We have good moments then bad ones."

"How bad?"

Roswynd shook her head and replied, "It is nothing like that. She has not harmed me physically at all." She played with the linen napkin on her lap and continued diving into the topic after keeping it to herself for the past nine days since the wedding. "Tharon was cold at the beginning, and now she is less standoffish, but she refuses to resolve what happened in the past."

"Unless the only resolution in her mind is taking down the House of Arrington," Gleda said.

"That is my fear," Roswynd said and sighed. "It is all rather confusing because she does thoughtful things." At Gleda's unconvinced look, she started ticking off examples on her fingers. "She organized the wedding, which was romantic if you remove the political nature of it. She gave me a beautiful ring that represents what I enjoy in life." She held up her right hand, then returned it to her lap. "Tharon gave me a wedding gift."

"A wedding gift?" Gleda's interest was piqued by the news.

"A bow. And she is teaching me archery."

Gleda gasped and leaned forward. "Is your father aware?"

Roswynd shook her head and echoed what Tharon told her. "He is no longer my Alpha."

Gleda chuckled and covered her mouth as she leaned back in the chair. "When he learns that Tharon gave you a bow, he will be cross with you both." She shook with silent laughter. "I wish I could be there."

Roswynd grinned, but it slipped as she thought about this morning. She fidgeted, until she decided to give in and announced, "We are going to become lovers."

"Pardon!" Gleda's voice boomed through the room, which caused the servant to hurry in to help them. Sighing, Gleda shooed off the servant and waited until the door closed again. "You said nothing happened on your wedding night."

Roswynd withheld the detail about Tharon's prank, knowing Gleda wouldn't understand Tharon's sense of humor. As pups, Roswynd lost count of how many pranks and jokes they pulled on each other, but the prank on the wedding night was something different and confusing even now. "Nothing happened then. But something happened last night… and this morning."

Gleda leaned against the table and reached across it for Roswynd's hand. "Tell me." Her brown eyes were bright from the streaming sunlight.

Roswynd chuckled and took her friend's hand. She recanted last night's fun and then told Gleda about her first orgasm this morning. Her face and chest were flushed from reliving the exhilarating memory. The slight dampness returned between her legs.

"She used her mouth?" Gleda whispered, withdrew, and slumped against the chair. She fanned herself and murmured, "Perhaps she is worth forgiving, then."

Roswynd's eyebrows hiked up at her friend's panting response to the story. "Why are you so—"

"Aroused?"

Now that Gleda said it, Roswynd had noticed her friend's magnified scent, even for a Beta. She squirmed in the chair and tried handling the strange situation between them. Gleda was often well composed and in control. Plus, a Beta's scent was supposed to be weaker than an Alpha's or Omega's. At least the open window provided fresh air to drown out the pheromones. "Well, yes."

"My apologies." Gleda drank water from the crystal glass to her right. She cleared her throat after setting the stemware down. "All the old and new gods know I love Byron, but he is dreadful with his tongue. He also refuses to practice."

"Oh," Roswynd whispered, blushing again the more she thought about Tharon between her legs this morning. Was she blessed to have an accomplished lover? At least, she assumed Tharon was well versed in all areas of sex.

"And you say you orgasmed too?" Gleda clicked her tongue once and shook her head.

"Have you not?" Roswynd asked, dumbstruck by the idea that Gleda might not have with Byron. What Tharon told her about the information from the books must be true.

Were Byron and Gleda the type of couple that focused on the male's orgasm?

"I have on rare occasions," Gleda replied. "I tend to not orgasm during penetration."

Roswynd wiggled in the chair. They had been friends since childhood, but they didn't often discuss sex because of Roswynd's inexperience. At the moment, Roswynd felt certain she would melt through the floor if Byron walked into the room. But Gleda's details interested Roswynd, who sat up more. "Then how have you orgasmed?" She hoped Gleda would explain more about sex and give away secrets that the books had failed to tell her.

Gleda grinned and folded her arms on the edge of the table. "When Byron is inside of me, I massage my clitoris. He seems to like it better when I orgasm with him in me."

The details churned through Roswynd's imagination. She saved it for later, if she and Tharon went further in their new relationship. But the conversation spurred her questions to life again. "Did it hurt the first time you were with Byron?"

"Yes, it burned for a little bit, but then that goes away." Gleda tilted her head in consideration, then added, "Sometimes it still can if he pushes at the wrong angle." She smiled but it turned into a grin. "But if Tharon is willing to use her mouth, then I suggest milking that for all it is worth."

* * *

After breakfast with Gleda, Roswynd returned to the castle with her two guards. She thanked them when they departed for patrol duties around the castle grounds. Inside the keep, she located Tharon in their bedroom, but her arrival had carried through the castle. Her father wanted to speak to her and Tharon at his office.

They met Garrett in the office on the third floor. Tharon hadn't been too far off the mark when she joked about a parade. Garrett decided a festival was in order to celebrate both the marriage and the cease-fire between the kingdoms. He also picked days for two short trips, one north to the mountain city called Montisgard, the other south to the city of Brickelwhyte. There were other cities and major towns, but they would have to wait until Roswynd and Tharon returned from Wulfbite. For now, the three city visits and the abbreviated festival would have to suffice. The festival would be held on the last week before they departed for Wulfbite.

For the week of Skywice, they would travel to Montisgard, which would take a full day, then stay two nights. They would spend all day touring the city and waving to the people. The next day they would travel back to Earna. For Brickelwhyte, Garrett planned to follow the same schedule, finding time between court sessions to leave the capital.

By the time they left the office, Roswynd was certain that her wife needed the horseback ride and archery to unwind from the demands imposed on them. Tharon was the lord commander in White Sommer. Even though Saxon was king, Roswynd suspected Tharon ruled the roost behind the scenes. Now in Wyndfeld, Tharon was subjected to Garrett's rule without question.

After changing into riding attire, Roswynd retrieved her bow and quiver, then handed them to Tharon. They escaped the keep before anyone could halt them. Deri readied their horses and brought them out of the stable without hesitation. Once free of the castle grounds and the city, Roswynd released a sigh of relief. Even Tharon appeared more relaxed in the saddle as they followed a trail into the Icecrown Forest. Roswynd was unsure where they were headed until Tharon took the lead.

They arrived at an abandoned water mill beside one of the rivers flowing from the White Razor Mountains. This same river had their favorite overlook farther upstream. They allowed their horses to graze without the face tacks while they set up a shooting spot. Similar to last time, Tharon marked out certain distances and used the north side of the water mill as their target.

Roswynd kept from rolling her eyes that she was shooting at another structure rather than a smaller target. While Tharon marked the lines, she strung her bow and smiled at her ability to do it faster than last time, but the best part of waiting was appreciating the view of Tharon's ass each time she bent over to drag the arrowhead through the ground to make a line. By the time Tharon had made all five marks, Roswynd was praying her arousal didn't call to Tharon.

Stepping up to the closest line, Roswynd and Tharon started the archery lesson. They warmed up first, then backed up to the next line after one round. Roswynd was growing more confident even though it was merely her second lesson.

The bow required a strong eye and steady hands. When she made it to the fourth line, she sensed some early fatigue in her arms, but she was determined to go farther.

"When can I shoot at a smaller target?" Roswynd asked after landing most of the arrows into the same area of a board on the water mill's side.

Tharon considered the request and canted her head. "Do you feel you are ready?"

"Perhaps. I will not know until I try." Roswynd started collecting the arrows. Tharon joined her, standing close by. Roswynd glanced at her wife and watched the biceps tighten against the tunic each time Tharon dislodged an arrow.

Tharon sensed the attention and looked at her wife.

Roswynd turned away and grabbed the last arrow, which had fallen to the ground rather than embedding into the wood plank. She noticed Tharon was already walking away to a different spot.

Tharon stood in front of a tree and measured out the paces from it, then marked the spot for Roswynd. "Here." When Roswynd stepped up, she slid the arrows into the quiver on Roswynd's back. "Now try."

"No advice?" Roswynd asked, eyeing her wife next to her.

Tharon put her hands behind her back and shrugged. "Sometimes the best learning is on your own." She grinned and waited for Roswynd to begin.

With a sigh, Roswynd nocked the first arrow and aimed for the single tree. She released the arrow, which embedded itself in the center.

Tharon rumbled but said nothing and watched Roswynd nock the next arrow.

Roswynd struck the tree again, but a bit higher. The third arrow almost missed and buried into the side. The fourth was a dud and pierced the ground about a step away from the trunk. The fifth one landed close to the first one. Roswynd continued one after another but slowed when Tharon moved behind her. She nocked an arrow but didn't draw it. "What are you doing?"

"Watching."

Roswynd rolled her eyes and drew the arrow, then aligned her sight on the tree. Behind her, she felt Tharon edge closer to her. Roswynd's eyelids fluttered for a second, then she released the arrow, which whizzed into the bush behind the tree. "Shit!"

"Distracted, Princess?" Tharon whispered next to Roswynd's left ear. "Let me assist you."

Roswynd growled and glared over her shoulder at her wife. "I do not require your help."

"I think you do." Tharon extracted an arrow and held it out to her.

Roswynd swiped it, nocked it, and lifted her arms. She drew the string back with the arrow but paused when Tharon touched her.

"Your last few arrows went higher than normal." Tharon placed a hand under Roswynd's outstretched arm that had the bow. Her other hand pressed on the underside of Roswynd's right arm. "When you start to release, you have been lifting your upper body, which changes the trajectory of the arrow." She placed both hands on Roswynd's hips and said, "Do not lean back, and hold your position."

Roswynd closed her eyes and clenched her lip between her teeth. Her wife was pressing into her, teasing her. She pictured Tharon between her legs again, pleasing her as she did this morning. A moan almost escaped her, but Roswynd blew out a breath. She concentrated, aimed again, and released the arrow, which sailed through the air and hit the center of the tree.

"Much better." Tharon placed a finger under Roswynd's chin and then tilted and turned Roswynd's head. "You want to lean back and arc your arrow when your target is farther away."

Roswynd made an agreeing sound and stared into Tharon's bright orange eyes. She was certain now that her arousal had caught Tharon's nose. There was no way to avoid the truth, especially when Tharon's lip curled back. Giving in, she whispered, "I continue to think about this morning."

"Mmmm." Tharon grabbed Roswynd's leather belt around her waist and yanked it, bringing Roswynd's side into Tharon. "Ask me."

Roswynd trembled and grabbed Tharon's waist with her free hand. She searched Tharon's features and wondered if it was normal to need this much. They'd fooled around only hours ago, but Roswynd was turning into a mess. The dampness between her legs was hard to ignore, and Tharon could make her feel so good. With her lips parted, she struggled to ask Tharon, especially out here in the forest. They were far from the city and people, but it was possible for someone to happen upon them. In the past, she and Tharon had played around the water mill and often came across strangers who picnicked here. Roswynd's stomach fluttered at the idea that they could be caught; two royals publicly fooling around was against traditions.

Tharon growled, bent down, and picked Roswynd off the ground. She lifted her wife to her waist, clenching both hands against Roswynd's ass.

Roswynd dropped her bow on instinct and grabbed Tharon's shoulders. She was panting and dropped her forehead against Tharon's head.

"You *need* it again. It is acceptable to ask me," Tharon told her in a rough, throaty voice.

Roswynd tangled her fingers in Tharon's hair and moaned before she whispered, "I do want you to do it again. I have been wanting it all morning. Please, Tharon." She pressed her lips against Tharon's brow but wished they were kissing, even though she wasn't ready to share such an intimate act.

With a throaty growl, Tharon carried Roswynd past the tree they'd used for target practice, and then a different tree's rough surface pressed into her back. The bark scraped against her, but she ignored it. All that mattered was getting Tharon's head between her thighs and that tongue against her clit. "Please, Tharon."

Lowering her wife, Tharon flattened her body against Roswynd, who was pinned to the tree. With nimble fingers, she unthreaded the fly of Roswynd's trousers, then shimmied them to Roswynd's hips. With her hand, she latched onto Roswynd's neck, but she was gentle and locked their gazes.

Roswynd swallowed and placed a hand against her wife's stomach. They'd known each other all their lives and been friends since they were able to form words. Even if the ten years of war dissolved their friendship, Roswynd's dangerous feelings for Tharon stayed alive underneath her anger for Tharon's betrayal. She was certain that if Tharon broke their marriage vows, she would have no strength left to survive. She had waited all these years to see and confront Tharon. Fragments of her held on to the dream that she would find a way to reach Tharon and reawaken her best friend rather than go to war again. If it was an impossible feat, then it was better to have a coldhearted Tharon than not have a Tharon at all. But Roswynd knew she was lying to herself; the reality of their future might end with her life.

As Tharon regarded her, Roswynd felt her wife's possessive Alpha nature rising to the surface. The war had divided them, separated them, and made them enemies. However, their marriage now unified them despite its political purpose. By law they belonged to each other, and Tharon was clearly pleased by the arrangement. If the war was rekindled, Roswynd was wife to the lord commander of White Sommer until the end of her days.

Tharon leaned in and dipped her head until her nose was near Roswynd's neck. She breathed in Roswynd's honey-like scent that pleaded for Tharon to taste and lick her. With a free hand, Roswynd reached back and clawed the tree behind her. Her eyes rolled back as Tharon continued to drink in her scent as if nothing else in the world were as delicious. Roswynd locked her knees in hopes to stay upright rather than make an idiot of herself. Each second was more maddening than the last one and left Roswynd shaken and needy. If Tharon didn't please her soon, she might try using her fingers as Gleda suggested.

"So excited and aroused," Tharon whispered. Her voice was thick, and it wrapped around Roswynd. "Very unbecoming of a princess." She hooked a finger in Roswynd's loose trousers and pulled them the rest of the way down. "Soon I will have you howling like the Omega you are."

Roswynd hadn't forgotten Tharon's mild howl last night after she helped Tharon orgasm. The deep, animalistic noise caused her stomach to flutter from the power of it. Tharon was a proud Alpha, who rallied against their royal upbringing to restrain that side of themselves. Roswynd found Tharon's Alpha thrilling and alluring. Biting her lip, Roswynd struggled with a moan, but it escaped and encouraged Tharon's smug look.

With thunder in her chest, Tharon began to lower to the ground, pushing back her swords. She paused to kiss Roswynd's stomach after lifting the white tunic. Once on her knees, she growled and wasted little time in pleasing Roswynd with her mouth. After a soft cry, Roswynd gasped and peered down at Tharon between her thighs, licking and sucking on her clit. She was trembling from top to bottom and choking on air while Tharon's tongue played with her throbbing bud. Within a minute, she had already hit one limit and dropped her head back against the tree. She cried out again as an orgasm swept through her, but Tharon didn't stop.

"Oh gods!" Roswynd dragged her nails down the tree trunk behind her. "Tharon!" She started to sink some, except Tharon's hand against her hip kept her pinned in place. Roswynd gulped more air as her body recovered from the first orgasm, which Tharon seemed to notice.

Tharon returned to sucking the sweet nub into her mouth, then flicked it a few times. Roswynd bucked against her face, but Tharon didn't lose contact and continued stroking Roswynd. Groaning and rolling her head, Roswynd lowered her gaze and admired Tharon working her sex so hard. She pulled up her tunic, tucking it under her waist belt, and exposing her flat stomach. She swept back Tharon's dark hair, and their eyes met for an instant. Tharon was clearly happy to ravish her like this, making Roswynd whimper.

Unable to resist any longer, Roswynd rocked her hips and ground into Tharon's tongue that brushed her clit. She groaned in pleasure and heat rippled through her belly, making her heart slam even more against her chest. Roswynd had never felt anything like this, and the brief thought of what it might be like to have Tharon inside her sat at the edge of her mind. But then Tharon's exquisite sucking vanished the fraying thoughts in Roswynd's mind. All she needed was to orgasm again, to hold on to this moment, and satisfy Tharon with her own howl.

Roswynd curled her back and pushed her head against the tree. She closed her eyes when Tharon growled against her pussy, and they came undone for each other. Roswynd's howl was soft, but it was deafening to their ears. The orgasm was stronger than the last one, giving her an overwhelming bliss. She could feel herself surrender a little more of herself to Tharon in that moment. As she started to slip, Tharon was there to collect her and hold her.

Tharon remained on her knees, but fell back onto her haunches as she pulled Roswynd into her lap. She tucked Roswynd's head into her neck, then omitted a soft, comforting sound while Roswynd trembled in her arms.

With her thighs pressed against Tharon's hips, Roswynd clung to her wife and dug her fingers into Tharon's shoulder blades. With big breaths, she inhaled Tharon's musky scent that left her in a daze while the orgasm's aftereffects consumed her.

Nuzzling and purring, Tharon waited for Roswynd to recover and snuck a hand under Roswynd's tunic. She rubbed a sensitive area of skin at the base of her spine.

Roswynd remained wrapped around Tharon, the single person who once understood her and accepted her. They were finally married, but they were more separated than they ever had been in their lives. In the moment, Roswynd tried to pretend that they were wed out of romance, madly in love and best friends. She squeezed her eyelids tighter from the slight sting, but her pheromones revealed her distress to

Tharon, who grumbled near her ear. She sensed from Tharon's tension that her wife was trying to figure out what to say or do.

Tharon tangled her fingers into Roswynd's bronzy hair and said, "It is not perfect, but we *are* together."

* * *

Date: 35 Striker 816G
(About 10 Years Ago)

Roswynd closed her eyes against the cold and wind that nipped against her exposed cheeks. She sensed her mother's hand against her back, trying to comfort her. Several tears had already frozen against her cheeks and chin when the service for Queen Edeva first started in the cemetery. There was no casket, or body, or even a single Blakesley here. Instead, the House of Arrington held a painful memorial for Queen Edeva, who had died fifty-six days ago.

Underneath the old curly willow tree, a beautiful white life-size statue of Queen Edeva had been placed on a stone base. At the start of the service, Layla had placed a holy crown over the statue's head, and then a priestess of Divine Cailean started the service.

Myla stood on the other side of Layla. Selwyn was next to their father, while Archibold and Josse remained with their aunts and uncles. Several extended family members had traveled from different regions of the kingdom to be part of the sunset service for Queen Edeva, who had been well loved by all. The only people missing were the members of the

House of Blakesley. Roswynd had hoped that the Blakesley family would come to Earna. Her father had invited them, but Roswynd gave up hope this morning when there was no word.

At first, hundreds of rumors had circulated about Edeva's sudden illness. Edeva showed strange symptoms the morning after the Howling Eagle ball. Everyone was convinced it was from the seafood, even though the suppliers were extremely careful when transporting the product from Stormbreaker Landing to Earna. Edeva had rested all day and insisted that the hunts begin despite her condition. However, everyone refused to leave the castle, especially as her condition worsened, prompting King Eustace to take her back to Wulfbite. It was the last time Roswynd saw or spoke to Tharon, who had been a wreck over her mother's illness.

Then the announcement came six days after the ball—Queen Edeva had died.

The hundred rumors transformed into a thousand as more gossip traveled from the Kingdom of White Sommer to the Kingdom of Wyndfeld. Queen Edeva had been poisoned, according to a report from a healer. King Eustace confirmed it in a letter to Garrett two weeks after the announcement of Queen Edeva's death. The House of Arrington was being accused of murder.

Did Tharon believe that Roswynd's family could poison Edeva?

Roswynd wiped her tears and rubbed her friendship bracelet that she shared with Tharon. For the past week, the bracelet felt more like bitter metal than the warm comfort that it had once been to her. It left a nasty pit in her stomach, but she had hope that Tharon would respond to her last two letters. Their friendship was unbreakable, and they could work through this. They had exchanged vows, especially to always be together.

The priest came to the end of his service and wished Queen Edeva a peaceful afterlife. Everyone echoed his sentiment, then one by one, they each placed a sprig of forewinter at the base of the stone statue. The violet berries on each sprig contrasted against the white of the stone and snow. Roswynd was the last person to put down her sprig, and then she simply stood there. Behind her, she heard soft conversations and murmurs, but her mind was on Edeva, who had been a second mother to her.

Part of her hoped it was all an awful prank and that Edeva was alive in Wulfbite. When she first heard the news from her father, Roswynd had cried all night and into the next day. She cried for Edeva and for Tharon. After three days of constant sobbing, Roswynd forced herself to write a letter to Tharon, then another and another until her tears turned the papers into a bleeding, inky mess. Several times she begged her father to let her go to Wulfbite to see Tharon, but Garrett denied her. No one from the House of Arrington was allowed into White Sommer. She didn't understand why at the time, until Edeva's death was blamed on Roswynd and her family.

Now standing here in front of the statue, Roswynd had no idea how to handle the future, which was confusing, painful, and dark. Every night, she prayed to the old and new gods for help and for peace. She prayed to the old goddess of friendship, Ælfwynn, and wished for her relationship with Tharon to hold together. More than anything, Roswynd needed Tharon to be stable. Edeva was Tharon's world, and now she was gone.

"Rossy," Layla called as she approached her from behind. "It is dark now, honey." She hooked her arm across her daughter's shoulders and pulled her into her side. Her mother's warmth was welcoming and Roswynd leaned in closer. Since Edeva's passing, her mother had withdrawn more each day. On several occasions, Roswynd had sought out her mother for comfort only to find her hiding and sobbing in a solar room. This evening was the first time in weeks that her mother offered Roswynd security after the horrible events. "These are dark times now."

Roswynd blinked, peered up, and memorized her mother's stricken features. Layla was no longer referring to the setting sun but rather the shadows cast upon their kingdom after Edeva's death. She opened her mouth but closed it when comforting words failed her. "Mother?"

After a soft rumble, Layla turned and knelt alongside Roswynd. She hooked Roswynd's hips and whispered, "Edeva's death will haunt us for years to come." Her voice was rough and even a bit hollow, but her glassy eyes held Roswynd's gaze. "One day you will see Tharon again. When that day arrives, you must remember that Edeva lives on inside of her."

"Y-Yes, Mother." Roswynd frowned at her mother's strange words, but she nodded regardless. She bit her lip and struggled to find a better response. Her mother's broken smile brought a sob from Roswynd. She launched herself into her mother's arms, held on, and buried her face into her mother's fur-covered neck. For several minutes, they breathed in each other's warm yet distressed pheromones, trying to seek peace with Edeva's death, yet instead finding heartache.

"It is time to go inside," Layla murmured, attempting to coax Roswynd back to the keep. She withdrew her head, started to stand, and clasped Roswynd's shoulder.

"Can I stay a few more minutes?" Roswynd asked and looked over at the statue. She needed a few more minutes alone with Edeva, even though she was certain she would spend more time with her in the future.

Layla bent over, kissed Roswynd's head, and hugged her. "We will be inside waiting for you." She released her daughter after a minute, then went on her way to the keep to join the somber meal to honor Edeva. Her walk was slow and somewhat unsteady.

Roswynd waited until her mother's soft footsteps faded before she collapsed in the snow in front of the statue. She covered her mouth and muffled her initial sob. "Please, Queen Edeva, come back." The icy snow's coldness seeped through her clothing, but Roswynd ignored it. She drew her knees to her chest and whispered, "Please come back for Tharon. Sh-She needs you more than anyone." Rocking back and forth, she pleaded with the statue to come to life, or for Edeva to rise from her grave in Wulfbite. Maybe if magic were alive, they could do something to save Edeva or pay magic's price to bring her back. "Please, please, please," Roswynd repeated until her throat was raw. She gasped between her pleas, causing her breath to form in puffs under the wall's torchlight.

Roswynd lowered her forehead to her knees. She squeezed the bronze bracelet around her wrist and whispered, "Tharon, please hear me." Bringing the bracelet closer to her lips, she continued calling out to her friend as if the magical jewelry would transport her message. "Everything is going to be fine. I swear. I am going to be there for you. I want to be there for you. Please let me." She squeezed her eyes shut, but the tears broke free again. "We did not do this to your mother. We love Edeva." Her chest tightened down, clamping over her pounding heart. "I love Edeva. Please know we did not do this. You must believe me."

Tilting her head back, Roswynd stared up at the stars and searched for a sign or response. Didn't the gods hear her praying and begging? Didn't they know that Edeva didn't deserve this death? Or that Tharon should not have to bury her mother like this? Gritting her teeth, Roswynd tried to hold back a cry, but it still escaped her. She dropped her head back onto her knees, and the bracelet's cold metal pressed against her lips. For weeks she pictured Tharon's broken features, and it pierced her heart every time. "I love you, Tharon… until the end of our days."

Tearless again, Roswynd dried her face and dragged herself from the cemetery and returned to the keep. Everyone in the dining hall was quiet, drinking and eating small bites of food. Roswynd stayed for an hour before she vanished to her room and collapsed on her bed. After she dozed off, her mother slipped into the room and changed Roswynd out of her dress, then into a nightgown. Roswynd murmured something to her mother, who curled up on the bed with her for the night.

Everyone told Roswynd that the day after a funeral service would ease her pain. They lied to her. The mourning continued to claw at her heart the next day. Layla tried to comfort her, but no one's words fixed it. Although she wanted to go for a horseback ride, Roswynd was expected to spend the day with her tutor. Her father had given specific orders that Roswynd was forbidden to ride until further notice. Her parents anticipated that she would ride off for White Sommer, and they ruined her plans to find Tharon. A few years ago she and Tharon had agreed to meet at Fairview Lake if their parents kept them apart. However, a grain of doubt wedged into the cracks of her heart about whether or not Tharon would meet her at the lake.

Such concerns about the future made it impossible for Roswynd to focus on her tutor's lessons. In the afternoon, her father asked her to come to her bedroom. She half expected a lecture about her studies, but his grim features worried her more.

"Roswynd, I received something from White Sommer today." Garrett revealed a pouch that had been hidden in his palm. "I..." He faltered and seemed unsure of himself.

Roswynd trembled when her father's voice cracked. He was an Alpha, strong and confident. This was unlike him, and it scared her. "Is it a message from Tharon?" Her hopes lifted until her father closed his eyes for a beat. "What is it, Father?"

Garrett swallowed loud enough for Roswynd to hear it, but he opened the pouch and turned it over. A bronze bracelet fell into his hand. "Th-There was no note. Simply the bracelet."

"No." Roswynd shook her head, then looked from her father to the friendship bracelet. "N-No." She backed up a step and stared at the jewelry as though it may kill her. "Why did she send it?" she asked with rising demand. "Why did she send it!"

"Roswynd, please try—"

"No!" Roswynd fisted her hands and glared at the bracelet. "I do not want it back!" Her eyes burned, but it was nothing compared to how the matching bracelet burned her soul. "Tell her to take it back!"

Garrett closed his hand around the bracelet, then approached his shouting daughter, who glared at him as if he were Tharon.

"Send it back!" Roswynd shoved her father away, refusing to accept that Tharon had returned the bracelet to her. Tharon would never break their vows. It was a mistake or an accident. Someone forced Tharon to do it. Perhaps Saxon stole it and was playing a cruel joke on her. "She would not return it!"

Garrett moved faster this time and picked up his daughter, who thrashed and screamed. He let her kick him while he went to the bed and sat on its edge. With Roswynd secure in his arms, he held her against his rumbling chest.

"She would not," Roswynd whispered, clinging to her father's tunic. Her rage cracked in half and released the agony that had become her new best friend over the past month. She lost count of how many hundreds of tears she had shed or how often she had wanted to curl up and die. "Please," she murmured and fisted her father's tunic, sobbing into his neck.

Tightening his arms, Garrett attempted to hush her and rocked their bodies. He promised her that everything would be better in time. Combing her hair back, he tried to comfort his daughter and used his pheromones to sooth her. Edeva's death was heartbreaking for Roswynd, but Tharon breaking their friendship vows opened an abyss. There was little that Garrett could do to protect his daughter or family from the cold truth that the House of Blakesley would become their enemy.

Roswynd was spent after her father placed her on the bed. She felt his kiss to her brow and a fur pulled over her, then heard the bolt sliding into place after he left. Drained and broken, Roswynd fell into a deep, dreamless sleep until first light. She woke feeling a little better than the past several days, until she saw Tharon's Bracelet of Ælfwynn on her nightstand. With it curled in her hand, she balled up on the bed, wept, and tried to tell herself it was a mistake.

How could Tharon break their vows? They swore to each other over a blood pact. Tharon had said they would stick together through the good times and the dark times.

Did it mean that Tharon believed that Roswynd's family murdered Edeva? Why couldn't Tharon talk this through with Roswynd? She was certain that if they discussed the events, they could work through it. Nothing could keep them separated, especially some lie about the House of Arrington poisoning Edeva. For days, she had expected to receive a letter from Tharon. A letter that held special wording that would signal for her to hold up their promise to run away together. Instead, she received the bracelet.

The longer Roswynd held Tharon's bracelet, the more her heart fractured and died from the truth. The reality that Tharon betrayed their friendship, that Tharon believed in a lie, and that Tharon hated Roswynd for Edeva's death. How could any of this happen to them? Why did the Divine cause this rift between the two kingdoms that were stronger together?

All Roswynd had left were sweet memories that were now open wounds on her soul. She wanted to put an end to her pain and to forget everything about Tharon. If Tharon was stupid enough to believe such a callous lie, then she had betrayed Roswynd, their friendship, and their love. Tharon was stupid and heartless. Tharon was blind and mean. How could she ever think Roswynd's family would murder Edeva? Tharon was no friend, nor even a worthy mate for Roswynd.

No, Tharon was a vow breaker.

Roswynd hurried off the bed and stumbled, but straightened her dress that she had slept in last night. She didn't care. She rushed across her room to her desk, yanked open the bottom drawer, and tossed out every letter from

Tharon. One letter after another flew and toppled to the floor, scattering all around her. Once they were all out, she yelled at them and kicked them, almost sliding on a few.

"I *hate* you too!" Roswynd cried at the letters. She had expected a message from Tharon, but not her friendship bracelet. It wasn't meant to be their future. She was supposed to receive a letter, begging her to meet Tharon at Fairview Lake so they could start a new life together. Instead Tharon had discarded her as if their friendship meant nothing.

"You betrayed me!" Roswynd stomped over to the fireplace, struggling with the searing burn in her eyes. She tossed in a few pieces of wood, then started a fire while her vision blurred from the tears. Once the fire was ready, she scooped up a handful of letters and stood in front of the flames. She prepared to toss them and cleanse them from her soul, but her grip increased with each heartbeat. Dropping to her knees, she curled over and clutched the letters to her chest.

"Please, *Tharon*," she pleaded, rubbing the broken seal of White Sommer on the top letter. She lay down, curled into the fetal position, and nuzzled the letters as if they were her best friend. "*Pl-lease*," she whispered between tears. Unable to burn the special letters, Roswynd instead gathered them all and stared at the stack for a moment. Her eyes wandered over to the bracelet that rested on her bed before lowering her eyes to the one on her wrist.

Closing her eyes, Roswynd gripped the Bracelet of Ælfwynn's clasp that Tharon had locked for her over a year ago. She clenched her teeth and stared down at the clasp shining back up at her. If she freed it, was she, too, betraying their friendship? Maybe it was all a mistake? Even though her heart wanted it to be an accident, her soul felt the pain of truth. Tharon had turned her back on their friendship and betrayed Roswynd.

Whimpering and whining, Roswynd forced her quivering fingers to push up on the clasp, which hung on for another heartbeat before it popped up and opened the bracelet. She wrenched it off, yelled, and dropped it to the floor. For a moment, there was a brief flash brighter than the fireplace's flickering. Roswynd took a deep breath and held herself together, even though a few tears fell onto her cheeks.

She gathered her strength, went to the desk, and retrieved a leather thong, which she tied around the stack of letters. Next, she retrieved the bracelets' original container. She returned the Bracelets of Ælfwynn to their small wooden box and closed the lid, cutting off their existence. Roswynd gathered the box and letters, then left the bedroom with her cape floating behind her.

Outside it was windier than yesterday, and the sun creeped over the horizon, signaling the start of another wintry day. The cold air was sharp against Roswynd's lungs, but she ignored it in her rush to the stable. The inside of the building was a little warmer, and a few horses greeted her with a neigh or whinny, especially the one she rode often. But she wasn't here to enjoy a horseback ride, as much as she wished she could go.

Roswynd hurried to the right and entered the side room that contained tools, tack, feed, and other supplies for the horses. She went to the tools and took a shovel.

"What are you doing?"

Yelping, Roswynd dropped the shovel and faced the groom, Deri.

"Princess Roswynd?" Deri covered his chest, then frowned at her presence in the stable. "I am sorry, my princess, but your father gave strict orders that you are not allowed to ride." He picked up the shovel and looked from it to Roswynd. Almost six years ago, he took over as the groom after the last one retired. Deri was excellent at his job and was favored by King Garrett and Roswynd.

"I know." Roswynd lowered her eyes and studied the shovel in his hand. "I simply would like to borrow your shovel." She hesitated but added, "Please."

Deri's frown deepened, and he lifted the tool. "Whatever for, my princess?" He balanced the tip against the cobblestone floor.

"I-I must bury a few useless trinkets." Roswynd tightened her arm around the items nestled against her chest.

For a moment, Deri regarded her, then rubbed the back of his neck. "I see." He peered over his shoulder, then asked, "Where might you be burying these items?"

Roswynd snuck a peek at the letters and container, then whispered, "In the cemetery, near the curly willow tree." Cemeteries were for burying dead things. Her eyes screwed shut again, but she contained her emotions.

Deri nodded and pointed at the letters in Roswynd's hold. "Is that what you wish to bury?"

"Y-Yes."

Deri took a step closer to the wall and leaned the shovel against it. "I will assist you, then. The ground is freezing over, so it will be tiring work." He offered a slight smile to Roswynd. "If you would like the help, my princess."

Roswynd raised her attention from the stone floor and softened at his kindness. "Yes, please."

Deri nodded and said, "Wait here. Let me collect my cloak and a lamp." He vanished into the next room, which was a small office space for breaks. In his arm was the cloak, but he also had a larger metal box in his hands. "Perhaps you would like to store those papers in here?"

Roswynd touched the metal box, then gave him a curious look.

"In case one day you wish to have these items again." Deri popped off the lid and showed off its depth.

Roswynd fidgeted and bit her lip, then asked, "Are you certain?"

"I am, my princess." Deri held out the open box in silent offer.

Roswynd deposited the stack of letters into it. There was exactly enough room for the wooden box, which contained the Bracelets of Ælfwynn and the other items for the ritual. She placed it inside last, then Deri slid the lid back over it and secured it. Deri took the shovel and a lamp, and she held the box. Together, they left for the cemetery.

The ground was covered in snow to Deri's shins. After Roswynd picked a spot, Deri allowed Roswynd to clear the snow first. When they reached the frozen ground, he received the shovel back and started fighting the frozen dirt. The hole wasn't big, but it needed to be deep enough to protect the box's contents from freezing. Once past the frozen layer, Deri returned the shovel to Roswynd, who dug slower due to her smaller size. Deri waited patiently and offered a few suggestions.

Roswynd felt a sheen of sweat over her arms and chest after twenty minutes of shoveling. "Do you think it is deep enough?"

Deri rubbed his chin with this gloved hand. "Perhaps a little deeper. Would you like me to finish it?" He smiled at Roswynd and held out his hand. After her nod, he took the shovel and dug a little farther, opening the hole more.

Going to the lantern, Roswynd reached up, turned it off, and pulled it free from the tree branch. The sun had come over the horizon well enough now. At least the morning's bitter cold was starting to wane.

"There we are," Deri proclaimed and stepped aside with the shovel. "How does that look, my princess?" He waited for her approval, but his face was still grim.

Roswynd peeked into the hole and nodded. "Thank you, Deri."

"You are welcome, my princess." Deri leaned the shovel against the tree. "I will leave you to it. But if you need any more help, I will be in the stable." He glanced at the statue of Queen Edeva, frowning more. "I was sorry to hear about Queen Edeva."

Roswynd shuffled on her feet and whispered, "I was too." She stared into the hole, unsure what else to say.

Deri didn't press her but squeezed her shoulder and departed the cemetery with the lantern.

Picking up the icy box, Roswynd turned it through her hands and blinked away the tears that threatened again. She had cried for so many days, one after another. Her soul ached and her heart was damaged. Not only was Edeva gone, but Roswynd had lost Tharon in the process. How would she find a way to keep going? Her past was entangled with Tharon, and her dreams for the future were meant to be shared with Tharon.

Crumbling to her knees in front of the grave, Roswynd stared at the metal box that contained endless words of friendship, stories, love, and promises. For every drop of pain she felt for Tharon there were equal parts of rage. No more now. Lifting the box higher, Roswynd let her lips hover near the lid, and with a hitch of her breath, she whispered, "Until the end of our days."

The metal box fit into the hole without resistance, snuggly and glinting in the morning sunlight before the first pile of dirt buried it.

Chapter 15

Date: 05 Fyrfall 826G
(Present Day)

Roswynd cheered for the final dueling swordsmen, who used small swords to defeat their opponent in a dramatic show. Around her, the huge audience cried out for the two swordsmen. The crowd loved both contestants equally, if their wild screams were any measure.

Tharon stood next to Roswynd, her arms folded and attention locked on the swordsmen in the center of the sparring pit. Even as an adult, she appeared fascinated by the art of fencing compared to cold, brutal fighting on a battlefield. Today was the final day of the festival to celebrate Roswynd and Tharon's marriage and the cease-fire between the two kingdoms. Earlier this week, people from all around the Kingdom of Wyndfeld had arrived in Earna to attend part or all of it.

After five consecutive days of celebration, Roswynd was ready for the peace and quiet of normal life. For the past fortnight, she, Tharon, and Garrett had traveled north to

Montisgard for a political visit, then they repeated the same trip but south to Brickelwhyte. Two days after they returned to Earna, the festival began. Around the sixteenth of Starfall, they were due to be in Wulfbite. The Divine only knew what Saxon expected her and Tharon to do there for the political marriage.

A roar of cheers brought Roswynd's attention back to the swordsmen. One of them was poked in the chest, earning the other one a point. Everyone yelled for the leading swordsman to take the win, but the duel wasn't over.

Roswynd leaned into her wife's space and asked, "Do you think you would be any good at a duel?"

Tharon grunted and leaned her hip against the wooden fence that separated the crowd from the contestants. "No, I fight with brute force." She canted her head and said, "But perhaps you would do well with fencing."

Roswynd opened and closed her mouth a few times, then peered up at her wife. "You think so?" She hummed and smiled at the playful gleam in Tharon's eyes. Over the past weeks, they had forged common ground, especially as they both were stuck waving, smiling, and being cheerful in front of the masses. On occasion they traded jokes or mild teasing that felt familiar, but Tharon's walls always returned when it became too familiar.

Then there was the bedroom situation. Most nights Tharon slept on the bed with Roswynd. She was naked every time, and it taunted Roswynd, who was unwilling to take the final step in their sexual relationship. They gave and took oral sex or used their hands, but never moved on to penetration.

Roswynd fantasized about Tharon slipping inside her, connecting them, and giving over herself. However, her fantasy was a lie, because it was *her* Tharon making love to her. And her Tharon was gone, buried, and dead. Somehow letting this Tharon take her, all of her, would feel like disgracing the memory of her best friend, and would break Roswynd.

Tharon seemed well aware of Roswynd's guarded heart. She didn't push Roswynd for more and only took what Roswynd gave willingly. Tharon also gave back without restraint whenever Roswynd asked her. In a short window, Roswynd had learned a lot about her sexuality, even though other parts of it remained in the dark. There were few days they didn't fool around, despite it being against royal tradition.

Fuck them all, Roswynd said, seething at the old traditions. She was an Omega, and Tharon was an Alpha. It was part of their natures. If she wanted Tharon's mouth between her legs or Tharon in her own mouth, then they would do it. Besides, the suppressant she took each month protected her from heats and pregnancy, if she ever went that far with Tharon. This morning, she had taken the suppressant when Tharon went for her bath. The suppressant was one discussion they never touched, even though Roswynd overheard Saxon demand that Tharon handle it. She considered why Tharon hadn't approached her about it, but assumed it was only a matter of time.

Another ear-crushing cheer came from the crowd when one of the swordsmen won the contest. He was declared the champion of the entire competition and was rewarded for his win. The people applauded him as King Garrett gave the golden trophy to the winner, who bowed to his fans.

Roswynd clapped and cheered for him. She had hoped he would win after watching him over the past two days. He was a skillful swordsman and also young, close to Selwyn's age.

All at once, people scattered from the stands, including the nobles around Tharon and Roswynd. They were at the very front and waited for the throng to thin out. Tharon shifted behind Roswynd, bent forward, and grabbed onto the fence on either side of Roswynd.

"Are you hungry?" Tharon asked, bowing her head close to her wife.

Roswynd placed a hand on her stomach, which had been queasy for most of the day. The suppressant often bothered her stomach for a day or two, but she needed to eat something. "A little."

Tharon closed the gap between their bodies, molding her front against Roswynd. "You have not eaten much today."

"Do I ever?" Roswynd asked and peered up at her wife. Tharon kept careful watch of Roswynd's habits but didn't pester Roswynd except when it came to eating. For some reason, Tharon focused on Roswynd's health. The attention warmed Roswynd's Omega, which in turn irritated Roswynd a degree. Since the first archery lesson, Tharon hadn't made another attempt to feed her. She was unsure if it was due to the disaster of the almost kiss or simply because Tharon wasn't alarmed yet.

"Do not encourage me to care for you in public," Tharon whispered in warning.

Roswynd huffed, but it was a fair warning from her wife, who would feed Roswynd regardless of the public outcry. Tharon might be willing to cross that line in public, but Roswynd wasn't about to around her father. "You made your point, Lord Commander."

Tharon raised an eyebrow at hearing her title. Over the past weeks, Roswynd had begun using it, avoiding Tharon's name when possible. Tharon had a habit of calling Roswynd "Princess," never once using Roswynd's name since their reunion at the wedding. How Tharon managed to evade using it was beyond Roswynd.

Straightening, Tharon offered her arm and waited for Roswynd to take it.

Roswynd took the muscular arm and was escorted from the viewing area now that the crowd had thinned. Together, they started back into the capital before the sun sank behind the mountains. They smiled at various people and played the part of a happily married couple.

"Roswynd!" Myla came racing up to them from behind. She had hitched her dress in her hands, making it easier to catch them.

"Hello, Myla." Roswynd smiled at her sister, who joined them on the walk back into the city. All around them the festival was in full swing with jesters, bards, vendors, and musicians. They headed to the city center where a small park and most of the excitement was.

"Did you see how handsome that winning swordsman was?" Myla flushed and threaded her arm through Roswynd's open side.

"Yes, his features remind me of Prince Drust from the illustration you received," Roswynd replied and giggled at Myla's feverish blush.

Myla shushed her sister, then looked around Roswynd. "Hello, Tharon." Her smile was bashful and her scent grew stronger.

"Evening, Myla," Tharon returned in a polite tone.

Roswynd jerked her sister closer and said, "Do not coo at *my* prince."

Myla laughed and nudged her sister, then shrugged. "You cannot blame an Omega for finding an Alpha attractive."

"Oh yes, I can," Roswynd argued, freed her arm, and tickled her sister, who squealed and jumped away.

Myla hurried a few steps ahead of them, turned, and walked backward. "When do you both depart for Wulfbite?" She looked between the pair, a slight frown creasing her lips.

"In about ten days," Roswynd replied. She then pointed at a cart sitting in the street and said, "Watch out, Myla." She almost broke free from Tharon, but Myla turned in time. She snared her sister's arm and pulled her close. "Are you going to miss us?"

Myla blew out a breath and nodded. "A month is a long time." She fidgeted with her girdle but said nothing else.

Her scent was all over the place, which meant she had concerns for Roswynd.

"It will go quickly," Roswynd promised and smiled at her sister. "I will write to you." She caught how Myla's eyes darted to and from Tharon.

"Your sister will be safe in Wulfbite," Tharon promised. She must have detected Myla's underlying stress about Roswynd going to White Sommer.

Myla remained quiet and played with her girdle. Roswynd yanked on Myla's arm again and said, "Do not fret. I will be fine." She smiled at her sister, who still had a frown. "Besides I am the lord commander's wife."

"Yes, but Saxon…" Myla let her voice fade off after she remembered who was with them. She looked away from the pair and studied the people around them.

"Saxon is a dick," Roswynd finished, ignoring her wife's rumble. Tharon's annoyance wasn't directed at Roswynd but more at the truth of the matter. She chuckled at Myla's big eyes, which cut to Tharon.

"He is a dick," Tharon agreed after a drawn-out silence.

Roswynd snorted, glanced at her wife, and nodded at their mutual agreement about something for once. She turned back to Myla and said, "Tharon can handle him. Everything will be fine and then we will be back here for the stout festival."

Myla crinkled up her nose at the mention of the infamous beer festival. "Gross." She and Roswynd traded grins.

They arrived at the park, which was busy and loud with festivities but being kept orderly by the city guards. The overhead streetlamps were lit as darkness fell over the city. Food and alcohol were plentiful, and the people were merry. Many approached Roswynd and Myla, then later their parents arrived for the festivities.

Hours later, Roswynd and Tharon ended up sitting on a stone wall at one end of the park. They had eaten one small snack, but now it was time for a late supper. Popping another shrimp in her mouth, Roswynd watched the citizens mingle, laugh, and drink. Pups raced around or listened to a bard's latest tale.

Tharon nudged her wife with an elbow and handed her the last two shrimps. Similar to past times, she was ensuring that Roswynd ate a decent meal after having noticed she ate little today. Her care left a warm burn low in Roswynd's belly. Before they left the keep, Tharon had tied two mugs to her side. Both were now full with the mead Roswynd had picked out. Tharon drank from hers, then handed over the other when Roswynd was ready for it.

Roswynd savored the sweet alcohol and was surprised Tharon drank it. They'd been together for almost a month, and she had noticed Tharon steered away from sweet things as compared to their youth. It was another thing Roswynd missed in their relationship, but she tried to not let it dull her mood tonight.

From their position in the park, Roswynd enjoyed the cheerfulness of her people after so many years of war. Even if the peace might be temporary, at least they had some kind of reprieve from the hardships of war. So many citizens had given up different things: fortunes, limbs, and lives.

"They are happy," Roswynd said after a while and indicated the people after Tharon studied her.

Tharon gazed about the park as her expression turned thoughtful. She lifted her right leg, pressing her boot flat against the side of the wall.

Roswynd finished off a turkey leg, then set it on the wall next to her and cleaned her hands on a linen napkin. "Do you mind dancing?" she asked. "Father said it would start soon."

Huffing, Tharon nodded, then returned to eating slices of deer meat. She washed it down with more mead and watched the citizens.

Rubbing her face, Roswynd sensed the alcohol already burning in her blood, but she wanted to dance once or twice before going back to the keep. A low but familiar cry caught her ear, and she looked over at her two younger brothers horsing around in the square. Selwyn wasn't far away, keeping an eye on them. For a moment, a memory from the Howling Eagle came to her.

"You remember that one ball where Josse lay down on the food table and Archibold threw pastries into his mouth?" Roswynd snickered into the mug near her mouth. "Father locked them in their rooms for weeks."

Tharon grinned and replied, "That hardly compared to the time you purposefully tripped Leith into a food table."

Roswynd gasped and covered her chest with a hand after she lowered the mug to her lap. "I did no such thing."

She mirrored her wife's grin, then she groused and whispered, "He was being a knothead toward you." Lifting the mug again, she muttered, "He deserved it."

Tharon chuckled and brushed her hands together after finishing the smoked deer meat.

"He left you alone after that," Roswynd whispered and returned the mug to her lap. "I bet he would piss his trousers if he met you now."

Tharon grunted and canted her head in Roswynd's direction. She remained quiet and ate a few cooked carrots from her bowl of food. Earlier Layla had brought them bowls and napkins so they could get food from the different vendors.

Roswynd was lost in the fantasy of Leith cowering under Tharon's towering form. Tharon was a far cry from the meek princess she had once been at the balls. One too many times Roswynd had to save Tharon from Leith's attempts to court her or bore her. Even today, Roswynd still despised that sniveling man, who was married to another noble.

"Are you ready to dance, Princess?" Tharon asked and pointed at the musicians returning to their instruments after a meal.

"Are you?" Roswynd wiggled her eyebrows at Tharon, who was still eating the last few items from her bowl. "Father did suggest we do at least one couples dance."

Tharon grumbled and huffed, then muttered, "Then I need beer."

Roswynd swatted her wife in the stomach and asked, "Is it so bad dancing with your wife?" She ignored Tharon's smirk and popped the last morsel of bread into her mouth. It was time to join in the dancing. Even if Tharon pretended to dislike it. Leaving their dishes for later, Roswynd dragged her wife out to the dancing area and started the fun.

They performed several line dances before the first couples dance began. Roswynd expected them to leave after the couples dance ended, but Tharon continued to dance. There were certainly a few good changes worth noting in Tharon, who was a more confident dancer than when they were young. Roswynd liked the difference and fell into the steps of a circle dance.

By the third couples dance, Roswynd was drained and in need of a drink. She could barely form any words, but Tharon understood her needs. Tharon scooped up their mugs from the wall and went in search of drinks.

Roswynd reclaimed her spot on the wall and was grateful for the sweet mead that Tharon brought her. "Thank you," she said after a deep draw of the mead.

Tharon had a beer, which she offered to Roswynd, who tasted a sip.

Roswynd hissed at the bitterness of the drink and shook her head. "How can you drink that?"

Tharon chuckled and continued enjoying the alcohol.

Chasing off the beer's flavor, Roswynd swallowed a large mouthful of the mead, which was sweet from honey and berries. She favored it in the summer over wine, but soon the mead would fade away for the winter. Stouts and wine would become the more favored alcohol for the next four months.

Roswynd finished her drink and rested the mug on her knee. Tharon slid off the wall, took Roswynd's mug, and went directly to the vendor with the mead and beer. Roswynd narrowed her eyes at how Tharon was plying her with alcohol. But when she had the refilled mug, she couldn't deny that she wanted more. The past weeks had been strenuous and wearing. However, the archery lessons and horseback riding had helped reduce some of the stress.

Tharon emptied her mug in a few large swallows and cleared her throat. "More?" she asked and held out her hand.

Snorting, Roswynd eyed her wife and peered into her half-empty mug. "If I have another after this one, you *will* have to throw me over your shoulder for the walk back to the castle." She groaned at Tharon's toothy smile. "Or is that your plan?" Her head was buzzing, and her limbs were heavy. "The lord commander carrying her Omega wife back like a claimed prize?" Apparently, her tongue was loose too.

Tharon hopped off the wall and stood in front of Roswynd. "Is that your darkest fantasy, Princess?" She placed both hands on either side of Roswynd and leaned in closer. "The lord commander forcing you over her shoulder as you struggle, being carried away and then being locked in a room, ravaged, and fucked until you are unconscious."

Roswynd had no idea if the alcohol or the crude conversation had overheated her. But the erotic fantasy made her thirsty. She took a quick swallow of the alcohol, then replied, "Perhaps." Her pheromones were the real answer, and they both knew it. Squirming, she tried to ignore the burn between her legs. "Is that yours, Lord Commander?"

"Perhaps," Tharon replied, then pushed off the wall and put space between them. Her scent was powerful, warm, and enveloping Roswynd from head to toe.

Roswynd drank the last of the mead and then handed the mug over to her wife, who lashed the mugs to her side again. After sliding off the wall, Roswynd touched Tharon's arm and waited to find her balance.

Tharon remained motionless while Roswynd settled into a standing position.

"I am fine." Roswynd turned and picked up their bowls but had to take Tharon's arm for support. "The mead seemed stronger than normal." Truthfully, she didn't drink too often, or too much for that matter, but the alcohol had overwhelmed her.

"You ate little today," Tharon reminded as they started their return walk to the keep.

Roswynd gave a soft sound of agreement and leaned some into Tharon. "I ate well at supper. And at least I am not slurring my words." She spotted her parents and gave them a brief wave before they left the square. Then a damn cobblestone bested her.

Tharon caught Roswynd with an arm around her waist.

For a second, Roswynd saw the temptation in Tharon's eyes to pick up Roswynd and put her over her shoulder. With a sigh, Roswynd straightened and said, "I am fine." For the most part, she was fine for the rest of the walk to the castle. But the stairwell inside the keep was another story. Roswynd ended up falling back into her wife's waiting arms, with a huge blush.

Tharon sighed, then scooped up her wife into her arms and cradled her.

Shrugging, Roswynd settled in for the ride up to the second floor and pointed upward. "That way, please."

Tharon rolled her eyes, hiked up the steps, and leveled a glare at a guard near the top.

The guard scurried off before he could be subjected to any growls or pheromones from Tharon.

"I must use the latrine first," Roswynd mentioned and chuckled at Tharon's fussy rumble. When they entered the garderobe, she slid out of her wife's arms, then realized Tharon was going to stand there and wait. "I can manage this alone." Tharon gave another soft growl, then stomped out of the room so Roswynd had her privacy. Roswynd smirked to herself because under all the dramatics, Tharon was toying with her. *At least she still has some remnants of her humor.*

After Roswynd was done, they walked to their room and started to prepare for rest. Roswynd found it rather difficult to get changed, cleaned up, and into bed. She groaned and collapsed into the waiting comfort. In the background, Tharon was moving about, but then the few oil lamps went dark. Next to her, Tharon's heavier form sank into the furs and blankets. On occasion Tharon would hold her, especially after they fooled around. But tonight, Tharon seemed content to lie on her stomach. Roswynd didn't even have the ability to consider it due to the alcohol putting her to sleep in minutes. For once Roswynd's sleep was deep and dreamless, until her bladder stirred her awake.

Roswynd was in the same spot and in the same position on the bed as when she fell asleep. In the darkness, she tried to focus on Tharon's form, but it was small… or perhaps not there? She stretched out her arm and came up empty-handed, which roused her more. Sitting up, Roswynd frowned, scanned the room, and said, "Tharon?"

Receiving silence, Roswynd rubbed her face and slid out of bed. The chilliness of the floor forced her awake more, but first she needed to handle her full bladder. Leaving the room, she traveled the hallway and passed a single guard, who straightened. Tharon was probably using the latrine already. However, the garderobe was empty. After relieving herself, Roswynd returned to the bedroom and frowned at the emptiness of it. Where in all the gods' names was Tharon?

With her back against the door and her hand on the bolt, Roswynd scanned the room for any clues, but it was hard to see much in the dark. She was about to check for Tharon's boots and swords, knowing she wouldn't leave without them. But then the coldness of the iron bolt in her palm prompted her. Turning, she stared down at the bolt and tried jogging her memory about its placement before she went to the garderobe.

Roswynd slowly pushed the pin down into the lock position and recalled she had to unlock it before she left for the garderobe. It was impossible to lock the bolt from the outside hallway, which meant that Tharon didn't leave from the bedroom door. With a furrow across her brow, she faced the room and called, "Tharon?"

Crossing to the nightstand, Roswynd lit a candle and then picked up the candle holder. "Tharon, if this is another prank, it is over." She searched the room, checked behind the divider, and went into the washroom, but found nothing. Holding her breath, Roswynd confirmed that Tharon's boots and weapons weren't here.

Tharon was gone.

A sickening feeling churned deep in Roswynd's gut. *Where could she have gone, and how?* With labored breaths, she tried to figure out the puzzle with her still-fuzzy mind. She never felt Tharon move or heard her get up from the bed. Could someone so large be so stealthy? If Tharon hadn't plied her with so much alcohol, Roswynd would have noticed something, as she had been a light sleeper all her life. Then it struck her hard, right in her chest.

Tharon had planned this.

Tharon was far from an idiot. She knew Roswynd was a light sleeper, and had pushed the alcohol on her to keep her asleep for the night, so then Tharon could carry out the rest of her plans. But Roswynd had no idea what those plans were. More panic set into her bones before it occurred to her that there was one place she hadn't checked—the damn balcony.

Roswynd hastened to it, set the candle holder on the floor, and opened the door. Perhaps she was being ridiculous and Tharon was outside, admiring the starry night. Much to her shock, the balcony was void of any life, similar to the moonless sky. At a loss, Roswynd turned a full circle in the middle of the balcony until something passed her peripheral view. Turning to her right, she squinted and caught the movement of rope. She rushed to the balcony's left side and followed the upward direction of the bizarre rope that went to a third-floor balcony.

"Sweet Gyldr, no." Roswynd was awestruck and stared at the fastened line that went from her balcony to the balcony of her father's office. "N-No, no." She shook her head at the absurdity of the scheme. But the rope shifting with the soft breeze was real. Covering her pounding chest, Roswynd panted and warred with what to do now. She needed to warn her father, but what if she was wrong? Worse yet, what if she was right, and Tharon was in her father's office right now?

Roswynd had to be sure for herself. There was no possibility that Tharon had climbed the keep to get to her father's office. Her heart refused to believe it, while her logic told her otherwise. She hurried into the bedroom, sprinted to the wardrobe, and threw on her trousers, tunic, and boots. On the inside of the wardrobe, she snared a ring of keys, one of which unlocked her father's office. About to rush out, Roswynd remembered one other important item and went behind the divider. She dug free the dagger that her father gave her on her wedding day, then finally bolted out of the room.

Trying to contain her burning need to run, Roswynd walked at a fast pace to the stairwell, went up to the third floor, and slowed upon seeing another guard. There were at least one, if not two, per floor who walked the halls at regular intervals. She wondered why they hadn't heard Tharon in her father's office. But Tharon was that fucking sneaky.

"My princess," the guard greeted in a hushed voice. "It is la—"

"I am aware," Roswynd cut him off, keeping her voice to a whisper. "I am going to my father's office. You will wait here until my return."

The guard straightened, nodded, and took a post next to the wall across from the top of the stairs.

Roswynd hurried past him and followed the dim hallway that had a single lit lamp. She slowed as she neared the office's locked door. Her racing heart was in her throat, and the keys slid in her clammy palm. With each step she took toward the door, her limbs shook more. She took a deep breath and steeled herself as she knelt in front of the door. For a moment, she peered through the keyhole and wished for Tharon to be anywhere but here. Her wish was shredded by the slight movement inside the room.

No, no, no. No! This cannot be! Roswynd gritted her teeth and tightened her hand on the dagger's hilt. Some foolish piece of her kept clinging to the possibility that it all was a bad dream. But her hand lifted the key and inserted it while she grabbed the bolt with her dagger hand. Taking two gulps of air, she willed Tharon to not be in her father's office, which held important documents about the Kingdom of Wyndfeld.

With a twist of the key, the lock released the bolt, which freely slid with a resounding click of metal.

Leaving the key in the keyhole, Roswynd drove the door open with her shoulder as she stood and entered the office. With the dagger at her side, she stared in horror at her wife standing behind her father's desk. Her heart thundered against her chest, causing her knees to tremble. However, she slipped into the security of her anger and glared at her wife.

Caught with a scroll in hand, Tharon placed it onto the desk without ever breaking eye contact with her furious wife. She came around the furniture but paused when she spotted the dagger and gritted her teeth.

Roswynd reached behind and closed the office door so that the guard wouldn't overhear their voices. Once the door shut, she whispered, "H-How could you do this?"

Taking small steps, Tharon closed the gap until Roswynd lifted the dagger, then she halted and waited for Roswynd's next move. "Return to bed," she said in a soft voice.

Roswynd laughed with slight madness and shook her head. "That was not an answer." She blinked against the initial sting in her eyes, refusing to cry in front of her enemy. "Tell me why you are doing this?" She fought to keep her voice down, not ready to alert the guard.

Tharon moved closer, but the dagger was pointed right at her face. She rumbled and raised her open hands. "Hand me the blade." Her pheromones had increased tenfold, trying to force Roswynd to submit to her.

Roswynd was too far lost in her anguish to crumble to Tharon's Alpha nature. Tharon's simple order sent her surging forward after her wife, who stumbled in reverse until her back hit the wall. Roswynd advanced without restraint and took a weak swipe at Tharon, who leaned to the side. Tharon latched onto both of Roswynd's wrists, but Roswynd's skin was slippery from sweat. Tharon held her next breath when the dagger's tip poked against her throat.

"Everything has been a lie!" Roswynd hissed between clenched teeth. She tried to free her left hand, but Tharon's hold was too strong. Her mind struggled to process the truth, but her heart was already crashing. For the past ten years, she somehow accepted that she could survive life as an unwed Omega or one day die at Tharon's hands when the war came to a bloody end. The political marriage gave her a measure of air after slowly suffocating over the years. However, she was silly to believe it was anything but an attempt to bring down her family.

Her father had been right.

Shaking her head, Roswynd trembled and whispered, "You wanted this marriage so you could further the war and kill my family. But I wanted to believe that the marriage might mean *something* to you!" She seethed and growled at her wife. "You *are* a vow breaker!"

"I have *not* broken my vows to you!" Tharon snarled back and shifted Roswynd's wrist, which caused the dagger's pointed end to slice through her skin. "I have vowed to shelter, cherish, and care for you through the light and darkness." Her orange eyes reflected her passion for once. "Tell me when I have not done these things?"

Roswynd lost control of her jaw as it fell open upon hearing Tharon's delusions. As she absorbed the harsh truth that Tharon believed her current actions were good and wholesome, it wrenched a spear into her heart. "Do you truly believe *this* is how I wished to be loved?"

"I never vowed love," Tharon replied in a rough voice. Her deceleration stole the last of Roswynd's will and hollowed her heart. "After the House of Arrington falls, I will continue to uphold my vows."

"No." Roswynd shook her head and growled again. "I will not let you and Saxon kill my family." Her family was all she had left at this point. Tharon had revealed her true intent, and Roswynd had the power to stop it. She had to simply call on the guard, who would alert the others and arrest Tharon.

"Are you truly going to break your vows to me?" Tharon whispered with a piercing gaze. "Can you stand by and watch them behead me?" Her hard stare had softened a fraction. "I think if you were going to betray me, you would have told the guards long before you came into the office."

The first tear started to fall onto Roswynd's cheek, then she shook her head. "Betray *you*? No, you betray *me* again and again!" She pushed the dagger forward but withdrew it when blood welled under it. "You *always* betray me!"

"I have not betrayed you," Tharon whispered, her voice even. Her pheromones were gentler, trying to coax Roswynd into a false calmness. "A long time ago, I swore to you that we would always be together until the end of our days. I have never given up on that vow. Now we are so close, but if you break your vows, then they will sentence me to death." She released Roswynd's wrists and placed them on her hips instead. "You simply have to walk out of this office and return to our bed."

Roswynd was panting and shaking against her wife's firm body. A yell for the guard was lashed down in her chest. It was true that the espionage was enough to have someone sentenced to death. It would be the perfect justification to kill the lord commander of the White Sommer Army and send a shock wave through their enemy kingdom.

Tharon would die, by Roswynd's hand.

Yet, Tharon made no vow to protect the House of Arrington. In fact she was certain Tharon had vowed to kill Roswynd's family for the death of Edeva. Roswynd would lose her parents and siblings in one stroke if she stood aside and allowed Tharon to continue her espionage. She stumbled backward and clutched her throbbing head.

For weeks Roswynd had attempted to reconnect with her best friend, who she was certain was buried deep within the lord commander. There were brief glimpses of her, but each time there was a break in her armor, Tharon caught the pinholes, sealed them back up, and blocked Roswynd once more. Tonight's trespassing supported Roswynd's worst nightmare—Tharon was the lord commander first and foremost. Roswynd had no more subtle ways to reach her best friend and rekindle any honest meaning in their relationship. With racing emotions, she considered whether there was *any* option left that she could use to break through the lord commander, reach her best friend, and truly correct their devastating course.

Tharon took a step but stiffened when the dagger was pointed at her again.

Roswynd growled at her wife and said, "You want me to choose between you or my family." Her vision was blurry from tears and agony. Brutal images of both her family and Tharon dying were too overwhelming. She lost to the panic building in her. "I cannot choose. I will *not* choose!"

Tharon clenched her jaw and held out her hands. "*Listen* to me. We will make this work." Even damaged they could still work, Tharon had told her once. But Tharon was wrong. Roswynd could no longer live on damaged. Breathing harder, Tharon tried to get closer to Roswynd. "Do not choose *them* over me after everything we have been through to be together finally."

Roswynd growled and clawed her scalp. Tharon's ideas cluttered her head further. "But *they* are my family, Tharon!"

"*I am* your family now!" Tharon whined and shifted closer, but Roswynd backed toward the door. "If *they* had not poisoned my mother, we would not be here right now."

"N-No, *this* is not family." Roswynd indicated the small space between them. Edeva's murder was never her family's fault. Tharon was echoing a horrible lie that had to have been burned into her mind at a young age. It was the only explanation, and that lie had fueled Tharon's ten years of rage. Nothing short of a miracle or a devastation could extinguish Tharon's relentless determination.

Roswynd fought against her downward spiral to oblivion. She wrenched her hair and clenched her teeth, then a snarl came free. In the distance, Tharon continued talking to her, but Roswynd's breaking heart was all she heard. "This cannot be happening," she murmured in a rasped voice and whined low. Regardless of which path Roswynd chose, everyone she loved would die, including her. Only one final choice could save her and her best friend—a sacrifice to save them all. If one Omega's death spawned such madness inside Tharon, then perhaps another could undo it?

"No," Roswynd repeated, cutting off Tharon's rambling. "I will not break my vows to you as your wife." She blinked through her tears and watched the frantic energy bleed out of Tharon. She swallowed and whispered, "And I refuse to betray my family either." Shaking her head and backing toward the door, she murmured, "But there is one last thing I can do." An eerie peace settled over her now that she accepted her fate and could move on from the incessant heartbreak. She refocused on Tharon's distraught features and saw a flicker of *her* Tharon in those beautiful orange eyes.

With a deep, calming breath, Roswynd declared, "Until the end of my days."

Epilogue

Date: 30 Striker 816G
(About 10 Years Ago)

"My little Alpha," Edeva whispered and cupped Tharon's cheek. Her features were paler than a ghost, her eyes foggy, and her smile weak. The dampness of her palm seeped through Tharon's skin and drained the remaining hope in Tharon's chest.

Her mother was dying, again.

"Please do not go, Momma," Tharon pleaded over and over until her voice cracked. She should have been stronger for her mother. But Edeva's frailness broke Tharon's thin layer of control. Similar to all the previous times, Edeva hummed a familiar tune and encouraged Tharon to come closer.

Tharon toppled into the bed next to her mother, curled up alongside her, and held on to the one being who loved her without a single condition. After Tharon tucked her head under her mother's chin, Edeva tangled a hand in

Tharon's thick tresses and continued to hum the warm tune from Tharon's early days.

"I love you, Tharon, so much."

"I love you too, Momma." Tharon choked and started to sob. "Stay," she murmured repeatedly until her throat was raw. But Edeva hummed back and rocked their joined bodies until her last breath. Tharon gasped when they went still, then she dared to poke her head out from the crook of her mother's neck.

Edeva's mouth was half parted, but her chest was unmoving now. Dark blood began to ooze from the corner of her mouth. Droplets of blood trickled from her eyes and nose. The fraction of life in her features was long gone. In seconds her face was sinking in, and her skin started to wrinkle. The horrid stench of death consumed the air in the bedchamber.

"Tharon!"

A firm hand gripped Tharon's shoulder and tore her from her mother's corpse. She was tossed to the floor, a useless and sobbing pup. Her father's shadow fell over her, and his voice vibrated in her head.

"The Arringtons are to blame for this!" Eustace pointed at Edeva's lifeless, half-decomposed body in the bed. "All of them will die!"

"N-No." Tharon clawed the cold floor underneath her. "It was *not* them!" Her Alpha roared to life inside her chest, needing to protect Roswynd. "They would never—"

"They murdered your mother!" Eustace took a step closer, knelt, and pushed into Tharon's face. "I am willing to bet Roswynd Arrington was the one to slip the poison to your mother. That clever little—"

"No!" Tharon bellowed and launched at her father, whose laugh now matched Saxon's maniacal cackle whenever he succeeded in tormenting Roswynd. However, she flew through her father and found herself sitting upright in her bed. From head to toe, she was coated in sweat, and salt was in her mouth. She was alone, like every night since her mother's death fifty-one days ago.

Tharon heaved for air, which seemed so thin. She was lightheaded and battling against the nightmare's hold, but it was impossible. Night after night, she waged war against the demons in her head and failed to undo the memory.

Her mother was dead and could never be returned to her.

Unable to hold back any longer, Tharon tilted her head back and wailed into the darkness of her room. She cared nothing about waking all those in Monales Castle. For weeks she had done everything to contain her anguish, tried to bury it like her mother, and ignored the growing blackness in her chest. Tonight she wanted the three Divine to hear her and to know her agony. Then perhaps the last Divine would bring her mother back to her.

However, Edeva never entered through the bedroom door.

Several voices hollered from the hallway, followed by banging on the door, which was thrown open. Someone was running across the floor, bare feet slapping against stone. The door boomed shut and a second pair of feet hurried across the chamber.

"Tharon!" Daisy hopped onto the bed followed by Holly.

"Tharon, you must stop," Holly insisted. Like Daisy, her cheeks glistened from tears. She raised her spread out arms and a blanket fell open. She dove forward and wrapped it around Tharon's upper body. The blanket's familiar and comforting scent enveloped Tharon in a heartbeat.

With a heavy gasp, Tharon inhaled her mother's warm scent that radiated from the blanket. The twins sat on either side of her, hugged her, and allowed their combined Omega scents to mix with their mother's own. Little by little, Tharon's wail turned into a soft sob that matched her sisters' whimpers. She choked on her next sob, nuzzling into Daisy first before turning her head and rubbing her scent into Holly.

"Ar-Are you hurting?" Daisy asked between gasps.

"Y-Yes," Tharon whispered and whimpered. "I miss her s-s-so m-much." She wished that Roswynd were here as well. If Roswynd were in her arms, then she might find a moment of silence in her head. But her father insisted that the Arringtons had murdered her mother.

"We do too," Daisy said between whines.

"We will stay with you tonight." Holly tightened her arm around Tharon. From birth, she and Daisy shared a bedchamber and were inseparable. But they shared a special bond with Tharon compared to Saxon, who claimed it was due to them all being females.

"We will stay," Daisy echoed and nuzzled Tharon's jaw. Her breathing was irregular and heavy.

"Stay," Tharon murmured and encouraged her sisters to crawl under the covers with her. She undid her mother's blanket, spread it out, and shared it with her sisters. The last sob faded from her, then a weak thrum started in the back of her throat when Daisy and Holly snuggled into her sides. With both arms under her siblings, Tharon drew them in as close as possible. The wonderful combination of Omega scents pacified her and held back the nightmare for the last few hours of darkness.

* * *

At dawn, Tharon struggled to leave her bedchambers, even though Daisy and Holly encouraged her to go to breakfast with them. She put on a dress without thought, washed up, and cleaned her teeth before stepping out of her room. Her twin sisters were waiting for her in the hallway.

Daisy took Tharon's hand and guided her through the castle to the great hall. Holly followed alongside and wiped her face several times. Even though their mother's funeral was over a month ago, their cheeks had yet to dry. But their father was strong enough to withhold his sorrow after the funeral and continue to rule the kingdom, which was stricken by its queen's sudden death. Saxon often attempted to hide his crying, but Tharon was well aware of his breakdowns.

The great hall was rather quiet despite being occupied by several lords, the chamberlain, the steward, and the seneschal. Today their father would hold royal court in the throne hall and make decisions that best benefited White Sommer. Most of the discussion would center around Edeva's death and how to respond to the murder. There was much talk about a possible war with Wyndfeld. The sheer idea sounded maddening to Tharon. For eight hundred years, the Kingdom of White Sommer and the Kingdom of Wyndfeld were allies. Her father was about to break with a tradition followed by every Blakesley generation—a dedication to fostering and deepening a relationship with Wyndfeld. Everything was going to change with a single order from Eustace. Tharon prayed her father would come to his senses.

Tharon took her usual seat at the table while Holly and Daisy sat across from her. They waited for their father and brother to arrive while the servants prepared the table for breakfast. Tharon kept her head down and played with her friendship bracelet. Over the past month, she had written and rewritten a letter to Roswynd but had yet to hand it to a messenger. The first letter had been a jumbled mess of emotions and run-on sentences. Tears had caused the ink to bleed. By the sixth rewrite, Tharon had better organized her thoughts and closed the letter with their coded sentence.

The coded sentence was simple in its wording and would never seem strange to one of their parents, if they read it. The sentence merely said, "I wish to see you soon," which would secretly signal to Roswynd that it was time to run away together. They would meet at Fairview Lake, which was near the village of Oldview in Wyndfeld. Once together, they would begin their new life that didn't involve their families, at least for a time. If her father decided to go to war with Wyndfeld, then Tharon was more than ever determined to send the letter to Roswynd.

"Good morning," Saxon muttered to his siblings when he arrived at the table. He had dark circles under his eyes and sighed when he sat at the table across from Tharon. After the twins responded to him, he stared at Tharon, who continued to ignore him. "Good morning, Tharon."

With a soft thrum, Tharon looked at her brother and responded to him before he became annoyed with her. "Good morning." She continued to spin the bracelet around her wrist while she considered the shift in her relationship with Saxon. Similar to her, Saxon had sleepless nights and cried often, even though he tried to hide it from them. Since their mother's death, Saxon hadn't played a single prank on Tharon, Holly, or Daisy. In recent weeks, Tharon noted a developing acidic note to Saxon's pheromones that had never been there. The harsh undertone wasn't directed at anyone, but it was stringing its way through his being.

"Where is Father?" Saxon asked them.

"He will be here soon," Holly replied.

Saxon frowned and seemed prepared to argue, except their father indeed passed through the open doors. He shifted in his seat, then relaxed a degree and greeted their father as his siblings did.

Eustace took his seat at the head of the table. He prompted the servants to bring out the morning meal. As the filled plates were brought out, he said, "Tharon and Saxon, I will be speaking to you both prior to court."

Tharon traded a befuddled look with Saxon, but she nodded at her father.

"Yes, Father," Saxon agreed and lowered his eyes to the food set in front of him.

Worrying her lip, Tharon tried to discern what her father wanted to speak to them about and hoped it wasn't about war. Her stomach clenched at the idea of going to war against the Arringtons. Did her father truly believe that Garrett and Layla had poisoned and murdered their mother? Had Eustace found proof that the Arringtons killed Edeva? Her stomach dropped at the possibilities. The food placed in front of her was suddenly unappetizing.

Eustace told his children to eat, but everyone poked at their food. He asked Daisy and Holly what their tutor had planned for them today. The chatter at the table continued in such a manner until no one could stomach anymore food. Eustace rose, which signaled for Tharon and Saxon to accompany him. On their way through the great hall, Eustace paused by his officials at another table and informed them to delay court until his arrival.

"We will retreat to the solar room," Eustace told his son and daughter as they followed him through the castle.

"Yes, Father," Saxon said and walked alongside Tharon. He glanced over at her, but she ignored him and fidgeted with her friendship bracelet.

The solar room was already warm, mostly from the curtains being drawn back. Eustace set about starting a fire while Saxon sealed the doors. Tharon took a seat in an armchair, and Saxon dropped into the settee. Eustace finished building the fire but remained standing near the fireplace after he faced his children.

"I have decided that White Sommer will be ending all relations with Wyndfeld." Eustace paused, placed a hand on the Sword of White Sommer at his hip, and studied Saxon first before shifting his attention to Tharon. "I will declare war against Wyndfeld, and the Army of White Sommer will begin to march at the end of the month."

Tharon parted her lips but a faint whine came out with her next breath. Her earlier dread coiled tighter in her gut, then her heart was pounding in her ears.

Eustace came closer and took the armchair between Saxon and Tharon. He released a strained sigh and continued his rationale. "Your mother's death must be avenged. She must have justice so she can be at peace in Freodlond."

Saxon was wringing his hands together, but he nodded and whispered, "I do not u-understand why the Arringtons did this." His voice quaked, then his leg shook up and down.

"Because they did *not* murder our mother," Tharon argued, sharp and fast. She glared at her brother, who followed their father's thoughts about the Arringtons. Whipping her head to the right, she turned her venom on her father. "How can you believe they did this to Mother? The Arringtons are a part of our family."

"How can I not?" Eustace countered and leaned toward Tharon. He touched her knee and squeezed it. "Tharon, I did not make this decision lightly. Everything points to the Arringtons' guilt."

"But is there proof?" Tharon asked, her voice growing thicker.

"Yes, our mother's body in a grave," Saxon replied in a snappy tone. "Can you not see, sister? Mother was in perfect health until she attended the ball. Her symptoms were consistent with poisoning." He scooted to the edge of the settee and leaned closer to Tharon. "Why can you not see?" A harsh but desperate note was in his voice.

Tharon shook her head and looked between her father and brother. Her father's pheromones were gentle, as if coaxing her into a false sense of calm. "Bu-But it could have been anyone at the ball."

Saxon huffed and declared, "Even if that were true, the Arringtons would still be guilty for allowing it to happen in their castle." He growled and fisted his hands. "They are to protect us when we are in Wyndfeld as we protect them here!"

"Saxon, be calm," Eustace ordered and allowed his Omega pheromones to permeate the space around them. Once Saxon's tense shoulders lowered, Eustace turned back to Tharon. "These are very difficult and confusing times, Tharon. I would not choose war if I thought the Arringtons were innocent."

"How can you be so certain?" Tharon asked in a pained voice and grabbed her father's hand on her knee. She wanted to plea for the Arringtons and convince her father that Garrett and Layla would never kill her mother. For generations the two royal Houses fostered an unbreakable relationship that many kingdoms looked upon with great respect. The Arringtons were loving people, and condemning Wyndfeld would also condemn White Sommer.

"I have spoken at length with our healer." Eustace placed his other hand over Tharon's own, covering the friendship bracelet. "Bifan is certain that the poison was administered to your mother at the ball. Your mother's ailments started that night after the ball."

Tharon shook her head and tears pricked behind her eyes. Her father's voice sounded more distant as he continued to speak the truths.

"I also spoke to a few of our nobles about the ball. One of whom distinctly recalls seeing a servant pour strange contents into your mother's..." Eustace's voice faded to nothing.

The uncontrollable ringing in Tharon's ears followed by the slamming of her heart overwhelmed her. She sprung from the chair, which fell back with a boom. "No!" She backpedaled from her family and almost tumbled into the roaring fireplace, except her father had hooked her arm. Tharon cried low and toppled to her hands and knees, gasping for air.

Eustace knelt beside her and cupped her cheek. "Breathe, Tharon." Again, he tried to use his Omega pheromones to settle her, but he was her sire rather than her bearer. Often his pheromones could ease certain levels of Tharon's distress, while Edeva's pheromones would extinguish them. The one other person capable of soothing her was Roswynd.

Tharon covered her heaving chest, closed her eyes, and willed her mind to calm.

"That is it," Eustace said and swept back Tharon's hair. He leaned in closer and murmured, "The truth hurts so, but we will continue to work even when we are damaged." Leaning his forehead against Tharon's temple, he said, "I need you to be strong now, Tharon. To be strong enough to accept the truth."

"But…" Tharon raised her head and revealed her glistening cheeks. He spoke gently to her even though his words were cold and harsh.

Eustace cupped Tharon's cheeks in his hands and said, "I know how you care for the Arringtons. We all cared for them. But they betrayed us, Tharon."

Tharon searched her father's features and saw the certainty in his eyes. He wasn't weaving a great lie; he was a king, a father, and a widower destroyed by the ugly truth about his wife's murder. For the first time, there were fine cracks in his calm facade that drew a deep ache from Tharon. The Arringtons had in fact done this, all of this, to her family. Forcing herself to believe her father, the one point she refused to accept was that Roswynd had anything to do with Edeva's death. It was Garrett and Layla or perhaps only Garrett, but it wasn't Roswynd's sin. Yet as she raised her head, she saw that her father and brother condemned the entire House of Arrington.

Eustace lifted Tharon to her feet and guided her back to the armchair that Saxon had picked up for them. He reclaimed his earlier seat between his children and said, "I wished to tell you both this news in private before I announce it to the lords."

"What of Holly and Daisy?" Tharon asked and started to turn the friendship bracelet on her wrist. Across from her, Saxon was glaring and rumbling low like an adolescent Alpha.

"I will speak to them this evening after they have finished with their tutor." Eustace folded his hands in his lap. He remained calm and even indifferent about the upcoming war. "They are very young. We will not speak much about the war against Wyndfeld." He looked between them and asked, "Yes?"

"Yes, Father," Saxon agreed without hesitation.

Tharon dipped her head in agreement and warded off the returning tears. She stilled her thoughts in hopes to survive the rest of the meeting with her family. Her body trembled as she worked to contain her natural Alpha response to the pending oblivion.

"Father, are we to sever all ties with the Arringtons?" Saxon asked. The darkness in his brown eyes indicated his rising disdain for the House of Arrington. They had murdered Edeva for power or spite.

Eustace nodded and said, "All communication with Wyndfeld must be approved by me first." His lips pulled downward when he focused on Tharon. "You are forbidden to write to Roswynd."

"But Father she is innoc—"

"She is an Arrington," Saxon cut off and pinned Tharon with a hard stare. "Treacherous Arrington blood runs in her veins."

Tharon popped up from the chair and Saxon attempted to match her, but he was younger and a hair shorter. She balled her hands at her side and prepared to defend Roswynd's honor. Eustace had risen and kept them both at bay before a dangerous wrestling match was sparked between them.

Saxon shook his head and asked, "Are you a treacherous Arrington or a Blakesley, sister?" The hardness of his features cracked, then his harsh pheromones retreated and allowed room for Tharon to breathe. He pointed at the bracelet and said, "Is your friendship more important than our mother's death?"

"Saxon," Eustace warned and halted his son's next attempt to prod Tharon. He released a low breath and said, "I must speak with Tharon alone." After a shuffle of his feet, Saxon nodded and departed the solar room in a calmer manner. Once he was gone, Eustace indicated for Tharon to sit again, then he took Saxon's earlier spot on the settee.

"Father, Roswynd *is* innocent." Tharon wanted to argue that all the Arrington children were innocent. How could they condemn Roswynd and her siblings for something their parents had done?

"That may be so," Eustace responded and remained quiet for a beat. He released a strained sigh and rubbed his brow. "However, she is an Arrington. We can no longer associate with any of them because they are our enemies now." When Tharon dropped her head, he reached over and gripped her hands resting on her shaking legs. "It is best that you begin to accept the truth and let go." He touched the bracelet on Tharon's wrist. "Or else you will never heal from the pain of your mother's death."

Tharon opened her eyes and studied her friendship bracelet through blurry vision. She swiped at the tears, glowered at the bracelet, and remembered the vows she had exchanged with Roswynd about a year ago. *But I love her.*

"It is time to start letting go," Eustace said and fingered Tharon's bracelet. He tilted his head up when Tharon met his gaze. His features were stern, and his voice was like iron, unbreakable and strong. Without speaking the command aloud, he was requiring Tharon to remove her bracelet and surrender her love for the Arringtons. Every drop of his pheromones willed Tharon to obey.

Tharon wondered how her father was capable of declaring war on people he had considered family all his life. Like she and Roswynd, Eustace had grown up with Garrett. But from the first day Tharon could form words, she knew her father to be an Omega dedicated to caring for his immediate family first. The Arringtons had murdered his wife and forever damaged his children. As the legends told, Gyldren knew no greater wrath than a betrayed Omega. As much as Tharon cared for the Arringtons, her own family came first.

"Tharon," Eustace whispered and turned over his hand, waiting.

Tharon swallowed and looked from his open palm to her precious bracelet. She had never removed it since Roswynd clasped it to her wrist that night on her birthday. The bronze bracelet reflected the firelight and hummed against Tharon's skin. She could refuse to give it to her father; however, she also didn't want to hurt him for choosing Roswynd over him. Even though they had butted heads, Tharon loved her father deeply.

It is a silly bracelet, Tharon chided herself. *Removing it means nothing. You can still love Ros without it.* A few tears fell from her eyes. Then her trembling hand seemed to move on its own. Her father's warm Omega pheromones attempted to lull her into a false sense of security. Slowly, Tharon squeezed the bracelet and loosened the clasp, which popped free. The bracelet's once brilliant color seemed to dull to a tarnished look.

Eustace released a shaky breath when Tharon placed the Bracelet of Ælfwynn into his hand. He closed his fingers around it and whispered, "Thank you." He wiped Tharon's tears away with his other hand. "I know that took great strength, Tharon. I am proud of y-you." A stutter entered his voice at the end.

"May I go now?" Tharon was holding her breath and fighting to stay whole in front of her father.

Nodding, Eustace tightened his hand around Tharon's own and whispered, "One day your mother will rest easy. I promise you, Tharon."

For a moment, Tharon heard her mother's voice drift through the room. She yanked her hand free, stood, and hurried from the room. She ignored her father's soft call and ran through the castle. The soles of her flats smacked against the stones as she darted around castle guards. Her legs carried her outside of the castle and across the grounds toward the stable.

You are forbidden to write to Roswynd, her father's voice echoed in her head. The letters between her and Roswynd were a lifeline when they couldn't see each other. The idea that she was cut off from Roswynd sent her spiraling out of control. Her father may forbid her to contact Roswynd, but she could take a horse, escape Monales Castle, and ride to Roswynd.

Tharon burst into the stable and scrambled down the first aisle of stalls. She went to her favorite horse, which her mother rode sidesaddle on occasion. The horse, Shamrock, neighed after seeming to sense Tharon's urgency. He danced in the stall and backed up a few steps when Tharon entered with him. In haste, Tharon grabbed the saddle from the wall and carried it to Shamrock.

"Princess Tharon."

Stiffening, Tharon looked over her shoulder at the groom, who appeared calm but had a serious note radiating from him.

"Please return the saddle." Centus placed his hands behind his back. He was older but rather tall, especially for a Beta. "Your father informed me that you are forbidden to ride."

Tharon lowered her arms with the saddle in front of her. She wanted to ask why, even though she knew the reason. Eustace was one step ahead of her, like any smart parent. Part of her considered pleading with Centus, but he would deny her. No one in the kingdom would contest King Eustace, especially someone directly employed by him.

Centus raised a hand and indicated the empty hangers for the saddle. "Please, Princess Tharon. It is for your own well-being."

"But…" Tharon lost her resolve as Centus's features hardened with determination. He would halt her attempt to ride off. Even if Tharon rode Shamrock bareback, she would have to get past the castle guards. Centus would alert the castle guards, then they would seize her. In the end, Centus would be punished for failing to uphold Eustace's order. Biting her lip, she blinked away the sting in her eyes and returned the saddle.

Centus opened the stall door and locked it after Tharon stepped out. "I am sorry, Princess." He escorted Tharon from the stable. "Perhaps in a month's time he will allow you to ride again." His scent turned sympathetic, but it was no consolation.

Tharon hurried from the stable and came to the center of the open grounds of the castle. She turned in a complete circle and studied the gigantic walls that separated her from the rest of the world, from Roswynd. There were guards everywhere, both on the walls and marching around or in the castle. A few beads of sweat rolled down her temple even though the weather was mild today. Once she came back to the gatehouse, she stared at the gates that opened into Wulfbite. With renewed strength, she marched toward the gatehouse and fisted her hands.

The guards were busy chatting among each other and with two visitors, probably a lord and his knight coming for the royal court. One guard waved on the lord and his knight, and they hurried along but the knight bumped into Tharon.

"Watch out, you little—"

"Alpus," the lord warned the knight. "Be kind to the king's eldest, Princess Tharon."

"Yes, Lord Erland," Alpus responded, although his scent held a wretched stench to it.

Erland pivoted to his right as Tharon brushed past them without care. "Princess Tharon, where are you—"

Tharon ignored them and focused on the guards, one of them stepping in her path.

"Princess, you must remain in Monal—" The guard yelped when Tharon stomped on his foot. His cry caused several other guards to whirl around and respond to the incident.

However, Tharon was lighter on her feet than the armored guards. She darted around two of them, ducked under another one, and bolted past the last before sprinting down the stone bridge toward Wulfbite. Behind her, people were hollering and then giving chase. But Tharon hitched her dress, bolted down the bridge, and was absorbed into the throng of people.

The city of Wulfbite was bustling due to the beginnings of springtime. The day was still cool with a slight breeze, but the weather was warmer than it had been. Many citizens were preparing for the spring and summer months, which were spent either farming, cattle herding, or logging.

As Tharon moved through the city, she zipped past people or carts and hopped over debris in the street. She was well aware of her location in the city and turned down an alleyway. With her back pressed against a home, she gulped in several mouthfuls of air. She bent forward, closed her eyes, and thought through her plans. Why had she runaway from Monales Castle? It was her home, where her family lived, and where she was born. Every hallway held a memory for her. But it was many of those memories that now constricted around her throat. Her mother was gone from the castle, and Roswynd could never return there.

Peering around the corner, Tharon studied Monales Castle sitting above the city. She was torn in half, to return home or continue southeast to Roswynd. Her father's heartbroken features from the funeral were burned in Tharon's mind. Daisy and Holly were hurting and sobbing every night. Saxon was grappling with a new level of anger that frightened even Tharon. Their mother had been the foundation to their family.

With a low whine, Tharon pushed off the building and continued down the alleyway that would take her to the next street. She stood on the sidewalk at the mouth of the alleyway and looked over her left shoulder. Traveling by foot to Wyndfeld, alone and as an adolescent, would be suicidal. Tharon turned to her right and headed north, following the tight pull in her heart. She broke into a jog and eventually departed the city. The busy road continued north, to the furthest reaches of White Sommer.

However, Tharon had a single destination that called to her heart. She turned off Howl Highway and followed a wooded lane that twisted and turned through the dense forest. Everything was familiar to her, triggering more warm memories that burned against her heart. Tharon swiped away the tears from her cheeks, growled, and ran faster until the first structure came into view. The lane was blocked by an old iron gate that was part of a stone wall, which was built many generations ago.

Tharon neared the chained gates and glared at the lock, but there was enough chain that she might be able to slip past. She pulled one gate forward and the other backward, opening a gap. Carefully, she wiggled her way through after sucking in her tummy. With a tumble, she landed on the other side, inside the estate's property. Tharon hopped onto her feet, brushed off some dirt from her dress, and hurried across the estate. The manor home was half built into a rock face and had been recently updated by her father. Going past the manor house, Tharon went around a few tall trees and approached the fenced-in garden that was budding with new life. Once through the fence, she cut across to the left and slowed upon seeing the newest pillar among all the rest. At the base of it, the ground had recently been spoiled by shovels.

"Momma?" Tharon called and edged closer to the white pillar that had her mother's name chiseled into it at the top. As she came closer, she reached for the highest carving of a young wolf who was playing with similarly aged pups. Biting her lip to hold back her sobs, Tharon followed the little wolf's story on the pillar. Her fingertips traced the next image of a preadolescent wolf, followed by a matured wolf, and then later a second wolf seated next to her mother's wolf. As the story wrapped down the pillar, the adult wolf had pups of her own and proudly watched her pups grow older. But then the story ended too soon, and Tharon collapsed to the damp ground with her knees pressed against her chest.

Tharon leaned against her mother's pillar and whined low, willing her mother to be reborn. "Please, Momma." She buried her face between her knees and whispered, "Please, come back." The only response was the soft creak of the trees' empty branches around the garden cemetery. Behind her were numerous other pillars for past Blakesleys over the generations. One nearby Edeva's had a prominent black wolf who died early.

"Please, please, please," Tharon whispered again and again until her throat ached. She rocked back and forth, trying to find any measure of peace from the anguish inside her. Her body was sore and weak. She was exhausted from her nights wrought with horrible dreams of her mother's death. But all her body's pain seemed trivial compared to the searing blade that constantly sliced her soul into tinier and tinier pieces. Tharon wondered if there would be anything left once it was done cutting away at her.

For the first few days after her mother's death, Tharon clung to the impossible dream that everything could be fixed. If her mother returned, everything would be okay again. Her father would forgive Garrett, the war would never begin, and Tharon could see Roswynd again. However, Edeva never rose from her grave.

The horrible truth was that King Garrett Arrington *had* murdered her mother.

Tharon released a low, threatening growl and wished Garrett were here now. She would launch into him, scream at him, and beat him bloody for killing her mother and destroying *everything*. The colors in Tharon's life were swept away by the coldness of her new world. Her two most important people were taken from her. As her snarl deepened, her vision was washed with red and heat. With a tilt of her head, Tharon howled with all her remaining strength. Deep inside, she could feel her Alpha growing and clawing forward in her chest. She found comfort in her Alpha's developing power.

"Father is right," Tharon whispered and pressed her hand against the ground near her mother's grave. "None of this should have happened to you. I am so sorry." She dragged her nails through the soil and whimpered for her mother. "We will give you justice. I will give you peace, I swear it." Closing her burning eyes, she murmured her promise a few more times to her mother until exhaustion overtook her. She had no idea how long she slept, until a few distant voices stirred her.

Tharon straightened against the pillar when she heard movement by the fence, which creaked low. She blinked twice and focused on the single castle guard entering the cemetery garden. He was tall and bulky, ever the Alpha.

"Hello, Princess Tharon." The guard moved slow and offered a gentle smile. Most male Alphas were boorish and also carried an unpleasant scent around them now that Tharon was maturing. But this Alpha was a little different, and perhaps that was the reason he was sent to locate Tharon on the property while the others remained by the gates. She could detect their scent on the breeze.

"Hello," Tharon said and rubbed the sleepiness from her eyes. She frowned at being caught and decided it was just as well. As much as she wanted to be with Roswynd, she couldn't abandon her family after what the Arringtons had done to them.

The guard took another step closer, then knelt down. "I am Pòl." He placed a hand against his leather-padded chest and said, "I am sorry that you lost your mother." He lifted his gaze to the pillar and frowned at it. "Queen Edeva was a great Omega." Focusing on Tharon again, he swallowed and whispered, "She still is."

"Yes… she is." Tharon played with the material of her dress and swallowed back a sob. She had cried every day since her mother's illness. But today would be the last one.

"I came to return you home." Pòl clasped his hands in front of him and asked, "If you are ready, may I take you home?"

Tharon clenched her jaw and looked down at the fresh soil where her mother's ashes had been buried over a month ago. After a deep breath, she licked her dry lips and looked over at Pòl. "Only if you will bring me here again?"

Pòl nodded and replied, "Whenever you wish, I will bring you here myself. I swear it on the bones of Gyldr." He rumbled and held out his gloved hand. His scent was calm and even open, never pushing Tharon to submit to him, even though he was the bigger Alpha.

"All right," Tharon murmured and placed her smaller hand in his. She was helped to her feet, but she turned to her mother's pillar. Her grip on Pòl's hand tightened, but if it hurt him, he didn't complain. Her mother's pillar gleamed in the sunlight and reminded Tharon of her mother's bright smile. Again, she gave her mother her solemn vow.

One day, Tharon would have justice for her mother, and then she would have Roswynd Arrington.

The End

Standalone Titles
The Iron Edge

About the Author

Lexa Luthor is an avid writer and reader of the Omegaverse trope especially F/F pairings. In her books, each main character(s) is a strong-willed female, who navigates difficult situations but always ends up finding love with their mate. Every tale has a twist and is gripping, sexy, and even a bit adventurous.

When not writing, Lexa enjoys binge watching television shows like Game of Thrones, Gentleman Jack, or The L Word. Her other favorite hobbies are playing cornhole, rooting for the Kansas City Chiefs, and laying around the pool in the summer. At times, Lexa finds time to read romances (both dark and fluffy) and great sci-fi books but nothing else can beat a steamy, downright erotic F/F romance with biting, knotting, and slightly possessive love.

Visit her website at LexaLuthor.com for more information and be sure to sign up for her newsletter for the latest release information, bonus material, and freebies.